Ana Huang is a #1 *New York Times, Sunday Times, Wall Street Journal, USA Today*, and #1 Amazon bestselling author. Best known for her Twisted series, she writes New Adult and contemporary romance with deliciously alpha heroes, strong heroines, and plenty of steam, angst, and swoon.

Her books have been translated in over two dozen languages and featured in outlets such as NPR, *Cosmopolitan, Financial Times*, and *Glamour UK*.

A self-professed travel enthusiast, she loves incorporating beautiful destinations into her stories and will never say no to a good chai latte.

T0373037

Also by Ana Huang

KING

OF

ENVY

ANA HUANG

PIATKUS

PIATKUS

First published in the US in 2025 by Bloom Books,
An imprint of Sourcebooks
Published in Great Britain in 2025 by Piatkus

7 9 10 8

A CIP catalogue record for this book is available from the British Library.

ISBN 978-0-349-43639-5

Printed and bound in Great Britain by Clays Ltd, Elcograf S.p.A.

Papers used by Piatkus are from well-managed forests
and other responsible sources.

Piatkus
An imprint of
Little, Brown Book Group
Carmelite House
50 Victoria Embankment
London EC4Y 0DZ

The authorised representative
in the EEA is
Hachette Ireland,
8 Castlecourt Centre,
Dublin 15, D15 XTP3, Ireland
(email: info@hbgi.ie)

An Hachette UK Company
www.hachette.co.uk

www.littlebrown.co.uk

To all the readers who like their fictional men a little unhinged. This one's for you.

Author's Note

The Serbian spelling and pronunciation of Vuk's last name is Marković.

However, since he never says his last name himself, it is spelled Markovic (without the diacritic over the C) throughout the book as English speakers tend to use the English pronunciation, which differs from the original.

Playlist

◄◄ ► ►►

Moth To A Flame
Swedish House Mafia ft. The Weeknd

Battle Scars
Lupe Fiasco ft. Guy Sebastian

Fashion
Sandra Resendes

You Right
Doja Cat ft. The Weeknd

Young and Beautiful
Lana Del Rey

Tearin' Up My Heart
*NSYNC

Baby (Acoustic)
Clean Bandit ft. Marina and Luis Fonsi

Obsessed
Zandros ft. Limi

Who Do You Want
Ex Habit

I'm Yours
Isabel LaRosa

Lose Control
Teddy Swims

Believer
Imagine Dragons

Undiscovered
Laura Welsh

I Got You
Bebe Rexha

Way Down We Go
Kaleo

Let the World Burn
Chris Grey

Content Notes

This story contains explicit sexual content, graphic violence, sexual harassment and assault, profanity, and topics that may be sensitive to some readers.

For a detailed list, please scan the code below.

CHAPTER 1

Ayana

"CONGRATULATIONS. HALF THE PEOPLE HERE WANT to kill you, and the other half want to be you." My fiancé's lips brushed my cheek. "Now *that's* an accomplishment."

"I'm not sure that's something to be proud of," I said out of the corner of my mouth. I kept my smile planted firmly in place. People were watching. "Especially the second part."

"When the guest list reads like a who's who of fashion, it is," he said. "Inspiring envy amongst this crowd is a talent. Embrace it, MOTY."

I huffed out a laugh. "I swear you're prouder of that title than I am."

MOTY was short for Model of the Year. Eight months had passed since I received the prestigious title, and Jordan still brought it up any chance he got.

"What can I say? It proves I have a good eye." He winked. "I remember when Hank told everyone he'd found the 'face of the century' at a random college party in D.C. Now look at you."

My smile wavered at the mention of my agent before I caught

myself. "I don't know about face of the century, but this definitely beats a sweaty frat house."

I took a sip of champagne and glanced around the outdoor garden. We were currently playing host and hostess at an end-of-summer cocktail party for Jacob Ford, the iconic luxury department store Jordan's grandfather founded more than fifty years ago.

Jordan gave me my big break as a model when he chose me to be the store's ambassador four years ago. The size and success of that one campaign had unlocked more doors than two years of casting calls and small bookings had. I owed my career to him and Jacob Ford.

He'd rented out a beautiful rooftop garden for today's party. The drinks were flowing, the sun was shining, and half the guests were staring at us, discreetly or not-so-discreetly whispering behind their hands. Jordan was right. Some of them definitely wanted to kill me.

Modeling was a cutthroat industry. My rise to fame over the past few years, coupled with my engagement to one of New York's most eligible bachelors, hadn't endeared me to many of my peers. Friends were few, and *genuine* friends were even fewer.

It was what it was, but sometimes, I mourned the life I would've lived were I not quite so visible.

"Uh-oh." Jordan straightened. "Missile incoming. Gird your loins, or she'll blast you to bits."

My brief bout of melancholy popped like one of the bubbles in my drink. I stifled another laugh even as I heeded Jordan's advice and braced for impact.

The indomitable Orla Ford was no laughing matter. While Jordan was the CEO of Jacob Ford, his grandmother was the majority shareholder and family matriarch. She ruled the Ford clan from her estate in Rhode Island, and her ability to bend half of Manhattan to her will from two hundred miles away was a testament to her force of character.

"You are the hosts of this party, yes?" she said as she drew close. The elegant eighty-four-year-old cut a sharp figure in her floral suit and signature diamond-and-emerald necklace, but up close, she looked exhausted. Her cheeks were sunken, and there was a slight shake in her hands.

Nevertheless, she stood tall and proud, her eyes narrowing as she awaited our response.

"Yes, Grandmother," Jordan said, all traces of levity gone.

"Then why are you giggling here in the corner like schoolchildren instead of *hosting*?" Orla clucked her tongue. "Dante and Vivian Russo are here. Stella Alonso is here. Go network. You're engaged now—you'll have plenty of time for couple activities later."

My face heated at the knowing tone she used to describe "couple activities." Jordan placed his drink on a nearby table and sped off. I moved to follow him, but his grandmother stopped me with a hand on my arm.

"Not you, dear. Not yet." She swept a discerning eye over me. "You look lovely."

"Thank you," I said, pleased. Compliments from Orla were rare, and I didn't take her approval lightly.

I wore a gauzy saffron yellow minidress from the store's in-house collection. My silk pressed hair cascaded past my shoulders in loose waves, and my gravity-defying heels put me two inches above Jordan's even six feet. They'd cost an absurd amount of money, but they were so beautiful I couldn't resist.

Everyone had their indulgences; mine were shoes and perfume. Also knitting, but my projects came out so misshapen I'd yet to admit *that* particular hobby to anyone.

"I wanted to speak to you because we don't see each other

in person often," Orla said. "I know you and Jordan have been engaged for quite a while now—sixteen months, I believe—but I..." She faltered. Her breath wheezed.

I almost reached for her to make sure she was okay, but she shook it off a moment later like nothing had happened.

"I haven't gotten a chance to properly welcome you to the family." She clasped my hand in hers. "For the longest time, I thought Jordan would never find the right partner. He's my only grandchild, and I was...concerned. He's certainly never dated anyone for longer than a few weeks. I worried that when he finally *did* bring someone home, it'd be some trollop off the streets. I'm very glad it's you instead." Orla patted my hand. "You're a beautiful couple. I know you'll take good care of him." She sounded sincere but a touch sad.

I purposely overlooked her use of the word "trollop"—the woman was in her late eighties, after all—and masked my confusion with another smile.

Orla wasn't a sentimental person, and she'd already welcomed me to the family at my engagement party over a year ago. Perhaps she'd forgotten?

"I appreciate that, Orla. You've been so kind to me since we announced our engagement. I'm, um, really excited to join the family."

If she noticed my small verbal stumble, she didn't mention it. "Of course, dear. I had to tell you in person. I couldn't count on my daughter to do it. The only thing she knows how to do is spend my money and take on increasingly appalling lovers." She glanced to the side. "Ah, there's Buffy Darlington. Excuse me, but I must go say hi."

Orla gave my hand one last pat before she left.

I blinked at the empty spot she'd vacated. What the hell just happened?

"You look shell-shocked. What did she say? Did she berate you for wearing heels that make you taller than me?" Jordan reappeared like a ghost materializing out of thin air now that his grandmother was gone. He loved her, but he was also terrified of her. "You know how picky she is about appearances. It doesn't look good when the woman is taller than the man. Blah, blah, blah."

"Well, I'm five-ten in flats, so that's going to be hard," I quipped. "But no, she didn't mention my heels." I gave him a quick summary of our conversation. "Also, I don't want to alarm you, but is she okay? She looks a little pale, and her hands keep shaking."

Jordan frowned. "I'm sure she's fine. She got the flu last week, and she's still recovering. Of course, she insisted on flying here for the party anyway. She loves any chance to brag about the company and our wedding." He gulped down the fresh glass of scotch in his hand. "Speaking of which, don't forget we have dinner with Vuk on Friday to go over some wedding stuff. I booked us a table at that new French bistro in the West Village."

The champagne soured in my stomach.

Vuk Markovic was Jordan's old college roommate and best man. I didn't know him well, but our previous interactions hadn't been the warmest. In fact, I was pretty sure he despised me.

I had no idea why. I was always friendly and cordial toward him, and I'd never paid attention to the rumors that the powerful CEO was possibly involved in shadier businesses than running the world's largest liquor and spirits company.

Jordan was one of the best guys I knew. We'd clicked while I was working on the Jacob Ford campaign, and we'd been friends since. He wouldn't ask someone to be his best man if they weren't on the up and up. Right?

"Friday in the Village. Got it," I said. "I'm kind of surprised he's not here today."

"Are you?" Jordan sounded skeptical. "Vuk hates parties. I'm pretty sure he thinks the seventh circle of hell is a black-tie gala with live music."

I laughed. "I don't know. He's attended a lot more parties this year. *Mode de Vie* even mentioned it in their profile of him last month."

"True, but I wouldn't count on that trend continuing. Vuk does what he needs to do for business and that's it. A garden cocktail party doesn't fall under that umbrella." Jordan cursed. "Shit. My grandmother's staring daggers at me again. I'm going to find some 'important' person to talk to before she stabs me with an ice pick. I suppose we can't be seen next to each other for the rest of the party, or she'll accuse us of not hosting properly."

"Same." We shook hands solemnly, our mouths twitching in an attempt to hold in our laughter. "Good luck, soldier," I said. "See you on the other side."

Jordan responded with a laconic two-finger salute. He disappeared into the crowd, and I took a final sip of my drink before I moved toward Stella Alonso and her husband.

I passed by Orla on the way. Her words echoed in my head.

You're a beautiful couple. I know you'll take good care of him.

I really did appreciate the sentiment. A lot of people thought she was scary—which she could be—but privately, she was warmer than others gave her credit for.

I returned her smile with another one of my own and ignored the quick twist of guilt in my gut.

Getting Orla's approval was a big accomplishment, but I suspected she'd be less benevolent if she found out the truth: that my engagement to her grandson was a complete and utter sham.

CHAPTER 2

Ayana

THAT FRIDAY, I SHOWED UP AS PROMISED AT THE BISTRO Jordan booked. The food was delicious, but sadly, it was hard to enjoy even a Michelin-starred meal when the person sitting across from you hated you.

He didn't say it, of course, but I could *feel* the animosity rolling off him in waves, and it took all my willpower not to flinch beneath his glare.

I took a sip of water and tried to avoid eye contact while Jordan rambled on about our wedding beside me.

"We secured the castle in Ireland, courtesy of Katrakis," he said, oblivious to the tension suffocating the table. "Seven hundred guests. Five days in the countryside. Then the Ethiopian ceremony afterward in the States. It's going to be the wedding of the year, and we're thrilled. Aren't we, sweetie?"

"Absolutely." I smiled.

The idea of spending a week with seven hundred people I barely knew made me want to crawl into a hole and die. That wasn't even counting the hundreds of guests my parents were inviting to the reception *they* were throwing for me in D.C.

Nevertheless, I had to play the role of excited fiancée. That was part of our deal. Jordan needed a wife to secure his inheritance; I needed money to get out of the soul-sucking contract my younger self had unwittingly signed in order to help my family.

Five million dollars upfront for five years of my life, plus an extra five mil once Jordan came into his inheritance. It was a mutually beneficial arrangement.

So why did I feel uneasy every time I thought about the ceremony?

"We've gotten RSVPs from almost everyone on the guest list." Garret's voice carried over the din in the restaurant. "Speaking of which, thank you for taking charge of the bachelor party. I know parties are...not your favorite."

Silence.

It was always silence.

I finally braved a glance across the table, where his best man loomed like an immovable mountain of muscle and scars.

Vuk Markovic.

CEO of Markovic Holdings, chairman of the Valhalla Club's management committee, and quite possibly the most intimidating person I'd ever met.

At six foot five, he towered over me even while sitting. His stern mouth and the vicious scar bisecting his otherwise devastating face lent him an air of quiet danger, but it was his eyes that sent goosebumps rippling over my skin.

Cold. Impassive. So pale a blue they were nearly white.

They met mine for a brief moment before Vuk flicked his gaze back to Jordan and responded with a few curt hand movements.

I'd learned American Sign Language in high school after my aunt lost her hearing, so I understood Vuk perfectly.

I'm your best man. That's my job.

Not the most enthusiastic reply, but I couldn't imagine Vuk expressing enthusiasm over anything. The man was made of ice.

"I know, but still," Jordan said. "I appreciate it. *We* appreciate it."

He squeezed my hand on the table; I faked another smile.

Nothing to see here. We were just another soon-to-be-married couple who were deeply in love with each other. *Obviously.*

A muscle ticked in Vuk's jaw.

His eyes touched mine again, and I fought another wave of chills.

Neither Jordan nor I had told anyone else about our arrangement. It was too risky. There were literally millions of dollars riding on our ability to sell our relationship, and as much as I hated keeping secrets from my family, I *needed* the money.

But sometimes, Vuk looked at us, at me, like he—

The blare of a ringtone derailed my train of thought.

Jordan grimaced. "Sorry, I have to take this." He removed his hand from mine and stood. "I'll be right back. No dessert for me if the server asks, okay, babe?"

"Yep. Got it." I hoped my reply sounded natural and not forced. Although we conversed easily one-on-one, our need to convince the world we were a happy couple put a strain on our interactions around other people.

Once Jordan was gone, Vuk and I lapsed into silence again.

"So," I said brightly, wishing not for the first time that Jordan had chosen someone less terrifying to be his best man. "What do you have planned for the bachelor party? Poker? Lap dances? Be honest. I won't get offended."

I didn't want to talk about the wedding, but I couldn't think of anything else we might have in common.

Vuk regarded me coolly. One hand wrapped around his glass, the other remained on the table, and God knew he hadn't engaged in a single conversation with me since we met over a year ago. I doubted he'd start tonight.

Okay then. I guess he didn't want to talk about the wedding either.

I held back a sigh and took an unenthusiastic bite of salad.

I'd just forced the greens down when a family of three passed by our table. The daughter, who looked like she was around seven or eight years old, stopped to gawk at Vuk.

"Mom, Dad, look at his face." Her stage whisper was hardly a whisper when she was standing less than a foot away. "Why does it look like that?"

"Don't stare," her father admonished. "It's rude."

"But those scars! They're *gross*."

"Emily!" The mother glared at her daughter before casting an embarrassed glance in our direction. "I'm so sorry. She's…" Boisterous laughter from another table drowned out the rest of her apology.

She placed a hand on the little girl's shoulder and quickly ushered her out of the restaurant. The father trailed after them, taking great care not to look at Vuk.

Cold metal bit into my palm. I hadn't realized how hard I'd been gripping my fork, and I had to physically force my hand to uncurl.

Vuk, on the other hand, hadn't moved an inch. If it weren't for the near-imperceptible tightening of his lips, I would've thought he hadn't heard the girl at all.

How often did people openly stare and whisper for him to act so unfazed?

My earlier annoyance softened with sympathy. I wasn't sure whether I should address what happened, so I let the silence stretch on while I debated what to say next.

Besides the scar on his face, Vuk had additional burn scars

wrapped around his throat. They peeked out from the neck of his shirt, and though they weren't as visible, they were enough to make the average person do a double take.

But the little girl was wrong. They weren't gross; they were simply a part of him. Some people had freckles and moles; he had scars.

Vuk's lips tightened further. *If my appearance disturbs you so much, we can end dinner early.* His movements were sharp enough to cut glass. *I wouldn't want you to lose your appetite.*

Blood rushed to my face. I was mortified that I'd been caught staring—the very thing the little girl had done—but his assumptions regarding my character made me bristle.

Did he think me so rude and shallow that I would blatantly judge the way he looked over dinner?

"I wasn't staring at you because of your appearance," I said. "You're sitting across from me. It's natural that I look at you. I wasn't even *thinking* about you."

It was a bald-faced lie, but I certainly wasn't going to share my real thoughts with him. I had a feeling he'd hate sympathy more than he would rudeness.

Vuk arched his brow a fraction of an inch.

"I wasn't." I lifted my chin. "I was thinking about...Ireland. And how excited I am to visit."

He looked unimpressed. *You've been to Ireland before.*

This time, I was the one whose eyebrows flew up. "How do you know that?"

I'd studied abroad in Dublin for a summer, before I was scouted and dropped out of Howard to pursue modeling full-time. It wasn't a secret, but it wasn't common knowledge either.

There was a short pause before Vuk answered. *Jordan told me.*

I frowned. I didn't remember telling Jordan about Dublin, but I could be wrong. The past year and a half had been such a blur that I barely remembered what life was like before I agreed to Jordan's marriage of convenience.

It was a long engagement, but I was marrying the heir to Jacob Ford. People expected us to have a lavish wedding, and those took time to plan.

Our ceremony was set for February, six months from now. After that, I'd receive my first five-million-dollar payment, and I could finally leave my agency.

They'd already taken too much of my money and soul; if I lost any more pieces of myself, I'd have nothing left.

"Are you bringing anyone to the wedding?" I asked Vuk.

Despite his public profile as a major CEO, he was notoriously private.

I knew he'd been born in Serbia and that his family moved to the U.S. when he was ten. He'd studied chemical engineering in college, where he met Jordan, and the pair had been roommates for their last two years at Thayer.

Some people called him the Serb because they said he hated being called by his real name, but I suspected that was just a rumor. Jordan always called him Vuk, and he never said a thing about it.

That was all I knew about him.

There was zero information about Vuk's personal life online, and I was oddly curious about his dating habits.

I'd never seen him out with a date, but he was rich, single, and powerful—the holy trinity, as far as half the women in Manhattan were concerned. He *had* to be dating someone, if only casually.

An indiscernible emotion flickered across his face. *Perhaps.*

"That's not really an answer."

If I had another answer, I would've given it.

I glared at him. "Do you get off on being difficult, or does it just come naturally to you?"

Both.

A small growl of frustration slipped out.

Vuk's mouth twitched. On anyone else, it might've passed for a hint of a smile, but the mere idea of Vuk Markovic smiling was so far-fetched, I was certain I was imagining things.

"I—"

A whoosh of air interrupted what I was sure would've been a thoroughly witty reply on my part.

"Sorry about that." Jordan sounded breathless as he settled back into his seat. I'd been so fixated on my conversation with Vuk, I hadn't even noticed his approach. "The call took longer than expected."

"Is everything okay?" I asked.

A furrow dug between his brows, and his previously neat hair stuck up like he'd been running his fingers through it.

"Not really." Jordan's voice was tight. "It's my grandmother. You were right. She's...not doing so well. I have to go to Rhode Island tomorrow to see her."

Orla had returned to her Newport estate after the party on Tuesday.

"What do you mean by not doing well?" I asked, concerned.

"I'm not sure. Her assistant just said I should go up and see her ASAP."

That couldn't be good.

My teeth dug into my lip. I wasn't close with Jordan's family, but I didn't want anything to happen to his grandmother either.

She was the reason for our arrangement. Orla had tired of waiting for her only grandchild to settle down, and she gave Jordan an ultimatum last year: marry within the next twenty-four months and *stay* married for at least five years, or she'd donate the entire family fortune to charity.

All one hundred and twenty million dollars of it.

Needless to say, Jordan had approached me days later with his proposition. I'd accepted, and here we were.

I have to go to Rhode Island tomorrow to see her.

The rest of his words suddenly clicked. "If you have to leave tomorrow, does that mean…"

"I can't make it to the cake tasting," he said apologetically. "I'm so sorry. I know how hard it was to get that appointment."

We were scheduled to fly to California tomorrow to meet with Sammy Yu, whose wedding cakes had become a status symbol for those in the know. Brides across the country waited *months* to get a tasting appointment. Couples literally booked a whole trip to San Francisco just to see him.

"No. It's okay." I shook my head. "We'll reschedule. Your family is more important."

"I doubt we'll be able to reschedule before the wedding. We're cutting it close as it is, and my mother will pitch a fit if we don't have a Sammy Yu cake at the reception." Jordan rubbed a hand over his face. "The shitty part is, she wants to take the jet to Rhode Island, so you can't use it for Cali. And I don't want you to do the tasting alone. If only…" His gaze slid across the table.

Dread suddenly coalesced in my stomach. *No.*

"Vuk, I know this is a lot to ask, but would you mind taking Ayana to San Francisco tomorrow?" A pleading note entered Jordan's voice. "You have your jet in New York, right? It'll only be for the weekend, and I'll owe you one."

I braved another glance at Vuk.

Any hint of warmth he might've shown earlier had disappeared. He resembled a stone statue, his mouth a grim slash as he stared at Jordan like the other man had asked him to peel off his flesh and fashion it into a carpet for me to walk on.

Okay, ouch. I knew he didn't like me, but he didn't have to look *that* horrified at the prospect of traveling with me.

"Please. I don't trust anyone else to go with Ayana, and you know how my mother is," Jordan said. "I'll never hear the end of it if we don't get this damn cake."

She can take the jet. Vuk didn't look at me. *I don't need to go with her.*

I bristled. While I appreciated his jet offer (sort of), I did *not* appreciate them talking about me as if I weren't here.

"I don't need a jet," I said. "I'll book a commercial flight like a normal person."

"That's too much hassle," Jordan argued. "You need to be back by Monday morning, and there've been so many cancelled flights lately because of that big IT outage." He turned to Vuk again. "Two days. That's it. You know my food preferences, so you can sub in for me at the tasting, and Ayana doesn't like flying alone."

I winced. My anxiety over flying wasn't a secret, per se, but it seemed too intimate a detail to share with Vuk.

Everything seemed too intimate to share with him.

His features twisted into a scowl. If he was annoyed before, he was downright irritated now.

Part of me hoped he'd say no. Yes, flying private was much more appealing than popping a Valium before a crowded flight, but Vuk and I had never been alone together before.

Even now, surrounded by dozens of diners in one of the city's hottest restaurants, he managed to suck all the oxygen out of the room. His presence was like a black hole—powerful, inescapable, and so all-consuming everything else paled in comparison.

Fine. His expression was pure ice. *I'll go. This weekend only.*

"Great." Jordan's relief was palpable. "I appreciate it, man." He squeezed my hand again. "Isn't that great, sweetie?"

"So great." I beamed so hard my cheeks hurt.

If I were an actress instead of a model, I'd get fired on the spot.

Luckily, Vuk didn't notice my pitiful attempt at feigning enthusiasm because he *still* hadn't acknowledged my presence.

It was like Jordan's return had flipped a switch. He'd gone from sort of carrying on a conversation to straight up ignoring me.

Okay. I could deal with that. I'd rather have a silent companion than one who didn't understand boundaries.

Besides, it was a cake tasting. It wasn't like Vuk was accompanying me to buy bridal lingerie.

One round-trip flight and one weekend in California. It'd be easy.

I reached for my water again, my ridiculously opulent engagement ring flashing beneath the lights. It wasn't my style at all, but Jordan had insisted on something showy "for appearance's sake."

Vuk's eyes narrowed. They bore a hole in the diamond before they slid up to meet mine.

A fresh wave of goosebumps scattered over my arms.

Easy. I swallowed. The water tasted like metal. *Right.*

CHAPTER 3

Ayana

GOOD NEWS: VUK DIDN'T KILL ME DURING OUR FLIGHT to San Francisco.

Bad news: We had roughly twenty-eight hours left together, and I couldn't guarantee his murderous tendencies wouldn't pop up sometime between a slice of chocolate cake and our return to New York.

Due to morning traffic and unforeseen storms across the Midwest, we took off and landed later than expected. We didn't have time to check in to our hotel before the tasting, so I freshened up in the jet's bathroom instead.

Moisturizer, check.

Lipstick touch-up, check.

Swap out my flats for a pair of killer Louboutins, check.

When Vuk and I finally left the jet, a black Rolls-Royce was already idling on the tarmac.

He waited for me to slide in first before he joined me—though "joined" was too generous a term for the way he sat as far from me as humanly possible. He was pressed so tight against the opposite side of the car, I was surprised he and the door didn't fuse together like some sort of weird billionaire-vehicle hybrid.

"I don't have a contagious disease," I said. "You *can* sit like a normal person. I promise I don't bite."

No response.

Shocker. He'd acknowledged me with two seconds of eye contact when I showed up for our flight and proceeded to act like I didn't exist.

I considered touching him briefly to see if he'd melt like the Wicked Witch of the West at my audacity, but since I wanted to arrive at the tasting in one piece, I pulled out my phone instead.

My plan to catch up on my favorite fragrance blogger's latest posts disintegrated when I saw the name flashing on my screen.

Four letters, instant stomach-churning nausea.

"Hi, Hank." I kept my tone even as I turned my back to Vuk and lowered my voice. He could still hear me, but the illusion of privacy was the only comfort I had in that moment.

Every time I talked to my agent, I wanted to crawl out of my skin. I couldn't believe there'd been a time when I thought he was on my side.

That was one of the hardest parts of growing up—realizing the people you trusted to have your back were often the ones stabbing it.

"Ayana." His oily greeting oozed over the line. "Did you make it to Cali okay?"

"Yes. We're on our way to the tasting now."

"Excellent. And I hear you're with Vuk Markovic?"

My shoulders tensed. I hadn't told Hank about my change in travel partner, but he knew. He *always* knew.

I was so paranoid about his inexplicable omniscience that I'd swept my apartment and devices for surveillance bugs a few months ago. I hadn't found anything, which was somehow worse than if I had.

"He was kind enough to fly with me after Jordan couldn't make it." I didn't ask how he found out about Vuk.

Hank pounced on the smallest sign of weakness, and if he picked up on how much his seeming omniscience unnerved me, he'd double down on it.

"How generous of him." A door slammed, followed by the sound of an espresso machine brewing in the background. "Well, I hate to interrupt your weekend…"

I almost snorted out loud.

He had no qualms about interrupting me when I was doing anything. He'd once insisted I run downtown for a last-minute casting call while I was in the middle of a dentist appointment.

"But I'm calling to make sure you'll be back in time for the Delamonte Cosmetics shoot Monday morning." *Or else.* Hank paused, letting his unspoken words fill in the silence before he continued. "They're a big account. The agency will be very upset if you jeopardize this campaign, especially given your recent distractions."

My nails dug into the leather seat. By "distractions," he meant my wedding preparations.

Hank and the agency's management hadn't been thrilled when I told them I was engaged, but they hadn't put up a huge fuss until this past month. That was when the wedding prep went into full swing and filled up my schedule. They'd been breathing down my neck ever since.

"I haven't jeopardized a campaign yet," I said. "I'll be back by Monday morning. Don't worry."

"Good. Because if you're not, we'll be forced to deduct the lost earnings and the cost of time and labor from your next paycheck."

Anger surged up my throat. I swallowed it before it spilled out in a deluge of curses that would make a trucker blush.

"Understood." Still calm, still even. I would *not* let him hear me panic.

He hung up, and I forced myself to take a deep breath before I unclenched my fist and dropped my phone back into my bag.

Hank hadn't called because he was worried I would miss Monday's shoot; he'd called to reassert his authority over me. To remind me that I was beholden to him because of the stupid contract I'd signed when I was nineteen and hadn't known any better.

My anger spread into my stomach and mixed with nausea.

Six more months.

I had to deal with him for only six more months. After that, I could break my contract and free myself from the agency forever.

I'd wanted to leave for years, but that hadn't been possible until Jordan came to me with his proposal.

I took another deep breath and faced forward again. I barely had time to compose myself before heat scorched my cheek, and I turned to see Vuk staring at me.

Was that your agent?

I'd known he could hear my end of the conversation, but I was so startled by his sudden desire to converse that it took me a second to respond.

"Yes. We were talking about—about an upcoming photoshoot."

You sounded upset.

First, he initiated conversation. Now he was concerned about my emotional state?

I almost checked the car for hidden cameras in case we were on a prank show, but Vuk Markovic would never deign to go near reality TV.

Instead, I did what I did best—I deflected.

"Not upset. Just a little stressed with everything going on." I flashed the same smile that'd landed me a coveted deal with Delamonte Cosmetics. "What about you? Anything exciting going on at work?"

Not the most inspired of topics, but it was the only one I could come up with on the fly.

What did he say to you?

So much for deflection.

"He was reminding me of Monday's schedule." I wasn't going to spill my deepest, darkest secrets to Vuk, of all people. Even Jordan didn't know how bad things were with Hank. "Why are you so interested in what he said? Don't tell me you're looking for an agent."

I meant it as a light-hearted tease, but Vuk's glower only deepened.

Hank Carson. That's his name?

I nodded, hiding my surprise. My agent's name wasn't something the average non-industry person memorized.

Vuk's face shuttered, turning cold and remote. A flicker of darkness passed through his eyes, and goosebumps peppered my flesh.

I crossed and uncrossed my legs again, my stomach warm despite the sudden chill. It was like he was imagining Hank's murder because...of me?

No. That couldn't be right. He didn't even like me.

So why did the thought of his hypothetical protectiveness send a tiny flutter through my chest?

Because no one has ever protected you since you moved to New York. Not without wanting something in return.

Clearly, I was delusional. There was no world in which Vuk would feel protective of me.

But the silence pounded as surely as my heartbeat, and there was a second, just one, when I thought he might—

A car horn blared outside. Vuk's expression hardened, and he sat back and took his phone out like nothing happened—because nothing *did* happen.

He'd confirmed my agent's name. That was all.

I turned and stared out the window while I waited for my rapid heart rate to return to normal. Eventually, my pulse calmed, and the world righted itself as we crawled through afternoon traffic.

Nothing happened.

Still, a whisper of warmth remained in my stomach for the rest of the ride.

We made it to the bakery with less than a minute to spare. The receptionist checked us in and led us to the back, where the tasting area was already set up with coffee, tea, and an assortment of cakes.

"Hi." Sammy Yu greeted us with a broad smile. He was a handsome man, tall and square-jawed with short dark hair and a laid-back demeanor. "You must be Ayana and Jordan. It's wonderful to meet you."

"It's great to meet you too." I shook his outstretched hand. "Jordan actually had a family emergency and couldn't make it. This is Vuk, his best man. He'll be, um, sitting in for Jordan today."

Vuk greeted him with a curt nod.

Sammy's eyebrows rose.

I guess it was unusual for a groomsman to take on such an important wedding activity, but Sammy was professional enough not to comment on it.

We settled into our seats. The receptionist brought out glasses of champagne, and I spent the next hour discussing the wedding with Sammy and sampling the cakes.

He'd created six flavors based on the preference profiles Jordan and I filled out beforehand.

Each and every one was mind-blowing.

No wonder people traveled out here to see him. I was afraid he'd be overhyped, but the cakes were definitely worth the hype.

"Once you choose a flavor, we'll tackle the cake design," Sammy said. "I'll send you a few sketches next week. Do you have a favorite so far?"

"I love all of them, but I'm leaning toward this one." I gestured at the raspberry almond. "Vuk, what do you think?"

He'd taken one bite of each cake and given exactly zero feedback for them.

That's your choice?

I frowned. "Do you not like it?"

It's not about what I like. His gaze sharpened. *Jordan hates almonds.*

Fuck. He was right.

Jordan's aversion to the nut had completely slipped my mind, but as his fiancée, I *should've* been on top of it.

That being said, why the hell hadn't he mentioned it on his preference profile? We'd filled ours out at the same time, so I knew he'd submitted his.

"Right. I guess we forgot to include it in our forms." I tried to play it off with a laugh. "We filled them in right after the Met Gala, and we were exhausted. I should've remembered today, but I have plane brain. You know how it is."

Vuk stared at me, his face dark with suspicion.

My pulse tapped a frantic rhythm against my veins.

It's fine. He doesn't know. So what if I forgot Jordan hated almonds? It was a small mistake. It's not like I threw his ring in the trash and said I hated him.

Even if Vuk found out about our arrangement, he wouldn't run to Jordan's grandmother and tattle on his best friend…unless he hated me so much he would use that as an opportunity to kill our engagement.

If it were anyone else, I would've dismissed the idea as far-fetched.

But this was Vuk Markovic. I wouldn't put anything past him.

After a tense, drawn-out moment, he shifted his attention back to Sammy.

I should feel relieved, but the knot in my gut only tightened. I couldn't shake the feeling that Vuk was adding the almond slip-up to some mental folder he'd compiled just for me.

Sammy watched us with a bemused expression. "So, no almonds. I'll make a note of that." He tactfully avoided commenting on my end of the conversation. "Do you have a second favorite flavor?"

"I think either the hazelnut with chocolate buttercream or the rose and Earl Grey." The latter was more aligned with my tastes, but this was a two-person decision. I attempted to engage Vuk again. "Which do you like better?"

It doesn't matter. I'm not the one marrying you.

I didn't lose my temper often. My parents taught me never to make a scene in public, and I tended to be more nonconfrontational than not.

However.

Vuk was being an *asshole*, and after a seven-hour flight, a phone call from Hank, and so much sugar I might've gotten a cavity, I was done tolerating his passive aggressiveness.

I signed my reply instead of verbalizing it. No need to make things awkward for Sammy.

I know that. I'm simply asking which one Jordan would prefer. Also—my hands cut sharp slashes through the air—*while I appreciate you taking the time to accompany me, I don't appreciate your uncooperativeness. You agreed to be here. Either act like a decent human being and pick a damn flavor, or leave. I'll find my way back without you.*

Sammy's eyes darted between us. The room was so quiet I could hear the receptionist typing up front.

Clack. Clack. Clack.

My heart thumped in rhythm with her jabs. I wasn't entirely convinced Vuk wouldn't storm out and leave me stranded in California, but he looked almost amused.

He tilted his head toward the rose and Earl Grey without taking his eyes off me.

Jordan won't care. But that one suits you more.

How did he...

Never mind. There were two choices. He had a fifty-fifty chance of landing on my favored one. It didn't mean anything.

"Option number two it is." I smoothed a hand over my skirt and smiled at Sammy. The poor guy was probably regretting taking us on as clients already.

"Perfect. I'll finalize the details with Vera up front. In the meantime, please." He gestured at the remaining spread. "Enjoy the drinks and food. I'll be back with more champagne to celebrate."

You've been holding that rant in for a while, Vuk signed after Sammy was gone.

My face flushed. "Only because you've been so...so..."

Uncooperative? I could practically hear his mocking tone.

I glared at him, but my biting response died a quick death when he reached up and brushed a thumb over my cheek.

I froze.

He'd never touched me before. Ever. He didn't even shake my hand when we first met.

My muscles instinctively tensed, torn between the impulse to flee and the desire to lean in.

His hand was rough. Strong. But his touch was surprisingly gentle as he rubbed the corner of my mouth.

Then it was gone, and oxygen flooded my lungs like I'd been holding my breath for hours instead of seconds.

I unconsciously touched the same spot he'd brushed. A ghost of warmth lingered.

Vuk's lips thinned. He wiped his hand on a napkin and tossed the crumpled paper into a nearby trashcan before scribbling something on a fresh napkin.

He pushed it toward me, his eyes cool.

YOU HAD FROSTING ON YOUR FACE.

Right. That made sense.

Heat scalded my neck and chest. What was wrong with me today? Why was I making our interactions into a bigger deal than they were?

Thankfully, Sammy returned at that moment and saved me from responding.

Vuk and I both declined one more glass of champagne. We wrapped up the paperwork, and fifteen minutes later, we were on our way to our hotel.

We'd booked Sammy's last appointment of the day. The sun was already setting by the time we left, and though we could've flown straight back to New York, staying overnight seemed preferable to taking a round-trip cross-continental flight in under twenty-four hours.

I put my body through enough during Fashion Week and unhinged photoshoots, so I tried to let it rest when I could.

"Mr. Ford and Ms. Kidane, welcome to the Winchester," the front desk agent chirped. I'd given her my ID for check-in, but I'd forgotten to change Jordan's name on the reservation. Neither Vuk nor I corrected her. "I see here that you're booked for one night in our Regal Suite. I'm happy to confirm that your room is ready. Here are your keys. The elevators are down the hall to your left. If you need anything at all, please dial zero for the front desk and we'll be happy to help."

I sucked in a sharp breath. *Shit.*

Jordan and I had booked a one-bedroom suite for appearance's sake. Unfortunately, I'd forgotten to change our sleeping arrangements after Vuk replaced him on the trip.

Beside me, Vuk went rigid.

"Apologies, there's been a last-minute change in plans. I should've mentioned this earlier, but it's been a long day." I gave the desk agent a sheepish look. "Can we add an extra suite to our reservation? We—that is, we'd like separate rooms if possible."

The agent's smile wavered. "I'm so sorry. The hotel is fully booked. There's a Riley K. concert this weekend and every hotel in the area is slammed. The Regal Suite is our only availability for the night. *But*"—she brightened again—"it does have a cot, so it sleeps two. Would that work?"

Vuk's hands curled into fists on the counter.

I gulped. I hoped he wasn't imagining strangling me. If we had to share the same room, I wanted to wake up in one piece.

"Miss?" the agent prompted.

"Um." I glanced at Vuk. One call from him would definitely free up a suite somewhere in the city. Hell, he could buy this entire hotel right now if he felt so inclined. But he hadn't offered, and I didn't want to ask. "That does work. Thank you."

Our suite occupied the top floor of the hotel. It boasted a living room, a dining room, a bedroom with an en suite marble bath, and yes, a cot.

A very small, flimsy-looking cot.

To be fair, it would've been adequate for anyone other than Vuk. The man was six-five and weighed at least two hundred pounds. He could crush that thing between his bare hands.

"You can take the actual bed," I offered. "I don't think you're going to, uh, fit on that."

I'm not taking the bed.

Fine. I wasn't going to argue.

As bad as I felt for him, I liked my silk pillowcases and Duxiana mattresses more. Sue me.

I was unpacking my toiletries and debating what to order from room service when the inevitable happened.

Vuk tossed his duffel onto the cot and sat.

The frame bowed with an ominous creak.

And, before either of us had time to register what that forebode, the cot promptly collapsed.

CHAPTER 4

Vuk

I'D ENDURED TORTURE BEFORE.

Knives, burns, shackles—I'd survived it all.

But this? This was *actual* fucking torture, and I had no one to blame but myself.

I glared at my laptop, willing myself to focus on my head of security's debrief instead of the closed bathroom door.

From where I sat in the living room, I had a direct view of that door, as well as the open suitcase filled with silks and lace in the bedroom. It was like she'd left it there on purpose to torment me.

The shower squeaked, followed by the sound of running water.

A muscle jumped in my jaw.

"…beef up our office security measures…" Sean's voice cut in and out of my thoughts.

I should've never agreed to accompany Ayana out here. Being near her in public was bad enough. Now we had to share not only the same room but the same fucking bed.

Due to its full capacity, the Winchester didn't have an extra cot to spare, so I was left to suffer for the night.

If only I'd found us another hotel earlier.

If only the greedy, selfish part of me—the one that'd foolishly wanted to be closer to her—hadn't won out.

If only.

"I didn't want to say anything until it's confirmed, but we have a lead on the person who started the Vault fire." Sean's update finally snapped me out of my escalating spiral.

I straightened, my pulse quickening. The fire was the only thing that could take my mind off Ayana these days, and Sean had just handed me a big fat distraction on a silver platter.

"We found traces of fiber that didn't belong to any of the workers or logged visitors at the site," he said. Sean was former Special Ops and had been one of Harper Security's top employees before I hired him for my personal team five years ago. He had the exact direct, no-nonsense attitude that I valued in my employees. "Given the state of the site after the fire and the bureaucratic red tape, it took us a while to dig through the evidence. Our guys didn't find the fibers until this morning."

I typed my reply in the chat. When we couldn't meet in person, we communicated via a secure encrypted network.

Any DNA evidence?

"No. However, we tracked down this photo from someone who was in the area around the time of the fire."

A picture popped up onscreen. A twenty-something blond in a Northwestern sweatshirt grinned into the camera. She was obviously a tourist, but I wasn't interested in her.

I was interested in the man in the background.

She'd captured her selfie right as he walked by. To the untrained eye, he looked like any other man going for a stroll.

To me, he looked like a man hiding something. The nondescript clothing, the relaxed yet alert body language, the angling of his face away from surveillance cameras—this was a professional.

A plain blue cap obscured half his features. He was around six foot two, Caucasian with a muscular build and dark hair. Black T-shirt, no identifiable logos.

Sean read my mind. "The shirt he's wearing is a potential match for the fibers," he said. "We pieced together the surveillance footage from surrounding businesses. We don't have a direct shot of his face, but when you take timing, clothing, and other relevant factors into account, he's the most likely suspect."

I examined the photo again and caught something I'd missed the first time—a hint of a tattoo peeking out from the sleeve of his shirt. He was too blurry and far away for me to make out the details, but that was nothing a good enhancer couldn't fix.

Once again, Sean picked up on what I was thinking. "We've enhanced the image and are analyzing the tattoo. It's difficult since we only see a quarter of it, but once we have the specs, we'll run it through our database."

I sent my reply. *Good. Chase it as far as you can. Money and time aren't an issue.*

I didn't care how many months or years it took; I was going to find the bastard who'd tried to kill me.

Earlier this year, during a walkthrough of the now-famous Vault nightclub where I was a silent partner, I'd nearly died during a "freak" fire. If the Vault's owner, Xavier Castillo, hadn't risked his life and dragged me out in time, I would be a pile of ashes.

Official sources chalked it up to old, faulty wiring, but the timing and method had been too coincidental.

I didn't believe in coincidences, and I definitely didn't trust the city investigators. I'd ordered my team to look into the fire themselves.

It was a testament to their loyalty that they'd never questioned me despite half a year of dead ends.

But we were getting closer. Like Sean said, the tattoo wasn't much, but it was something, and that was all I needed.

The bathroom door opened.

I exited out of the video call without another word and shut my laptop before Ayana even stepped foot in the bedroom.

"Sorry for hogging the shower," she called out. "It's all yours if you want it."

I glanced over. My teeth clenched as a visceral bolt of heat streaked through my blood.

Fuck.

She wore a gold silk robe that flowed past her knees. It was perfectly modest, but it didn't matter.

Makeup-free face.

Bare feet.

Glistening skin.

The sight of her fresh out of the shower was so goddamn intimate, it hit me like a punch in the gut.

I could handle her in a fancy gown or a swimsuit, but not like this. Not when the only thing that separated us was an expanse of carpet and my own fraying self-control.

She was my friend's fiancée. I had no business noticing the lush curve of her lips, or fixating on the bead of water dripping down her neck.

And I certainly had no business imagining my mouth following that water—down, down the slender column of her throat and into the shadow of her neckline.

But I'd always done things I had no business doing. No one had ever stopped me.

No one had ever dared.

I leaned back, my face impassive as Ayana walked over to grab her phone off the table. The sleeve of her robe grazed my arm when she reached across me.

An electric current ran the length of my body, intensifying my loathing, and I turned my head so I didn't have to breathe her in.

Some women had a signature scent, but Ayana wore a different fragrance every time. Sweet one day, sultry the next.

Tonight, there was no perfume—just the soft whiff of coconut from her shampoo and the natural scent of her skin.

I craved it as much as I hated it.

"Sorry," she apologized again. "I forgot I left my phone out here."

Stop apologizing.

Her eyes flew up to mine.

Two sorrys in two minutes is a bit much when you don't have anything to apologize for.

I didn't like the restrained, obsequious version of Ayana. It wasn't her. I wanted to see the version that'd bitten my head off back at the bakery—and who was glaring at me now like she wasn't sure whether she should agree with me or slap me.

Satisfaction leaked into my chest. *That's more like it.*

Granted, I could've worded it less like an asshole, but the more I kept her at arm's length, the better.

Why do you have to be back in New York by Monday morning?

I switched subjects, hoping the conversation would distract me.

Long legs, high cheekbones, rich brown skin, and dark eyes that gleamed with a mixture of intelligence and playfulness— even if she weren't a well-known model, Ayana would turn heads walking down the street.

But the majority of her allure for me didn't rest on her physical looks. It was the way she moved, with a natural grace that couldn't be taught; it was the way she laughed, so whole-heartedly and joyously that it could chase away the darkest shadows. And it was the way she glowed, like there was a fire inside her that was just waiting to be unleashed.

Fame or not, Ayana Kidane was born to shine.

"I have a photoshoot for Delamonte Cosmetics." She took the seat across from mine. Her midnight-black hair fell in waves past her shoulders, and her skin glowed beneath the suite's dim lights. She appeared oblivious to my inner turmoil. "I'm their newest beauty ambassador and this is my first shoot with them, so it's a big deal."

A big enough deal that her agent would call her on a Saturday to harass her about it.

I couldn't hear what he said, but I'd heard her end of the conversation. I remembered the way her nails dug into the seat and the tension underlying her voice.

It'd been more than stress; it'd been fear.

Hank Carson. I rolled the name over in my mind as I asked my next question.

Modeling. That was your childhood dream?

"Not exactly." She traced an absentminded finger over the table. "I loved beauty and fashion. I even convinced my parents to get me a *Vogue* subscription when I was eleven. But I didn't see myself as a model. I wanted to be…well, a lot of things. A pediatrician. A psychologist. An interpreter. I ended up studying chemistry and pre-med at Howard until I went to a friend of a friend's party at Thayer. Hank was there and scouted me. The rest is history."

I knew all this already. I'd watched every interview and read every article she'd ever been mentioned in.

But I relished hearing her share the details with me herself, though the trace of bitterness in her voice told me there was more to the story than she let on.

For a model who'd graced the cover of countless magazines and commanded the runways in New York, Paris, and Milan, she didn't appear too thrilled.

"What about you?" Ayana's eyes were bright with curiosity. "How did you get into the alcohol business?"

It was infuriating, the way my heartbeat thrummed at the faintest sign of interest from her.

I studied chemical engineering.

"That's not exactly a direct pipeline to running a multinational empire."

I also studied business on the side.

I didn't give her my whole, boring backstory, which was that I'd worked for a small distillery in my Virginia hometown in high school. I'd hated how it was run, so I'd saved enough money to buy it outright after college. After I took it over, I'd used my knowledge of chemical engineering to revolutionize the vodka-making process. Markovic Holdings was born, and it kept growing until it became what it was today.

"You could've led with that." Ayana's expression turned thoughtful. "Vuk Markovic as an engineer. I don't see it."

I ignored the thrill of hearing my name leave her lips and raised a questioning brow instead.

"It's hard to picture you as anything other than a leader. I can't imagine you…" she trailed off.

Can't imagine me what?

"I can't imagine you hunched over in a cubicle, developing manufacturing processes. That's all," she finally said. There was an odd hitch in her voice. Embarrassed, maybe, but also a little breathless.

What can you imagine me doing?

On the surface, it was an innocent question, but my hand movements were deliberate, almost lazy. They dared her to answer.

I was treading a dangerous path.

Here, in this room, with nothing except a small table separating us…it would be so easy.

She was so close I could reach over and slide that robe down her shoulders. Run my hands over her skin and see if it was as soft as it looked. Slide my tongue into her mouth and see if she tasted as sweet as I imagined.

The silence stretched.

Ayana's lips parted. There was no question she'd picked up on the subtle suggestiveness of my question—her eyes were wide, and I could see the wild flutter of her pulse at the base of her throat.

I expected her to walk away and end this charade once and for all. Women like her would never be attracted to monsters like me.

But she didn't.

She stayed seated, and she looked at me...she looked at me in a way she had no right to when she was wearing another man's ring—with awareness bordering on heat.

My blood burned hotter for an entirely different reason.

That *fucking* ring.

The diamond glittered in my peripheral vision and tossed a bucket of ice water over the moment.

She was engaged. I was the best man. And though I'd crossed many lines and twisted many morals in my life, loyalty was the one value I held fast to.

I stood abruptly, severing eye contact.

Ayana startled. "I—"

I didn't wait for her to finish.

I crossed into the bathroom and slammed the door behind me. My pulse rattled alongside the walls.

I was rock-hard, but I didn't touch my engorged cock.

Instead, I cranked the water as cold as it would go and let the icy drops pelt my body.

Self-inflicted punishment, perhaps, or simply masochism, just like my inability to stay away from the woman in the other room.

I rested my forehead against the tile wall and released a long, controlled breath.

It didn't help.

My mind still buzzed from whatever the hell happened out there. I was wound so tight, one more word from her would've made me snap.

If she were engaged to anyone except Jordan, I might've let it happen, consequences be damned.

But he was my friend, and once upon a time, he'd saved my life. That was the only reason I'd agreed to be his best man.

I was loyal to the people who were loyal to me.

Still, loyalty wasn't enough to tame the ugly green beast inside me. I had more money and power than Jordan, but I envied his ability to create and maintain normal relationships. He could glide through life without others gawking at him like he was a zoo exhibit, and as much as I despised most human interactions, there were days when I craved a normality I'd never have.

I resented his privileged upbringing, with its silver spoons and easy access. He'd never been forced to trade in his soul for money. He'd never lost the people he loved.

Most of all, I resented the fact that he had *her*.

I gritted my teeth.

Between the fire investigation and running a multibillion-dollar corporation, I had better things to do than obsess over my friend's fiancée. But like I said, my good judgment paled when it came to her.

Jordan and Ayana. The happy fucking couple.

Something unspooled in my gut—a slow, insidious poison that crawled into my throat and made me choke.

No matter how hard I tried, I couldn't dispel it because of them.

Because they were getting married.

Because I saw her first.

Because she was his when she should be mine.

CHAPTER 5

Ayana

"WAIT. YOU'RE SHARING A BED WITH VUK MARKOVIC?" Sloane's disbelief crackled over the line. "How did that happen?"

"I told you. I forgot to change the reservation and every decent hotel in the area is booked out for the Riley K. concert." I glanced at the bathroom door. The water was still running. Vuk had been in there for forty minutes, and I was trying *really* hard not to imagine what he might be doing. "And technically, we haven't shared the bed yet. It's just...an inevitability for when we do sleep."

"He really broke the cot just by sitting on it?"

"Yep." For a five-star hotel, the Winchester wasn't making the best impression.

I could practically hear her head shake in response.

Sloane Kensington had been my publicist for the past year and a half. She'd become a friend as well, so much so that I'd asked her to be one of my bridesmaids. I'd been pleasantly surprised when she agreed.

The sad truth was, I didn't have many friends in the city. I had plenty of fashion acquaintances. We worked the same shows, attended the same parties, and ran in the same circles, but I wouldn't consider them true *friends*. They weren't people I'd turn to when I was having a bad day, nor were they people I wanted to celebrate my wins with.

Thankfully, I had Sloane, who understood that world without being entrenched in it.

"As long as your hotel situation doesn't end up in the press, we're fine," she said. "The last thing we need is a scandal before Fashion Week."

"Trust me. I have no intention of causing any sort of scandal."

That being said, intentions and reality didn't always align.

What can you imagine me doing?

The memory of Vuk's question sent a frustrating tingle down my spine. The way he'd sat, his legs spread, his gaze cool yet mocking, like a predator lazing before a hunt.

It made me envision things I had no right envisioning, if only for a moment.

I barely knew him.

I wasn't sure I liked him.

And yet, his presence was so imposing that reacting to him was an inevitability, not a choice.

I shifted in my seat and glanced at the bathroom again.

"Ayana?" Sloane prompted. "Did you hear me?"

I blinked, my attention returning to the call at hand. "Sorry, can you repeat that?"

"Your interview with *Luxury Brides*. Can you confirm Jordan is okay with the schedule change?"

"Yes, we'll make it work."

Luxury Brides magazine was doing a huge profile on our wedding. They were sending their top correspondent to Ireland for on-the-ground coverage, but they wanted to do some preliminary interviews first.

I was already dreading it.

There was a short pause before Sloane surprised the hell out of me. "Are you sure you want to go through with the wedding?"

"Of course. Why wouldn't I?" I laughed, the sound pitched a decibel too high.

"You don't sound too excited whenever the topic comes up."

Nerves danced over my skin. I thought I'd done a good job playing pretend, but Sloane had always been too observant.

I'd also gone to her for advice when Jordan first came to me with his proposition. I hadn't revealed the business aspect of our arrangement, but I had expressed my hesitation about marrying him. I'd framed it as being torn between my gratitude—he'd given me my big break as a model—and my heart. I cared about him, but was that enough?

Sloane had advised me to listen to my gut; I'd listened to logic instead.

Not everyone had the privilege of following their heart.

"I'm just overwhelmed," I said. "I didn't realize how much went into wedding planning. It's stressful."

I wasn't sure she believed me, but she didn't press the issue. "As long as it's what you want." Sloane paused again. "If you need to talk to someone, I'm always here. I'm saying that as your friend, not your publicist."

That was as sentimental as Sloane Kensington ever got.

Emotion tangled in my throat. I forced a smile even though she couldn't see me. "Thank you. I appreciate that."

The moment soon passed, and we went over a few more publicity-related items before hanging up. It was past midnight on the East Coast, but she worked twenty-four seven.

I was about to check my email when the shower squeaked off.

My heart rate jumped, and I quickly averted my gaze when the door opened so it didn't look like I'd been waiting for him to come out.

Bare skin flashed in my peripheral vision, but I kept my eyes firmly planted on my phone.

At least, I tried.

Vuk bent down to fish something out of his suitcase. The muscles in his back flexed as he pulled a shirt over his head, and I glimpsed what looked like a tattoo on his inner arm before the shirt covered it.

What was the tattoo of? A symbol, a quote, a name, or a date? I wasn't going to ask, but I was desperate to know.

I fought an annoyed groan.

I had no frame of reference for my sudden awareness of him. It wasn't lust, per se. It was…intrigue? Curiosity? Morbid fascination?

It didn't matter. They were all shades of the same thing. *Inappropriate.*

Engagement of convenience or not, I was being paid millions to act like a doting fiancée. I wasn't going to ruin my plans over a few stray thoughts.

"How do you want to do this?" I asked after he was safely clothed. I nodded at the bed.

Vuk gave me a sardonic look. *It's a bed. We sleep in it.*

"I know that. But it's…You know what? Forget it." I stalked into the bathroom with a huff.

I changed into my pajamas and spent the next half hour doing my nightly hair and skincare routine while Vuk did whatever he did. Brooding and plotting how to murder me in my sleep, probably.

I didn't understand how he and Jordan were friends. Jordan was so gregarious and easygoing, and Vuk was…not.

After I layered on the necessary serums and creams, I brushed my hair, plaited it, and secured it with bobby pins. I wrapped it all up in a silk scarf before I reentered the bedroom, where I found Vuk sitting next to the bed, reading.

It was some sort of crime thriller, and I almost asked him about it before I caught myself.

I'd made enough overtures for the day. He was rude half the time, and I wasn't a glutton for punishment.

If he didn't want to converse like a civil person, I wasn't going to force him to.

I climbed into bed and deliberately turned my back to him. Petty of me, sure, but this way, I didn't have to notice how irritatingly attractive he looked with a book in his hands.

I never would've pegged him for a fiction reader, but I didn't know much about him at all. Even his answer about how he'd gotten into the alcohol business had been vague.

I stared at the clock on the nightstand. Half past ten.

Pages rustled, followed by the soft thud of a book landing on wood. A moment later, the bed dipped, and body heat engulfed me.

I stiffened, afraid that if I breathed too hard, we might touch.

It didn't matter how big the mattress was. We could be sleeping on opposite sides of the room and that would still be too close.

The comforter slid over my bare skin as Vuk settled into bed.

I squeezed my eyes shut and wished I'd worn something other than my skimpy satin pajama shorts.

I also wished I'd brought a book or my knitting needles to bed. That way, I'd have something to focus on besides the infuriating hulk of a man next to me.

Since I didn't, I simply lay there, restless, until I finally drifted off into an uneasy sleep.

———

Vuk

It was three in the morning, and I'd done fuck all since I turned off the lights besides stare at the ceiling and listen to Ayana breathe.

Her body had relaxed, and her breaths had evened out hours

ago. She was clearly sleeping soundly while I was tormented by the far-too-small gap between us.

Under normal circumstances, the hotel's king-size bed was enormous. Under my current circumstances? The Pacific Ocean wouldn't be large enough.

I could still feel her warmth.

I could still smell her shampoo.

I could still imagine how easy it would be to close the distance between us and kiss her until she was wet and wanting.

My teeth ground together. I closed my eyes and forced myself to think about something, *anything*, else.

The performance of Blackcastle—the London football club I'd bought—this season.

The investigation into the fire.

The goddamn burger I'd ordered from room service earlier.

None of it worked.

In the quiet hours between midnight and dawn, my worst impulses took precedence, and I couldn't do a damn thing about it.

I turned my head, my eyes so attuned to the dark I could easily make out the curve of Ayana's shoulder and the gentle swell of her hips beneath the comforter.

She slept so close to the edge she was practically falling off it—a reminder that I wasn't, and never would be, her fiancé. I was a placeholder on this trip. If Jordan were here, they'd probably be cuddled together like fucking sea otters.

They weren't moving in together until after the wedding, but I assumed they spent most of their nights in his house.

This was a normal occurrence for him. He wouldn't blink an eye at going to bed with her every night and waking up next to her every morning.

The thought ground through my head. The darkness closed in to the point where I almost choked on it.

Thankfully, my phone lit up with a silent notification right at that moment and dragged me out of my spiral.

Sean.

I forced a breath through my nose and opened his email, impatient for a distraction. The man slept as few hours as I did, which worked well for our relationship.

His message contained a single sentence.

The files you asked for are attached.

Satisfaction eroded some of my gnawing envy. This was why I paid him enough money to finance a West Village brownstone and his son's private school tuition. He did his job, and he did it well.

I opened the encrypted documents and scanned the contents. One was a full dossier on Hank Carson. The other was a similar report on his agency, Beaumont Model Management. It was named after its founder and owner, Emmanuelle Beaumont. Ayana had been signed with them her entire modeling career.

After her call with her agent, I'd asked Sean to send me everything he could find on Hank and Beaumont. At first glance, everything looked normal, but my gut told me there was something off about the agency.

I hadn't paid much attention to them before, but Ayana's anxiety over Hank's call had been a red flag. So was their clean record, now that I was looking at it. Besides the usual complaints of overwork and delayed payments, their profile was almost *too* clean.

For an agency that'd been around for two decades, there should be some sort of scandal or rumors of impropriety. This was fashion; the industry was a breeding ground for abusers.

Either Emmanuelle was a saint and Girl Scout rolled into one, or she had a damn good team covering her tracks.

That being said, the dossiers were only the start. There were financial records to sift through, clients to track down, and a complicated web of relationships and favors to untangle.

I'd do that myself. I wanted Sean focused on finding the arson suspect, and anything Ayana-related was mine. No one else touched it.

I exited out of the files and was putting my phone back on the nightstand when she stirred.

I froze.

She mumbled something—maybe I was hearing things, but I could've sworn she said *peanut butter*—and rolled over to her other side. The movement brought her within inches of me.

I stiffened. Before I could place some much-needed distance between us, she draped her leg over mine and sighed.

Her bare skin burned through my sweatpants like they weren't there. My body's reaction was so visceral, so instantaneous, that I jolted away without thinking. My shoulder slammed against the nightstand and sent a shock of pain down my arm.

Ayana startled awake. "What happened?" She sat up, a thread of panic running through her drowsy voice. "Is everything okay?"

I turned on the lights and tossed the covers off. My pulse hammered in my veins. *Everything's fine.*

My feet hit the floor. I grabbed my key card and phone again and stalked toward the door.

"Then why are you up at"—based on her pause, I assumed she was checking the clock—"three-thirty in the morning?"

I turned to glare at her. *I'm going to the gym.*

"At *three-thirty* in the morning?"

Yes. Hell, I'd sleep in the gym if I could. Anything to get away from her and erase the memory of her body against mine.

My expression chilled. *Go back to sleep, Ayana.*

I didn't wait for a response.

I left the room and headed straight to the hotel's lower level.

The fitness center was open twenty-four hours, but it was deserted at this time of night.

Ayana probably thought I was an asshole with mood swing issues. She wouldn't be wrong, but the more she disliked me, the better.

The only thing worse than having the woman you were obsessed with hate you was having her try to befriend you.

I grabbed a pair of dumbbells. My skin still buzzed from our brief moment of contact, but I ignored it.

Instead, I channeled all my pent-up frustrations into a punishing workout. If Sean were here, he'd berate me for being reckless with my body, but fuck that. He wasn't the one who had to sleep in the same bed as his friend's fiancée.

After an hour of weights and cardio, I finally stopped the treadmill and sank onto a workout bench. Sweat poured down my face and back, and my muscles screamed with fury.

I welcomed the ache. It gave me something else to focus on besides the mental image of Ayana in a white lace gown. I'd managed to push it aside during my workout, but now that I was sitting still, it came roaring back.

I rested my forearms on my knees, my heart thundering in my ears. The mirror opposite me reflected my glare.

Even after all these years, my reflection was a kick in the gut.

The scar across my face had faded from an angry red to a pinkish white, while the burns around my neck had settled into a purplish pink. The ruined skin was as healed as it would ever be, but it wasn't the aesthetics that made my insides twist.

Whenever I looked at myself, I remembered his screams. Smelled the reek of burning flesh. Felt the pain clawing at my face and throat.

Some things stay with you no matter how much time has passed.

Back then, I didn't have the money and medical access I had now. Even if I had, I would've left my scars alone.

They were my price to pay for what happened—rage and guilt and horror all packaged into a monstrous visage for everyone to gawk at. A warning to stay away, and a reminder of what I'd done.

Even if Ayana wasn't engaged to Jordan, she wouldn't be mine. We belonged in different worlds.

But there were moments—days—when I didn't give a fuck. She *belonged* by my side. And she was right there, only floors away, like the universe had dropped her in my lap on purpose to fuck with me.

My lip curled.

I tore my eyes away from the mirror and entered the adjoining bathroom, where I turned the water on full blast and took my second cold shower of the night.

CHAPTER 6

Ayana

VUK WAS ALREADY AWAKE AND DRESSED BY THE TIME I woke up the next morning. Perhaps he hadn't gone to sleep at all, but if the lack of rest affected him, I couldn't tell.

He sat at the living room table, drinking coffee and reading the newspaper while I got ready. Broad shoulders and rough edges, his shirt open at the collar to reveal a sliver of lightly tanned skin. Not a trace of fatigue marred his glacial features.

I didn't bother saying good morning. He didn't deserve it after last night.

Petty of me, I know, but I was tired of getting rebuffed. I didn't believe for a second that he suddenly got the urge to work out at three a.m. He just didn't want to be near me.

We checked out of the hotel and rode to the airport in silence.

Vuk's staff was ready for us when we arrived, and it didn't take long before we were in the air and on our way back to New York.

I swallowed my nausea and avoided looking out the window at the clouds below. I'd taken an anti-anxiety pill before wheels up, but it took a while to kick in. Until then, I was stuck with rampant images of plane crashes and twisted debris.

My apprehension over flying wasn't debilitating. If it were, I wouldn't have been able to do my job.

However, it did stress me out to the point that I was secretly a wreck unless I had a companion to distract me. My aunt had nearly died in a plane crash when I was fifteen. After her accident, I'd delved down a rabbit hole of crash research, and the images I'd seen had seared themselves into my brain. Every time I stepped on an aircraft, I was convinced those would be the last moments of my life.

Vuk, on the other hand, seemed perfectly at ease. He sat across the aisle, his head tipped back and his eyes closed. A welcome glass of champagne sat untouched on the table in front of him.

"Why do you hate me so much?" My question cut through the silence with one neat slice.

I would say it just slipped out, but it'd been simmering beneath the surface for months. There was no better time to ask the hard questions—and to distract myself from my sick imagination—than when we were trapped on a six-hour flight together, I suppose.

Vuk opened his eyes and turned his head. His expression was unreadable. *You think I hate you?*

"Don't you?" I gestured between us. "You go out of your way to avoid me. When you can't avoid me, you barely acknowledge me. You'd rather spend the night in a hotel gym than in the same room as me, for Christ's sake. And don't try to feed me any bull about how you don't like anyone. There's a marked difference between the way you treat me versus other people." I took a deep breath. "I know I don't come from a rich family, so maybe you think I'm not good enough for Jordan. Regardless, we're engaged, and we *are* going to get married. You're the best man. The least you could do is act civil until the wedding is over."

My frustration spilled out in its full glory.

I was *sick* of his hot and cold attitude. While I'd read him a similar riot act at yesterday's tasting, we were alone now. I didn't have to hold back, and it was time to tackle the root of his issues with me once and for all.

Something dark flickered in Vuk's pale eyes. He turned away deliberately and wrote something on a notepad.

A moment later, he unfolded himself from his seat, and I instinctively sank deeper into mine. My heart rate kicked up when he moved toward me.

Why had he written his reply instead of signing it? Had I finally pushed him over the edge? Was he going to murder me right here on his private jet?

There was no one else around except for the pilot and flight attendant, both of whom were in his employ. I doubt they'd come running to my aid.

Vuk stopped in front of me. He was so tall I had to crane my neck to look at him.

I held my breath as he unclenched his fist and dropped the crumpled note in my lap. It wasn't until he disappeared into another cabin that I allowed myself to relax and read what he wrote.

My pulse fluttered at the words scratched in bold black.

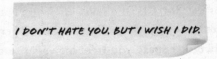

I DON'T HATE YOU. BUT I WISH I DID.

Vuk didn't explain his note; I didn't ask.

Someone wishing they hated you was almost worse than actual hate, and I was too exhausted to chase him down for an explanation. Trying to pry a direct answer out of him was like trying to pry blood out of stone.

Hours later, while he locked himself in the bedroom suite, I stared at my bank account.

Objectively, it wasn't terrible. I made a substantial living compared to the average person, but I knew what *should* be in the account versus what was *actually* in there. There was a huge disparity between the two.

Beaumont paid for all my costs and expenses up front—hotels, transportation, test shots back when I was a new model. So on and so forth. However, like most modeling agencies, they expected full repayment for those costs, and I was indebted to them for years until I booked enough high-paying jobs to climb out of that financial hole. Sort of.

My post-debt years with Beaumont had been marked with late or missed payments, excuses, and subtle threats whenever I tried to chase them down. I was still owed money for jobs I completed a year ago.

Unfortunately, the modeling industry was a largely unregulated one. Financial exploitation and other forms of abuse ran rampant, and there wasn't much the models could do.

I was lucky to have a decent nest egg and family close by. Even so, I was held captive by my contract, which prohibited me from leaving the agency without "mutual consent." If I did, I had to pay them an eye-watering sum for breaking their terms. It was money I couldn't spare—not when New York was so expensive and my income from modeling was so unstable. I was doing great now, but future success wasn't guaranteed. That was why I needed the money from my arrangement with Jordan—to buy out my contract, cover my legal fees, and maintain a financial safety net. I exited out of my bank account and typed out a text to Hank.

> Checking in on the Crystal Water payment. The shoot was eight months ago, and I still haven't gotten the money.

Fifteen minutes passed before he replied.

HANK

> Sorry babe, don't know anything about it. You'll have to take it up with accounting.

I knew that would be his answer, so I didn't bother following up. I just wanted a paper trail.

I set my phone aside and finished my water. Despite my upcoming payday from Jordan, my stomach was in knots. So much could go wrong between now and February.

What would happen if I couldn't get out of my contract? Would I be stuck with Beaumont forever until—A sudden jolt sent my phone crashing to the ground. Plates clattered in the kitchen galley, and a flash of lightning streaked through the gray skies outside. The jet shook so hard I felt my bones rattle.

Just like in my morbid imaginations earlier.

Oh God.

Bile surged as every thought about Hank, Beaumont, and my finances flew out of my head. The only thing I could focus on was the nauseating rise and dip of the aircraft.

How high were we in the air? Thirty, forty thousand feet? How long would it take before we plummeted to earth and exploded into a fireball?

Vuk strode into the main cabin, his expression tense. He managed to walk steady despite the shaking—was it normal for turbulence to last this long?—and he took the seat beside mine without a word. Behind him, the flight attendant strapped herself to her designated seat.

The seat belt. Right. I should do that.

I barely heard the pilot's warning about staying seated as I fumbled with my seat belt. The clasp kept slipping out of my sweaty palms.

Why won't the damn thing *close*?

I felt a small brush of air as Vuk reached over and snapped the seat belt in place for me.

"Thank you." The words scraped past a dry throat.

Before I could say anything else, the plane suffered another massive jolt. This time, I couldn't hold back a scream, and I instinctively grabbed Vuk's hand.

He tensed, but he didn't pull away.

Breathe.

I forced myself to count to ten, over and over, until the shaking subsided. Only then did I relax, though adrenaline continued to pump through my blood.

It was also then that I realized I was still squeezing Vuk's hand. He glanced at where I touched him, his jaw tightening.

"Sorry." My face flushed. "I don't deal well with turbulence."

I moved to pull away, but his fingers curled, trapping my hand in his. His skin was rough and warm, his hold steady.

The breath vanished from my lungs for a second time. I opened my mouth—to say what, I wasn't sure—but at that moment, the jet rattled again.

The chicken and spinach I'd had for lunch tossed in my stomach. I couldn't take much more of this. If my adrenaline kept dipping and spiking, I was going to throw up all over the custom-engraved tray table.

Thankfully, the aircraft steadied soon. Gray turned to blue outside the window, and the pilot came over the PA system to assure us we'd made it past the expected turbulence. It should be smooth flying ahead.

Once the PA system clicked off, Vuk dropped my hand like a hot potato.

I wiped my palm against my thigh, hoping it would stave off the tingles. It didn't.

"How did you know?" I assumed he'd held on to me when I tried to pull away because he knew we would hit another patch of rough air.

When you fly enough, you sense these things.

That seemed like a stretch, but honestly, I wouldn't be surprised if he possessed supernatural powers. There was something unnervingly forbidding about him.

To my surprise, Vuk stayed beside me despite the pilot's all-clear. His gaze slid from my sweaty face to my tight-knuckled grasp on my knee.

Like I said, I didn't deal well with turbulence.

We were landing in an hour or so, and it would take that long for me just to recover.

You're afraid of flying, but you chose modeling. It wasn't a question.

"Chose" was a strong word, but I let it slide.

"I'm not afraid. I'm uneasy." Okay, sometimes I was afraid, but *most* of the time, I was uneasy. "It usually helps when I have someone to talk to. They keep my mind off the fact that we're trapped in a little tin box in the sky because some genius decided it would be a good mode of transportation."

A hint of amusement glided through Vuk's eyes. *What do you talk about?*

"Anything. Everything. Movies, memes, current affairs." Then, because I couldn't resist, "How some people blow so hot and cold you don't know where you stand with them."

Vuk ignored that last part and fixated on the last topic I would've expected from him. *Memes.*

"Yes. Like the Kermit the Frog memes? Or the guy blinking nervously?" I spent a lot of time waiting and doom scrolling at casting calls, so I was well-versed in internet jokes.

Whenever I found a good one, I sent it to my sister, but she was usually so busy with her kids or her nursing job that she didn't respond until days later.

I sent a funny video to Jordan once and spent half an hour trying to explain the joke to him. I never sent him one again.

Vuk slanted a sideways glance at me. *I know what memes are.* A pause. *What do you and Jordan talk about when you fly together? Specifically.*

The short answer: we didn't. I tried to calm myself by reading my favorite fashion and perfume blogs while he worked. I couldn't tell Vuk that, though.

"Family." It was the first thing that popped up in my mind. "Our families," I clarified. "And, um, how they're going to be one family soon."

I internally cringed. I sounded like an idiot.

If Vuk agreed, he didn't show it. *Tell me about your family.*

I paused, surprised to realize how long it'd been since I talked about my family with anyone outside of it.

"They live in D.C.," I said. "I have two older siblings, Liya and Aaron. Liya is an ER nurse at Thayer Hospital, and Aaron works at the restaurant my parents own. They're grooming him to take over after they retire in a few years."

What kind of cuisine?

"Ethiopian. They're from Addis Ababa, and they opened the restaurant when I was a teenager because they missed the taste of home. There's a huge Ethiopian community in D.C. so there were already quite a few restaurants, but none of them can make sambusas the way my father makes them."

I smiled wistfully at the memory of our weekly Friday night

dinners, when the whole house was redolent with the aroma of chicken and spices. Liya, Aaron, and I would bicker over our chores while my father cooked and my mother set the table.

We would often have guests over too. Our house was a revolving door of aunts, uncles, cousins, and family friends, many of whom brought *their* friends for a taste of my father's famous cooking.

I loved New York, but in D.C., I had a community. After six years in Manhattan, I was still struggling to find my footing.

I called and texted my parents often, but it wasn't the same.

"We have a big extended family," I added. "They live up and down the East Coast, but every holiday season, we have a big reunion at my grandparents' place in Maryland."

I'd missed several reunions over the years because of work. They were so used to it by now they didn't bother pressuring me to "take time off," which made me feel even worse.

The flight attendant came by to offer us more food and drinks. Vuk and I both declined before he focused on me again.

Who's your favorite sibling?

I side-eyed him. "Are you trying to get me in trouble?"

He shrugged, a shadow of a smirk playing around his mouth.

I didn't know what to make of his sudden interest in my personal life. I hadn't forgotten his earlier note: *I don't hate you. But I wish I did.*

But he wasn't acting like he wanted to hate me. He was acting like he genuinely wanted to know more about me.

We were apparently blowing hot again. As much as I hated his mood swings, it'd been so long since I'd had a real conversation about anything other than work and the wedding. It was...nice.

Vuk's mouth flattened into a straight line again. *Why Jordan?*

I blinked, so thrown off by the sudden switch in topic it took me a minute to respond. "I don't know what you mean."

Why did you choose to marry him?

Choose. That word again.

I supposed I *had* chosen to marry him, but like my modeling career, it was out of necessity more than anything else.

My entire adult life had been shaped by circumstances out of my control.

A rock lodged in my throat. I crossed my legs and smoothed a hand over my skirt, stalling for time.

I wasn't a fidgeter, but Vuk's questions—his very presence— set me on edge. I felt like I was teetering on the precipice of ruin. One wrong move, and everything would come crashing down.

"Why wouldn't I marry him?"

Deflection 101: answer a question with a question and hope they moved on.

Vuk's gaze bore into mine, so cold it burned.

That's not an answer, Ayana.

I'd never heard his voice, but the phantom sound of my name sent an electric shiver down my spine.

"He's nice." I suppressed a wince at my milquetoast description. "We've known each other for a long time, and we enjoy each other's company. He's exactly the type of person I should marry."

I wasn't selling our love story at all, but in my defense, no one had ever asked me why I was marrying Jordan. The model and the fashion CEO. To most people, the answer was obvious.

Unfortunately, Vuk wasn't most people.

If we use your logic, I would've married Jordan before you. I've known him a long time, and I enjoy his company.

I would've teased him about almost making a joke had it not been for the strange sparks dancing beneath my skin. "That's a lie. You don't enjoy anyone's company."

Wrong.

"Name one person whose company you enjoy. Besides Jordan."

Does he not count as "anyone?"

"Not for the purposes of this conversation. I'm trying to prove a point."

Which is?

"You don't like people."

People in general, no. His gaze dipped for a moment before meeting mine again. *But there are exceptions.*

A haze thickened in the air. It smoldered with every inhale.

Vuk wasn't talking about me. He couldn't be, not based on the way he'd treated me in the past.

But he'd joined me on this trip.

He'd held me when there was turbulence.

And when he looked at me, I felt like a living, breathing person. Not a mannequin. Not a cash cow. Not a role model for girls I'd never asked to be a role model for.

Just a regular human with interests and a life outside the one my agency constructed for me.

I don't hate you. But I wish I did.

The haze crisped at the edges and burned away my previous notions of Vuk's feelings toward me. Did he—

The seat belt sign dinged. The pilot's voice crackled over the intercom. "We've begun our descent into New York City. If you need to use the restroom or other facilities, please do so now. We'll be landing shortly."

The haze cleared. Oxygen rushed back into my lungs, and when I glanced at my phone, I was shocked to see an hour had passed since the turbulence started.

My conversation with Vuk had done more than distract me from my near-death panic; it'd made me forget it entirely.

When I looked up again to thank him, he was already gone.

CHAPTER 7

Vuk

I COCKED MY GUN AND AIMED.

BAM. BAM. BAM.

Every shot punctured the paper target's head and heart with clean holes until I ran out of bullets.

Afterward, Sean came up beside me and examined the target with arched brows. He held a file in his hand. "Feel better?"

Not even close. Not when my weekend with Ayana continued to weigh on my mind.

Instead of responding, I simply reloaded my gun.

We were the only people at the Valhalla Club's shooting range. It was one of the club's less popular facilities, which made it the perfect place for us to brush up on our skills and discuss private matters.

Truthfully, guns weren't my favorite weapon. They were too impersonal. If you hate someone enough to kill them, have the balls to do it up close, where you can see the light die in their eyes.

Professionals and psychopaths aside, it separated those who killed for purpose and those who killed out of impulse. Only the former possessed the conviction to follow through when they could feel their victim's last breath on their skin.

That was why I preferred knives. They were precise, versatile, and always personal.

However, when I needed to blow off steam or take my mind off a certain supermodel, guns would do.

"I have news that'll take your mind off whatever you're pissed about," Sean said when I remained silent. He handed me the file. "We identified the suspect's tattoo. Seventy-five percent match based on what was visible in the photo. It's the most we could hope for given what we had to work with."

I put my gun down and opened the folder. It contained a single blown-up photo of the tattoo in question: a black scythe with a hissing viper twisted around the handle.

My blood ran cold. There was only one organization whose members got inked with that specific tattoo.

The Brotherhood.

"Obviously, this complicates things," Sean said. "At least now we know for sure the fire wasn't an accident and that they're after you. We understand their motive."

I shut the folder and dropped it on the table. ***Do we?***

My last bloody altercation with the Brotherhood happened almost thirteen years ago. We'd existed in uneasy mutual peace since then. They left me alone; I let them live.

So why the hell were they coming after me again after all this time?

"Not the exact motive," Sean amended. He'd learned ASL after I hired him, so he understood me perfectly. "But we will figure it out. Have you received any unusual communication recently? Noticed anyone new or suspicious lurking around? Mail courier. Delivery person. Electrician. Anyone who fades into the background that could get temporary access to you."

I shook my head. I was trained to look out for suspicious behavior. If I'd spotted something, I would've told Sean immediately.

"That's what I thought, but I had to double-check." Sean's lips thinned. The Brotherhood wasn't your average two-bit criminal operation. My head of security was worried, and I didn't blame him. "I've already put together a plan to increase our security measures. Do you want me to put a detail on Willow too?"

Willow was my former right-hand woman and long-time assistant. She'd been my mother's best friend, and after my parents died, she took care of me like I was her own son.

She'd retired earlier this year and moved to Oregon. Her health wasn't so good anymore, and her daughter recently gave birth to her first grandchild. She wanted to spend more time with family. I'd respected her wishes and gave her a hefty severance package as a goodbye gift.

We still talked regularly, but we didn't see each other as often as we used to. I hadn't replaced her with a new assistant yet either; I didn't trust anyone enough.

No. We don't work together anymore, and she's in Oregon. They won't go after her. I paused, then added, *Don't change our hard security measures yet either. We don't want to tip them off that I know.*

Sean's eyes widened. "We'll be sitting ducks," he argued. "Our current security is excellent, but against the Brotherhood... they could attack again at any minute."

They could do a lot of things. But they haven't.

Things had been ominously quiet since the fire. No attempted assassinations, no freak accidents. I'd started second guessing my instincts about the fire being intentional until Sean confirmed the Brotherhood's involvement.

Knowing them, they were waiting for me to slide into complacency before they struck again. That gave me another month, perhaps more.

Like me, they were nothing if not patient.

Upgrade our soft security measures, including cyber and surveillance. We'll play it off as part of our annual assessment. Also change our passcodes, locks, etc. But I do not want any visible additions to manpower.

Nothing would alert the Brotherhood more than additional guards around my house and offices.

"Understood." Sean retreated to his lane, and we fired off another dozen rounds before we turned in our equipment.

No one blinked an eye when we entered the club's main building. Sean only had access because he was my guest, but the other members were used to seeing him around. Even if they weren't, they were smart enough not to question who I brought here and why.

The Valhalla Club was the most exclusive members-only society in the world. Some people were born into the privilege of membership; I'd fought and clawed my way in.

But I was here, and I'd landed the directorship of the club's management committee. The position rotated between high-level members every five years, and I was nearing the end of my term. Nevertheless, I still had access to director perks including unlimited guest passes and near-free rein of the facilities.

I'll find out what the Brotherhood wants. Sean and I passed a well-dressed trio on our way to the foyer. A visiting prince from Europe, the CEO of a telecommunications company, and an exorbitantly wealthy cosmetics heiress turned entrepreneur, respectively. They took one look at us and scurried down the hall. *You deal with the suspect.*

Sean nodded.

After he left, I took the elevator up to my office. Besides my extracurricular activities, I had my own company to run, as well as Valhalla business to take care of.

My head pounded as I poured myself a glass of Markovic vodka, neat. I tossed it back in one swallow.

It was only after I finished my third glass that I braved a look at the most hated part of my body.

Not the scars, not the burns, but the tattoo inked on my inner bicep: a black scythe with a viper curled around the handle.

———————

If I had a choice, I'd devote the entirety of my time to hunting down the Brotherhood again.

Unfortunately, obligations must be met, which was how I found myself at the Vault that Friday.

The nightclub had skyrocketed to notoriety since its grand opening five months ago, and an invitation to its Tastemaker nights—which granted attendees early and exclusive access to the best events in food, fashion, literature, and more—was the hottest ticket in town.

As a silent partner, I contributed capital but stayed out of its day-to-day operations. Those fell on Xavier Castillo, the heir to the Castillo beer fortune and now the most powerful name in New York nightlife.

"Good to see you, Vuk." He slapped a hand on my shoulder. "You'll be happy to hear business is booming. I'll have last quarter's reports to you on Monday."

I nodded, indifferent. My partnership was more a formality than anything else. I didn't count on it being a major revenue stream, though I was impressed by how well Xavier was running things.

When he first came to me last year with his idea for the Vault, I'd dismissed him. The former playboy had a reputation for frivolity, indolence, and debauchery, none of which were qualities I looked for in a business associate.

However, he'd impressed me with his tenacity and vision for the club. Even after the fire set construction back by weeks, he'd pulled things together in time for its splashy grand opening in the spring.

I'd invested well.

But I wasn't here to bask in the Vault's success. Tonight's Tastemaker event was a coveted first look at Lilah Amiri's new collection ahead of New York Fashion Week.

Jordan had returned from Rhode Island and asked me to meet him here to discuss an "important matter." He was constantly trying to get me to leave my house, hence the insistence on meeting at parties and restaurants.

But tonight? I would've come even if he hadn't invited me.

After Xavier excused himself to make the rounds, I scanned the room. It was packed with a who's who of the fashion world, but I skipped past the nameless models, designers, and magazine editors in search of...

There.

My gaze zeroed in on the corner where Ayana stood with Jordan. They were speaking with a leggy blond in a blue dress—Sloane, Xavier's girlfriend and Ayana's publicist.

A silvery peal of laughter carried over the music and settled low in my gut.

Ayana's laugh was what had grabbed my attention the very first time I saw her. It was infectious, joyful, and full of life—the antithesis of how I lived my own life.

But I couldn't stop thinking about it. I couldn't stop thinking about *her*. And the more I watched her, the deeper my obsession grew, until its vines were so twisted up inside me, I couldn't hack them off without killing myself too.

Ayana said something that made Jordan grin. He wrapped his arm around her waist and whispered something in her ear. She laughed again, her smile flashing white in the dimly lit club.

I took a deliberate sip of whiskey, my eyes trained on the angle of her body and the placement of his hand.

The alcohol washed down my throat, burning away the toxic green fumes of envy and leaving a bitter aftertaste in their wake.

Seeing her with Jordan was torture; not seeing them and letting my imagination run wild was worse.

Either way, I was fucked.

A group of raucous partygoers quieted as they came near. They skirted around me, giving me a wide berth.

Besides Xavier, Jordan, and a small handful of other people, no one approached me at events. It was exactly what I wanted.

I had little use for small talk and even less use for ass-kissing. I was here for one reason and one reason only.

I tipped my glass back and finished my drink without taking my attention off the couple in the corner.

Jordan said something else to Ayana before leaving her side. His hand grazed her hip on his way out.

The empty glass cracked in my hand.

In six months' time, I'd have to watch them kiss. Marry. Fuck off to the type of happily ever after that was never meant for people like me.

The glass shattered.

The conversations near me lulled, followed by an outburst of gasps and whispers. Two staff members immediately appeared to take the broken glass out of my hand and sweep up the broken shards.

"Many apologies, Mr. Markovic," one of them said. A small tremble ran through his voice. He avoided looking me in the eye while his colleague did his best to fade into the background. "Please, let us get you a Band-Aid for that cut. If you'll follow us…"

I glanced at the smear of blood on my hands. I'd barely felt the pain before he brought it up.

"We'll make sure to double-check the integrity of all our glasses…"

Oh, for fuck's sake.

I shook my head, cutting him off. The incident wasn't his fault, and it damn sure wasn't the glass's.

I grabbed a napkin to stave off the bleeding and waved the men away. They disappeared without question.

The music was loud enough that only the people in close proximity to me noticed what happened. Ayana was still chatting with Sloane, but the other woman left a minute later.

Ayana was alone.

She sipped her drink and looked around the room, her gaze skimming over me before she did a double take.

Our eyes met. A soft glow of surprise illuminated her face, and the sting from my cut receded.

She took a step toward me.

However, before she made it any further, a man with slicked-back hair and a red shirt cut into her path. She came to an abrupt halt, her mouth hardening.

The man didn't have to turn around for me to recognize him. *Hank Carson.* Her agent.

Something dark and unpleasant slithered through my veins.

I'd been going through his and Beaumont's files. I hadn't pinpointed why they'd raised red flags yet, but I would. Until then, it would be interesting to see their dynamic play out in person.

So I watched.

And I waited.

CHAPTER 8

Ayana

"HANK." I MASKED MY DISPLEASURE WITH A TIGHT smile. What the *hell* was he doing here? "I didn't think you were the clubbing type."

He smiled back, all sophistication and artificial charm. He was objectively a handsome man, but I'd seen behind his mask and found the sight revolting. "I'm not, but it's a Tastemaker event. Considering how many of my girls are here, I figured I'd make an appearance."

There were a dozen other models from Beaumont in attendance. I'd exchanged brief hellos with them when I arrived, but everyone was too busy schmoozing to hang out with people they deemed competition.

"How thoughtful," I deadpanned.

"I heard the Delamonte shoot went well on Monday." He returned his attention to me. "You received a rave review from the photographer."

"I told you you didn't have to worry."

It was my first major beauty campaign, and I'd been a ball of nerves going into the shoot. Luckily, the photographer and crew had been fantastic, and everything went off without a hitch.

"Hmm." Hank's eyes bore into mine. "Where did you go after you wrapped?"

My breath stalled.

No. He couldn't know. I'd been so careful.

He knows everything, a voice whispered in my head. It was the same voice that'd told me it was a bad idea to head to a contract lawyer's office after I finished the Delamonte Cosmetics shoot. I should've waited until Hank was out of town.

I'd dismissed my misgivings as paranoia. How could Hank have found out? I'd chosen a law firm that had no ties to the fashion industry, and their office was across town from Beaumont's. My agency couldn't possibly have spies in every business in Manhattan, though it certainly seemed that way at times.

My gut knotted.

"I ran some errands, worked out, then went home," I said.

"What kind of errands?"

"Dry cleaning, groceries, the post office." All true, though I'd left one notable stop out. I adopted a playful tone. "Why the sudden interest in the mundane details of my life?"

"I'm invested in the lives and well-being of all my girls. As your agent, it's my job to have a holistic view of everything that goes on in your life. You know that."

Yes, because my post office runs were so integral to my success as a model. What bullshit.

"Speaking of which, I have good news." Hank smoothed a hand over his tie. "Sage Studios called. They're booking you for their denim campaign."

My heart leapt. "That's great!"

My dislike of Hank didn't override my pleasure at booking a job. Although modeling hadn't been my childhood dream, I'd grown to love it.

"Yes. You haven't done a big commercial clothing campaign

in a while. Prestige is great, but commercial pays the bills." Hank clucked his tongue. "Wentworth will be thrilled. He's been wanting to shoot you again for ages."

My smile melted. "Wentworth...Holt?"

"Is there another Wentworth who matters in fashion?" Hank's tone indicated there was only one answer. *No.*

The knots in my gut constricted further. "I told you I don't want to work with him anymore."

"It's a good thing what you want doesn't matter." Hank delivered his response so casually that I would've questioned whether he meant what he said had I still been a new model. "Wentworth is the most influential fashion photographer working today. You *will* shoot with him, and you *will* stay on his good side."

My fingers strangled my water glass. "I don't care. He's a predator."

The industry was filled with them, but everyone turned a blind eye. It was a tale as old as time: the more powerful they were, the more they got away with, and Wentworth Holt was Powerful with a capital P.

If he refused to work with a model, her career was all but over. Unfortunately, he also had a reputation for being a little *too* hands-on at his shoots—and not in a professional way.

"Have you witnessed inappropriate behavior firsthand, or are you repeating gossip and lies?" Hank asked coolly.

"I've seen how he's treated other models on set. He's made *me* uncomfortable on set."

Wentworth wasn't stupid enough to try anything with other people around, but he certainly toed the line of what was appropriate. The last time we shot together, he groped me and tried to play it off as "adjusting" my outfit—which was the stylist's job.

I hadn't worked with him in over a year after I expressed my concerns to Hank. I foolishly thought that meant the agency was taking my boundaries into consideration for once, but I should've known better.

"Making someone uncomfortable is not *predatory behavior*." Hank scoffed. "This is fashion, and you're a star, babe. So suck it up and stop whining." He raised an eyebrow. "You don't want to develop a reputation for being difficult, do you?"

I gritted my teeth. Reputation was everything, and rumors that a model was "difficult" could tarnish even the brightest of careers.

Before I could reply, Hank's smarmy smile fell off his face. He glanced over my shoulder, his expression now one of trepidation.

I was about to turn and see what had him so spooked when I felt it.

His presence at my back, cool and commanding. The faint smell of whiskey and leather. The soft brush of his shirt against my arm.

He didn't utter a word; he didn't need to.

Awareness warmed the nape of my neck.

"I'm going to check on Vlada." To his credit, Hank managed a half-convincing facade of calm. "I'll email you the details for the Sage Studios campaign."

He disappeared into the depths of the club, and I waited until he was out of sight before I finally faced the person who had him scampering away like a frightened rabbit.

My heart gave a small thump.

"Vuk Markovic at a nightclub." I covered my breathlessness with a playful smile. "Will wonders never cease?"

He lifted an eyebrow. *I'm a partner here. I've been to nightclubs before.*

"Only for business. Not for anything fun."

He'd been at the grand opening, and that was it.

I didn't realize you kept such close track of my comings and goings.

"I don't, but it's difficult not to notice you when you're there." I meant it in a matter-of-fact of way, but I didn't realize how suggestive it sounded until the words left my mouth.

Vuk's eyebrow rose another inch.

Heat scorched my cheeks. "I mean, because you're so big. Height-wise," I added hastily. "Obviously, I'm not talking about anything else."

Obviously.

His mouth tipped up. Was he *laughing* at me?

I attempted a glare, but it was impossible to be angry when I'd brought this on myself. Besides, he didn't appear to be mocking me. It almost felt like we were…flirting.

The thought wasn't as off-putting as it should've been.

"Tell me." I set my glass down on a nearby table. "If you weren't here tonight, what would you be doing? Brooding in a corner somewhere or terrifying peasants and children?"

His eyes glittered with amusement. *I can do both right here. I'm a good multitasker.*

An image of what that multi-tasking might look like flashed through my mind for a millisecond.

Hands and mouth. Rough kisses and fisted hair.

Nothing at all to do with brooding or children.

I swallowed past the dryness in my throat.

"You talk a big game, but I've yet to see it in action." I picked up my water again and prayed he didn't notice my flustered tone. "What do you do besides scowl and boring business stuff?"

I play bingo.

The answer was so swift and unexpected, I nearly choked on my drink. "Excuse me?"

Bingo. It's a game where players match the numbers called to the ones on their card.

"I know what bingo is." I glowered, unsure whether he was

serious or having fun at my expense. "You're telling me that's what you do when you're not running a multibillion-dollar corporation?"

Among other things.

"Where, exactly, do you play bingo?" He had to be joking.

Senior centers if I'm feeling social. At home if I'm not. He shrugged. *My staff enjoy the game as much as I do.*

I tried to picture Vuk Markovic playing a rousing game of bingo with his staff in that giant mansion of his.

I could no more imagine a lion breaking out into dance in a tutu and tiara.

Still, the image of Vuk enjoying something so mundane was oddly charming. It lent him a rare sheen of normality—if he wasn't lying about the bingo, that was. I still wasn't sure.

"How old did you say you were again?" I teased. "Eighty?"

Bingo is a game of chance. No complexity required. It's the perfect activity to help me unwind after making decisions at work all day.

I never thought of it that way. "Do you win often?"

Vuk's mouth curved a fraction more. His eyes glittered, pale and sharp as crystals. *I always win.*

On anyone else, the arrogance would've been astounding. On him, it was a mere fact of life.

Vuk Markovic always got what he wanted.

The party swirled around us. Lilah's preview was scheduled to start soon, and Hank was still lurking somewhere, but it was impossible to focus on those things when exhilaration fizzed through my veins.

As much as I liked Lilah, I'd spent all week dreading tonight's event. I didn't want to make small talk with industry people, and I only came because Jordan asked me to. Hank's unwelcome appearance solidified my dread.

For better or worse, Vuk's presence wiped that away in one fell swoop.

When I first moved to New York, I'd dated casually. However, none of the men were interested in anything more than a one-night stand or a trophy girlfriend. The more I advanced in my career, the worse my options got, and now that I was engaged, I couldn't even *attempt* to date anyone else.

I wasn't trying to date Vuk—this was not a man who "dated" anyone—but when I was around him, my world opened up again. The potential, the possibilities…the rush of *what if*.

He gave me a glimpse at what my life would look like if it were mine again.

Vuk stepped closer to allow another attendee past. His shirt grazed my chest, ever so lightly, and little fireflies danced all over my skin.

His eyes appeared darker up close. More heated.

"There you are." The sudden sound of Jordan's voice was the equivalent of getting tossed out into a snowstorm after cozying up by the fire all night.

I jerked back, my heart skittering even though Vuk and I hadn't been doing anything wrong.

Vuk's expression wiped blank as Jordan came up beside me. He'd returned from Rhode Island that morning, just in time for tonight's highly anticipated preview.

He hadn't updated me on his grandmother's health yet, but he had alluded to the fact that we needed to discuss something important.

"Vuk! Good to see you." Jordan clapped his friend on the shoulder. "I was just looking for you."

The other man responded with a cool nod. All the banked heat I thought I'd detected earlier was gone; not a trace of emotion marred those features carved of ice and stone.

The corners of my world folded in again. Possibilities blinked out one by one like stars dying in the night.

Once more, I was Ayana Kidane, the supermodel and doting fiancée.

I wanted to scream.

"The preview is about to start, so this is perfect. There's something I need to tell you. *Both* of you." Jordan rubbed a hand over his mouth. His eyes were slightly bloodshot, and unease trickled into my bloodstream. "As you know, my grandmother got sick last week, but it wasn't a passing illness. She was diagnosed with a lung disease. Apparently, she found out last month but hadn't told us. I spoke with her doctor, and the prognosis isn't good. He said she likely won't be mobile by the end of the year." His tone was bleak. "I spent the week with her, and after much...discussion, she made her wishes clear."

Concrete blocks piled up in my stomach. *Oh no.*

"She wants us to move the wedding up," Jordan said. "I'm her heir, and her wish is to see me marry while she's still fully functioning. She doesn't want to risk waiting until February."

His words formed a strange bubble in the air. Despite the noise from the rest of the club, you could've heard a pin drop in our tight circle.

Vuk stood so still one could've mistaken him for a statue. If it weren't for the tiny flare of his nostrils, I would've thought he hadn't heard Jordan at all.

Meanwhile, a storm of emotions tumbled through me.

Guilt that I'd been thinking only of his friend while his grandmother was dying. Shock at the Ford matriarch's request. And, most of all, that crushing dread again.

"Move up the wedding?" My voice sounded strained to my own ears. "To when?"

Jordan sighed. "October," he said, sounding as happy about it as I felt. "Two months from now."

CHAPTER 9

Vuk

I HAD SEVERAL PROBLEMS—THREE, TO BE EXACT.

One was the Brotherhood's reemergence in my life. A week had passed since my meeting with Sean, and we were no closer to tracking down the suspect or figuring out the Brothers' goals.

Two was my CFO's monotone drone as he discussed Markovic Holdings' latest fiscal quarter. He was competent, but his voice could put a bear on cocaine to sleep.

Three...

My jaw ticked.

Jordan and Ayana's wedding, now scheduled for the end of October.

Six months, I could somewhat deal with. Six months was in the new year, far enough away that I could dismiss it as a near-distant possibility.

Two months was concrete.

Two months made me want to burn the whole fucking church down.

We're done for the day.

My dismissal popped up in the chat and brought the proceedings to a crashing halt.

The members of my executive team gaped at me. Apparently, they couldn't conceive of why I wouldn't want to listen to them discuss earnings and dividends for hours on end.

"But sir, we haven't..." The CFO faltered at my glare. "Of course. I'll send the full reports to you right away so you can review them at your leisure."

I logged off, restless. The thunderstorm outside matched my mood and cast a dreary gray pall over my home office.

At least I wasn't at my corporate headquarters, suffering constant interruptions. I hated the song and dance of corporate life. The bowing, the scraping, the ass-kissing from yes-men who would leap into an ocean of piranhas if I told them to.

I'd built Markovic Holdings from the ground up after college. At first, the challenge had intoxicated me. The money and status that came with it also provided an additional buffer in case the Brothers went back on their word and sought retribution.

However, after thirteen years of stocks, mergers, and product launches, I was so bored I'd contemplated shooting someone just to liven things up.

Perhaps I should pay Hank a visit and use him as an example. Ayana's discomfort around him at the Vault hadn't escaped my notice, but he still held the keys to her career. I couldn't make my move yet.

When I did, it would be thorough. It was better to take one's time and do something properly than rush into it—no matter how badly I wanted to smash Ayana's agent's face in the minute we returned to New York.

Instead, I settled for opening the dossier on Beaumont again. I had my network looking into the Brotherhood, but the organization had overhauled its operations over the years. Some of my old sources were dead; the others were cast out in the cold.

It was taking longer to get answers than I would've liked, but I would get them. Until then, I needed something else to take my mind off the fucking wedding.

I reviewed the Beaumont files for the third time. I'd sifted through the rest of their available records, but I kept coming back to the initial dossier.

I still hadn't pinpointed what tripped my inner alarms the first time I scanned them. A connection my subconscious seized on, perhaps, or a name my memory stashed in a dusty drawer.

Whatever it was, it was important, and it went beyond Ayana.

After half an hour and no progress, I tossed the dossier aside and poured myself a glass of scotch. Everything I'd consumed since the Vault tasted like shit, but I downed the drink anyway.

My home study was custom-built to my standards: large, secluded, and quiet, with a window overlooking the back courtyard and a maze of halls separating it from the main rooms. It brimmed with furniture and books but few personal effects.

The only nod to my past came in the form of a framed diploma from Thayer. It was where Jordan and I met.

If we'd never met, I wouldn't be his best man. I would be freed from the torture of watching him and Ayana walk into a room together.

But if we'd never met, I wouldn't be a CEO; I'd either be trapped with the Brotherhood or dead.

In a way, I owed everything I had to him, but I would give it all up for one thing—one person—in exchange.

If I'd said something about Ayana after I first saw her, would he still have pursued her?

If he hadn't, would she be by my side instead?

No. I would've kept watch from afar, she would've gotten

engaged to some other bastard along the way, and unburdened by the debts of gratitude or friendship, I would've killed him.

Instead, I was trapped in a hellish limbo where I couldn't act either way. I couldn't have her, and I couldn't kill him.

I finished a second glass of scotch and returned to my desk. Loathing turned my blood to acid.

My obsession with Ayana was a double-edged sword. I craved her presence even when it drove me mad; I fixated on her absence even when it consumed my thoughts.

Whether she was near or far, I suffered.

I picked up the Beaumont dossier and read it. Again.

Perhaps it was the alcohol or the desperate need to forget October's festivities, but the words formed a different shape this time around. Clearer, more distinct.

I skimmed past the agency's origins and zeroed in on the founder's bio.

Emmanuelle Beaumont, née Élodie Beaumont. Early fifties, born in a tiny town in France, changed her name to be more "fashionable" after being scouted on vacation in Paris when she was a teen.

Élodie. France. The timeline…

The connections snapped into place as ice chased away the burn from the alcohol.

It could be a coincidence, but like I said, I didn't believe in coincidences.

I grabbed my phone and messaged Sean.

> I need you to dig into something for me. Immediately.

CHAPTER 10

Ayana

"DO YOU KNOW WHY YOU'RE HERE, AYANA?"

Don't panic. "Hank said you wanted to discuss my career goals going forward."

Emmanuelle leaned back, the picture of stylish sophistication. Her smile formed a bold slash of red across her face.

At age fifty-two, the owner of one of Manhattan's preeminent modeling agencies could've passed for a woman half her age. Not a single wrinkle marred her porcelain skin; not a single hair dared stray from her sleek blond bob. She possessed the same elegance that had made her such a phenomenon in her modeling heyday, but there was a sharpness to her that prevented me from relaxing in her presence.

She reminded me of a beautiful serpent lying in the grass, waiting to strike.

"Yes. It's your six-year anniversary with us," Emmanuelle said. Her lightly accented voice was as smooth and crisp as her perfectly tailored blazer. "You've achieved enormous success over the years, and I couldn't be prouder."

"Thank you." I crossed my legs and forced myself to maintain eye contact.

Emmanuelle's inner sanctum was deceptively warm. Small potted plants lined the shelves next to her desk; photos of her husband and son dotted various surfaces.

In all my years with the agency, she'd called me into her office twice—once when I signed with her, and once after I booked my first multimillion-dollar campaign.

It was enough for me to know the welcoming decor was a trap.

"I wouldn't be where I am without you," I added. I knew how to play the game. "Your mentorship over the years has been invaluable, as has Hank's hard work and guidance."

It was a bald-faced lie. My real mentor was Fabiana, the former Brazilian supermodel who'd taken me under her wing after we met at the Model of the Year awards five years ago.

Admittedly, we no longer talked as often now that she was remarried and traveling around the world with her new husband, but she'd personally done far more for me than Emmanuelle had.

"I'm glad to hear that." Emmanuelle didn't blink an eye at my obligatory flattery. "Perhaps that's why I'm confused to hear that you've been unhappy with your compensation timelines. That doesn't sound like the attitude of a grateful model, does it?"

Bone-deep cold stole through me.

Crap. I had to tread carefully.

My engagement to Jordan afforded me a semblance of leverage, but until we were married and I got my money, Beaumont held all the cards.

"Of course I'm not unhappy. I'm so grateful for all the agency has done for me over the years." I placed as much sincerity as I could into my voice.

Pushing Hank was one thing; antagonizing Emmanuelle was another. She was one of the most powerful and well-connected people in fashion. The last time one of her models pissed her off, the girl disappeared overnight. The agency said she returned to

Wisconsin for "mental health reasons," but rumors abounded about what really happened.

I was skeptical of the sensationalism, but one could never be too careful. Regardless of what happened to the girl, it was a well-established fact that Emmanuelle could ruin anyone if she put her mind to it.

"As you know, I'm in the midst of wedding preparations," I said. "Part of it includes discussing my finances with Jordan. That was how the status of my payments came up."

"I see." Emmanuelle's smile returned. "I'm sure those payments pale next to the Ford family fortune, but I understand why you'd want to bring something to the table. I'll speak to accounting. We wouldn't want to tarnish your big day with such a little hiccup."

My fingers curled around the edge of my chair. That *little hiccup* was my career and financial well-being. "I appreciate that. Truly."

"Good. I'm glad we're on the same page." Emmanuelle returned her attention to her computer. "You can go."

I stood and walked toward the door. My skin felt like it was stretched too tight over my body.

"One more thing." Her voice stopped me dead in my tracks. "The denim campaign with Wentworth Holt. Will that be an issue?"

Ugly little shards wedged into my chest. "No." My mouth formed an approximation of a smile. "Not an issue at all."

I spent the entire elevator ride down picturing Emmanuelle and Hank's faces when I quit. I wanted to take a hammer and smash those big glass windows of hers on my last day here. Return every bit of gaslighting and condescension they'd thrown at me tenfold.

The simmer in my blood matched the alarming violence of my thoughts.

I forced a deep breath through my nose. I couldn't afford to get too worked up. Even if I quit, I had to maintain my professionalism.

Once you reached a certain height, people looked for any

excuse to tear you down. I'd be damned if I handed them the opportunity myself.

That was why I'd agreed to Jordan's proposal. It gave me enough money to buy out my contract, and covering my financial bases with Beaumont before I left was the only way I might appease Emmanuelle enough to keep her from badmouthing me all over town. When she talked, people listened, and as much as I despised the bad actors in fashion, I loved the actual art of modeling.

My relationship with the camera, the way I came alive when the shutter clicked, the exhilarating rush of slipping in and out of different personas the way I slipped in and out of dresses—those things were *mine*. I couldn't lose them.

The late summer heat steamed off the sidewalk when I finally exited the building. It was at least ninety degrees, the air so thick and muggy it condensed like soup in my lungs.

I had two hours until my fitting at the Stella Alonso showroom, so I stopped by a nearby café for caffeine first. Fashion Week started tomorrow. Between the grueling prep and wedding anxiety, I was running on little sleep these days.

The café was packed, but I took solace in the rush of people. The noisier it was, the easier it was for me to retreat into myself.

I stared at the chalkboard menu and tried to calm my racing heart.

I'm fine. Everything was fine.

Emmanuelle hadn't banished or blacklisted me, and she didn't know about my plans to leave. If she did, she would've been less subtle with her threats.

As for the wedding...well, that was another matter.

It was Thursday, nearly a full week after Jordan dropped his bombshell at the Vault. Since then, it'd been a scramble to update our logistics and notify the guests and vendors.

Jordan and I agreed that moving the reception up on such short notice was impossible, so we settled on an alternative: a small, intimate ceremony for our closest friends and family in New York, followed by the Irish and Ethiopian receptions in February, as originally planned. His grandmother cared more about the vows than the party.

My parents freaked out when they first heard about the change in plans, but since the church ceremony shouldn't affect the party they'd planned, they eventually calmed down.

Logistics aside, getting married earlier than planned shouldn't be a big deal. Most brides and grooms would probably welcome it. The sooner the wedding, the sooner they could spend the rest of their lives together. An earlier date also meant I'd get my money faster. If I was lucky, I'd be out from under Beaumont's thumb before the holidays.

But Jordan and I *weren't* spending the rest of our lives together, and October loomed in a way February hadn't. Even the prospect of leaving my agency couldn't untangle the knots in my chest.

"Miss?" The cashier's prompt brought me back to the present. I'd made it to the front of the line without noticing. "What would you like to order?"

"Oh, sorry," I said, flustered. "Just a large green tea. Hot. Thank you."

I paid and stepped back—straight into the person behind me. I whirled around, but my second apology in as many minutes died when I saw the dark buzz cut and blue eyes.

"Vuk." My pulse ratcheted up again. "What are you doing here?"

He raised his eyebrows and glanced at the espresso machine. *Right.* Coffee. Duh.

I composed myself while he placed his order and joined me next to the pickup counter.

He was dressed for work in a black suit, no tie, but that didn't dampen the air of danger he exuded. It was in the way he moved, the way he stood, the way his eyes took in every last detail of his surroundings.

No amount of tailored clothing could hide the fact that he was made for the battlefield, not the boardroom.

"Did you have a meeting nearby?" I asked.

I hadn't seen Vuk since he abruptly excused himself after Jordan's announcement. I imagined he was busy doing CEO things and planning the bachelor party, so it was strange to see him in here in the middle of the day. The café was nowhere near his house or his office.

He nodded but offered no elaboration.

Shocker. The day Vuk willingly shared information about himself was the day I willingly wore Crocs in public (i.e. never).

"Green tea for Ayana!" the barista called out.

I picked up my drink and hesitated. Despite his reticence, Vuk's presence calmed my earlier nerves—probably because I was too busy overthinking every detail of our interaction to focus on anything else.

"You're welcome to join me if you want." I threw out the invitation on impulse and sat at a recently vacated table nearby. "I have some free time before my next appointment. I could use the company."

I'd brought my knitting materials. I'd planned to work on my latest project (a hat made from a beautiful cerulean yarn I'd picked up in Scotland) before I ran into him, but I'd rather talk to him than knit.

I wanted to know him better. He was Jordan's best friend, which meant we'd be around each other for years to come. He'd also accompanied me to California and calmed my nerves during the flight back. Strangely, I wanted to see more of that side of him. The softer, gentler side, though nothing about Vuk could be considered particularly soft *or* gentle.

Despite my invitation, I didn't expect him to say yes. It was a workday, and he had better things to do than hang out with me.

I'd already resigned myself to my own company when he grabbed his coffee before the barista had a chance to call his name. He ignored her double take when she saw his face and took the seat across from mine.

He was so large and the chair so small, he resembled a giant sitting on doll's furniture, but his warning stare told me to keep that observation to myself.

I fought a smile. "I would've thought a big-shot CEO would have his assistant fetch his coffee. How down-to-earth of you to get it yourself."

I always pick up my own drinks. Less risk of them getting poisoned that way.

I stared at him. "Are you serious, or was that a joke? Actually, never mind." I held up a hand. "Don't tell me. I don't want to know."

People weren't really running around poisoning rival CEOs, were they? Yet the idea somehow seemed more plausible than Vuk Markovic making an honest-to-God joke.

His mouth tipped up, but his eyes remained impassive. *How's the wedding planning going?*

My chest deflated while my mouth maintained a smile. "It's going great. The church ceremony is small, and Vivian is on top of it." Jordan and I had hired Vivian Russo, a well-known luxury event planner. She was also one of Sloane's best friends, and I had full faith in her to execute the big day flawlessly. "We'll get everything done in time. It's going to be a beautiful ceremony."

I'm sure you're thrilled. You've been counting down the days, haven't you?

Vuk's trap unfolded so casually I would've missed it had I not spotted the near-imperceptible tensing of his shoulders.

He was testing me. Why? Had he picked up on my horror at the Vault before he left? Or was he still suspicious about my almond slip-up at the cake tasting?

Either way, he was watching my face like a hawk.

"Well, I obviously wish we were getting married under better circumstances, but what bride doesn't dream of her wedding day?" I hoped he didn't notice the slight shake of my hand when I brought the cup to my mouth again.

Just minutes ago, I'd convinced myself an earlier wedding was a good thing for various reasons, but Vuk's words sent those rationales scattering like leaves in the wind.

I *should* be thrilled. After all, a platonic marriage wasn't that different from my current (nonexistent) love life, and I was getting paid for it to boot. Plus, Jordan and I were good friends, and we had fun together. There were far worse things than being married to a good friend.

But friend didn't equal lover, and platonic didn't equal romantic.

At the end of the day, it wasn't love. Not the kind that I would be thrilled about.

Once again, that's not an answer. Vuk hadn't touched his coffee. His attention was wholly focused on me, and I suddenly empathized with how bugs under a microscope must feel.

"It is. Why are you so obsessed with my thoughts and feelings regarding the wedding anyway?" A hint of irritation snapped into my voice.

It wasn't like me to lose my cool, but every time I extended an olive branch, he used it to browbeat me with his arrogance. What happened to small talk and pleasant conversation?

I want to know if you're in love with Jordan.

"Why?"

He's my friend. You're marrying him. Connect the dots.

It was incredible how quickly I went from being happy to see him to wanting to slap him.

"You," I said, squeezing my cup so tightly a drop of liquid splashed over the side, "can be a real jerk."

I've been called worse. The bastard didn't even blink. *Answer the question, Ayana. Are you in love with him?*

Yes. One word, one syllable. It was a simple enough lie.

The response hovered on the tip of my tongue, yet I couldn't bring myself to say it. I chose a workaround instead.

"I love Jordan, and I'm marrying him." I took a steadying breath and squared my shoulders. I wasn't *in love* with Jordan, but I did love him—as a friend. "So unless you have a legitimate or *personal* objection to our union, I would appreciate if you stopped interrogating me about it. It makes me uncomfortable."

The earlier crowd had dispersed, leaving the café empty save for us and two baristas. My voice traveled the length of the small space, but the staff studiously avoided looking our way.

Perhaps they were too scared of Vuk, whose jaw had tensed so much I was surprised his teeth didn't crack.

Noted.

That was it. No pushback, nothing else to be said.

My brief burst of indignation popped. "Thank you." Something passed through my chest that I couldn't name. It was tight and heavy, but it was gone so quickly I paid it no mind.

I searched for a new topic of conversation. "The bachelor party is next weekend. Have you figured out what you're doing yet?"

Yes.

"Okay. So what's the big plan?"

This is the second time you've asked me about the bachelor party. Vuk finally took a sip of his coffee. *You say I'm obsessed. Maybe I'm not the only one.*

Blood rose to my neck and chest. "I am not obsessed. I'd hardly call one repeat question *obsessed*."

Whatever helps you sleep at night.

"Keep it up. I *will* take off my heels, and I *will* stab you with them," I threatened.

Vuk leaned back and stretched like I'd offered him a day at the spa. *What if I said there'll be strippers at the party?* His lazy stare didn't lose any of its original sting. He could pierce armor with those eyes. *Would you be upset?*

I couldn't care less. I'd only asked about the bachelor party because it was the first thing that popped up in my head, but it was hard to summon any real interest in Jordan's stag night activities.

When we made our arrangement, we'd agreed that the other person could do what they wanted with whomever they wanted as long as they were discreet. Ironically, neither of us would take advantage of that loophole.

Jordan wasn't interested in romantic relationships with anyone ever, and I was too paranoid for an affair, even one sanctioned by my husband. I didn't trust any potential lover to keep his mouth shut. The last thing I wanted was scandal or for Jordan to be humiliated.

Of course, I couldn't tell Vuk any of that.

"It's entertainment. It doesn't mean anything," I said. "Everyone has strippers at their bachelor party, and I trust Jordan won't cross the line. If he does, I'm sure you'll rein him back in. That's what the best man is for."

A scowl fell over Vuk's face. He appeared deeply displeased at the prospect of playing babysitter.

It occurred to me then that Jordan wouldn't be the only one entertaining strippers. Vuk would be there too.

The tight feeling returned, this time for an entirely different reason.

He didn't strike me as a lap dance type of guy, but as the best man, he was expected to participate in the festivities. Besides, how well did I really know him? He could be a regular at the Vermilion Lounge, the city's most high-end strip club, for all I knew.

An image of Vuk sitting in a dark VIP room while a busty dancer ground against him flashed through my mind.

The tea's aftertaste turned sour, and I quickly pushed the cup away.

Vuk watched me quietly. ***If you were my fiancée, I wouldn't look at another woman. Entertainment or not.***

Somewhere in my lungs, a bubble of oxygen collapsed.

If you were my fiancée...

The sentiment brushed over my skin, soft yet rough.

I'd never heard Vuk speak. Few people had.

According to Jordan, Vuk stopped talking verbally to most people after an undisclosed incident in his past. But the shock of his words was so potent he might as well have touched his mouth to my ear and poured those twenty-three syllables straight into my bloodstream.

If you were my fiancée, I wouldn't look at another woman. Entertainment or not.

Vuk's gaze narrowed.

I wondered if he could read the thoughts scrawled across my face. If he heard my pounding heartbeat or noticed the telltale heave of my chest when I couldn't hold my breath anymore and expelled it all in one great rush.

Time slowed. The whir of espresso machines retreated into a dull background roar.

Then he straightened again, and the thread holding this moment aloft snapped with disorienting swiftness.

Noise rushed back in, punctuated by the jingle of bells above the door as a new customer walked in.

Hypothetically speaking, of course. Vuk's expression was one of impersonal civility.

"Of course." I managed a bright tone. "Well, I hope you have fun next weekend. That's when I'm having my bachelorette too."

He started to sign a response, but he froze halfway. His attention snapped to something over my shoulder, and his face darkened with such animosity I instinctively recoiled.

I have to go. He pushed back his chair. The metal screeched against the tile floor. *Thank you for letting me join you for coffee.*

I stared, mouth agape, as he disappeared out the door. I was so thrown by his abrupt departure that I didn't dwell on the novelty of his first-ever thank-you to me.

I spun around and searched out the window for what might've caught his attention. Nothing stood out.

The only thing I saw was a pizza delivery guy, Vuk's retreating back and, further down the street, a tourist in a blue baseball cap.

CHAPTER 11

Vuk

SAME HEIGHT. SAME BUILD. SAME CAP AS THE MAN from the surveillance photos.

From the back, my target was a dead ringer for the mystery Brother, but his gait gave him away. It was too hesitant.

Nevertheless, he was another thread in the Brotherhood's web. It was the only thing with the power to tear me away from Ayana.

He turned left onto a side street. I followed him, keeping enough distance for discretion but not so much I risked losing him. My pulse drummed in my ears.

He'd been tailing me all day. I'd picked up on it immediately after I left the house, but I'd lost him somewhere between the Upper East Side and Beaumont's headquarters.

He didn't pose an immediate threat—if he wanted to kill me, he would've tried the instant I stepped outside my house—so I'd pretended not to notice. But passing by so deliberately when I was with Ayana was a clear fucking violation. I didn't want her anywhere near their radar.

The Brotherhood usually didn't drag innocent civilians into

their business, but one could never be too careful. Their rules of engagement might've changed over the years.

I should've slipped into Beaumont's office like I'd originally planned instead of changing course to follow Ayana when I saw her leaving their headquarters, but I couldn't resist. An extra moment alone with her was worth the disruption—unless it put her in danger.

The man in the blue cap slowed his pace while I kept mine steady.

The street we were on was so narrow it wouldn't fit even the smallest car. Shuttered windows and graffitied walls lined the grimy path, and a stray cat scampered behind a dumpster when I approached. Otherwise, there was no other sign of life.

Blue Cap nearly reached the end of the street before his self-preservation instincts kicked in. He whirled around, his expression like that of a rabbit who sensed a predator looming.

It was too late; I'd already caught up with him.

He swung at me, but I easily dodged the hit and slammed him against the wall. My forearm pressed up against his chain. He flailed, trying to throw me off, but his struggles gradually weakened as he ran out of energy and oxygen.

Considering how he'd gone out of his way to provoke my attention at the café—he had to have known I would see him through the window and follow him—he was putting up a valiant effort to escape.

Either he was an imbecile, or he was arrogant enough to think he'd escape my notice.

However, his sloppiness confirmed what I'd suspected: he wasn't a Brother. The organization may have changed over the years, but they would never slack so much with their recruits.

I narrowed my eyes, taking in Blue Cap's reddening face. He reeked of fear.

There was no one else around. If I exerted a little more pressure on his windpipe…

"Wait!" he choked out. "This isn't what you think. I'm not—"

I pressed my forearm harder against his throat and watched him claw at my hold with cold apathy.

No, I wouldn't kill him yet. He was a source of information, but even sources needed some extra motivation.

I waited until his face morphed from red to deep purple before I eased my hold.

He gasped, his chest heaving with great deep breaths. "I'm not here to hurt you," he wheezed. "Someone paid me to follow you and get your attention. He said—he said I couldn't just come up to you. I had to make you come to me."

See? Nothing loosened the tongue faster than the fear of death.

"Why?" My voice sounded guttural after years of little use. I hated wasting words on unimportant people, but it was necessary in situations like this.

"I don't know!" Tears welled in Blue Cap's eyes. "He paid me a thousand dollars in cash to wear this cap and pass along a message. He gave me your home and office addresses. I really needed the money, so I didn't ask questions."

The man in the photo must've known Blue Cap's resemblance to him would catch my attention. The hat was the cherry on top.

"The—the note is in my pants pocket. Left side." Blue Cap looked like he sorely regretted agreeing to what he thought was easy money.

He could be lying. The Brothers weren't above faking victim-hood in pursuit of their goals, but I'd developed a finely honed radar for bullshit.

He was telling the truth.

Even so, I kept my arm on his throat and my senses on high alert while I retrieved the note. It came in a plain white envelope with my initials printed on the front in black Times New Roman font. Simple, generic, untraceable.

"Describe him," I commanded.

"He approached me outside a bar last night. It was dark, and he had a hoodie and sunglasses on. I couldn't see—" Blue Cap choked as I cut off his air once more.

"Wait! Wait." He panted. "I—I do remember that he was around my height. Similar build. He was maybe in his late twenties or early thirties? It was hard to tell, but...but he smelled like motor oil. Like a mechanic or something."

Interesting.

I filed that information away for further inspection. There were several abandoned garages around the city that could be used as a safe house. It was worth looking into.

Blue Cap didn't have any more useful intel, so I released him with a cool threat not to speak a word of this incident to anyone. I didn't tell him what I would do if he broke his promise; I didn't need to.

I waited until he'd scurried off before I opened the envelope. Blue Cap's wallet with his ID rested in my pocket. He hadn't even noticed me take it.

Sean could run his name through our database later; for now, I was focused on the contents of the note.

One sentence, typed in the same generic black type as my initials.

Find me before they do.

CHAPTER 12

Vuk

THE NOTE CONTAINED NO FINGERPRINTS, NO DNA, AND no way to identify who'd sent it or where they'd bought the card stock.

My team's lab analysis results confirmed my suspicions, but we were missing something. I was sure of it.

Find me before they do.

It'd been a week since I chased down Blue Cap. His background check turned out to be as dull as his wits; he really was just an unfortunate soul the mystery Brother had picked out to do his dirty work.

If the Brother wanted me to find him, he would've left a clue. A search of the abandoned auto repair shops in and around the city had yielded nothing. If he was moonlighting as an actual mechanic, that broadened our search radius by miles.

I turned over the details of the situation in my head.

The facts: The man from the photo was a member of the Brotherhood, he was still in New York, and instead of hiding, he wanted to get my attention. He should know I wouldn't let the Vault's fire slide, so his motive for doing so had to outweigh his desire to live.

The unknowns: The reason for the Brotherhood's sudden interest in me again, whether the mystery Brother was acting on his own or with the leadership's approval, why he didn't seek me out himself, and who "they" were. It could be the Brotherhood; it could be someone else.

There were far too many unknowns for my comfort.

As if shit wasn't complicated enough, I also had to deal with work, the wedding, and my hunch about Beaumont while Sean investigated Blue Cap's motor oil clue.

I blinked away the mental image of the note and refocused on my computer screen. It was playing a video of Stella Alonso's latest runway show. I'd already watched it, but I liked having it on while I worked.

New York Fashion Week had just ended, and while I would never attend the shows in person, I kept up with select ones online.

Stella, Delamonte, Prada, Saint Laurent, Dior. They all had one thing in common.

The music's bass dropped, and my pulse tripped in anticipation.

A second later, Ayana appeared on the runway in an ethereal lavender dress. Her skin glowed effortlessly beneath the lights, and loose curls peeked out from an ornate headpiece. The headpiece shadowed half her face, but I'd watched her walk enough times to recognize her distinctive strut.

The Ayana Kidane on the catwalk was a different person from the one who'd invited me for coffee and teased me about bingo. Her persona morphed with every show, oscillating from playful and flirty to haughty and regal. A goddess to suit every mood.

But no matter what role she slipped into, onstage or offstage, she maintained a spark that was entirely her own. It was that spark that kept me coming back over and over again.

Waiting. Watching. *Obsessing*.

The video ended. I contemplated replaying it for a third time, but a new text interrupted me first.

JORDAN

Checking in on the bachelor party prep

JORDAN

We good to go? Let me know if I need to do anything

Reality ground my momentary pleasure into dust. The bachelor party was this weekend, a fact I'd tried to forget even as I confirmed the plan with other attendees.

No. Everything's set

JORDAN

Are you sure? Because you've never planned a party before

JORDAN

Minus the Great Halloween Incident our junior year

I scowled. Jordan was the only person who could've convinced me to throw that disastrous party in college. He was always encouraging me to "loosen up and have fun." I'd finally caved to his incessant pleas, and look what that'd gotten us—a formal disciplinary hearing with the school, a permanent ban from the local supermarket, and two hundred rolls of toilet paper that we couldn't give away fast enough.

Had it been fun? Sort of, while it lasted.

Had I loosened up? No.

I told you never to bring that up again

JORDAN

Right. But I'm just saying, you hate parties. So if you do need help, I'm more than happy to pitch in.

A low growl rumbled in my chest.

I did hate parties, but I'd agreed to be the best man. I wasn't going to pawn my duties off on someone else, no matter how much I loathed the task.

Thankfully, Jordan was laid-back when it came to parties. Give him a strong drink and good music, and he was happy. It was one of his best qualities. Despite his wealthy background, there wasn't a pretentious bone in his body.

> Ask me if I need help again and I'll change our plans to camping. With bears.

JORDAN
> ...

JORDAN
> You're on top of it. Got it. No more questions from me.

I set my phone aside and tried to refocus, but now that the bachelor party and, by extension, the wedding were on my mind, I couldn't get them out.

Jordan and Ayana.

Ayana and Jordan.

The walls of my office closed in. Pressure suffocated my chest, and I suddenly couldn't stand to be inside anymore.

I logged out of my computer, grabbed my jacket from the back of my chair, and stalked out of my office.

My staff fell silent as I passed, their wide eyes tracking my path to the elevator like they were afraid I might snap if they took their attention off me.

The elevator doors opened. Two junior marketers were already inside, but when they saw me, they leapt out as if it were on fire.

"Sorry, Mr. Markovic," one of them said. "It's all yours." He stared a bit too long at my scar before his friend elbowed him. He quickly looked away, his face crimson.

I stepped into the elevator without replying. It stopped at two more floors on the way to the lobby, but no one else entered.

Outside, the city teetered on the brink of another thunderstorm. Rain had shrouded the streets in gray the past few days, and despite a promising morning of sunshine and blue skies, today was proving to be no exception.

I breathed in the fresh air, letting it calm the flames licking at the insides of my stomach. Sean would lose his mind if he saw me out in the open like this amidst the Brotherhood threat, but I'd never hid from anything or anyone in my life. I wasn't about to start now.

I had taken care to wear Kevlar-reinforced clothing and carry a concealed weapon with me, but I knew the Brothers wouldn't take me out with a quick bullet in public. They'd want something more personal.

Five minutes later, I found myself in front of a familiar storefront. According to one of Ayana's interviews, it was her favorite juice bar in the city.

I hadn't planned to come here—I hated juice—but my feet had a mind of their own.

*Or...*My pulse sped up when the door opened and a stunning brunette stepped out. *The universe has its own plans.*

What were the odds I'd show up at the exact same time Ayana was leaving?

She stopped short in front of me. She carried a green juice in one hand and her phone in the other. "First the café, now the juicery." Her eyes gleamed with surprise. "Mr. Markovic, are you following me?"

No. My answer came out terser than intended. *My office is nearby. I'm on my lunch break.*

"I know. I was joking." Ayana pocketed her phone and hitched the strap of her bag higher on her shoulder.

A beat of silence passed between us.

Her heels put her four inches closer to my eye level, but otherwise, she was dressed down in a T-shirt, jeans, and makeup-free face. Even so, she was the most beautiful woman I'd ever seen.

I'm sorry for leaving so abruptly the other day. My movements were stiff. *An emergency came up.*

"It's okay. I had to leave for a fitting anyway." She cocked her head. "A thank-you *and* an apology in the same month. It must be winter in hell."

Don't get used to it.

"I wouldn't dream of it."

More silence.

I stepped closer to allow a mother and her son past. Ayana's mouth opened, then closed without a word.

All the while, the impending storm gathered overhead in billowing dark clouds.

And yet, neither of us moved to leave.

I had a mile-long to-do list back at the office, but I could stay here with her forever. Just us, just like this.

A drop of water landed on my cheek, jarring me back to reality. Several others fell in rapid succession, and that was our last warning before the skies finally opened up and shattered the peace.

Torrents of rain poured down like the wrath of God, flooding the streets and soaking us to the bone.

"Shit!" Ayana squealed and ran for the scaffolding across the street. She used her purse as an umbrella until she was safely under shelter.

I followed her, less concerned about myself than I was about her running in heels, but I shouldn't have worried. She made it without so much as a stumble.

"I guess that was our fault for not taking cover earlier," she said breathlessly. The scaffolding provided some reprieve, but the slant of the rain continued to sprinkle us with droplets. "I *knew* I should've brought an umbrella today. I hate getting caught in the rain. My shoes get—" She cut herself off with an embarrassed laugh. "Sorry, I'm rambling. I'm sure you don't care about what happens to my shoes."

I care about everything relevant to you. The thought passed, silent and fleeting, before I locked it away.

How are you getting home?

"The subway," Ayana said. "If the rain doesn't let up soon, I'll call an Uber."

The nearest subway station was blocks away and prone to floods during heavy rain. I grimaced at the mental image of her packed into a train with drenched, unvetted strangers.

No need for an Uber. I'll drive you.

"That's not necessary. I—"

My car isn't far. I shrugged off my jacket and handed it to her. **Use this for cover instead. Your purse looks expensive.**

Ayana crossed her arms. "Are you always this bossy?"

Yes.

"It's not an endearing trait, you know."

I know.

She huffed and made no move to take the jacket from me.

At this point, she had to be refusing out of sheer stubbornness. How could a filthy train or paying surge pricing to sit in a stranger's car compare to a free ride home?

Rats are more likely to come out in the rain. Don't be surprised if you run across a family of them in the station. I paused, then added, **Have you seen a subway rat? They're the size of cats.**

Ayana faltered. "I haven't, but that's not true. You made that up."

I cocked an eyebrow as if to say, *Maybe, but do you* really *want to chance it?*

"You—" A nearby shout interrupted her. Someone's umbrella had lost its battle with the wind and flipped inside out. The umbrella wielder was soaked and, in an unfortunate coincidence, wearing all white.

Ayana eyed them with trepidation. "Fine," she said. "You can drive me home, but only if you let me ask you three questions during the ride. You have to answer—*truthfully*."

I almost smiled. No one else would've dared bargain with me so brazenly.

I'm doing you a favor, yet you're the one making demands?

"Yep." She gave an elegant shrug. "It makes no difference to me. If you don't want to answer, I'll just take my chances with the giant, rain-summoned rats."

My almost smile morphed into an almost laugh.

I offered my jacket again in silent agreement. She took it, her mouth curving.

"What about you?" she asked. "If you duck, we'll both fit under the jacket."

The jacket wasn't large enough to cover both of us.

It's just water. I'll be fine.

I led her away from the safety of the scaffolding and toward my office's garage. I rarely drove in the city, but I'd taken my car that day in hopes of searching some of the garages myself after work. That would have to wait.

A passing bus trundled through a large puddle and sent a spray of water our way. I instinctively turned my body to shield her while she grabbed my arm with her free hand. I flinched, and she withdrew with haste.

"I'm sorry. I didn't mean to—"

Don't worry about it. I picked up my pace, my heart

pounding, but even the rain couldn't wash away the impression of her touch.

We reached my car without further incident. I unlocked the doors, and Ayana lowered the jacket from her head as she slid into the passenger seat.

I turned on the seat warmers while she took in the all-black Italian leather, state-of-the-art dashboard, and custom details.

"Very Batman-esque," she said.

Sounds like an insult.

"Only if you take it as one." She sank deeper into her seat with a sigh. "You're right. This is better than Uber."

I'm always right.

"Always humble too," she said dryly. She gave me her address, and I put it in the GPS for appearance's sake. I already knew where she lived.

We rode in silence out of the garage and onto the street.

It was my first time being truly alone with Ayana since we were forced to share a hotel room three weeks ago. Even then, I could shut a door between us or escape to the gym.

Here, there was no reprieve. No doors, no passersby, no phone calls to distract us from each other's presence.

There was only the scent of her perfume and the warm inquisitiveness of her stare.

It was an exquisite hell of my own making.

"First question," Ayana said when we arrived at a red light. "What's your family like? I told you about mine, but I don't know anything about yours."

Family.

Faint screams echoed in my ears. The smell of charred flesh crawled into my lungs, and my stomach heaved.

My knuckles whitened around the steering wheel as I forced the bile down. It was only after the wave of sickness passed that I released the wheel to answer.

There's not much to tell. I had two parents and a brother. That's it.

The patter of rain against glass filled the car.

"Had?" Ayana said softly.

Is that your second question?

I hated talking about my family. My parents died of natural causes—my mother of heart disease, my father of cancer—so it was easier to think about them. My brother, on the other hand...

The tattoo on my inner arm burned.

"No," Ayana said. Even softer this time, almost tentative.

I relaxed my grip on the wheel. I hadn't realized I'd clutched it again.

The light turned green, and we inched forward again. Traffic had slowed to a crawl thanks to the rain. What should've been a twenty-minute ride was turning into forty minutes.

My staff was probably wondering where the hell I was, but one of the perks of being the boss was not having to answer questions.

Unless, apparently, they came from Ayana.

She appeared deep in thought until we reached another red light. "Okay, second question. And it's not about your family, I promise." She cleared her throat. "Are you dating anyone?"

My gaze flew to her face. She appeared composed, but I detected a trace of nerves as she shifted beneath my scrutiny.

Define dating.

"You're in your thirties, and you need me to define dating for you? Classic guy move."

I didn't take the bait. I simply sat and waited.

After a minute, she sighed and clarified. "I mean, is there someone you're involved with romantically on a regular basis?"

Define involved.

Ayana scowled. "You *know* what I mean."

I don't. Are you asking about dinner dates, Ayana, or are you asking about fucking?

Her sharp intake of breath made my mouth curve.

I shouldn't have taken as much pleasure in her discomfort as I did. But she was the one who started this, and perhaps I wanted her to feel what I felt when I was near her—unbearable, agonizing tension, the type that condensed the world into a bubble around us and made it hard to even fucking breathe.

Ayana swallowed. She shifted again, the subtle clench of her thighs belying her even tone. "Both."

I made her wait.

It was only after the light turned green and a cacophony of honks erupted behind us that I turned away with a simple answer.

No.

I had my needs, but they paled next to my disdain for the insipid song and dance of modern dating. The women who threw themselves at me did so for money and power, and I had zero desire to watch them not-so-discreetly swallow their revulsion in hopes of becoming a billionaire's wife.

Even if a genuine, suitable interest came along, it didn't matter.

I only wanted one person, and they weren't her.

Ayana fiddled with the jacket in her lap. She didn't say another word until we arrived at her building half an hour later.

"You never give a direct answer," she said. "It's not so hard just to say 'no, I'm not dating anyone,' is it?"

You seem to have a strange fascination with my love life.

I didn't allow myself to examine the reason why. That wouldn't lead to anything good for either of us.

"It's not fascination, it's curiosity. They're different," she said with remarkable dignity. "I only ask because there's zero information about your personal life online, and Jordan barely tells me anything."

My mood darkened at the sound of his name.

I wanted to lean over and crush my mouth against hers until she didn't remember her own name, much less his.

I wanted to wrap her legs around my waist and make her scream for me and *only* me.

I wanted a lot of things I couldn't have, so I settled for mocking indifference instead.

Do you spend a lot of time researching me online?

"Only when I'm bored. I also spend a lot of time researching knitting patterns and watching cat videos, so don't feel too special. You're less interesting than both those things."

It happened so suddenly I hardly noticed it until the sound left my throat. A rumble of laughter—mine.

My first genuine laugh in possibly years.

The shock of it immobilized me for a moment. I *never* lost control like that, and Ayana's response hadn't been the funniest or the most surprising. However, it was so adorably spiteful I couldn't help but give in.

The delight that lit Ayana's face made me wish I was the type of man who laughed easily, if only so I could see her smile more often.

A knock interrupted our moment of camaraderie. The doorman must've grown tired of us idling outside her building.

My amusement died.

Ayana rolled down the window. "Hi, Bernard. Can you give us an extra minute please? I'll be out soon."

"Ms. Kidane, I'm afraid…" He faltered when I glared at him behind her back. "One minute. Of course."

He retreated, and Ayana faced me once more. "Thank you again for the ride and the jacket."

You're welcome.

I expected her to leave right away, but she lingered, crossing and uncrossing her legs again like she was silently debating something.

Few things surprised me anymore. I was trained to expect the unexpected, and yet, nothing could've prepared me for the next words out of her mouth.

"Do you want to come upstairs to my apartment?"

CHAPTER 13

Ayana

DO YOU WANT TO COME UPSTAIRS TO MY APARTMENT?

My question hung in the air. It snuffed out the remaining warmth from Vuk's laugh, but it was too late to take it back.

"To dry off," I added hastily. "You're soaked, and it'll take you at least another forty minutes to get home in this traffic."

It seemed like a reasonable offer to me, but based on his frown, you would think I'd asked him to shoot a newborn kitten.

"You don't have to." I filled the heavy silence with more rambling. "I suppose your clothes have already dried, but it's that stiff sort of dry, you know. From the rain. You might catch a cold or something." *Stop talking. Now.* "But like I said, no pressure. It was just a suggestion if you, um, want to take it."

Heat poured off my face.

I was already kicking myself for asking about his love life earlier, and I was only digging myself into a deeper hole with my incoherent pitch.

My intentions were innocent, but it sounded like I was desperate to get him upstairs to do something other than laundry.

A muscle twitched in Vuk's jaw.

After another beat of interminable quiet, he pulled away from the curb and into the attached garage.

He was coming upstairs.

Anticipation sank beneath my skin as we parked and took the elevator to the twentieth floor. Vuk was the first man I'd invited to my apartment in months besides the maintenance guy. The platonic nature of his visit didn't matter; my nerves rattled all the same.

We reached my apartment. I unlocked the front door and pushed it open. "Here we are. Home sweet home."

I'd lived with roommates my first four years in the city until I saved up enough money for my current place: a cozy one-bedroom with fantastic views. It was close to the subway and filled with natural light, which were my two musts when I'd been apartment hunting.

The monthly rent was absurd, but it was worth it. Giant windows overlooked Manhattan, and one of them even came with a deep window seat for reading and daydreaming.

Bold splashes of colorful art adorned the walls. Natural-fiber rugs covered the pale wood floors while hanging plants added a touch of greenery to the space. A thick orange blanket I'd knitted on a sleepless night draped over the back of my couch.

The blanket wasn't my best work, but it was the first knitting project I'd ever completed, and I was damn proud of it.

I glanced at Vuk as he stepped inside. His gaze swept around the airy space, and I tried to imagine it through his eyes. What did he see when he looked at that blanket or the collection of empty perfume bottles lining the living room shelf?

It was impossible to tell.

We took off our shoes, and I gave him a quick tour of the apartment. Living room, kitchen, the corner I'd set up for photos and virtual interviews. I purposely avoided the bedroom.

"The bathroom is over there." I gestured down the hall. "I can throw your clothes in the dryer while you—*oh*."

Vuk pulled his shirt over his head. *I'll keep my pants on.* He didn't look at me. *Where's the laundry room?*

I swallowed past a dry throat and wordlessly opened the closet containing one of the most coveted items in Manhattan: an in-unit washer/dryer. No one had an actual *room* for laundry unless they were Markovic-level rich.

While Vuk tossed his shirt in the machine and selected the appropriate settings, I tried not to stare. I really did.

However, it was impossible not to indulge in an eyeful when he was standing less than a foot away. His back was turned, giving me ample cover to admire the sculpted architecture of his torso.

Muscle corded his arms and back, and his shoulders spanned the width of the doorway. His thighs were tree-trunk thick. When he finished with the dryer and pivoted toward the bathroom, I glimpsed a light dusting of hair that trailed over his chest and disappeared into his waistband.

A maddening rush of awareness zipped down my spine. How dare my hormones miss the memo that I wasn't supposed to ogle my fiancé's best man? And how dare he walk into my apartment and take up so much *space* that I could scarcely breathe? It was downright rude.

I forced myself to wait until the door closed behind him before I walked to the kitchen and busied myself making two cups of tea.

I'd seen men shirtless before. Hell, I'd seen *Vuk* shirtless before.

But never in such close proximity. Never here, in my apartment, steps away from where I—

"Shit!" I cursed as the mug overflowed and tea scalded my hand. I took it as a sign that even the universe didn't approve of my inappropriate thoughts.

By the time I finished cleaning up, Vuk had exited the

bathroom. He joined me in the kitchen, his presence so domineering it instantly demanded attention.

"Here. I made you some tea." I pushed a steaming mug across the marble island and resolved not to look anywhere below his chin. "It's a special Ethiopian blend my mom made. It should warm you up while we wait for your shirt to dry."

He stared at the drink, which came in a smiling gray kitten mug. I had a brief vision of him throwing the poor ceramic kitty against the wall, enraged by its cuteness, but he picked it up without comment. It looked absurdly delicate in his hand.

I bit my lip to hold back a laugh.

Vuk glanced around the kitchen. *Your apartment doesn't look the way I'd imagined it would.*

"Do you spend a lot of time imagining my apartment?" I teased, echoing his earlier remark about me looking him up online.

Perhaps it was the lighting, but I could've sworn the faintest wash of pink tipped his ears. When I blinked, the color was gone.

I must've imagined it. Vuk Markovic didn't blush. Ever.

Most models don't collect animal mugs or allow so many colors into their decor.

Most models? How many models' apartments had he been in?

The need to know itched beneath my skin, but I didn't give him the satisfaction of asking.

"First of all, that's an overgeneralization. Second of all, not everyone bows at the altar of minimalism," I said, pushing the image of him with Polina or Indira or Vlada out of my head.

I swept my eyes over emerald green cabinets, copper cookware, and white tiled walls. I'd painted the cabinets myself, and I'd have to paint them back when I moved out. It was worth it; I couldn't stand their old sterile white color.

"When I first moved to New York, I shared a model apartment with other girls from the agency," I said. "It was the blandest, most colorless place you could imagine. We didn't know how long we'd last here, so it didn't make sense to spend time and money decorating." Both things had been in short supply back then. My current situation came with its own set of problems, but I would never miss those early days of cattle call castings and constant rejections. "When I finally got my own place, I wanted the exact opposite. So I filled it up with everything I loved, even if those things don't match."

I was of the firm belief that a home should feel like a home. Books should be read, couches should be sat on, kitchens should be used. A house wasn't a museum; it was a tapestry of who we were and the lives we'd lived.

Yet you'll have to move again soon. Vuk paused. *Unless Jordan is moving in with you.*

My smile dissolved. "No. He's not."

Jordan and I had agreed to move into his Upper East Side townhouse after we got married. I should've already started packing, given our new wedding date, but I hadn't opened a single suitcase.

I wasn't dreading it. I'd just been busy with Fashion Week. That was all.

"It'll be great," I said. "I'll have so much more...space." Stuffy, formal, antique-ridden space.

Jordan said I could redecorate to make myself feel more at home, but what was the point when I had to move out of *that* house in a few years too?

"How did you and Jordan become friends?" I steered the conversation toward safer waters. "I know you were roommates, but lots of college roommates don't keep in touch this long after graduation." I'd asked Jordan, but his answer about them "bonding after a while" had been too vague to satisfy me.

Vuk's expression was so austere I couldn't believe it belonged to the same person who'd laughed earlier. *If I answer, that'll be your third question.*

I groaned. You'd think I was torturing a confession out of him instead of asking for basic background info.

Still, a deal was a deal.

I hesitated, debating whether that was worth using my third question. Perhaps I should ask him something deeper, like how he got his scars or why he chose not to speak, but that seemed too invasive. We didn't know each other that well, and I didn't want to force him to discuss something that would make him uncomfortable.

I *could* also ask what he meant by his note on the plane. It sat in my nightstand drawer, and I revisited it more often than I cared to admit.

I don't hate you. But I wish I did.

His answers for what it meant could vary, and I wasn't sure I wanted to know any of them.

I nodded, giving him the silent go-ahead. I really was curious about his history with Jordan. They were as different as night and day, and their friendship surprised me more than anything else I'd learned about Vuk so far. Well, besides the bingo thing, which I wasn't fully convinced he was being honest about.

We weren't friends at the start. We were civil, but I was too quiet and he was too loud. We had…different interests. Then I got into trouble, and he saved my life.

I sucked in a breath. "He never told me that."

Vuk shrugged.

"What happened?"

We'd passed the three-question mark. Given how private he was, I had no right to pry, and he had every right not to answer. But there was something about this moment—the rain falling outside, the cooling mugs of tea, the gentle hum of the dryer in the background—that created a sense of intimacy.

Or perhaps it was the sight of him in my kitchen, looking entirely at home amongst the alphabetized spices and gauzy curtains. He was too rough, too cold, too masculine—and yet, he fit perfectly.

An island of calm amidst a sea of uncertainty.

I got involved with the wrong crowd. I owed them money, and they weren't the type of people you wanted to owe money to. When Jordan found out, he paid the full amount, no questions asked. Another shrug. *The rest is history.*

Considering Vuk's usual reticence, he'd basically offered me a gold mine of information.

I tried to parse through it all.

Now I understood why Vuk was so loyal to Jordan despite their differences. He must feel indebted to him.

But what "wrong crowd" could Vuk have been involved with in college? A gang, the mafia, or some other criminal organization? Those were the most likely options. As scary as the IRS could be, they didn't go around killing people who owed them money.

Vuk's mouth curled at my prolonged silence. *Ask me.*

"Ask you what?"

Who I owed money to.

His eyes were chips of ice set in a face of stone.

It wasn't hard to believe he'd been involved in questionable activities in his past, but it didn't matter.

I shook my head. "No."

Vuk's eyes flared with surprise.

"If you want to tell me, you can," I said. "But whatever happened, happened over a decade ago. It worked out in the end, and what's past is past. It would be unfair of me to reopen old wounds unless you were comfortable discussing them."

Those glacial eyes melted, giving me a glimpse of the man who'd laughed so beautifully and unexpectedly earlier. Compelling him to lower his guard was one of my greatest triumphs and not one I expected to repeat, but I missed the sincerity of that moment all the same.

If this is reverse psychology, it won't work. I won't tell you if you don't ask.

I snorted, torn between laughter and exasperation. "I don't expect you to—I meant what I said. But I appreciate how manipulative you *think* I am." I threw that last part in for jest.

You're a lot of things, Ayana. Manipulative isn't one of them.

My amusement died as quickly as it'd bloomed.

It was strange, how clearly I heard his voice when he'd never uttered a word to me.

My hand curled on the counter. My engagement ring felt unbearably heavy, and I wanted nothing more than to yank it off. One moment of freedom. That was all I needed.

Vuk's gaze dropped to the diamond. A noticeable chill swept through the air.

When his eyes returned to mine, the weight of the ring doubled.

I lived in front of cameras for a living. Everywhere I went, eyes followed. Watching, dissecting, judging. I molded myself into what other people wanted me to be because that was my job, and I was used to being the object of scrutiny.

But no crowd or camera made me feel the way Vuk did—like I was myself again. Like I was *seen*.

A loud beep dragged our eyes away from each other.

The dryer cycle was finished.

I dropped my hand and stepped back, my heart thrumming faster than it should've. "I can get—"

I was interrupted by a knock on the front door. My brow furrowed. I wasn't expecting anyone, and I'd lived in the city long enough to be wary of unannounced visitors.

However, Vuk's presence made me braver than I would've

been otherwise, so I checked to see who was at the door while he fetched his shirt.

My stomach bottomed out when I peeked through the peephole.

Slicked-back hair. Tanned skin. A shiny Rolex on his wrist.

What the fuck? When did my agent start making house calls?

I debated leaving him in the hall and pretending I wasn't home, but that would only put off the inevitable. It was better to rip off the Band-Aid and get this over with.

I steeled myself and opened the door. "Hank. What are you doing here?"

I didn't have it in me to feign politeness. My home was my sanctuary, and I did not appreciate him ruining it.

For once, he didn't insult me with fake platitudes about how he was checking in on me because he was *so* concerned about my well-being, but his unsmiling face sent a cold sensation crawling down my throat. "We need to talk."

CHAPTER 14

Vuk

WHILE AYANA ANSWERED THE DOOR, I WENT TO THE dryer and retrieved my shirt. I pulled it over my head, my mind seething with the mistakes I'd made today.

Offering Ayana a ride. Agreeing to come upstairs. Telling her about my past with Jordan. Fucking *laughing*.

All perilous missteps that drew me closer to her orbit when I should've been keeping my distance.

I'd sold her a half-truth about the Brotherhood and what I needed Jordan's money for, but if she'd asked me for details, I might've told her—not everything, but enough that she would look at me the way other people did. Like I was a monster in a man's clothing.

In her eyes, I was a better man than I would ever be, and I was too selfish and masochistic to disavow her of that notion.

If I couldn't have all of her, then I'd hoard the piece of her that still offered me a glimpse of hope for redemption.

The low murmur of voices from the entryway intruded into my thoughts. One male, one female.

Ayana and who? Jordan? An overly friendly neighbor?

Who the fuck was visiting her in the middle of a Wednesday afternoon?

The possibilities dug under my skin.

I shut the dryer door and headed into the living room. Ayana's back faced me, but I spotted the tension pouring off her body from a dozen feet away.

"I went there to consult on something for the wedding. That's all," she said. An edge ran beneath her calm tone.

"I see." The oily response made my molars slam together. *Hank fucking Carson.* I'd recognize his sleazy voice anywhere. "I find that interesting, considering Brown, Kermit & Wells specializes in business contracts. Specifically, breaking them."

"Marriage is a contract, and it's certainly business for quite a large number of people." Ayana's voice chilled another degree. "I love Jordan, but I would be foolish not to protect myself."

I love Jordan.

A vicious pressure swelled in my throat. I forced it down, but the toxic green residue lingered like a stain that refused to fade.

"That's good to hear." Hank's tone smoothed enough to hide most, if not all, of his skepticism. "I simply wanted to check in and make sure we were on the same page. Emmanuelle would be upset if she heard you were planning to leave."

I'd heard enough.

I came up behind Ayana, my body coiled with pent-up tension. Hank was already on my radar after their limo call in California, and I'd waited patiently for the right time to strike.

But my patience was fraying, and if he didn't remove the threat from his voice when he talked to her, I was going to rip his tongue out, patience be damned.

Hank opened his mouth, but it froze into a shocked O when he saw me. To his credit, he stood his ground this time instead of running off like he had at the Vault.

"Mr. Markovic. What a surprise." He recovered, his gaze sliding between me and Ayana. A curious gleam entered his eyes. "I didn't realize you and Ayana were so close."

"We ran into each other earlier, and he was kind enough to give me a ride home in the rain." She responded before I could. "I invited him up so he could dry off. Now, if there's nothing else you'd like to discuss, I have a kickboxing class in an hour."

"Of course. I wouldn't want to get in between you and your workout." Hank's lips pursed. "It's a shame you'll be missing Paris and Milan this year because of your wedding."

A warning noise rumbled up my throat.

He flinched, and he took a small step back before quickly adding, "A wedding which I'm sure will be beautiful." He glanced at me again. Behind a veil of fear, the gleam in his eyes turned speculative.

I bet he was already spinning a thousand stories about why I was in Ayana's apartment—stories he would then use to manipulate her into doing his bidding.

I'd met men like Hank before. I'd killed men like Hank before. I knew exactly how they operated.

He must've sensed the danger brewing in the air because he jerked his gaze away and left with a hasty goodbye.

Ayana shut the door with more force than necessary. She faced me, a crinkle of irritation digging into her brow. "Sorry about that. I had no idea he was going to drop by."

Does he make a habit of showing up at your house unannounced?

"No, which is why I was so surprised." She sighed. "He got wind that I visited a law firm a few weeks ago. They're known for getting their clients out of iron-clad contracts, and he suspected I had plans to leave Beaumont."

A cold whisper rattled through my veins. My team couldn't confirm my hunch about the founder, which worried me more than if they'd proved me correct. Either I was overthinking the connection I'd made with the dossier, or Emmanuelle Beaumont was in league with people good enough to wipe her history clean.

Either way, Ayana was better off without the agency, but they wouldn't take too kindly to losing her.

Are you? Leaving Beaumont, I clarified.

She hesitated. "I'm thinking about it." Caution underlaid her words. "There are a lot of considerations at play, which is why I consulted a lawyer. I didn't mention it to Hank for obvious reasons. If I stay with Beaumont but they find out I'd been thinking about leaving, the career repercussions would be…dire."

I wasn't familiar with the intricacies of the modeling world, but I knew that certain agents wielded disproportionate power. Emmanuelle Beaumont was one of them.

I studied Ayana. She'd curled her hand around the doorknob again, perhaps unconsciously, and she met my gaze so steadily it was as if she were forcing herself to make eye contact so I wouldn't think she was lying.

She wasn't happy with Beaumont—that much was clear. But based on the few interactions I'd witnessed between her and Hank, I bet she'd already made up her mind about leaving. She just didn't want to say it out loud yet.

Why do you want to leave?

"Turning the tables on me with the questions, I see." Ayana's brief smile faded. "I've been with Beaumont my entire career. They've done a lot for me, but I think it may be time for me to branch out. Plus, Hank is…Our personalities and working styles aren't a good match."

There was more to the story than she was telling me. There always was.

I'd heard horror stories of the way agencies treated some of their models. Perhaps Ayana's success protected her from the worst of it, but even the biggest names weren't immune to exploitation and abuse in an industry with so few regulations.

The general public thought celebrities could do whatever they wanted, but many were beholden to their agencies, labels, and other powers that be.

Something dark and insidious stirred in my gut. I needed to dig deeper into Ayana's relationship with Beaumont, but right now, I had a more pressing question: if Ayana didn't want her agency to know she was leaving, how did Hank find out about her visit to the lawyer?

"I'm not sure how he knew I met with a lawyer." It was like she'd read my mind. She dropped her hand from the doorknob and touched the pendant at her throat. "But I shouldn't be surprised. He knows everything."

My eyes narrowed. *Explain.*

Her hesitation lasted a beat longer than normal. "He just has a way of finding things out," she finally said. "For example, he knew you were with me in California instead of Jordan. He mentioned it during our call, but I hadn't said a word to him about it. There are other things too—little details about places I've gone and people I've met outside work. I haven't asked him about it because I don't want him to know it bothers me." She let out a rueful laugh. "Maybe I'm being paranoid, but I feel like if I call him out on it, he'll double down. And he'll be more careful about whatever he's using to keep track of me so I'll never find out how he does it."

Ice spread through my veins, cold but *searing.*

"Before you ask, yes, I've swept my apartment and devices for bugs," Ayana said. "I didn't find anything."

How often do you check? I kept my hand movements tightly controlled even as the beast inside me frothed at the mouth to hunt Hank down.

Her expression turned sheepish. "Um, twice total?"

Christ. My team swept my house, car, offices, and devices

daily. Old habits died hard, and the corporate world could be just as ruthless as the criminal one.

There are certain surveillance devices that basic bug detectors won't pick up on. I should know—I've used them myself. *I'll have my team do their own check. They'll be discreet, and we'll get to the bottom of it.*

Ayana released a shaky breath. "Thank you," she said. "I appreciate it. Truly."

I'll be in touch. I reached for the door.

"You're leaving already? I mean, you haven't finished your tea," Ayana added hastily.

I almost smiled for the second time that day.

I wanted to stay. She was clearly shaken from her encounter with Hank—which was exactly why I needed to leave.

I'll finish next time. I opened the door. *I have some business to take care of.*

Hank lived in an apartment on the west side. It was a strikingly average building for a man who flaunted expensive watches and blustered as much as he did, but the contrast tracked with what I knew of human nature.

The smallest men compensated in the biggest ways.

I parked a few blocks away and entered the no-doorman building with no issues. My search for the mystery Brother would have to wait another day; I had a more pressing issue at hand.

One text to Sean had turned up Hank's address and license plate number, while an educated guess led me to believe the agent had gone straight home after leaving Ayana's place.

His senior agent role at Beaumont meant he had more flexibility to work from home. It was too late for lunch and too early for dinner, and Ayana's apartment was relatively far from the neighborhoods where fashion types usually met. If he'd had a packed afternoon, he wouldn't have had time to see her *and* make it to his meetings. Ergo, his most likely location was at home.

One knock proved me right.

Hank opened the door, still dressed in the same shirt and tacky watch he'd sported earlier. His eyes rounded when he saw me. "What are you—hey!" He yelped when I shouldered past him. "You can't just come in like that! You're trespassing!"

I ignored his caterwauling and assessed his apartment with a dispassionate glance. It was an open space, so there were no walls dividing the living room from the kitchen and dining areas. Flat-screen TV, magazines stacked on the coffee table, dirty dishes in the sink. The typical bachelor pad.

"Get out or I'll call the police." Hank fumbled with his phone, his hand shaking. "Right now."

I strode to the kitchen and plucked an apple from the fruit basket.

"Did you hear me?" His voice pitched higher. "I'm calling the police!"

I pulled a knife out of the wooden block.

Hank's face paled, but he didn't dial 911. It would take time for the police to get here, and I could do a lot in a short amount of time.

His tone turned coaxing. "Is this about Ayana? Because I swear, I was only there to check up on her. She's one of my most important clients. I care about her well-being."

Funny how fast he switched up. He didn't seem so tough now that he didn't have an easy target to intimidate.

I slowly peeled off the apple's skin with the knife. The methodical motion restrained my rage, but the more Hank babbled, the more those restraints frayed.

His voice reminded me of his conversation with Ayana. His conversation with Ayana reminded me of how upset she'd been— and of what I'd overheard before I made my presence known.

I love Jordan.

The keen edge of the blade tore through the apple's flesh. A chunk of it fell into the sink next to the pieces of skin.

Had she been lying, or had she been telling the truth? I'd convinced myself she wasn't as excited about the wedding as a bride should be.

Perhaps I'd been wrong.

The last piece of skin landed in the sink. I took a bite of apple while Hank fell silent. He appeared to have realized his odds of survival were better if he didn't talk so fucking much.

I didn't take a second bite. Instead, I walked toward him, knife and apple in hand. My steps echoed against the bare wooden floors.

Hank inched back until he hit the couch. His gaze darted toward the door, clearly gauging his odds of escaping before I reached him. They weren't good.

I stopped a foot away. Up close, Hank's eyes were slightly bloodshot, and he reeked of cologne. He stared up at me, his face several shades paler than normal.

My rage simmered and swelled. It strained at its leash, begging me to let it loose and carve out my frustrations on a man who was little more than an overblown bully.

The wedding. The Brotherhood. The stress on Ayana's face when she'd been talking to him.

All that would feel so much better with a little slice or two.

My gaze flicked from Hank's face to his hand, to the couch, and back again. A crinkle formed between his brows before realization dawned.

He opened his mouth, then shut it and rested a shaky hand on the top of the couch.

I shook my head and notched my chin up. He hesitated before turning his hand palms up. Beads of sweat dotted his hairline.

I placed the apple in his palm—softly, almost gently.

A beat passed. The crinkle in his brow smoothed, and his shoulders relaxed. "If you—"

He cut off with a piercing scream as I brought the knife down. It happened so swiftly Hank didn't get a chance to react before I drove the blade straight through the core.

His scream was still ringing in the air when the tip of the blade met human flesh. Blood stained the fruit, its faint coppery scent mixing with the smell of urine as Hank pissed himself.

He held the apple, seemingly catatonic with shock as I stepped back. The knife quivered from the residual force of my violence before it finally stilled.

If I hadn't stopped when I had, it would've torn through muscle and bone and rendered his right hand useless.

My lip curled. I'd merely nicked him, but his near brush with mutilation had wiped away all his false bravado. His skin resembled wax paper as he shook like a lone leaf in the wind.

He had no problem threatening or spying on Ayana, but push back a little and he pissed himself.

Pathetic.

I left him in his apartment, covered in piss and blood, and calmly made my way back to my car.

If I'd had my way, I would've taken things a few steps further. However, Ayana was the last person he'd been seen with—her building's security would've documented his arrival—and I didn't want to place her in the middle of a murder investigation.

So no, I couldn't deal with the agent the way I wanted yet, but I'd accomplished what I'd set out to do.

What happened in Hank's apartment proved you didn't always need words to communicate.

He'd heard my warning loud and clear.

CHAPTER 15

Vuk

"YOU PULLED IT OFF!" JORDAN SLAPPED ME ON THE shoulder. "Shit, I'm proud of you, man. This night is awesome."

I made a non-committal noise in response. We had vastly different definitions of "awesome."

It was Saturday, the night of the much-dreaded bachelor party. Jordan was having the time of his life, and I would rather throw myself into a pool of battery acid. It would be a miracle if I got through the night without murdering someone.

While Jordan went to get another round of shots, I stuck by my spot in the corner. We were only at stop number two of my meticulously planned itinerary, and I couldn't stop checking my watch. *At least* four more hours of fuckery before the night ended.

Christ. Someone shoot me already.

The only bright spot of the night was how happy and easy to please Jordan was. Thinking about him and Ayana together made my gut churn, but as his friend, I really was glad he was enjoying himself.

He'd explicitly stated he didn't want anything extravagant for the bachelor party—no travel, no ridiculous activities or performances—so I'd stuck to the tried-and-true trifecta of music, alcohol, and women.

Our first stop had been the VIP room of the Vault, which Xavier had reserved just for us. Top-shelf liquor and a famous DJ from Iceland devolved into the sticky floors and tacky neon lights crowding our current dive bar location.

For someone who'd grown up surrounded by luxury, Jordan had a soft spot for the hole-in-the-walls. The Soggy Bottom was right up his alley, though the same couldn't be said for everyone in the bachelor party.

"What an...interesting bar." Kai Young grimaced as a scantily clad brunette tilted her head back to guzzle beer from a funnel. Beside her, a pair of fratty-looking guys bumped chests and hollered like imbecilic gorillas. "How did you find this place again?"

He looked more bemused than anything else, but out of all the attendees, the aristocratic British media tycoon was the least likely to willingly step foot in this establishment.

I shrugged, too irritated by the noise, the people, and the night in general to respond.

There were eight of us in total—me, Xavier, Jordan, his friend Will from boarding school, his cousin Topher, and a handful of business associates/close acquaintances. In New York society, even personal events like bachelor parties and weddings were little more than excuses for networking.

As the CEO of a media empire, whose fashion publications counted Jacob Ford as a major advertiser, Kai belonged in the networking category. So did Dante Russo, the CEO of a luxury goods conglomerate.

The eighth and final member of our group was the only one who straddled the line between friend and acquaintance. Killian Katrakis was a close family friend of the Fords, which was why he'd agreed to let them host the wedding at his famous ancestral estate in Ireland. However, he was eight years older than Jordan, and the two rarely hung out except at family functions.

While Kai left to join Jordan at the bar, I tossed back a glass of straight vodka. The cheap alcohol burned a fiery path down my throat.

We had three more stops after this—two bars and the gentlemen's club at Valhalla. It was leagues above the Vermilion Lounge in terms of class and quality, but that wasn't why I'd added it to our itinerary.

I wanted to see what Jordan would do when faced with temptation—if he would stay loyal, or if he would stray. If he'd stay respectful or let his eyes and hands wander beyond what was acceptable.

It was manipulative of me, but I'd never claimed to be a fucking saint.

"What crawled up your ass and died?"

I ignored Dante as he came up beside me. Besides running the Russo Group, he was also next in line to take over Valhalla's managing committee. We'd worked closely for months to prepare for the transition, so I was more familiar with him than many of the other attendees.

That didn't mean I wanted to talk. I hated parties, and I hated small talk.

Dante followed my gaze to where Jordan was laughing with Xavier and Topher. "The groom seems to be having a good time. Any reason why you're looking at him like you want to kill him?"

I pivoted my glare to the Italian and typed out a response on my phone. *Shouldn't you be at home with your wife and daughter?*

Never mind that Jordan had invited him. He didn't have to accept.

Dante's smirk fell as he returned my glare. "I should," he grumbled. "But Josie's with her grandmother, and Vivian is having a girls' night." He appeared unreasonably disappointed about being separated from his family for the night.

I didn't get it. Who wouldn't want a break from a screaming baby?

I returned my attention to the bar. In less than two months, Jordan and Ayana would be married.

She would move into his house. Sleep in his bed. Wake up next to *him* every morning and kiss him sweetly every night.

One day, they'd have children too, and they would be tied together forever, even if they divorced.

The vodka churned in my gut. I slammed my empty glass on a nearby table so hard I heard a small crack.

Dante's eyebrows rose. He wisely kept quiet, but his speculative gaze remained on me as Jordan and the rest of the party joined us.

"You look like you could use another drink." Jordan handed me another vodka. His face had flushed crimson, a sure sign he was drunk. "C'mon, loosen up a little! This is a great night."

I took the drink and downed it in one gulp.

Ayana's bachelorette was tonight too. What were they doing? Were they also at a bar, or were they at a strip club?

A mental image of some oiled-up male dancer grinding against her flashed through my head. My hand curled, itching to reach into my mind and pull the imaginary asshole off her.

Will grimaced. "I can't believe you drink vodka straight. That's…" He trailed off when I looked at him. "Cool," he said hastily. "Super cool."

"How are you feeling about the wedding?" Kai asked Jordan. "The big day is coming up soon."

A shadow crossed Jordan's face. "I'm excited, but I wish the circumstances were different," he said. "At least my grandmother will get to celebrate with us."

Everyone made an obligatory noise of sympathy for the ailing Ford matriarch.

"It'll be nice to get the ceremony out of the way so you can enjoy the reception," Killian drawled. The electronics and telecommunications titan lounged against a nearby railing, drawing the attention of several bachelorette parties nearby. "My staff is thrilled that they can finally plan a wedding at Westford, considering they've given up hope on me."

Westford was his family's castle in County Mayo, and Killian was an infamous bachelor who'd publicly vowed never to marry. That didn't stop every other woman in Manhattan from trying to lock him down—a feat that had proved useless over the years.

"Any advice from the married men in the group?" Topher clapped a hand on Jordan's shoulder. "He's never had a long-term relationship before Ayana. We need to prepare him before he makes a fatal marital mistake. I'm not flying all the way to Ireland for the reception so he can get divorced a month later."

Laughter and chuckles all around.

A quick divorce. Now *there* was a thought. I took solace in the possibility, no matter how remote it seemed.

"Hey, have a little more faith in me," Jordan protested. "Ayana and I get along great. We've never even fought."

"That's because you've never been married yet," Topher countered.

"My advice: don't listen to anyone who says you have to get along with your in-laws," Dante said. "The less you see them, the better. In-laws are assholes."

"No," Kai corrected. "*Your* in-laws are assholes. Mine are lovely."

More laughter as Dante scowled at his friend.

His wife Vivian was on notoriously rocky terms with her father. He was the one who'd arranged her marriage to Dante.

Though Dante and Vivian's relationship had worked out, there were whispers that Francis Lau had pulled some underhanded maneuvers before the wedding that landed him on both his daughter and son-in-law's eternal shit list.

"I like Ayana's parents, so I don't think that'll be a problem," Jordan said. "They're so nice, and they make the best food."

Dante opened his mouth, but Kai cut him off. "Don't listen to Russo. He doesn't know how to let go of a grudge," he said. "My advice is to listen, be patient, and never, ever rearrange your wife's books without permission." Kai frowned. "You would think alphabetical order by title makes sense, but apparently, it's not 'aesthetically pleasing.'"

"Why would you rearrange her books?" Xavier looked appalled. "That's rule number one of being in a relationship, married or not. Don't touch their shit. If I tried to reorganize Sloane's stuff, I wouldn't be here right now. I'd be dead."

"She was on deadline, and I was trying to be helpful," Kai said defensively.

"Well, it was a stupid move." Xavier turned to Jordan. "I'm not married, but personally, I think the key to a happy marriage is sex every day. Sometimes twice a day."

My teeth ground together. *Fucking Xavier.* I couldn't kill him, but I sure as hell could think about it.

"Jesus." Topher groaned. "No one has any *actual* practical advice? J, you're so cooked."

"Look on the bright side." Killian grinned at an increasingly nervous-looking Jordan. "If you get divorced, you can get tips from Davenport on how to win her back. It worked for him."

"Where is he anyway?" Xavier asked. "He's in town."

"It's his old wedding anniversary." Dante smirked. "You can bet he's not missing *that* celebration again."

Dominic Davenport was a powerful Wall Street financier

whose wife divorced him two years ago. They'd remarried less than a year later. I wasn't privy to the details of their divorce and reconciliation, but based on Dante's dig, I assumed it had to do with their anniversary.

I really didn't give a shit. I had enough problems of my own without taking on other people's.

While the rest of the group continued to tease Jordan about marital life, I swept my eyes across the bar.

My team was still coming up empty in our search for the mystery Brother. I wasn't worried enough about a Brotherhood hit to double down on security for the night—I was with some of the most powerful men in the city, and the organization wouldn't want a public mess—but I had to stay alert.

The clock was ticking. Sooner or later, the Brotherhood would make a move again. My job was to find them, neutralize them, and figure out what the hell they wanted before that day came.

Topher left to use the restroom—at least, he tried. He bumped into one of the other patrons along the way, and the air seemed to quiet as the man turned and glared down at him.

"You got a problem?" he growled. He was nearly as tall as me and twice as wide, with arms that could double as tree trunks and a grizzly beard that covered half his face.

"No problem." Topher held his hands up. "I was just trying to get by."

"Yeah? Well, you made me spill my drink." The man slammed his glass on the closest tabletop. His dilated pupils and the stench of alcohol on his breath told me he was wasted. "You think you can just walk around and knock into people because you want to 'get by?'"

Jordan's cousin looked like a deer caught in headlights. He was a trust fund baby who was half the size of Grizzly; a fight between them could only go one way.

"It was an accident, but I can see why you're upset." Kai stepped in, ever the voice of reason. "How about we buy you a new drink and call it even?"

Grizzly sneered. "How about no?"

He shoved Kai. Hard.

Kai glanced down at where wet handprints marred his previously immaculate shirt. When he looked up again, his face had hardened into stone. "That," he said, "was a mistake."

What happened next escalated so quickly no one could've provided an accurate account if they'd tried.

Grizzly swung at Kai, who dodged his drunken attempt and hit the other man somewhere that made him double over. One of Grizzly's friends jumped into the fray only for Dante to haul him back before they could make it a two-on-one fight. The rest was a blur.

More people joined the growing brawl. A crowd formed, jeers erupted, and I caught sight of the bar's bouncer shoving his way through the crowd to get to the culprits.

If it had been any other night, we might've been able to salvage it with a few bruised jaws and egos.

Unfortunately, I was already on edge, and when one of Grizzly's other friends tried to bait me, something inside me snapped.

"Why are you just standing there? Too scared to fight?" he taunted. His gaze fell on my scars. "You'd think an ugly motherfucker like you would—"

I grabbed him by the neck of his shirt and threw him against the railing. The cheap wood splintered from the impact, and his howl of pain was so loud even the other brawlers stopped to stare.

Red tinted my vision. A familiar buzz filled my ears as I stalked toward the asshole.

I made it halfway before someone grabbed me from behind. They locked their forearm across my throat, trying to restrain me, but I easily tossed them off. The guy went flying into a table of half-empty glasses. The table crashed to the ground, sending little shards flying everywhere.

The music stopped as screams filled the bar. The bouncer finally made it to the center of the melee, but when he tried to break up the fight between the bachelor party and Grizzly's friends, someone socked him in the eye.

And that was when everything really went to hell.

CHAPTER 16

Ayana

"WHAT DO YOU THINK THE GUYS ARE UP TO RIGHT NOW?" Indira asked. "Getting lap dances? Drinking in a bar somewhere? We should join them."

"That's not how bachelorette parties work." My older sister Liya gave her a stern look. We shared the same high cheekbones and rich brown skin, but she was shorter and had softer features. "This is Ayana's night. *Stop* thinking about the guys and celebrate *her*."

Indira shrugged, looking sheepish. She was one of the few models I considered a friend rather than a colleague. We didn't hang out every week, but we were often booked for the same jobs, and we spent a lot of time bitching and commiserating about the industry.

"Sorry, but I can't help it. Have you seen the guest list for the bachelor party? It's like a who's who of the hottest men in New York." She cast a quick glance in my direction. "Not that I'm not having fun with you guys. This is, like, the chillest bachelorette ever." Her tone indicated that wasn't necessarily a good thing.

My cousins all lived out of town and couldn't make the new

bachelorette date, so there were only five of us in the group: myself, Indira, Sloane, Liya, and my ride-or-die hairstylist Kim.

We were having dinner at a restaurant that was famous for its kitschy decor, extensive cocktail menu, and great-looking servers. It was a popular spot for bachelorette parties, as evidenced by the many sash-and-tiara-wearing women scattered throughout the lively space.

I'd eschewed both the sash and tiara, but I did dress up in a gorgeous new Stella Alonso dress and my favorite heels. I might not be marrying for love, but that was no reason not to look my best at my own bachelorette.

"Okay, enough *chill* for the night," Kim said. She was in her late forties, but she had a more vibrant social life than half the twenty-somethings I knew. "We've been sipping cocktails like we're at a goddamned book club. It's time to liven things up a bit."

Liya crossed her arms. "How? There's no dance floor."

As my maid of honor, she was the one who'd planned our night: dinner followed by a customized escape room and late-night cocktails at a jazz speakeasy. I wasn't a big clubber, and I made Liya swear she wouldn't take me anywhere near naked abs or penis-shaped desserts. Our current itinerary was perfect, even if it was too "chill" for Indira.

"Like you need a dance floor to dance." Kim scoffed. "But that wasn't what I had in mind. If we're going to spend the night together, we should get to know each other better. Think simple, fun, raunchy…"

"Like a drinking game!" Indira's face brightened. "How about Never Have I Ever? It's a classic."

"I don't know." Sloane wrinkled her nose. "I haven't played that since college."

"That explains it," Kim said. "No offense, hun, but you look like you could use about three more drinks and some major loosening up. Unclench your ass. It'll feel better."

Her tone was warm and teasing. Nevertheless, I shot a nervous glance at Sloane, who did not and would not ever take shit from anyone. She was a little more uptight than the rest of my friends, but I'd known her long enough to confirm she could let her hair down and party if she wanted to, especially after she and Xavier started dating.

To my surprise, Sloane let Kim's comment slide. "I *could* use another drink," she agreed. "It's been a hell of a week at work."

"So it's settled." Indira clapped her hands. "Never Have I Ever it is."

We ordered a fresh round of margaritas, and Indira kicked things off after I declined to go first.

She thought for a second before announcing, "Never Have I Ever had a foursome. Yet."

Kim took a demure sip, eliciting gasps around the table. "What?" She shrugged. "The early 2000s were a wild time."

After *that* surprise, the game went into full swing. Each admission was raunchier than the last, and when it was finally my turn, I couldn't think of anything good that hadn't already been said.

"Never have I ever...had multiple orgasms from a partner in one night." It was the best I could come up with, but the last thing I expected was for everyone else to drink. I gaped at them. "Seriously? You're telling me you've *all* had multiple orgasms? That's statistically impossible!"

Most women would be lucky to get one orgasm from their partner, much less two or more.

"Experiment enough, and anything's possible," Indira said. "I will say, I tend to have better luck with women than men on that front. They're better at getting down to business, if you know what I mean."

"I got lucky and met a *very* talented French guy when I was studying abroad." Kim fanned herself. "Gerard. Phew! I still think about that man from time to time."

We turned our attention to Sloane, who shook her head. "I'm not discussing my sex life in a restaurant with banana-shaped lamps. But..." She lifted one shoulder, a glint of mischief brightening her cool blue eyes. "I will say I have no complaints in that department."

"You. Don't say a thing," I warned my sister. "Or I'll never look at Nathan the same."

I couldn't imagine my calm, quiet brother-in-law...*no*. I shuddered. *Don't go there.*

Liya laughed. "No details, but all I'll say is, sometimes it takes a little guidance. When you're comfortable with someone, you're not afraid to tell them what works and what doesn't. It makes things more enjoyable all around."

"You need to tell Jordan to step up his game." Kim clucked her tongue. "I know you're in love and all, but I've seen that man dance. Poor thing has the rhythm of a sentient washboard."

I shouldn't laugh, but a giggle slipped out before I caught myself.

If they only knew how irrelevant this conversation was to my current sex life. Jordan could be the world's best or worst lover, and I'd have no idea. We hadn't done more than kiss for appearance's sake...and we were getting married in a month.

My amusement sobered at the thought of five years of celibacy. I couldn't bring myself to entertain the idea of an extramarital affair, not even a husband-sanctioned one, but...

No buts. This is what you signed up for. It's too late to second-guess yourself now.

"You know what you need?" Indira leaned forward. "You need to spice up your sex life. When you get *too* comfortable, that's a problem too. Try a threesome."

"You shouldn't be encouraging her to bring a third party into the bedroom during her bachelorette," Sloane said. "But I agree

KING OF ENVY | 139

with spicing things up. Try having sex somewhere forbidden like his office."

"*Or* bring out the props," Liya said. "Like handcuffs or nipple clamps."

I almost choked on my drink. "*Liya.*"

"Don't 'Liya' me. I've been married for ten years. If we didn't find ways to keep things interesting, we'd die of boredom."

"Ain't that the truth." Kim cackled. "I knew a drinking game would be a good idea. That being said, check with Jordan before you go crazy on sextoys.com. He doesn't look like the type of man who'd be down for handcuffs *or* nipple clamps."

"He does scream 'soft and gentle,'" Liya mused. "There's nothing wrong with that, but that's not the type that's usually super adventurous in the sack."

"Looks can be deceiving." Sloane's cheeks were flushed a deep pink. The margaritas had gotten to her. "According to one of my friends, it's the quiet ones you have to watch out for."

"Oh, I believe it. You know who fits that description?" A sly smile spread across Indira's face. "Vuk Markovic."

This time, I really did choke. I erupted into coughs as tequila and lime juice shot up my nose.

I recovered as quickly as I could, but my eyes were still watering when the rest of the party zeroed in on Vuk's name.

"Who's that again?" Kim asked. "The name sounds familiar."

"Jordan's best man." Indira pulled something up on her phone and handed it to the stylist.

"Ohhh. Now *that* looks like a man who can fuck shit up." Kim's eyes twinkled. "Just my type."

"You're married to an accountant," I said.

"You ever seen an accountant during tax season?" she countered. "They can be scary."

"Oh, come on, Ayana." Indira nudged my leg with her foot.

"You can't tell me you aren't curious about Vuk. He has that hideous scar, but it kinda adds to his appeal. Danger is sexy."

I bristled at the word *hideous* and resisted the sudden urge to throttle one of my few friends in the city. "I haven't thought about him in that way at all," I said stiffly. "I'm engaged. Remember?"

How did we end up here? I hadn't signed up to discuss Vuk's sex life this evening—or ever. In fact, the less I thought about him, the better.

"So? That doesn't make you a nun. Besides, I bet even a nun would have unholy thoughts about that man." Indira sighed. "Say what you will about his face, but that body? Whew. Anyway, that's what doggy style is for, or I can turn the lights off when we're having sex. If he didn't have those scars, he'd be really hot, but I wouldn't want to look at his face when I'm about to come, you know?"

Blood rushed to my face and neck. A strange ringing sounded in my ears as my hands curled around the edge of my seat. Instinct told me not to touch my fork or knife lest I end the night in jail for murder.

"There's nothing wrong with his scars." The bite in my voice was so scathing it surprised even me. "They add character."

"Yeah." Indira gave me a strange look. "That's what I said."

"You did—"

"Let's move on." Sloane swiftly interjected. "Our escape room is in half an hour, so we should head out soon. I'll get the server."

We paid and left the restaurant. I hung back from the group, flushed and irritable from our last conversation topic. The ringing had faded, but my heart continued to pound.

Who was Indira to talk about Vuk like he was a zoo animal? Would she like it if someone said they'd turn the lights off before sex so they wouldn't have to look at her face? No. It was...it was rude and despicable and plain *wrong* to talk about people like that.

Just because Vuk had money and power didn't mean he was made of stone. He had feelings. And sure, he was probably the last person on earth who needed someone to defend him in his absence, but—

"You know who's *not* put off by Vuk's scars? Polina. She's been trying to get her claws into him for forever." Indira fell into step beside me, either oblivious or indifferent to my anger. "She's been attending every event in the hope that he'll be there. That girl is determined."

Polina was a fellow model who was notorious for her string of high-profile relationships, including a brief fling with British soccer star Asher Donovan a few years ago.

My stride faltered. The prospect of Vuk dating Polina edged out my irritation toward Indira. "That's an awful strategy. He hates public events."

Plus, he and Polina wouldn't mesh at all. Her "see and be seen" mentality would drive him up the wall.

That being said, she *was* stunning. Vuk didn't strike me as the shallow type, but most men wouldn't turn down a gorgeous blond supermodel if she were throwing herself at them.

My dinner threatened to surge back up my throat. I shouldn't have drunk so many margaritas.

"He doesn't hate events as much as he used to." Indira winked at a passing group of finance bros who ogled us with unabashed desire. "I've seen him out and about way more than I used to. He was even at that fashion party in London last year."

I remembered that party. I was supposed to attend, but I ended up bailing for a last-minute brand dinner with Versace.

"Whatever," I said. "I don't really care." I sped up so I wouldn't have to talk to Indira anymore.

The escape room was only a few blocks from the restaurant, so we'd opted to walk instead of taking a cab. It seemed as if all of downtown Manhattan was out tonight; we could barely make it past the throngs of people crowding the sidewalks.

Kim squinted at a nearby group of men standing outside one of the bars. "I'm not wearing my glasses so I could be wrong, but...isn't that your fiancé?"

I paused and focused on the group in question. Several of the men sported cuts and bruises. One of them held an ice pack to his cheek while another argued with an exasperated-looking cop. Silent police lights bathed the group in flashes of red and blue.

I blinked, my brain too overstimulated to focus on any one person in particular.

Sloane beat me to a reaction by half a second. She stopped next to the group and gasped. "*Xavier*?"

Her boyfriend turned. His dimples winked into view even as a sheepish expression crossed his face. "Hey, Luna. This, uh, isn't what it looks like."

She crossed her arms. "It looks like you and the rest of the bachelor party got into a fight and got kicked out of the bar."

Xavier paused. "Okay, then it's exactly what it looks like."

"I swear, I—" Sloane zeroed in on the bruise marring his jaw. "You're hurt. Where's your ice pack? You!" She pointed at a random guy loitering nearby. "Get me an ice pack."

"Lady, I don't know who you—"

"Ice pack. Now."

The guy withered beneath her glare. He gulped and rushed into the bar like the hounds of hell were at his heels.

I never would've pegged Sloane for the fussy type, but the sight of her boyfriend's injury must've triggered some latent protective instinct.

"It does hurt," Xavier said solemnly as she brushed her fingers over his jaw. "Can you kiss it right...there." He sighed when she pressed a soft kiss to the bruise. "Much better."

I should've taken a cue from Sloane and gone straight to Jordan, but I found myself searching for a dark buzz cut and pale blue eyes instead.

Nothing.

My stomach sank, but I shook it off and quickly found Jordan. He was standing near the edge of the group with his cousin Topher, whom I'd met at our engagement party.

Topher had a gash on his forehead, and Jordan didn't look much better with his black eye. A weak smile carved through his surprise when he saw me. "Fancy seeing you here."

"Oh my God. What happened? Are you okay?" I rushed to his side and gently touched his face. I winced at the mottle of black and blue skin; his shiner was brutal.

"Yeah. Topher bumped into some drunken idiot who tried to pick a fight with him *and* Kai," Jordan said. "Then Dante got involved, the other guy's friends got involved, and, well, things escalated."

I slid a glance at the Italian, who was close enough to hear Jordan's explanation.

"The asshole had it coming," Dante said without a hint of remorse.

"Vivian is *not* going to be happy," Sloane warned. She glared at Xavier, her expression morphing from concern to admonishment. The guy she'd recruited earlier had returned with an ice pack, which Xavier held to his jaw. "And you. You should've known better than to get involved."

"All for one, one for all." Her boyfriend appeared equally unrepentant. "I couldn't leave my friends to fend for themselves."

"This is what happens when testosterone and alcohol mix." Liya shook her head. She and Kim were observing the scene with bemusement while Indira was busy flirting with Killian Katrakis. "What happened to a good ol' fashioned private party with strippers?"

"Uh, that was next on our stop." One of Jordan's boarding school friends grinned. What was his name? Wyatt? Walker? *Will.* That was it. "Not that I mind chatting with beautiful ladies such as yourselves." He ran his eyes over our group.

"I'm also married, but I appreciate the compliment," Kim said. "Keep 'em coming."

Will looked like he was about to do just that when his gaze shifted to someone behind me. "Yo, Markovic, we're still hitting up Valhalla, right? I've always wanted to see what it's like inside."

I almost whirled around before I caught myself.

I refocused on Jordan, absentmindedly stroking his face while my entire body tensed in anticipation of Vuk's approach.

A wisp of cool air brushed my back. Goosebumps popped up all over my arms, but I waited a full three seconds before I dropped my hand and turned.

I knew he was there before I saw him; his presence was impossible to miss. That didn't stop my pulse from skipping when I looked up at him.

Unlike the rest of the party, Vuk was unscathed from the fight. Not a bruise or cut in sight.

He ignored Will's question and stared down at me. A muscle jumped in his jaw.

He seemed pissed, but I hadn't even said or done anything yet.

"We were passing by when we saw you guys," I said, driven by the need to fill the silence with something other than the pounding of my heart. "How much trouble are you in?"

The cops were gone, but the bouncer looked like he wanted to haul everyone into a back alley and beat them up.

None. We sorted it out with the police. Vuk was definitely pissed. I could just tell by the way he moved.

His gaze dropped. He dragged his eyes up my legs and over my bare shoulders before focusing on my face again.

Warmth tingled in the aftermath of his scrutiny. It was like stepping into a hot shower after a snowstorm—my entire body reacted whether I wanted it to or not.

"Let me guess." I hid my shiver with a flippant smile. "You intimidated them until they agreed to drop the issue?"

'Intimidated' is a strong word. I persuaded him.

"Mm-hmm. No wonder you refused to tell me your plans for the bachelor party. I didn't have a bar brawl on my bingo card, especially not at a place called..." I squinted at the neon green letters buzzing over the entrance. "The Soggy Bottom."

The Fighting Pit was already packed. Vuk delivered his response with such a deadpan expression I almost believed he was serious until I caught the tiny smirk playing around his mouth.

I forced the curve of my own lips into a straight line. "Was that a joke?"

He stared back at me, his eyes giving nothing away, but his face had finally softened. Whatever pissed him off earlier was no longer an issue.

"Ayana." Indira sidled up to me. Killian was gone, and she'd turned her attention to Vuk like a missile homing in on its target. "Why don't you introduce me to your friend?"

She didn't wait for my response before she inched closer to Vuk and held out her hand. "I'm Indira, one of Ayana's friends from modeling." She paused, as if to give him time to process the fact that she was a model. "You may have seen me on the latest cover of *Mode de Vie*."

Vuk eyed her outstretched hand. He didn't take it, and I felt a pinch of satisfaction at his utter disinterest.

Indira was undeterred by his lack of response. "It looks like you and me are the only single people in the group." She was so focused on flirting with Vuk that she seemed to have forgotten about Killian, who was also single. *Like you weren't the one mocking his scars earlier,* I fumed. "We should grab dinner sometime. There's this great place in SoHo..."

I tuned her out as my nausea returned tenfold. Jordan had returned to his conversation with Topher while I spoke with Vuk, but I needed a distraction. If I didn't get away from him and Indira soon, I'd vomit all over her four-inch Louboutins.

"I hate to break up the party, but can we get back to the *real* parties?" Liya asked pointedly. "We are so late for the escape room."

"You're going to an escape room for a bachelorette?" Will scoffed. "That's so boring."

"If you want excitement, I can always hack off one of your balls," she said, her voice sugary sweet. "I'm a nurse. I'm good with a range of medical instruments."

He paled and immediately covered his groin with his hands. "No way. Didn't you have to sign a hypocritical oath or some shit?"

"It's the Hippocratic Oath, and that's only for doctors." Liya left out the part where nurses recited a modified version called the Nightingale Pledge. "Lucky for you, I don't have time to deal with your genitals tonight. Ayana, come on. We really need to go."

I hesitated. We weren't doing anything except milling around and talking, but I was strangely reluctant to leave.

"I have a better idea. Why don't we merge our groups?" Indira said. "We're already together. We might as well make it a big party. The more the merrier and all that."

"I agree," Topher said quickly. He eyed the supermodel like she'd just stepped out of his dreams. "We should definitely stay together."

"No complaints from me." Kim shrugged.

A chorus of agreement rippled through the group.

"Stop. You're forgetting that this isn't up to us." Sloane

silenced everyone with an icy glare. "This is Jordan and Ayana's night. Let them decide." She turned to us. "What do you think?"

Jordan and I exchanged glances.

I didn't want to play the loving fiancée during my bachelorette, but we were with our friends. Surely that gave us leeway to do our thing. Not every couple was glued at the hip all the time.

"I'm good with merging," I said. "Like Indira said, the more the merrier."

"Same, but no more bars, okay? I'm all barred out for the night." Jordan pointed to his black eye as proof.

After we gave our consent, we had one more problem to solve. Where, exactly, were we going to go? Bars and clubs were out, and our group was too big for the escape room.

Suggestions for mini golf, karaoke, and a casino night flew through the air until Xavier stepped in.

"Wait. I have the perfect idea." He grinned, his eyes alight with mischief. "But we're going to need three more girls."

CHAPTER 17

Vuk

KARMA WAS A BITCH WITH DIFFERENT FACES. Sometimes it was an attempted assassination; other times, it was a fucking laser tag night with my friend, his fiancée who I was secretly obsessed with, and a model who clung to me like a barnacle. Oh, and a bunch of drunken people I didn't care about.

I would've preferred another assassination attempt.

After the cops broke up the fight at the Soggy Bottom—though not before Kai broke Grizzly's nose and I sent two of Grizzly's friends fleeing into the night—I'd easily sorted things out with the police. Multiple witnesses confirmed that Grizzly was the one who'd thrown the first punch, and the names of the people in the bachelor party were enough to get the cops to back down.

We did get banned from the Soggy Bottom for life, but none of us were too choked up about that.

However, the last thing I'd expected was to run into Ayana and her friends. When I came out of the bar and saw her caressing Jordan's face, I'd wanted to hit something again.

Jealousy ate me alive, and now I had to spend an entire goddamn night watching them act lovey-dovey with each other.

I glared at Jordan while Xavier ran through the rules. He'd taken over my role as the party leader, not that I gave a shit.

"Boys versus girls. Winners take home bragging rights." Xavier looked around at the eclectic group of billionaires, supermodels, and assorted friends and family. In order to make the teams even, he'd recruited several of Sloane's friends to join, which was how Vivian Russo, Isabella Young, and Sloane's other client Maya ended up in the mix. Everyone looked ridiculous in the laser tag vests, myself included. "We all clear on the rules?"

"It's laser tag," Kai said. "I'm sure we'll figure it out."

"I've never played laser tag," Will mused. "But I do love video games. They're kinda the same thing, right?"

Dante's lip curled. "Petition to swap him out for Viv. At least she understands the difference between virtual reality and actual reality."

His wife grinned. "Not a chance. I look forward to beating you too much."

His eyes gleamed. He bent his head and whispered something that made her cheeks flush.

"As if you'll win." Jordan scoffed. "We got this in the bag."

"Care to wager on it?" Ayana tilted her head. "Losers cover the tab for the rest of the night."

Everyone had gone home to change before meeting up again at Area 56. Ayana's black T-shirt and sleek pants were somehow even more enticing than the dress she'd worn earlier, and she'd ignored the venue's suggestion about not wearing heels—her leather boots added at least three inches to her height.

"Done," Jordan said. "You're awfully confident for someone who's never played laser tag before."

She arched an eyebrow in return. "Who says I haven't?"

"Touché." He kissed her on the cheek. "Well, if you win, I'll happily buy you drinks all night."

My nostrils flared. I jerked my eyes away and stalked toward the entrance to the arena without waiting for the others.

Were we here to play, or were we here to fucking mess around?

The others took my cue and filed in after me.

According to Xavier, Area 56 was the best indoor laser tag venue in the tri-state area. Excellent service, state-of-the-art technology, a VIP room where customers could feast on top-shelf liquor and gourmet bar food in between games—it had it all.

I didn't care about the extras though. I just wanted to shoot something, even if it was with a fake blaster.

Once the doors shut and the game started, everyone sobered up fast. We were a competitive bunch, and while covering the bar tab wouldn't put any of us in the red, none of us wanted to lose.

I split from the rest of the guys and hunted on my own. I didn't want anyone slowing me down or giving away our position.

Music blasted from hidden speakers. I inched my way from barrier to barrier, keeping my eyes peeled for long hair and familiar forms.

Only a few minutes elapsed before I sighted my first target. I raised my blaster and shot Isabella straight in the heart.

"Dammit!" she wailed. "Out in the first round. All those hours spent watching action movies for *nothing*."

I didn't wait to hear the rest of her grumbles. I moved on, managing to "kill" Liya and Maya before the first two back-to-back matches were over.

Current body count: eight. Four men (Topher, Xavier, Killian, and Jordan) and four women (Isabella, Maya, Liya, and Indira) were out, leaving the game tied.

We had a twenty-minute break before the last match. Our group was too large to fit at one table, so we split into two neighboring tables.

I ended up with the last people I wanted to sit with—Jordan, Ayana, and Indira.

"We were playing Never Have I Ever at dinner earlier," Indira said after we got our drinks. She slid a sly glance in my direction. "We should play another game. I suggest Truth or Dare."

"We're adults. We're too old for drinking games," Dante grumbled.

"It's *because* we're adults that we should do it," Xavier countered. "Nostalgia is a drug, Russo. Give into it."

For fuck's sake.

I never played these insipid games in college, and I had no desire to do so now. Unfortunately, the majority ruled, and they voted in favor of Truth or Dare with one caveat: no passes allowed. You *had* to answer, or you had to carry out the dare.

I tuned everyone out until the turn landed on Ayana.

"What's it going to be?" Kim's eyes sparkled. "Truth or Dare?"

"Truth."

"What's the wildest place you've ever had sex?"

My glass paused halfway to my mouth. I set it down without taking a sip and leaned back, my eyes trained on Ayana.

She froze. Her eyes darted to mine for a fraction of a second before she cleared her throat. "The wildest place I've ever had sex, was, um…it was…"

Anticipation hung in the air. Jordan shifted, looking wildly uncomfortable while my pulse drummed to a steady, dangerous rhythm.

"It was a department store dressing room," Ayana said. "Bergdorf's. The, um, evening wear department."

"Oooh." Kim perked up. "Sex *and* couture. I love it. Good job." She winked at Jordan, who responded with a tight smile.

The rhythm of my pulse took a decidedly violent turn.

Whoever invented this game should die. If they were already dead, they should die again. Horribly.

Ayana dared Indira to share her phone's search history with the group—Jesus, that was a lot of shopping—and then I was up.

"Vuk." Indira turned to me. "Truth or Dare." She emphasized her question with her hands to indicate which was which.

I swallowed my irritation and nodded at her left hand. Dare.

Her grin suggested she'd been hoping that would be my answer. "I dare you to kiss someone at this table."

She was the only other single person at the table. It was a clever ploy, considering the game's no-pass rule.

"Damn." Jordan laughed. "She got you."

Beside him, Ayana stiffened, her neck and shoulders lined with tension.

I regarded Indira coolly. She was attractive enough from an objective standpoint, but I had more interest in kissing a slug than her—and I hated it when people tried to trap me into doing something I didn't want to do.

I kept my eyes locked on hers while I reached over and slowly, deliberately, took Ayana's hand.

A noticeable hush fell over the table.

I lifted her hand to my mouth, brushed my lips across her knuckles...and lingered. The faint scent of sweet almond filled my senses.

I'd imagined kissing her for so long that even the brief touch of my lips on her hand was enough to make my heart pound. Blood rushed in my ears, and every cell in my body ignited.

I wanted to pull her to me and give her a real kiss—my tongue in her mouth, her hair in my fist, her moans in my ears.

I wanted to lay her out on the table and feast on her until she was begging for more. Until she was crying out *my* name and it was clear to every single fucking person at this table, in this city, in this *world* that she was mine and mine alone.

I wanted everything I couldn't have, and every moment I

couldn't steal, but for the space of a heartbeat, I almost believed she wanted it too.

Ayana's fingers curled. Their slight tremble accompanied a ragged breath so soft it could be mistaken for a ghost.

It was only then that I dropped her hand and sat back, my eyes still on Indira's. I didn't glance in Ayana's direction.

Indira's lips parted. She wore a glazed expression, cobbled from equal parts disappointment and desire.

A thick, underwater silence blossomed in the wake of my audacity before Xavier's laugh broke it.

"That's why you need to be specific with this stuff," he said. "Or else people will find loopholes."

Indira had, in fact, forgotten the biggest loophole when it came to dares like hers—she hadn't specified what kind of kiss. By choosing Ayana, I'd misled people into thinking I took a cop-out, because what kind of impudent asshole would hit on his friend's fiancée in front of him?

When I finally looked at Ayana, she was staring at me with an unreadable expression. She glanced away before our eyes met, but there was no mistaking the rapid rise and fall of her chest.

My blood heated. For better or worse, I wasn't the only one affected by the kiss.

Our break ended, and we returned to the arena for the final match. It went much quicker than the first two rounds. I had pent-up energy to burn, and people were freshly drunk and/or distracted by their partners.

Within ten minutes, everyone got eliminated except me, Ayana, and, surprisingly, Will.

Music continued to blast overhead. Shadows flickered over the walls, and now that a majority of players were gone, the arena took on an almost ghostly feel. Barriers loomed around me, each one potentially hiding an enemy.

It was a silly game with fake guns and low stakes, but that didn't stop a sense of déjà vu from crawling over the nape of my neck.

I was suddenly reminded of another night, when music played in the background and death or worse waited around the corner.

The screams. The fear. The *smell*.

My vision darkened. A metallic taste flooded my tongue, and the scent of smoke teased my senses.

I tightened my grip on the blaster. *It's not the same.* This wasn't the past, and this wasn't home. This was a laser tag game filled with cardboard structures and people I knew. That was all.

I forced my breaths to slow.

Even if they were here, there wasn't anyone else they could take from me except—

A noise rustled behind me, and my instincts took over. I didn't think; I didn't even check who it was.

No one snuck up on me. Ever.

I spun around and slammed them up against the nearest wall. Their blaster clattered to the ground as I grabbed their wrists and pinned them over their head, immobilizing them. My other hand wrapped around their throat and squeezed.

Adrenaline pumped into my blood, clouding my thoughts and making me squeeze and squeeze until a gasp penetrated the haze.

I stared down at the person pinned beneath me. My vision gradually cleared, and horror trickled through me as the contours of her face took shape.

Long dark lashes. Huge eyes, bright with fear. Sculpted cheekbones and a full, lush mouth so close I could feel the soft pants of her breaths.

Ayana.

CHAPTER 18

Ayana

I COULDN'T BREATHE.

Every attempt to draw more oxygen failed, and I was growing alarmingly lightheaded, both from the hand around my throat and the weight of his body pinned against mine.

Vuk loomed over me, his face twisted into a scowl that had my self-preservation instincts screaming. His eyes were ablaze with some dark emotion I couldn't discern, but it was like he wasn't there. His mind was detached from his body, lost somewhere I couldn't reach.

He didn't see me; he saw a nameless, faceless threat he needed to neutralize.

Spots danced in front of my vision. Fear punched through my chest along with a strange, infinitesimal, and completely misplaced sense of euphoria.

It was there one second and gone the next, but the shock of it was so great I managed a small gasp.

The sound seemed to snap Vuk back to his senses.

Awareness slowly seeped across his face, followed by horror. He immediately loosened his grip, and I gasped again, my lungs burning from the sudden influx of air.

Tears prickled my eyes—a physical reaction more than an emotional one, as every muscle in my body loosened with relief.

Vuk stared down at me, his face stark. Despite his relaxed grip, his hand was still on my throat, and my arms were still pinned above my head. His body molded so tightly to mine I felt every ridge and muscle.

My heavy pants steadied as my breathing gradually returned to normal. I didn't push him off me.

I *should've* felt scared. If Vuk hadn't returned to his senses when he did, I would've blacked out or worse. But there was a part of me that, somewhat delusionally, didn't believe he would hurt me no matter the circumstances.

I had no data to back up that feeling. No rhyme or reason. It was simply instinct.

Vuk's eyes traced my face. He wasn't the type to ever show regret, but the tick in his jaw revealed his turmoil over what happened.

"I'm okay," I whispered. "It's okay."

His throat flexed with a hard swallow. He moved to release his hold on me, but I instinctively freed one hand and grabbed his wrist, making him still.

His eyes flared with surprise, and the tiny flicker of heat from earlier sparked to life again.

I didn't consider myself a fear junkie. I hated horror movies, avoided dark streets at night, and regarded Halloween with the wariness one might approach a feral cat. My sex life had been pretty standard up to this point, and I'd never fantasized about breath play.

But something about this moment flipped a switch inside me. Maybe it was the alcohol, or maybe it was just *him*.

The memory of Vuk's mouth on my skin resurfaced. It had been a featherlight kiss, so brief and chaste it hardly qualified as a kiss at all. Yet my body ached at the reminder, and my hips tilted upward on their own.

Vuk had wedged his thigh between my legs, immobilizing me, and the slight movement of my hips added unbearable pressure against my core.

The flicker of heat ignited into a full-blown fire. Goosebumps peppered my skin, and it took every shred of willpower not to grind against his leg like a lioness in heat. My breaths turned erratic again as I fought to control my inexplicable arousal.

What was *wrong* with me? My fiancé was waiting for me in the other room, and I was having fantasies about his best man—dirty, filthy fantasies about what would happen if I gave in to my desires, and what he could do to me while I was pinned underneath him.

The flames pulsed low in my belly.

God, there must be a special place in hell for me.

Darkness bled into Vuk's eyes again. I hadn't released his wrist, and he must know—must suspect—what effect he had on me.

My mouth dried.

I wasn't sure how much time had elapsed, but it was so dark, and the music was so loud, that time seemed to slip away altogether.

We were in our own world. Nothing else mattered.

Vuk pressed his knee up—no more than a centimeter, the movement so subtle it didn't shift the rest of his stance in the slightest.

But that was enough. The renewed pressure sent a burst of pleasure through me. It crawled through my blood, lighting me up from the inside out.

Vuk's palm closed around my throat again—not enough to cut off my air, but enough to draw out a small, humiliating moan.

I shouldn't like this, but *fuck*, I did.

My hand slid from his wrist to his shoulder. Vuk lowered his head, his face a terrifying mask of sharp edges and cold, brutal intensity as he watched me rub shamelessly against him, all restraint gone.

I barely noticed. A flush of heat spread across my skin, and the world blurred, narrowing to the pinpoint between my legs. Pressure built and built, climbing higher and higher until—

A burst of footsteps penetrated my haze.

Vuk flinched back like I was on fire. His head jerked to my left as his vest vibrated, indicating he'd been hit.

Mine vibrated a second later. A shudder ran through my body, but I gritted my teeth and forced myself to straighten.

I faced the intruder, my core throbbing, my skin so sensitive from my ruined orgasm that the vibrations echoed like lurid taunts.

"I won!" Will beamed at us and did a little jig. "Fuck, I won!"

He seemed too high on victory to realize this was a group game and that by hitting Vuk, he'd tagged his own team member out.

It didn't matter. I was the last woman standing, so they would've won either way.

I dragged in a shaky breath. I'd completely forgotten we were playing laser tag. How much did Will see before he tagged us out? Did he...when I...

Heat scorched my cheeks. I peeked at Vuk, who'd reverted to acting like I didn't exist. He brushed past me toward the exit without so much as a glance.

Oh God.

The reality of what I'd done hit me like a freight truck. I'd basically dry humped Vuk Markovic in a fucking laser tag arena. And he hadn't stopped me.

What did that mean? Maybe he'd been so surprised he hadn't known how to react, *or*—wishful thinking—he hadn't known what was happening at all.

The chances of that were slim, but it wasn't like we'd kissed or taken our clothes off. I didn't even get to come, thanks to Will. It was basically like nothing happened. Right?

I let out a small groan. My excuses sounded flimsy even to myself.

I followed Vuk and Will upstairs to the VIP room, where the rest of the group was waiting for us. I was convinced my brush with infidelity was painted all over my face, but no one seemed the wiser.

"Great job, babe." Jordan stood and kissed my cheek.

I forced a smile. My gut knotted with guilt as I accepted his kiss while the phantom of another man's touch lingered on my skin.

My attention drifted to Vuk again. I realized with a jolt that he was staring right at us. His eyes slid from Jordan back to me again, and his mouth curled into a mockery of a smile that made me flush all over again.

I yanked my gaze away.

He knew what I'd done. But he didn't have to be such an asshole about it.

Thankfully, we didn't stay long now that the game was over. Since the girls lost, they covered the night's tab and refused my attempts to contribute.

"This is *your* night," Sloane said firmly. "You're not paying a dime."

Arguing with her was like arguing with a brick wall, so I didn't bother.

We all filed outside except for Vuk, who stayed behind to take a video call. Everyone said their goodbyes and went home, leaving Jordan and me alone for the first time since he returned from Rhode Island.

He waited until the taillights from the last cab disappeared before he spoke. "How are you feeling?"

A brisk breeze swept the lingering flush off my skin. "Cold and tipsy," I said, earning myself an amused snort. I smiled before I mused, somewhat apprehensively, "Six more weeks."

"Yeah." Jordan shoved his hands in his pockets. "You ready?"

No. "Are you?"

"As ready as I'll ever be."

We stood quietly, listening to the sounds of traffic and the chatter of passersby. We usually conversed so easily, but we were both lost in our own thoughts tonight.

"How's your grandmother doing?" I asked, finally breaking the silence.

"As well as could be expected. You know her," Jordan said with a half smile. "She's tough, and she's been on my ass about marrying since I finished grad school. Our wedding has made her a very happy woman, all things considered."

That was a silver lining, at least. But now that we were on the topic of family... "Will you tell your family the truth after our arrangement is over?"

His smile morphed into a grimace. This topic was territory we rarely broached, but I knew how much his secret weighed on him. No matter what happened with our marriage, I wanted him to be happy. I didn't think that was possible unless he told his family why he'd chosen a marriage of convenience over one of love.

"I don't know. I want to, but I have a feeling they won't take it well, and I'm not ready to deal with that," he admitted. Another lukewarm smile. "Ask me again in five years."

"I'll put it in my calendar," I said.

Jordan laughed, but I didn't press him any further.

It was his life; he should do things on his own timeline. Besides, I understood why he was so hesitant. He was his family's only heir. How could he tell them that he had zero interest in romantic relationships with anyone? He'd had sex, and he'd experimented with different relationships, but he didn't need or want a life partner. He definitely didn't want kids.

That was why he'd come to me for our arrangement. I already knew his secret, which he'd confessed to me one night over drinks in Milan. That'd been years ago, right after the end of my Jacob Ford campaign, and I'd proven to be one of the few people in his orbit who'd never tried to use, manipulate, or seduce him in some way.

There was also no way I'd fall for him or expect a traditional marriage with him, which made me the perfect partner for his purposes.

It was a mutually beneficial arrangement, but part of me wished it wasn't necessary. I couldn't help but feel a little sad that Jordan couldn't share such an important part of his life—and himself—with his family.

"You never told me why you needed the money from our arrangement," he said. "Care to clue me in?"

"Does anyone really need a reason for wanting money?" I deflected. Although I trusted Jordan, he was far too involved with the industry for me to risk sharing my plans. There wasn't anything he could do about my contract anyway, and I didn't want to drag him into my mess when his grandmother was sick and he had his own company to run.

"No. But when someone like you is willing to give up half a decade of your life for it, there's usually a strong motivator involved." He shrugged. "You're beautiful, smart, and successful. You could find a better, richer love match than me any day of the week."

Love match. Right.

I tilted my head back and stared at the sky. It was impossible to see the stars over Manhattan, but I liked to imagine a sea of them out there, twinkling down at us like benevolent angels. Watching the drama and travails of mankind as we stumbled through life searching for purpose, meaning, and the tiniest shred of happiness.

"Maybe," I said. "But it doesn't really matter now."

Were there richer men than Jordan? Yes. Were they better men or a potential soulmate? Who the hell knew.

I glanced at the laser tag entrance. Vuk was still inside.

My mind flashed, unbidden, through our interactions over the past month.

The seamless way his presence fit in my kitchen. The small tug at my stomach every time I saw him. The touch of his lips on my skin and his hand on my throat.

It wasn't so much who he was but how he made me *feel*—like I wasn't alone, like I was alive, and the world was rife with possibilities instead of obstacles.

If he'd been the one who proposed a marriage of convenience, would I still feel this sick leading up to the wedding?

"I'm going to head home," Jordan said. "I can call you a cab."

I shook my head. "I'll walk. My place isn't that far."

We exchanged goodbyes. Then he left, and I was by myself again. For some reason, I couldn't bring myself to leave yet.

Now that everyone was gone, I felt...empty. They'd filled me up with their energy, and without their excitement, I was just sad and exhausted. Not exactly the way a bride-to-be should feel after her bachelorette.

I'd had fun, but it hadn't escaped my notice that I barely knew half the people present tonight.

I'd lost touch with my friends from high school and college. Time and distance had eroded those relationships, and I had nothing to take their place. Maybe if I did, I'd feel less adrift.

I had exciting news and no one to share it with; I had shitty days and no one to commiserate with. Not on a deep level, anyway. It was like a thick glass wall existed between me and everyone else. I could see them, but I couldn't reach them. If I had a true emergency, I wouldn't know who to call outside my family.

All because I'd exchanged my version of what I wanted for... this. The glamour, the fame, the money (which wasn't really that much after taxes, agency fees, and other expenses). Most people would kill for my life, but I often wondered what it would've been like if I'd finished school and became a doctor or chemist instead.

It might've been better, it might've been worse, but at least I would've felt free.

The door to the laser tag venue opened. Vuk exited, his face set in stone once more. I didn't know what call he had to make this late on a Saturday night, but whatever it was, it'd pissed him off.

Our eyes met. The events of the night passed between us, heavy with unspoken words.

A muscle jumped in Vuk's jaw. He turned and left without saying goodbye.

Follow his lead and walk away, Ayana.

I stared after him. Remembered the thrill of his lips on my hand and the electric high of our moment in the dark. It was the most alive I'd felt in a long, long time.

When he disappeared around the corner, something inside me snapped. I ran after him before I lost my nerve. "Wait!"

He stopped mid-stride, his back still to me. The street was quieter than the main avenue outside the arena, and I could hear the thundering of my heart as I walked toward him.

I'd worn high-heeled boots against the venue's advice because I was most comfortable in heels. They were usually a confidence booster, and they gave me a sense of control over my life.

None of that confidence or control was present tonight. Nerves hummed in my veins, high-pitched and strained, but it was too late to back out.

Vuk finally turned and watched me approach, the picture of indifference. Shadows played over his face, twining around knife-blade cheekbones and a cruel, stern mouth.

A month ago, being alone with Vuk Markovic on a dark street would've given me a panic attack. But somehow, somewhere, that had changed.

If I could choose anyone to be with at that moment, I would choose him.

I stopped a few feet away, my heart in my throat. "When you kissed my hand during the game, was it a cop-out or...was it something else?"

I cut straight to the chase. It was too late, and I was too frustrated to do anything else.

My heart pattered to an uneven beat as I awaited his response.

Not a single flicker of emotion marred Vuk's expression. *What would that 'something else' be?*

"You tell me." I'd never been this forward with anyone, but we'd been dancing around each other for weeks.

It was time to address the elephant in the room, once and for all.

Vuk peeled himself out of the shadows and into the light. His steps echoed in the empty street, and a strange twist of anticipatory fear curled through me.

It was the same feeling that'd consumed me in the arena. The knowledge that I was teetering on the precipice of danger, and that the fall would be both the most terrifying and most exhilarating thing I'd ever experienced.

It took him three steps to close the distance between us. The threat of an oncoming storm lurked behind those cold, blue eyes. *Why are you here, Ayana?*

This was my last chance to make up an excuse. That would be the safe, smart thing to do.

But I was tired of being safe, and smart, and every other thing that hadn't gotten me anywhere except here—trapped in a gilded cage and bound to a man I didn't love.

Why did everyone else get to do what they wanted while I had to do what was "right?" Why couldn't I chase a piece of my own happiness when I'd spent so much of it in pursuit of others' dreams and goals?

I just wanted *one* thing for myself. One spark of connection that made life exciting again.

My breaths puffed in the cool night breeze. I took a tiny step closer, my chest brushing his with every exhale.

Vuk's muscles visibly tensed, but he didn't move away.

Anticipation streaked through my blood. I was climbing, inch by inch, to the top of a roller coaster and waiting for the inevitable drop. That sudden, giddy rush—there was nothing quite like it.

Emboldened, I placed a hand on his shoulder and stood on tiptoe, letting reckless courage guide me as I tilted my chin up and—

Vuk's hand shot up and manacled my wrist. His palm burned into my skin. "Don't."

The word scraped across my senses and hit me straight in the gut.

He spoke. Verbally. To me.

The air evacuated my lungs. His voice was deep and gravelly, exuding control but laced with emotion.

Shock swept my attempt at a kiss aside like debris in a flood.

Vuk didn't talk unless he felt like he had to. Even Jordan hadn't heard him speak much since college.

So why did he choose tonight to break his silence?

I stared up at him, taking in the strained set of his mouth and the painful grip around my wrist.

Don't. The tortured sound rang in my ears, and it was in that moment that the truth set in with painful, wrenching clarity.

That wasn't the command of a man who didn't want me; it was the plea of someone who *did*.

Vuk Markovic wanted me, and it was killing him that he couldn't have me, even when I offered myself to him. *Especially* when I offered myself to him.

The knowledge sent a dizzying rush through me. "Vuk…" I breathed.

He squeezed my arm to the point that I almost cried out. He brought his mouth next to my ear, his voice so low and rough it made me shiver. *"Kada te konačno budem, poljubio nećeš više nositi njegov prsten na ruci."*

I didn't understand a word he said, but I picked up on the sentiment. It sounded like a threat and a promise all rolled into one.

Vuk released me for the second time that night.

He left me standing there in the dark, breathless with want and aching for more.

CHAPTER 19

Vuk

THE LAST BOTTLE EXPLODED INTO A SHOWER OF glass.

I'd beaten my record of hitting all twelve bottles in under a minute, but I didn't get any satisfaction from it. I was still wound tight, my emotions swinging between fury and regret like some fucked-up pendulum.

It'd been six days since the bachelor party.

Six days of replaying the way Jordan kissed Ayana on the cheek and the way she'd smiled at him in response.

One hundred and thirty hours of remembering the way her body arched into mine.

Eight thousand-plus minutes of revisiting how she'd almost kissed me.

And an eternity of what-ifs over what would've happened had I not stopped her.

What the hell had she been playing at, doing that on the night of her bachelorette?

I didn't believe for a second that Ayana would jeopardize her engagement to Jordan for no good reason. And I sure as hell didn't believe she'd been so overcome by her sudden desire for me that she couldn't help herself.

I set up a new row of bottles.

I was in no mood to socialize, so I'd retreated to my makeshift shooting range at home instead of visiting the one at Valhalla. After the bachelor party, I didn't want to talk to anyone for at least two months.

I was about to start my second round of shooting when the door opened. Sean entered, his expression somber.

My staff had been avoiding me all week. They'd worked for me long enough to pick up on my foul moods, and they knew any human interaction would only piss me off more.

If Sean made it past Jeremiah, my butler and the ultimate authority over who got past the gates and who didn't, it was important.

I pulled off my headset and waited.

"We found something." Sean cut straight to the chase. "A SIM card in an abandoned garage uptown. We picked it up and traced it back to the point of purchase. The odds of it being helpful were slim, but we got a hit." Satisfaction glinted behind his exhaustion. He'd been chasing the mystery Brother nonstop for weeks, and it'd taken a physical toll on him. "Devin Rhoades. An alias for a known member of the Brotherhood."

The air stilled as every cell of my body locked on to that piece of information like a shark sensing blood in the water.

"This is everything we could dig up on him." Sean handed me a file. "The man is a ghost, which is expected given his affiliation. But look at his last name."

I opened the folder to a clear photo of the mystery Brother. He stared straight at the camera, his face a map of brutal planes and cold green eyes. Early thirties, American, Caucasian, last seen in New York City. He'd operated under multiple aliases, but the earliest name on file came from his foster care records.

Roman Davenport.

"Yes." Sean accurately read my stunned silence. "*That* Davenport. He and Dominic were assigned to the same foster home in Ohio when they were in their teens. Dominic went off to college, and Roman disappeared off the grid. The details of his Brotherhood recruitment and training are unknown, but he resurfaced about six years ago in France. Rumor has it he was responsible for the hit on a local crime lord there. Decapitation. It made quite a statement."

I quietly digested the influx of information.

Roman and Dominic Davenport were foster brothers. The same Dominic I'd done business with, frequented events with, and exchanged civilities with at Valhalla.

Dominic never talked about his family or his pre-college years. My gut told me he wasn't involved with the Brotherhood, but in situations like these, I couldn't discount anything.

What's Dominic and Roman's current relationship like?

"Unclear," Sean said. "As far as we can tell, they lost touch after Dominic left for college. However, these are our preliminary findings. We'll have to do a deeper dive, but I wanted to notify you about our discovery right away." He paused.

I cocked an eyebrow at his hesitation. It was unlike him. *What else? Spit it out.*

"Do you remember the Sunfolk scandal two years ago?" he asked.

I nodded.

The scandal was one of the biggest crime stories to hit mainstream news in recent years. A member of an unnamed mercenary organization had leaked a redacted contract between the Sunfolk Bank CEO and the mercenaries to get rid of Sunfolk's competition by any means necessary (i.e. murder).

The contract had spread like wildfire online. Most of the details had been blacked out, but that didn't stop rumors and conspiracy theories from flourishing. Sunfolk's CEO had died under mysterious circumstances in prison, but someone else stepped in to buy the bank when it was flailing: Dominic.

The pieces fell into place. *You think the Brotherhood is the organization from the contract.*

"Yes. And I think Roman may be the one who leaked it." Sean's mouth pressed into a thin line. "I can't confirm anything yet, but given the timeline and the players involved, it makes sense."

It did, and fuck, I wish it didn't.

Dominic's involvement would add an extra layer of complication. We weren't friends, but we ran in the same circles. I tried to keep my past and present separate, and he was too intertwined with my present life to have ties with my past one.

Pull on that thread. I want daily updates.

Sean nodded. "One more thing. As your Chief of Security, I would be remiss if I didn't emphasize how important it is to increase protection measures both here and at your office. We've implemented the soft security upgrades as discussed, but if the Brotherhood is keeping an eye on you, they may already be privy to our search for Roman. They'll know that *you* know they're after you, which means another hit may be imminent."

He was right. Again.

I hated having armed guards around me. The more people involved, the greater the chances of a leak and the greater the odds of betrayal. It'd take only one slip-up or one traitor to bring things crashing down. It didn't matter how well they were vetted; most people could be bought. Unless I had an established history with them and they'd proved their loyalty, I didn't trust anyone.

Fortunately, there were other ways to protect myself besides hired muscle.

No bodyguards. Enhance the other measures. I can take care of myself, I added when Sean opened his mouth to argue.

He sighed, but he didn't press the issue. "Consider it done."

After he left, I stayed at my makeshift shooting range and tried to connect the missing pieces of the puzzle.

Roman. Dominic. The Brotherhood. The Vault. What was the through line?

If Sean was right and Roman was the one who'd leaked the contract, he would be the organization's number one target. Contract killers relied on their reputation for business; a leak of that magnitude would destroy their credibility. The public may not have a name, but those in the shadows had a way of sniffing out secrets.

If Roman was the organization's target, why would he try to kill me on their behalf? Perhaps he'd gone rogue, but we'd never crossed paths before. He had no reason to personally want me dead.

Finally, there was that damn note. *Find me before they do.* Was the Brotherhood the "they" he was referring to?

My head pounded with open-ended questions and a thousand possibilities.

I couldn't focus, so I cleaned up the range and went upstairs to my office. I kept my gun on me.

My wing of the house was separated from the main rooms by an enclosed walkway. Other than cleaning and maintenance, my staff left it alone unless I called them, which was exactly how I liked it. I'd bought this property on the Upper East Side specifically because the layout offered me more privacy than the penthouses and brownstones so many of my peers loved.

I stepped into my office, ready to tackle some of the actual work I'd been neglecting while I obsessed over the bachelor party, but the hairs on the back of my neck instantly stood up.

Something was wrong.

More specifically—*someone was here*.

The sixth sense that'd helped me survive multiple scrapes over the years kicked in before I even noticed the shadow on the wall, or the fact that the chair was turned the wrong way.

By the time the intruder spun to face me in *my* fucking chair, I'd already raised my gun and pointed it straight at him.

He settled deeper into the chestnut leather with a smirk. "That's not a very polite way to greet your guests."

I cocked the hammer.

"You could shoot me." He sounded bored. "Or you could find out why I'd risk breaking into your house."

"I prefer option one," I growled.

I hated wasting words on dead men walking, but I sure as hell wasn't going to lower my weapon. Talking was the only viable way to communicate in this situation.

"So he speaks." His smile lacked humor. "I know you know who I am, which means you also know we have a mutual interest: the Brotherhood. Like I said, you could shoot me, or you could listen to what I have to say. I have a feeling it'll answer quite a few questions you've had recently." He slowly raised his hands. "No weapons. I just want to talk."

My finger twitched. I was tempted to pull the trigger and shoot him anyway, the Brotherhood be damned. Hell, he could be a distraction. There could be other members in the house right now, storming the halls and terrorizing my staff while I was busy in here.

It was unlikely, given the utter lack of alarms raised, but it wasn't impossible.

The fact he'd successfully broken in was not fucking good, but I would deal with the security breach later. I had more pressing matters at hand.

He stared back at me, unflinching.

Bastard. He held a trump card, and he knew it. He was my

only active link to the Brothers at the moment, which meant the satisfaction of blowing his head off wasn't worth the intel that would die with him.

I lowered the gun an inch and gestured for him to start talking.

"That's what I thought." Roman Davenport leaned forward, his eyes glittering in the dying afternoon light. "Before we get into the details, I have a proposition for you."

CHAPTER 20

Ayana

"CUT!" WENTWORTH LOWERED HIS CAMERA AND frowned. "Ayana, babe, you're not *focusing*. Where's the fire? Where's the passion? Where's the *it factor* that made you Model of the Year, hmm? I don't see it, sweetie."

I am not *your babe* or *your sweetie.*

I bit back my tart response. If I acted with anything except the utmost professionalism, I'd be labeled "difficult to work with."

Plus, as much as I hated to admit it, he had a point. My head wasn't in the game. Two hours into the Sage Studios denim shoot, and we'd yet to nail any of the photos. I hadn't struggled this much during a job since I got food poisoning in Milan and vomited all over a ten-thousand-dollar gown.

"Sorry." I forced a smile. "I'm ready. I'll focus."

Wentworth stared at me for a second before he heaved an exaggerated sigh. "No. Everyone, take five. Get some fresh air, bang it out in the fucking bathroom. I don't care. But when we're back on set, I need you *all* at the top of your game, you hear me? Let's go!" He snapped his fingers. "Chop, chop!"

The crew of assistants, stylists, makeup artists, and hairdressers dispersed. Chatter filled the studio, and a few people threw sympathetic glances my way as I headed for the nearest window.

I cracked it open an inch and sucked in a greedy lungful of cool September air. I hadn't eaten since the green smoothie I'd downed for breakfast, and I was feeling a little lightheaded from the stress and hunger. Wentworth barking orders in the background didn't help. God, I despised that man.

He'd acted professionally so far, but his mere presence creeped me out. I'd seen and heard too many things to be fully comfortable around him, even if we were surrounded by other people.

If only Vuk were here. The thought floated, unbidden, through my head. He had nothing to do with the fashion world, but as intimidating and infuriating as he was, he made me feel safe. I was certain that if the apocalypse happened tomorrow, he'd know exactly what to do to keep us alive. He was that capable.

Unfortunately, he was also the reason I was bombing this shoot.

It'd been almost a week since Vuk left me standing on the street after I tried to kiss him. The more I thought about it, the more guilt and embarrassment ate me alive, yet I couldn't *stop* thinking about it.

The way he'd looked at me, his grip on my wrist and the rough words he'd whispered in my ear…

I hadn't understood what he said, but it didn't matter. The memory sent a warm shiver down my spine. Every damn time.

The makeup artist approached me. "We're shooting again in a minute. Let me touch you up first."

"Of course." I swallowed my turmoil and closed the window. "Thank you."

While the team fussed over my hair and makeup, my mind drifted back to last weekend.

I hadn't seen or spoken to Vuk since, and I was starting to

second-guess my gut. Maybe he wasn't attracted to me. Maybe the alcohol had made me delusional, and I'd simply manufactured the vibes I'd felt.

If that were true, he was probably disgusted by my shameless-ness. To him, I was nothing more than someone who'd tried to cheat on her fiancé weeks before her wedding.

If that wasn't true, and he really was attracted to me...well, that didn't change much, did it? Unless he was willing to jeopardize a thirteen-year friendship for short-lived gratification.

I let out a soft groan. This was all so much easier when I was drunk.

The hair and makeup team finished their touch-ups, and I took my place again in front of the camera.

Wentworth looked me up and down. "Beautiful," he said, his eyes lingering a little too long on my chest and legs. "But that isn't enough. Let me see that famous Ayana Kidane spark."

The sooner I nailed this, the sooner I could leave, so I pushed aside my discomfort and all thoughts about Vuk and the wedding.

If I could shoot a winter campaign in Iceland wearing a backless gown and stilettos while I was on my period, I could do this.

I took a deep breath and let the rest of the room fade away until it was just me, the camera, and the rhythmic click of the shutter. The rest of my life might be a shitshow, but this? This was my element.

For the next few hours, I posed and improvised and played off the rising energy in the room. I didn't have to think; I just let my body flow into the positions naturally.

French electronic music played in the background, underlaying Wentworth's exclamations of "Gorgeous!" and "Perfect!" We stopped intermittently for more touch-ups and wardrobe adjustments, but the shoot went so smoothly, we finished before sunset.

"Good job, everyone," Wentworth said after we wrapped. "This campaign is going to be smashing."

I changed and checked my phone while the crew packed up. I had new messages from my family and Indira—who was asking, *again*, whether I could set her up with Vuk—but nothing from Vuk himself...which made sense, considering I'd never given him my number.

But the disappointment stung all the same.

"Fantastic job, sweetie. I knew you could do it." Wentworth's voice in my ear made me jump. I jerked my head up to find his face inches from mine, and iron restraint was the only thing that kept me from kneeing him in the balls.

"We had a rough start, but it turned out well, yeah?" His smile had the opposite of its intended effect.

Objectively, Wentworth was decent-looking. He was in his early forties with thick brown hair, brown eyes, and rugged features. Not the type who would have trouble finding female company—until the women got to know him.

Whatever attractiveness he possessed was immediately counteracted by his arrogance and general sleaziness.

"Yeah." I took several discreet steps back. "I'm glad we got the shot."

I glanced around and realized everyone had left besides us. I mentally kicked myself for not leaving as soon as the shoot wrapped; no model wanted to be alone with Wentworth.

"We should celebrate." He closed the distance between us again. Now that he didn't have an audience, he didn't seem so concerned with being professional. "My apartment isn't far. I could order food. Champagne. Other things." The last two words dripped with suggestiveness.

The army of spiders crawling over my skin multiplied. "No, thanks." I took another step back, but the wall behind me prevented me from going any further. "I have another appointment soon. In fact, I should—"

"Really?" Wentworth arched his eyebrows. "Hank told me this was your last job of the day."

Dammit. Fucking Hank.

He'd been suspiciously quiet since he showed up unannounced at my apartment. Usually he would've called at least four times to check in on me, but it'd been crickets.

Maybe it was because he knew I was onto him about his spying. As promised, Vuk had sent his team to sweep my apartment and devices for bugs earlier that week. They'd found one on my phone and one in the Beaumont-branded pen I took everywhere. They couldn't trace them directly back to Hank, but I knew he was responsible.

Vuk's team had gotten rid of the bugs and left me a scanner that allowed me to check for "untraceable" devices on my own. The information blackout would've tipped Hank off, though he'd been quiet since before then.

I didn't want to confront him about the surveillance yet. I wasn't sure what I was waiting for; I just knew it wasn't time.

Meanwhile, I had another industry asshole to deal with.

"It's not a job. It's a…facial appointment," I lied. I hiked my purse higher on my shoulders and eyed the distance to the door. It wasn't far, but Wentworth blocked my direct path.

"I heard you're getting married in a month or so." He closed in enough for me to choke on the overpowering scent of his cologne.

"I am," I said with a tight smile. "Now if you'll excuse—"

"Is that why you've been so distracted? I have to say, I expected more from you." Wentworth shook his head. "Professionalism matters."

My temper reared, but I didn't take the bait. I refused to give him that opening.

"There's been a lot of chatter about your wedding," he said casually. "Like how the church ceremony *really* got pushed up because of a scandal and not because of Orla Ford's health. Pregnancy, child out of wedlock, that sort of thing."

"Whoever is saying that is wrong," I said shortly, too irritated to keep up pretenses. "Like I said, I have a facial appointment soon, so I really need to go."

I tried to sidestep him, but he was too fast. "There are other rumors too," he said, blocking my path again. "Like how you and your fiancé aren't even having sex. It must be difficult. Physical intimacy is important in relationships." He touched my arm, his breath billowing across my face.

His pupils were the size of quarters.

He's high. The realization struck me hard. I didn't know what he'd taken after the shoot, but Wentworth was absolutely high out of his mind.

A cold dagger of fear slipped between my ribs right as he moved, quick as lightning. By the time I reacted, it was too late.

His mouth crushed against mine. He placed his hands on the wall above my head, caging me in while his tongue probed at the seam of my lips.

I was so stunned by the abrupt turn of events that I could only stand, immobilized, while Wentworth Holt kissed me without consent.

I should push him off. Scream, cry, *something*. But there was a part of my brain that couldn't quite process what was happening.

We heard stories and we glimpsed things, but within every person lived the small, unshakeable belief that they were the exception. What happened to others couldn't possibly happen to them. Disaster was possible, but not probable.

So for all the concerns I'd raised about him and all the

discomfort I felt, I never truly thought he would be bold enough to make such a move.

Wentworth mistook my lack of response as encouragement. He kissed me harder, one of his hands dropping from the wall to caress my shoulder.

The feel of his palm against my bare skin shocked me out of my stupor.

My stomach heaved, and a swift surge of rage swamped every other emotion. In that moment, I didn't care about my job or reputation. Men like Wentworth Holt had been taking advantage of others for far too long, and I was *sick* of it.

I shoved him off me and slapped him. The resounding *whack* echoed through the empty studio.

"Don't *touch* me." My heartbeat slammed hard enough to bruise. A sticky, sour film coated my tongue, and the lights buzzed like wasps in my ears.

Compared to other models, I'd been "lucky" so far when it came to creeps like Wentworth. I'd been the subject of suggestive stares and comments, and I'd endured the occasional wandering hand, but no one had dared be this brazen—until now.

Wentworth's face twisted with an ugly scowl. He wasn't used to hearing *no*, and the combination of rejection and drugs turned him into an even more monstrous version of himself.

He lunged for me again. I tried to dodge him, but I had limited space and he had the superhuman strength that came from being high.

He grabbed hold of my arms and pushed me against the wall. A scream rose in my throat, followed by a fresh wave of fury.

I was hungry and exhausted after the all-day shoot, but *fuck him* if he thought that meant I would let him do what he wanted without a fight.

When Wentworth tried to kiss me again, I summoned all my

strength and headbutted him. The sickening crunch of bone mixed with his howl of pain.

Blood fountained from his nose and dripped onto my skin as I pushed him aside and scrambled for the door.

"You bitch!" He grasped my arm on my way past. His hand was slippery from the blood, and I was able to twist out of his hold.

I didn't give him time to try to corner me again; I didn't even think. I acted on instinct and slammed my knee into his groin as hard as I could.

Wentworth doubled over with a high-pitched howl. Just in case that wasn't enough to incapacitate him, I swung my bag into his face. It was my Shoot Day bag, and it was stuffed to the brim with makeup, travel-size hair products, a water bottle, a physical planner, a phone charger, snacks, a backup pair of heels, and a thousand other things I kept on me in cases of emergency.

All that to say, the bag was heavy as hell, and I heard a deeply satisfying thud when it connected with Wentworth's face.

I didn't wait to see if the hit knocked him out completely or simply slowed him down.

I turned and booked it outside. We were on the sixth floor, but I took the stairs instead of the elevator because I needed to move, needed to *keep* moving in case he caught up with me and made me pay.

My lungs were burning by the time I reached the lobby and burst into the middle of Chelsea.

A passing couple gasped when they saw me emerge, frazzled and blood-stained, but in true New York fashion, they left me alone. I ignored the curious gawks of other passersby as I sped walked far, far away from the studio. I passed street after street and made turn after turn until I lost all sense of direction.

I finally stopped at a random corner by a Chase bank. My

calves ached from how fast I'd been walking, and it wasn't until my vision fogged that I realized my cheeks were wet.

My chest heaved with silent sobs. I tried to wipe the tears away, but they just kept coming, and I eventually gave up.

I sagged against the wall. My earlier boost of adrenaline drained away, leaving my limbs so heavy I could hardly stand.

I'd been running on fumes for months, and my altercation with Wentworth had sapped me of my remaining energy.

I stared straight ahead, the world muddling into a blur of people and traffic.

On a day-to-day basis, when I had a packed schedule to follow and mindless entertainment to distract me, I could convince myself I was okay. But when I was alone, stripped raw and vulnerable, I could no longer deny what I'd refused to acknowledge: I was exhausted. Physically, mentally, emotionally.

My life was spiraling, and every attempt to regain control only put it further out of reach. First, it was signing Beaumont's contract to save my family from financial duress. Then it was agreeing to marry Jordan to get out of that contract. Now I had my feelings for Vuk and the Wentworth situation to deal with. I was sure he was going to try and twist what happened to make me look like the villain.

A migraine bloomed behind my temple.

I should file a police report. Call Sloane. Figure out what to do when my agency came down on me for "attacking" Wentworth when it'd been self-defense.

I'd long disabused myself of the notion that Beaumont was on my side. To them, models were at the bottom of the hierarchy because there was a never-ending supply of us.

Somewhere, always, there was a pretty young girl with stars in her eyes and dreams of fame and fortune—or, at the very least, of ways to put food on her family's table.

So no, Beaumont wouldn't take my side when they inevitably found out what happened. They'd keep it hush-hush and figure out a way to placate Wentworth.

I angrily swiped the back of my hand across my face again. The rational part of me recognized that I should get off the street before someone took and uploaded a picture of me crying to the internet.

I was well known, but thankfully, I wasn't famous enough to warrant a horde of paparazzi following my every move. That didn't mean I was safe from candid photos taken by random passersby.

I sucked in a long, calming breath and tried to think. What should I do next?

I didn't want to go home to an empty apartment; I wanted to be with someone I trusted. But who did I have, really?

Jordan was the obvious choice from a practical perspective, but I didn't want practical. I wanted emotional support, and that wasn't something I turned to him first for.

Kim was working, and Indira was a definite no. She'd understand the predicament, but she was too close to the industry. Sloane would be too logical about it, and my family would *freak out* if they knew what happened. My father would probably come up and kill Wentworth himself. I didn't want to place that emotional burden on them when they already had so much work and reception planning on their plate.

My tears finally slowed to a trickle.

If I were honest with myself, there was only one person I wanted to see. It made no sense, but few things in my life did anymore.

So, before I could talk myself out of it, I headed to the nearest subway station and took the train uptown, toward the most dangerous man I knew.

CHAPTER 21

Vuk

I HAVE A PROPOSITION FOR YOU.

Roman's words hung in the air. He lounged behind the desk, seemingly uncaring, but the sharpness of his stare suggested my answer meant a hell of a lot more to him than he let on.

"I want to take down the Brotherhood," he said. "And I want your help to do it."

I raised my gun again.

"I know, I know. You might be thinking, why would you want to help me?" If Roman was fazed about staring down the barrel of a Glock, he didn't show it. "I was the one who set fire to the Vault. I almost killed you. So I can see why you'd be a little—"

A gunshot exploded.

The bullet streaked past him and embedded itself in my wall. A warning—one so close his hair ruffled just the tiniest bit from the speed and proximity of the call.

Roman paused. "Upset about that," he finished coolly. "It wasn't personal. I owed the Brotherhood a debt, and I paid it. If I hadn't, we both know what would've happened to me."

My mouth thinned. Unfortunately, I did know firsthand what

it meant to owe the Brothers. That didn't change the fact that the bastard tried to *kill* me using my biggest weakness.

White-hot fire bubbled in my veins. I wanted to toss the gun aside, take out my favorite knife, and paint the walls with his blood.

My baser instincts demanded I give in to them, but in the end, rationality prevailed.

Roman lived—for now.

"On that note, I'll cut straight to the chase. The longer I'm here, the more likely it is they'll find out I've initiated contact with you." He flicked his eyes around the office like the Brothers themselves were hiding in the shadows. "The Brotherhood wants you dead. *Badly.*"

No shit. Tell me something I didn't know.

My silence communicated my unimpressed displeasure.

"It's not for the reasons you might think. The organization is at war." Roman offered another mirthless smile at my twitch of surprise. "Gallo died last year. His protégé Shepherd took over, but a faction of the Brothers strongly opposed his leadership. It split the group in half, and now they're battling for control. Instead of carrying out hits on each other—which would obviously be detrimental to the overall health and longevity of the Brotherhood—they've determined a prize for winner takes all." Roman inclined his head. "You."

The revelation sank into my skin like razor blades.

He didn't elaborate, but I could fill in the rest of the blanks myself.

I'd been the biggest thorn in the Brotherhood's side for years. I was the one that got away—a living and breathing reminder of their failure.

They were one of the world's most elite groups of assassins and contract killers, and I was the only person in their hundred-year history to face them head-on and win.

Killing me would restore their honor. Most importantly, the side that succeeded would've demonstrated the qualities they valued most: Strength. Skill. Power.

"I stayed with Shepherd. The devil you know and all that. He tasked me with killing you and making it look like an accident. I may have purposely slacked on the job, but it was convincing enough that they didn't suspect a double-cross."

"Why?"

The smart move would've been to take me out and earn himself a spot in Shepherd's good graces. Then again, with the Brotherhood at war, those good graces didn't mean shit if the other faction won.

This was all assuming Roman was telling the truth. I had no way of verifying in the moment, so I had to operate like he was until I checked out his story. Thoroughly.

"The enemy of my enemy is my friend." He shrugged. "I don't pledge allegiance to either faction anymore. I want out from under both of them. But I can't take them on my own, which is why I need your help."

I waited.

"I provide the intel and inside knowledge. You provide the money and resources," he elaborated. "I would've waited for you to find me first, but circumstances have changed, and your men were taking too damn long. So I left a little clue at the garage to speed them along."

Roman glanced around my office again. He was either an Oscar-winning actor, or he was genuinely jumpy about the Brothers finding him here. "I haven't fully earned back the Brothers' trust after a previous indiscretion. They're keeping close tabs on me, and I couldn't risk making direct contact until they were...distracted."

"Seems like they have reason not to trust you." It was a bright red flag. First rule of survival: don't trust a double-crosser. If they could betray their previous allegiances, they could betray you. But if the Brothers were privy to his general whereabouts... "Who's the 'they' from your note?"

Find me before they do.

Roman's face shuttered. "Someone I crossed paths with while I was hiding from the Brotherhood."

A world of secrets hid behind those words.

I'd bet my entire company that his "previous indiscretion" was the leaked Sunfolk contract and that was the reason he'd been hiding from the Brothers. What drew him back out, and who had he crossed paths with? Who had the power to unsettle an experienced killer?

All intriguing questions, but not ones I had time to delve into right now. Until I verified what he'd already told me, I would keep things simple.

"If you take out the leaders of both factions," I said, "you become the new de facto leader of the Brotherhood. Convenient."

Roman said he wanted out from under both of them; he hadn't said he wanted out, period.

The organization followed old world pack rules. The strongest rose to the top. The members wouldn't follow anyone else.

If Roman killed Shepherd and the leader of the other faction, he would be the strongest, and leadership would pass to him unless someone challenged him.

"Smart. I was right to come to you." A genuine smile touched his mouth. "Yes, I have deeply selfish reasons for why I want the leadership role, but it'll be beneficial for you too. Once I take over, the animosity between you and the Brotherhood will be wiped. Forever. I'll make sure of it."

"You expect me to believe you?"

"Of course not. But my word is better than nothing." Roman nodded at my gun. "Your truce held as long as the Brotherhood feared you. Unfortunately, that same fear has turned you into their biggest target. The only reason they haven't made another move on you yet is because of certain...developments in the war. Distractions. Once they sort those out, they'll be after you again."

"What developments?"

He let out a soft laugh. "Nice try. I've already told you enough. If you want more, you'll have to give something in return." Roman studied me. "Your old sources on the Brotherhood have dried up. They're dead or retired. I'm your only active link to the organization, and I'm the only one who can tell you when they plan to strike again. Shepherd's faction, anyway, but I'm sure I can infiltrate the other side as well."

He was careful not to name the other faction. More information he was holding over my head, or a sign of his bullshit?

I quietly dissected my options.

If Roman was lying, and I agreed to help him, he could lead me straight into a trap. However, he'd successfully broken into my house. If he was in league with the Brothers, they would've attacked by now. It wouldn't make sense for them to draw things out—unless, of course, they wanted to make a show of it. Humiliate me first by proving how gullible I was to believe Roman's lies, then torture me. It was unlikely, but it was possible.

If Roman was telling the truth, this was my best shot at survival. I'd played defense since I found out the Brotherhood was involved in the fire because I had no choice; I was operating in the dark. With Roman's intel, I could finally go on the offense.

As for the consequences of Roman taking over the organization...that was a problem for another day.

"So?" His eyes pierced mine. "Do we have a deal?"

My old sources may have dried up, but the Brotherhood's civil war was verifiable if I knew where to look—which I did.

I'd have to triple-check every word that came out of Roman's mouth. Until then...

I pulled the trigger.

He didn't get a chance to run. His body jerked from the force of the bullet, and he released a sharp hiss when it tore through his shoulder. Blood bloomed on the front of his shirt and dripped onto the leather armrest.

Goddammit. That was my favorite chair.

Roman glared at me, his face white with pain. But he didn't scream. He got bonus points for that.

"I could've aimed for your heart," I said. "I'll be in touch regarding your proposition. Now get the fuck out of my house before I change my mind."

CHAPTER 22

Ayana

VUK'S MANSION RESEMBLED ITS OWNER: LARGE, IMPOS-
ing, and cloaked in silence.

It was one of the rare Manhattan estates with enough space
for a front courtyard *and* a backyard, all of which were nestled
behind giant black iron gates.

I'd visited once before with Jordan. I'd been so intimidated
by the sheer size and unwelcoming facade that I'd spent the entire
dinner on edge. The lovingly home-cooked, gourmet roast had
tasted like cardboard.

That'd been a year ago.

This time, the sight of the gates filled me with relief. I wanted
to lose myself behind the security of the thick stone walls and
locks. I wanted a bubble where the outside world didn't exist, and
men like Wentworth Holt couldn't touch me. Most of all, I wanted
to see the one person who could possibly make me forget what
happened, if only for a short while.

I pressed the call button by the entrance and waited for
someone to pick up. The sun had set, and twilight bathed the
street in cool blue silence.

This was one of the safest neighborhoods in New York, but I'd still rather be inside than outside.

"Can I help you?" A crisp, vaguely British-accented voice floated out of the intercom.

"Hi. I'm here to see Vuk. Markovic," I added inanely, like there was another Vuk that could've possibly resided on the grounds. "I'm a, um, friend."

Perhaps "friend" was stretching it, but "his friend's fiancée who tried kissing him after he almost accidentally choked her to death on the night of her bachelorette" didn't have quite the same ring.

Also, when I put it like that…I winced. God, I was fucked up.

"I see." The voice sounded politely unimpressed. "I'm afraid Mr. Markovic is busy at the moment, but I'll let him know you were here. What's your name?"

"Ayana Kidane." I swallowed past the embarrassing thickness in my throat. I wasn't going to cry just because Vuk couldn't see me when I showed up at his house unannounced. What had I expected? That he would be sitting there waiting for visitors? He was a CEO and the managing director of Valhalla. He had more important things to do.

A long pause followed my response.

To my shock, the gates buzzed open a minute later, followed by a slightly warmer reception. "Please come in."

I was confused as to what made the gatekeeper change his mind. However, I wasn't going to look a gift horse in the mouth, so I entered the courtyard and walked to the entrance.

A tall, white-haired man in a black suit waited for me by the front doors. I didn't remember seeing him during my last visit. Then again, Vuk had greeted us himself, and the only staff I'd interacted with were the servers.

"Ms. Kidane, welcome," he said. "I'm Jeremiah, the butler. Please, come with me. Mr. Markovic is waiting for you."

Less than a minute had passed since he buzzed me in. How did he have time to inform Vuk already?

It doesn't matter. I wasn't here to study Vuk's household operations.

I followed Jeremiah inside. I'd cleaned up in a department store restroom before I came, but I couldn't fix my tear-swollen eyes or wipe away the stain of Wentworth's mouth on mine.

My steps faltered for a beat, and I hoped Jeremiah didn't notice the slight shake of my hand as I adjusted my bag.

We passed through the foyer and into the main living areas. It was exactly as I remembered. Long marble halls wound around grand rooms dedicated to every activity under the sun. There was a billiards room, a screening room, a sitting room, a living room (I still didn't know the difference between this and a sitting room), and a room that appeared to have no purpose other than to display different musical instruments.

After a good ten minutes, we finally stopped in front of the library. The doors were ajar. Jeremiah gestured for me to enter. Once I did, he shut them behind me with a quiet *snick*.

I waited until his footsteps faded into the distance before I breathed normally again. Vuk hadn't given me a full tour the last time I was here with Jordan, and I'd never seen the library before.

It was beautiful—shelves and shelves of leather-bound books, an emerald carpet so thick I couldn't hear myself walk, and giant windows overlooking the backyard.

Vuk sat at one of the rosewood tables. His laptop was open in front of him, and a deep furrow dug between his brows. However, it smoothed a fraction when he saw me.

He shut his laptop abruptly and stood, his gaze sweeping over my face and the tight-knuckled grip on my bag. His eyes sharpened.

What's wrong?

I opened my mouth. Nothing came out.

I just dropped by to say hi. I have some things to go over for the wedding. I want to talk about last weekend.

I'd rehearsed a dozen different excuses during the train ride. I'd decided it would be better if I didn't tell Vuk about Wentworth because, truth be told, I was a little scared of what he'd do. I didn't want him to get into trouble.

But now that I was here, the excuses I'd concocted died in my throat. To my absolute horror, tears welled up instead.

For a brief moment, I thought I could control them. Then a sob tore loose, and that was it.

I broke down, my shoulders heaving, my stomach cramping from the force of my cries. My earlier tears were nothing compared to this. I'd unconsciously held back because I'd been in public, but now that I was in a safe place, it all came rushing out.

The anger, the disgust, the fear and frustration and anxiety—every emotion that'd plagued me over the past year and more flooded the room. It wasn't just Wentworth; it was *everything*. He was simply the straw that broke the camel's back.

Every gasp for more oxygen failed; every tremble begot more trembles. Chills blanketed my skin, and I was drowning so deep in my anguish that I didn't notice Vuk's approach.

Strong arms wrapped around me and held me close. I instinctively buried my face in his chest, taking solace in his warmth and faint, slightly smoky scent. His heart beat a steady rhythm beneath my cheek.

I thought his walls and gates were what made me feel safe, but they weren't. It was *him*.

After minutes or hours or perhaps days, my tears slowed to a trickle. I pulled back, my eyes and throat raw. "I'm sorry." I sniffled. "I didn't mean to come in and cry all over you like that. I didn't—I didn't even say hi first."

Don't apologize. His movements were measured, but I detected something I'd never seen before in his eyes: panic. *Tell me what happened.*

I swallowed. Despite my earlier convictions, I didn't want to lie to him. Not when he was so worried, and I was so desperate to confide in someone.

What was the worst he would do, assuming he did anything at all? Call in some favors to get Wentworth blacklisted or rough him up a bit? The other man deserved it.

"I was at a photoshoot, and the photographer…" I hiccupped. "After everyone left…he tried to…he…" It took several tries, but I finally got the words out. I told Vuk what happened, starting with Wentworth's advances after the shoot and ending with my escape. The more I spoke, the stiller Vuk became. By the time I finished, he resembled a statue, his eyes so cold and flat, the hairs on my neck stood up.

"He touched you," he said softly. There was no inflection or emotion. Just pure ice.

It was so unsettling, I didn't dwell on the fact that this was his third time speaking to me. "He didn't…other than the kiss, nothing happened." I wasn't trying to defend Wentworth, but Vuk's eerie calm made me more nervous than if he'd raged and punched something. "I'm okay."

That wasn't true. I was physically fine, but my mind and emotions were all over the place. Nevertheless, I felt leagues better than when I'd first arrived.

I braced myself for a further interrogation into the day's events. To my surprise, it never came.

Vuk typed something on his phone and guided me to the nearest table. I sat, confused, until two staff members showed up minutes later with silver trays. They placed them in front of me and removed the warming domes to reveal a steaming mug of tea, an assortment of fruits and pastries, and, oddly enough, two jars of peanut butter. One creamy, one crunchy.

Eat. Vuk sat across from me after his staff left. *It'll make you feel better.*

As if on cue, my stomach growled. I really was starving. "How did you know?"

You were at a photoshoot all day. I doubt they were feeding you properly.

Warmth trickled into my stomach. "And the peanut butter?" It was one of my guilty pleasures.

You mentioned it in your sleep when we were in California. I figured you'd like it.

"I was talking about peanut butter in my sleep?" I asked, mortified. "That's so—just kill me now."

A smirk softened Vuk's mouth. He didn't say anything else as I tore into a croissant and dipped the apple wedges in peanut butter. Screw the calories. I was going to eat whatever I wanted today and worry about it later.

I was grateful Vuk didn't ask more questions about Wentworth. I'd gotten the incident off my chest, and it was nice to eat in silence without rehashing my trauma.

This was exactly what I needed at the moment.

I took a sip of tea. My eyes winged up at the taste. "This is almost exactly like the tea I gave you at my house."

Vuk shrugged. *I liked it, so I had someone recreate it as closely as possible.*

"How? It's my mom's custom blend. She won't even tell *me* everything she puts in it."

I have my ways.

Of course he did.

"Must be nice," I mumbled. I had to go back to D.C. if I wanted a refill.

Its comforting familiarity sent a wave of nostalgia crashing through me. If only I were home. I missed the simplicity of my younger days, when there was nothing my mother couldn't soothe with a hug and a hot drink.

Vuk smirked again, but the coldness never quite left his eyes. Wentworth was still at the top of his mind.

Meanwhile, there was another elephant sitting in the room with us. I debated whether to bring it up, but we had to talk about it sooner or later. I might as well rip all the Band-Aids off at once.

"About last Saturday," I said tentatively. "I didn't—"

Nothing happened last Saturday.

I startled at his terse reply. He hadn't hesitated for a single beat.

Was I delusional? Had I imagined what happened on the street?

No. I hadn't been *that* drunk. I'd definitely tried to kiss him, and he'd definitely stopped me. I didn't know what he'd said in Serbian, but I heard what came before that, loud and clear.

Don't.

Vuk was giving me a graceful way out by pretending nothing happened. That was, by all accounts, the best-case scenario for both of us.

So why did I feel so disappointed?

He switched subjects. *Did you tell anyone else what happened with Wentworth?*

"Not yet." Warmth rushed to my cheeks. "You're the first person I've told."

The naked vulnerability of my admission fluttered between us like torn diary pages in the wind.

Vuk's eyes softened the tiniest bit.

"I'll have to tell Hank and Sloane," I added quickly. "I have to check in with Hank soon anyway. I haven't heard from him all week."

Really? Vuk's expression was neutral. *How odd.*

"Yeah." I finished my tea and pushed the mug aside. "Thank

you for the food and for listening to me, but I should go. I've taken up enough of your time."

Why didn't you go to Jordan first?

I froze. Logically speaking, I *should've* gone to my fiancé first. But how could I tell Vuk that he was the one I'd wanted to see, not Jordan?

"I will tell him later," I lied. "But he has, um, a huge board meeting at work today, and I didn't want to distract him."

Vuk's eyes narrowed. It was a flimsy excuse, but fortunately, he didn't press the issue.

I was already halfway out of my seat when I collapsed again at his next question.

Are you angry?

"What?"

About Wentworth.

My jaw tightened. "Of *course* I'm angry. He assaulted me, and I'm not the first model he's harassed. I wish—" I stopped myself and took a deep breath. "It doesn't matter. Anger won't get me anywhere. I have to deal with things the...the practical way. Although I am happy that I probably broke his nose."

I hoped it never reset properly and the asshole had to walk around with a crooked nose for the rest of his life. He was so vain, it would kill him.

Vuk stood abruptly. *Come with me. I have something that might help.*

The fact I didn't question him was a testament to how much I'd come to trust him.

My chest prickled with curiosity as I followed him out of the library and downstairs to...

I blinked, unsure what I was looking at.

The basement-level room was twice the size of my apartment, but it was empty save for a table in the middle and crates full of junk. Broken bottles and bottle caps littered the far side of the room, and there was a faint, acrid smell. Almost like burnt toast, but a little smokier.

Vuk walked over to a black chest and popped it open. He motioned for me to join him.

I did. I peered inside, half-expecting to see a dead body or something. Instead, I found a helmet, vest, goggles, and gloves.

My brows pulled together. "What…" I paused and looked around again. It suddenly clicked. "Wait. You have your own rage room?"

He lifted his shoulders. *It comes in handy sometimes.*

I'd heard of venues where people paid to vent their stress and anger by smashing breakable objects. I'd never been to one, but I'd always been intrigued by the concept. It was definitely better than picking a fight in a bar or lashing out at the people around me.

I eyed the crates of dishware and old electronics surrounding us. My parents had raised me to value our belongings. The thought of indiscriminately breaking those items made me squirm—until my eyes fell on an old camera.

It wasn't the same brand or model Wentworth had used. It wasn't even the same color. But the mere sight brought me back to the studio, to the ugliness of his hands on me and the entitlement he'd displayed.

That old fury bubbled to the surface again, grinding and swelling against my insides until I thought I would burst.

I grabbed the safety gear and put it on. I made sure to tie my loose waves back before I put on the helmet so they didn't get matted. Once I was finished, Vuk handed me a baseball bat and retreated outside without a word.

The door shut.

I stared at the once-empty table. Vuk had piled it with items while I was suiting up. There were wine glasses, dishes, a TV, and that stupid camera. The TV's dark screen faced me, reflecting my trembling form.

What had Wentworth seen when he looked at me? Someone he could take advantage of because the system was created in his favor. Someone like the other girls, who kept their mouths shut and played nice because they were afraid of rocking the boat.

I didn't blame them for not coming forward. The world wasn't kind to those who dared speak up.

But that didn't mean it was right.

I approached the table, my pulse pounding. With my gear and the bat in hand, I didn't look as helpless as I often felt. I looked like someone who fought back.

I took a deep breath, swung the bat, and *slammed* it down on the camera. It broke apart with a terrible crack.

Unsatisfied, I moved on to the TV. I hit it again, and again, and again until the screen was so smashed, it was barely recognizable as a television. After that, I vented my frustration on the dishes, the bottles, the ceramic ornaments. Nothing was safe from my rage.

Yet the fire inside me remained, clawing, desperate for a way out. My heart ran wild. Sweat drenched my skin, and my muscles ached from the force of my blows.

But I kept swinging, taking perverse pleasure in the shower of glass and ceramic shards until finally, *finally*, there was nothing left for me to break. Only then did I stop.

The bat clattered to the floor. I placed my gloved hands on the table and bent over, my chest heaving. The goggles had fogged up, and beads of sweat rolled down the side of my face. My arms were so sore I struggled to lift them.

It wasn't comfort; it was something even better.

Catharsis.

CHAPTER 23

Vuk

"SIR, YOU CAN'T GO IN THERE. SIR!" THE ASSISTANT scrambled after me, his shiny loafers squeaking against the marble floors.

I ignored him the way I ignored the other staff gawking at me as I stalked through Beaumont's office.

I'd waited all weekend for this, and my patience had reached its limits.

After Ayana finished with my makeshift rage room on Friday, I'd driven her home and made sure she was safely inside her apartment before I formulated my plan.

It'd taken every ounce of restraint not to find Wentworth fucking Holt that same night and kill him. But there was something I needed to do first, and acting on impulse was never a good idea.

I stopped at the corner office and walked in without knocking.

Emmanuelle Beaumont didn't appear surprised by my arrival. She must've gotten a warning call from the front desk.

"Vuk Markovic." She waved off her assistant, her eyes glinting with amusement when I closed the door in the man's face. "What a surprise. To what do I owe the pleasure?"

I took the seat opposite hers and eyed her dispassionately.

She was, objectively, an attractive woman, but I'd dealt with enough snakes in my life to recognize one when I saw it.

Behind that polished veneer lay the cunning mind of a viper. She hadn't risen to the top of her field by playing nice, and I would've admired her for it had her ruthlessness not affected Ayana.

I cut to the chase and slid a pre-written piece of paper across her desk. It contained two words: **Wentworth Holt.**

"What about him?" Neutral tone, neutral expression, but she was clued in to what happened. I sensed it in her placidness. That was the calm of someone who was trying too hard to pretend they didn't know what I was talking about.

There was a ceramic cup full of basic ballpoint pens next to me. I bypassed those and plucked the five-hundred-dollar personalized Montblanc straight out of her hand.

Emmanuelle's mouth tightened, but she was smart enough to stay quiet.

I wrote my answer in precise black strokes.

He assaulted Ayana after Friday's photoshoot.

Writing it down brought my rage to a high simmer again. Only cowards attacked people who they didn't think could fight back. Wentworth knew the power he wielded, and he'd used it to take liberties he had no right taking.

It was the worst sort of gutlessness.

"That's interesting." Emmanuelle's expression shifted back to neutral. "Wentworth called me this morning, screaming about how Ayana assaulted *him*. He has the injuries and ER records to prove it. He said he's on the verge of pressing charges."

Let him.

She stared at the words on the paper. The implied threat behind them hung heavy in the air.

When she spoke again, caution edged her voice. "I'm not his

boss, Mr. Markovic. I don't let him *do* anything. I have no control over his decisions."

But you have control over your agency's bookings. The simmer had reached a boil, but I kept it contained for now. *Don't put any of your models in a room with that man ever again.*

"That's quite a demand for someone who doesn't work in fashion and whom I've never spoken to before," Emmanuelle said. She studied me. "You're Jordan Ford's best man, correct?"

I responded with a cool stare. We both knew the answer.

"I'm curious." She ran a sharp red nail over the black text on the paper. "Why are you the one here discussing the situation and not her fiancé?"

Because she's fucking mine.

Jordan was her fiancé in name, but I was the one she'd turned to first. I was the one who understood what she needed—not comfort, but vengeance. I was the one who would kill and die for her in the same breath.

No other man could match that, ring or no ring.

I smiled. It lacked the emotion of a true smile, and it was a deliberate facsimile of the real thing. The motion twisted the scar around my mouth.

Emmanuelle swallowed. A flicker of revulsion crossed her face.

I stood, and she blanched when the metal legs of the chair screeched against the floor.

I walked out without answering her question.

I waited until I hit the sidewalk before I pulled out my phone and logged into an encrypted app.

I'd wanted to confront Emmanuelle about Wentworth, but I'd had another ulterior motive: the tiny surveillance device I'd stuck to the bottom of her desk while she'd been distracted by my note.

It was currently broadcasting loud and clear from her office.

I was about to pocket my phone when it buzzed with a new text.

SEAN

We're ready for you.

This time, my smile was almost genuine.
The day was looking up already.

———————

Forty minutes later, I arrived at an industrial neighborhood deep in Brooklyn. Unlike the trendy areas closer to the city, this particular corner of the borough was a collection of graffiti and empty streets. Abandoned warehouses squatted along cracked sidewalks paved with grime. Even the skies here loomed grayer overhead.

The chances of anyone randomly wandering by were slim to none.

I parked behind warehouse number five and entered through the back exit.

Sean was already waiting for me outside the old storage room in the back. "We picked him up on his way home," he said. "No one saw us, and we kept him blindfolded the entire time so he doesn't know where we are."

Good. I reached for the door handle. I was hungering to get in there, but my security chief stopped me.

"One more thing." His voice lowered. "I investigated your... friend's claims. No one would give me a straight answer, but they heavily suggest that he's telling the truth. The entire underworld's on edge. They're rarely so jumpy unless something big is happening." Sean rubbed a hand over his mouth. "We could try to hire the Brotherhood through a proxy and see what happens, but that would be risky."

I agree. No proxy. A proxy could be traced back to us. If they were caught, the Brothers would torture them for information, and it didn't matter how tough the subject was. Everybody broke, sooner or later.

I'll take care of that situation going forward. Wait here until I'm finished.

I'd told Sean and *only* Sean about Roman's visit. He'd been appalled and outraged that someone had successfully broken into my house. It'd taken him less than an hour to find and patch the security breach. Roman had snuck in as a member of our bi-weekly gardening service, and the guard in charge of screening all visitors had slacked on the job. He'd been fired immediately and replaced with someone more senior.

It was a stupid mistake we couldn't afford to make with the Brotherhood back in the mix.

Sean also hadn't been thrilled to hear about Roman's proposition. However, he knew my relationship with the Brothers was complicated, and he'd refrained from passing judgment beyond several warnings not to trust Roman.

"Understood," he said. "I'll keep a lookout."

I twisted the handle and entered the storage room.

I'd bought the warehouse years ago using a shell company. Its ownership was buried under so many layers of paperwork it would take an entire team of top-notch forensic accountants years to trace it back to me.

I'd left most of the warehouse as it was, but I'd soundproofed certain rooms, including the storage space. It was impossible for people inside to hear what was happening outside and vice versa.

Acquiring and retrofitting the warehouse without tipping anyone off about its true ownership had been a pain in the ass, but it was worth it.

The warehouse was for special cases. I didn't visit it often, but it had its uses.

The man inside straightened when he heard me enter. He was tied to a chair with a blindfold on.

I walked over and calmly removed the piece of cloth with a gloved hand.

Wentworth Holt stared up at me, his face pale. A flicker of recognition passed through his eyes.

"What is this?" His voice shook. "What's happening? You need to help me! You need…" He trailed off when I retrieved a piece of paper from my pocket and placed it neatly in his lap.

It was a printout of his schedule last Friday with the Sage Studios photoshoot circled in red.

Wentworth was a predator, but he wasn't stupid. It took less than a minute for the puzzle pieces to click.

"Is this about Ayana?" He let out a nervous laugh. "Listen, man, I don't know what she told you, but *she* came onto *me*. She was practically begging me to—"

His words cut off with a howl when I slammed my fist into his face. I was pleased to note his nose hadn't fully healed from Ayana's headbutt, and it easily broke again from my punch.

The pain must've been excruciating.

"I didn't even do anything!" Wentworth shouted. Blood and tears poured down his face. "It was just a stupid kiss. You can't… you're a businessman, right? I recognize you from the papers. You can't do this. It's…I…this is kidnapping!"

One, I hated people telling me what I could and couldn't do. Two…

I typed out a reply on my phone. *It's only kidnapping if you're not dead.*

The second my implied threat sank in, Wentworth's eyes rolled so far back in his head that I could see only the whites, and he fainted dead away.

Oh, for fuck's sake.

I stared down at his limp form. My lip curled with disgust.

What was it with these men in fashion? First Hank, now Wentworth. They loved terrorizing other people, but they couldn't handle a fraction of what they dished out.

They thought Ayana was weak, but she was a thousand times stronger than they were.

I checked my watch. I had a tuxedo fitting and a meeting with Singapore in two hours.

Instead of wasting time, I slapped Wentworth awake and ignored his babbles of terror as I picked up a hammer from a nearby table. I untied his arms and placed his right hand on the table.

It was his dominant hand—the one he used to shoot photos, and the one he'd used to touch Ayana. To grab her and hold her down while he tried to take what wasn't his.

It was the hand he used to make her fucking cry.

Wentworth must've read the intentions scrawled across my face because his pleas reached a fever pitch. He wasn't stupid enough to try and escape, but his cries only added to the icy rage tunneling through my veins.

I pictured Ayana's tear-streaked face. Replayed the sounds of her sobs. Remembered the way she shook in my arms.

Crimson washed across my vision, and I let all that pent-up rage *explode* as I smashed the hammer onto Wentworth's hand.

The sickening crunch of bone was so loud I heard it even over his inhuman screams.

I tossed the hammer aside and channeled the rest of my anger with my fists. Knives and guns were nice, but when it came to venting, nothing beat an old-fashioned pummeling.

Wentworth's sobs fell on deaf ears. How many times had he ignored someone when they screamed for him to stop? It didn't feel so fucking good when he was on the receiving end, did it?

Sweat coated my skin. My knuckles were bruised and battered from the beating, but I kept going until his wails faded and he passed out again.

Only then did I stop.

I stepped past his broken body and signaled for Sean to take care of him. The worst of my rage had abated, but a tint of red lingered in front of my eyes.

Wentworth had gotten off easy. I wanted to cut off his dick and make him choke on it, but that would've been too messy. So I left him with a bloody face, a shattered hand, and an unspoken warning never to go near or even *think* about Ayana again.

It went without saying that any attempt to tell people what happened today would not end well for him. Maybe Emmanuelle could connect the dots given the stunt I'd pulled in her office, but Wentworth's fate was a subtle warning for her as well. She was smarter than him, and she'd keep her mouth shut.

By the time I left the warehouse, my breaths had calmed. Ayana would never know what I did. She didn't need to; all she needed to know was that the problem was taken care of.

No one hurt her and got away with it.

Now that Wentworth was taken care of, my attention shifted to another loose end.

All signs pointed to Roman telling the truth about the Brotherhood's civil war. He could be lying about the details, but I didn't have the luxury of nitpicking when there was a target on my back.

He'd left his burner phone number for me before I kicked him out of my house for good the other day. I sent him a short but succinct message.

I'm in.

CHAPTER 24

Ayana

I'D ADMIT IT—I CHICKENED OUT.

I didn't tell Sloane, Jordan, *or* my agency about Wentworth. I'd had every intention of doing so, especially when I was convinced he'd turn around and try to paint me as the bad guy, but a week after the incident, he vanished into thin air.

He'd canceled all his bookings, leaving a swarm of angry editors and brands in his wake. He didn't provide details, and he didn't give people a way to contact him after he disconnected his phone and deleted his email account.

It'd been two weeks since the Sage Studios photoshoot, and no one knew where he was. Even if he tried to make a comeback, he'd pissed off so many powerful people who now had to scramble and find a new photographer at the last minute that his standing in the fashion world would never be the same.

Neither Hank nor Emmanuelle mentioned what happened at the shoot. Either they didn't know, or they didn't care. Both were plausible.

Whatever the case might've been, Wentworth's disappearance rendered my initial plan moot. I'd already vented my feelings in the rage room, and I didn't want to rehash the events with anyone else besides Vuk. It was too emotionally draining.

I had my suspicions about what—or rather *who*—caused Wentworth to vanish, but at the end of the day, it didn't matter. I just wanted to put the incident behind me.

Luckily, I had plenty to distract me, including my upcoming wedding in three weeks and tonight's gala at the Valhalla Club. I wasn't a member, but Jordan was.

"Are you okay if I dip out for a minute?" he asked after we entered the ballroom. "I need to talk to Dante about something."

"Go ahead. I'll be fine." I waved a hand around the lavish room. "I have plenty to keep me entertained."

The gala was ocean-themed, and the organizers had somehow installed life-size aquariums on both ends of the room. There were free-flowing drinks, a live orchestra, acrobatic performers, and a fifteen-foot-tall ice sculpture of Poseidon. All the guests were dressed to the nines in varying shades of blue, green, and silver, including me.

After much deliberation, I'd selected a seafoam green silk tulle gown with a strapless bodice and a gorgeous, frothy skirt that cascaded to the floor in graceful layers. I'd kept my jewelry minimal except for a pair of show-stopping gold and green quartz earrings that grazed my shoulders and my engagement ring. The effect was simple but striking.

"Great." Jordan gave me a distracted smile. "I'll be right back."

While he spoke with Dante, I wandered over to the main bar and ordered a water with a twist of lime. I'd slacked on my diet the past few weeks, and I was on a strict alcohol ban until the wedding.

"Tell him that's unacceptable." A furious voice brought my attention to the woman sitting a few stools down. "*No*, I will not co-chair with Sebastian Laurent. I don't care if he's the last man on—Mom. Please." Her sigh encompassed a world of exasperation. "I understand, but can we discuss this later? I'm at the Valhalla gala. Okay, yes. Yes, I know. Good night."

She hung up and rubbed her temple.

She was beautiful in a natural, effortless way. She had the shiniest hair and the longest, thickest lashes I'd ever seen. Her toned, athletic body was clad in an exquisite blue dress, and her smooth brown skin and sculpted cheekbones gave some of the models I knew a run for their money.

She also looked oddly familiar. With a start, I realized she'd been at my bachelorette. She was one of Sloane's other clients.

She must've felt my eyes on her before she dropped her hand and glanced at me.

"Sorry," I said, embarrassed. "I didn't mean to eavesdrop, but...you're Maya, right? I think you were at my bachelorette."

It was an odd way to meet. Most brides wouldn't allow strangers to join their premarital celebrations, but nothing about this wedding was normal.

"I was." Maya brightened. "Thanks for letting me tag along. I was with Vivian since she's planning my birthday party, and when the call came in, I *had* to come. I hadn't played laser tag in ages." Her expression turned sheepish. "I hope it wasn't weird, since we..."

"Barely know each other?" I smiled. "It's okay. It was a fun time, and I enjoy meeting new people."

"Good. I know we've technically met, but I'm going to reintroduce myself anyway." She held out her hand. "Maya Singh. Happy to be a backup bridesmaid if you need one since I've already crashed your bachelorette."

I laughed and shook her hand. "Ayana Kidane. I'll add your name to my backup roster."

Maya's grin widened. Sloane had introduced us at the laser tag venue, but there'd been so many people and so much going on that we didn't get a chance to really talk.

Singh. It was a common surname. But given her presence at Valhalla, Maya had to be one of *the* Singhs—a large and extraordinarily wealthy family who'd made a killing in the frozen foods industry. They'd since expanded their empire to include snacks, beverages, and confectionaries, among other things.

Basically, you couldn't walk into a single supermarket or convenience store without seeing at least a dozen brands that fell under the Singhs' corporate umbrella.

"Well, I'm invited to the Ireland reception, so you'll see me regardless." Maya shook her head. "I can't believe the church ceremony was moved up by several months. I understand why it's necessary, but you're better than me because the change would've sent me spiraling."

"It's not ideal," I admitted.

"Are you excited about the reception at least?" Maya signaled the bartender for another drink.

"Of course." My voice pitched a little higher than I would've liked.

"It's okay. You don't have to bullshit me. I know what those big weddings are like." She rolled her eyes. "When my older sister got married, my parents invited *everyone* they knew. I kid you not, there were two thousand guests at the Indian ceremony. My sister never even met half those people, but they *had* to be on the guest list or it would be 'socially unacceptable.'"

"There's going to be seven hundred guests at ours. It's not two thousand, but I feel you." I grimaced. "That receiving line is going to be torture."

"Wear comfortable shoes and bring hand sanitizer," Maya advised. "Or just drink so much champagne they all blur into one giant conga line of smiles and congratulations."

I laughed again. I wished we'd had a chance to talk more at my bachelorette. There was something about her that instantly put me at ease.

Our conversation gradually shifted from wedding woes to travel, fashion, and our mutual dislike of pumpkin-flavored foods and drinks (it was fall, so they were everywhere, but I was a sweet potato person).

Maya was surprisingly down to earth for someone whose family was worth several billion dollars. It was also nice to finally chat with someone who had zero ties to my work. She wasn't involved in the modeling world, and we didn't have a professional relationship. She was just someone I clicked with.

"I wish Sloane would've introduced us earlier. You're way more fun than half the people I'm forced to deal with on a daily basis." Maya sighed. She glanced over my shoulder, and her perfectly shaped brows rose a centimeter. "Wow. The Serb is here. Now *that's* a surprise."

I whirled around before I could stop myself.

Despite the hundred plus people crowding the ballroom, I spotted Vuk immediately. The air seemed to warp around him as he entered. Space and time bent to the indomitable force of his presence, and he was the picture of devastation in his black tuxedo.

My pulse fluttered.

I quickly looked away before he caught me staring. Still, my back tingled with awareness. It didn't matter how near or far he was; I always felt it when he was in the same room.

"*Oh.*" Maya's eyes widened. "He's headed our way."

"Really? I mean…" I took a gulp of water. "Interesting."

I hadn't seen Vuk in person since the rage room. I'd wanted to text him multiple times over the past two weeks, but I kept chickening out. What would I say anyway?

Hey, thanks for letting me smash shit in your basement. By the way, do you want to come over for tea sometime?

No, thanks.

"Oops. Never mind." Maya was still invested in whatever

he was doing behind me. Vuk didn't attend galas often, so his presence was always a novelty. "I was wrong. He's talking to the Davenports."

My chest pinched with disappointment. I peeked behind me again. Vuk was, indeed, talking to Dominic and Alessandra Davenport.

He was facing my way. This time, his eyes slid toward me when I turned. The corner of his mouth tipped up in a knowing smirk.

Shit. Caught red-handed.

Warmth curled around my neck and ears. I yanked my gaze away and finished the rest of my water.

When did it get so hot in here?

"Are you okay?" Maya asked. Her brow furrowed. "You look a little flushed."

"Mm-hmm." *Don't look back. Don't look back.* "Actually, I, um, have to use the restroom, but I'm so glad we were able to chat. This was fun. We should exchange numbers in case you want to grab brunch or hang out sometime. If you want," I added quickly.

I fought the urge to cringe. Making friends as an adult was like dating—equal parts awkward and mortifying, but when it worked out, it was worth the discomfort.

Maya's smile dazzled. "I'd *love* to."

After I got her number, I left the ballroom. I really did need to use the restroom, but I had an ulterior motive.

I deliberately passed by Vuk on my way out. I didn't look at him, but the heat of his gaze seared into my skin.

Thankfully, there was no line at the restroom. I quickly used the facilities and touched up my makeup. When I exited, the hall was empty.

I deflated. Perhaps I'd misread the situation. Perhaps—

The ballroom doors swung open. Broad shoulders and crisp black lines filled the frame. Just like that, my heart beat faster again.

Vuk's gaze came my way, cool and assessing.

I ignored him and walked upstairs, my pulse thudding with each step. The second floor was deserted. I kept walking until I reached the doors at the very end of the hall.

The roar of my pulse grew louder. I inhaled a small breath and, with a quick twist of the door handles, stepped inside the Valhalla Club library. Moonlight trickled through the stained-glass windows; hushed silence stretched from the plush carpet to the triple-height ceiling.

I felt rather than heard Vuk enter behind me. A moment later, the doors shut with a soft click, and a shiver ran from my head all the way to my toes.

"You should be downstairs." His rough voice pebbled my skin with goosebumps.

I finally turned. "So should you." I kept my voice light and airy. "You're the one who followed me."

Vuk regarded me from half a dozen feet away. His face was hard and unsmiling. *Tell me to leave.*

"No."

The word traveled between us on a thread of defiance. I hadn't come this far to back out now. If he wanted to leave, he'd have to do it himself. I wasn't going to give him an easy out.

Vuk released a sharp exhale. *You didn't get dressed up to hang out with me in a library.*

Maybe not, but I'd be lying if I said I hadn't hoped Vuk would make an appearance tonight.

"Once again, you're the one who followed me here," I said, knowing full well I'd baited him into doing so.

And you're the one who wants me to stay.

Also true.

The seconds ticked by without a response from me or a movement from him. The silence stretched, smoldering with all the banked heat and breathless yearning we shouldn't want.

Vuk's gaze slid from my face down to my throat and over my chest. It skimmed past my stomach and hips and dragged, leisurely, over the length of my legs before coming back up to meet my eyes.

All the breath swept out of me in one soft wave. A thousand fireflies danced over my skin in the wake of his scrutiny. It'd been so warm, so *intimate*, that I felt it as surely as a lover's caress.

Why did you come to me first the other week?

I was so light-headed it took me a moment to piece together his question. He was asking about Wentworth.

"Because you're the one I wanted to see in that moment." The truth came out easily. In another time or place, I might've lied, but we were beyond that. "There's no other reason. That was it."

Vuk's throat moved with a hard swallow.

"Wentworth vanished," I added softly. "Do you happen to know anything about that?"

No. The glitter of satisfaction in Vuk's eyes told me otherwise. *But I imagine justice found him.*

A shiver dripped down my spine.

His involvement in the photographer's disappearance should make me uneasy. Wentworth operated on pure ego, and whatever Vuk did had to have been extreme to make the photographer go underground. But I'd gone unheard for so long, and I'd been fighting alone for so many years, that Vuk's decision to take matters into his own hands made me feel protected more than anything else.

"Do you think he's alive?" I asked cautiously. That was the one line I didn't want to cross.

Vuk shrugged. *If he's smart and takes care of himself.*

"I see." I licked my lips. His eyes dropped to my mouth again, and the earlier heat came roaring back to life.

My breath shortened, and any thoughts about Wentworth, work, or the world outside this room dissolved beneath the weight of Vuk's gaze.

Whatever he saw in my face made his darken. *You're getting married this month.*

"I know."

The quiet admission erased any plausible deniability I might've had. I couldn't use alcohol as an excuse tonight. I knew exactly what I was doing.

It would be different if I still thought Vuk hated me or was tolerating me for Jordan's sake, but the events of the past few weeks proved he wanted me too—no matter how much he tried to hide it.

And yet, here we were. Trapped on opposite sides of an ocean, separated by our loyalty to a man who'd done nothing wrong. I'd made a promise to Jordan, but the scope of that promise didn't encompass *this*.

Genuine feelings. Heady possibilities. The tease of a world that'd long been out of reach.

"Do you remember when you asked me whether I loved him?" My quiet question made Vuk's eyes flare. "The truth is, I don't. Not romantically."

This time, his body trembled from the force of his exhale.

"He doesn't love me either," I said. "He never has."

The library was so silent I could hear the weight of my admission as it slid off my shoulders and drifted to the floor. I was bare and naked with vulnerability—half my heart in my throat, the other half in my hand.

After all the pretense, the lies and deception and denial, this was where I'd ended up. Right where I wanted to be.

"Why are you telling me this?" Vuk's voice was cool, but the fire in his eyes blazed hot enough to make my toes curl.

Why *was* I telling him this? What was I hoping for? That he would admit he had feelings for me? That he would sweep me off my feet and make all my problems disappear with a snap of his fingers?

He had the power to do that, but I didn't want a magic fix. I wanted...

Him.

That was all this was. I didn't care about his money or power. I didn't care about his dubious actions toward Wentworth or other people who deserved it. I didn't care about yesterday, tomorrow, or three weeks from now.

I only cared about this moment, right here, with the two of us.

"Because I want you to know," I said. "And because I...I don't want you to feel guilty."

"About what?"

"About what I want you to do right now," I whispered.

Vuk closed the distance between us with slow, deliberate steps. His normally pale eyes were the color of midnight in the dim light, and he moved with the coiled grace of a predator on the hunt.

I held my ground even as fear and desire throbbed between my thighs.

He stopped inches from me. "What you want me to do." His tone was lethally soft. "And what might that be?"

The scent of his cologne stole into my lungs, robbing me of words. I licked my lips again. My gaze touched his mouth, and a tortured noise rumbled past his throat.

It was the first tangible sign he was losing control.

The flames pulsed hotter; my skin drew so tight I felt every minuscule shift in the air. The atmosphere was so dense, the tiniest spark could set it ablaze.

"Take off your ring." Vuk's harsh command was a shot of whiskey straight to my veins.

Fever gripped me, making me dizzy. My skin flushed, and there was a slight shake in my hand as I slid the diamond off my finger.

He watched, his eyes dark and merciless, as the tight band finally popped free.

I placed it on the table behind me. It'd barely hit the mahogany surface before Vuk grabbed the back of my neck and swallowed my gasp with his mouth.

The flames exploded into a wildfire. Smoke and heat raced through my blood, consuming me from the inside out. His skin was the only cool reprieve in a world ablaze, and my hands roamed over him, desperately seeking something to appease this aching, insatiable *want* inside me.

Vuk groaned. He lifted me up and set me on the table, his kiss ravenous, almost punishing. When I wrapped my legs around his waist, urging him closer, he nipped my bottom lip in a light warning.

"Careful, *srce moje*." His voice rasped against my sensitized skin. "Or you'll fucking kill me."

My fingers curled around a fistful of his shirt. "Good," I breathed.

Vuk squeezed. His fingers dug into the sides of my neck, and an embarrassing moan escaped before his mouth covered mine again.

This. *This* was what I'd been missing. I couldn't put a name to it before because I'd never experienced it, but it was wild and reckless and everything I imagined a kiss would be.

This was the type of kiss that made time stop. I never wanted to leave. I never wanted it to end.

My soft pants mingled with his heavy breaths. His palm burned into my skin as it slid over the curve of my shoulder and down, down past my waist to—

A loud crash yanked us out of the moment and dumped us into a vat of ice water.

Vuk's touch disappeared. Goosebumps popped up in the resulting chill, and our eyes flew to the door.

The noise had come from the hall. Whoever made it hadn't come in *yet*, but the boisterous laughter followed by a giddy giggle proved we weren't the only ones who'd snuck out of the ballroom in search of privacy.

Vuk's attention returned to me. My high from the kiss came crashing down at the ice in his eyes.

Reality had set in.

His gaze swept over me. A muscle ticked in his jaw, and his throat flexed with an unspoken curse before he tore his eyes away and left. The doors shut behind him, harder this time.

He didn't have to say the curse for me to hear it. *Fuck*.

As in, what the *fuck* had we done?

The laughter in the hall faded. Whoever it belonged to wasn't coming in here.

So I sat there, my heart racing, my hair and dress mussed from the most thorough ravishing of my life. My ring had fallen onto the carpet, where it glinted accusingly up at me.

I should've felt guilty. My fiancé was probably downstairs looking for me while I was busy kissing his best man. If Vuk and I hadn't been interrupted, we would've done more than kiss.

I let out a small breath. I didn't move to pick up the ring.

Yes, I *should* feel guilty, but I didn't.

It was hard to regret what happened when I'd never felt so beautifully, wonderfully alive.

CHAPTER 25

Vuk

IT TOOK ALL MY WILLPOWER TO WALK AWAY FROM Ayana in the library. It took even more not to reach out to her in the week after our kiss.

I literally had to have my cyber team install a fucking code that would wipe everything from my devices if I emailed, called, or texted her first. It was that bad.

I'd made a lot of mistakes in my life, but kissing Ayana? It was the biggest damn mistake I'd ever made.

If I hadn't kissed her, I wouldn't have known. I'd have suspected, but I wouldn't have *known* that she wanted me the way I wanted her. I wouldn't have tasted her desire or heard her fucking moans.

That knowledge spelled the beginning of my end because there was only one obstacle left between us, and my loyalty to him grew more tenuous every day.

I glanced at Jordan. He scrolled through the movie options in his den, his brow furrowed with concentration. He'd called and said he needed a break from the wedding prep. We usually hung out at my house because I avoided going out in public whenever possible, but I'd opted to visit him today instead of the other way around.

Ever since Roman's break-in, I'd locked down security at home and limited access to everyone except essential staff. Ayana was the only person on my Always Receive list.

I wasn't worried about Jordan being a security threat, but I suspected the Brotherhood had eyes on my house. I didn't want to throw any potential targets their way.

Roman was still pissy about me shooting him and refused to confirm or deny the Brothers' surveillance efforts. He said he'd gotten called away on business, but he'd promised to give me a heads-up when Shepherd's faction was planning to strike again. He couldn't guarantee solid intel for the other faction.

I trusted the bastard as far as I could throw him. So far, everything he'd told me came up clean, but blindly trusting someone like Roman Davenport was the equivalent of signing one's own death warrant.

I'd cornered Dominic at the Valhalla gala to gauge whether he was aware of his former foster brother's comings and goings. It didn't seem like he was, but I was keeping an eye on him anyway.

The Brotherhood, Beaumont, the Davenports...at this point, I might as well run my own spy ring. My security team was already stretched thin, and I hoped nothing blew up in our faces before we solved one of our other problems first. We didn't have the manpower or the time to train new people.

"I give up. You pick." Jordan tossed the remote aside and took a swig of beer. "I have decision fatigue."

I didn't give a shit what we watched. I wasn't in a movie mood, but I'd rather stay in than leave the house. Despite Roman's assurances, I was on edge.

Events like the Valhalla gala were somewhat acceptable

because they had high security and vetted guests; movie theaters and other public places didn't.

Nevertheless, I scrolled through our options and picked a random heist film. Hopefully the distraction would loosen the knots in my gut.

I don't want you to feel guilty.

He doesn't love me either. He never did.

Ayana's admission was seared into my brain. Was it true, or was it wishful thinking on both our parts?

"You've been awfully quiet all day," Jordan said. "Everything okay?"

I gave a curt nod. *I just have a lot on my mind.*

"With work? You have a new product launch coming up, don't you?"

I made a noncommittal noise. My marketing and sales teams were on top of the launch, so I wasn't worried about that. I needed to give everyone at my company big fat bonuses at the end of the year; I'd pulled back from the office, and they'd picked up the slack without missing a beat.

But if Jordan thought my brooding had to do with work, I wasn't going to correct him.

"Did you think we'd ever be here?" he mused. "You, the CEO of a multibillion-dollar corporation. Me, on the verge of getting married." He drained the rest of his beer. "Our twenty-one-year-old selves would've never believed it."

People change. I stared at the opening credits onscreen. After a beat of deliberation, I added, *You never told me why.*

"Why what?"

Why you're marrying Ayana.

When he first dropped the engagement bombshell on me, I'd been so stunned I hadn't asked questions. I'd simply gone straight to the shooting range and let my feelings fly in a hail of bullets.

Of all the people in the world, he had to choose *her*. The only one I wanted.

I knew Jordan and Ayana had been friends for years, but I never suspected their feelings were romantic. The engagement had completely blindsided me, and Jordan had been cagey about when the shift in their relationship occurred.

But according to Ayana, the relationship hadn't shifted at all. If I hadn't been so intoxicated by her last night, I would've asked why they were getting married if they didn't love each other.

This was my chance to get the answers I needed.

Jordan hesitated. He cracked open a fresh bottle of beer, brought it to his mouth, and swallowed before answering. "Why else would anyone marry? For love."

We both know there are other reasons people get married.

"Not in my case."

So you love Ayana.

He shot me a sideways look. "What's with the questions today? Did something happen?"

Call it curiosity. I hadn't questioned him before because I didn't want to hear him wax poetic about their relationship. That was my mistake. *Remember Hungary?*

"Oh man, you just unlocked a shitload of memories." Jordan laughed.

We'd visited Budapest for spring break our senior year of college. Our last night there, we'd stumbled across a wedding in our hotel. We'd crashed it and spent the night partying with the guests, whom we'd conned into thinking we were the groom's distant cousins from America.

That was one of the last times I'd felt so carefree.

"What a trip." Jordan stretched his legs. "I can't believe that was more than twelve years ago. Time really does fly." He glanced at me again. "Why'd you bring it up?"

When we left the wedding, you told me you'd never marry. Granted, he'd been drunk off his ass, but he'd said it with such conviction that I'd believed him.

"I was young and stupid," he said now. "I didn't mean it."

I narrowed my eyes, trying to gauge whether he was lying.

Jordan had dated occasionally over the years, but before Ayana, none of his relationships lasted more than a few weeks. He'd also never expressed a desire for marriage and kids.

However, that was all circumstantial.

"What about you?" he asked in an obvious bid to change topics. "Will the great Vuk Markovic ever tie the knot?"

My face shuttered.

That depended on what happened in two weeks. If Ayana and Jordan got married, then that was it. If they didn't…

We'll see.

The wedding plans were going full speed ahead. There was nothing to suggest the ceremony wouldn't happen—unless I stopped it.

I tipped my head back and downed the entire bottle in one long gulp. It did nothing for me.

Fuck, I needed something stronger than beer.

"I envy you," Jordan said quietly. "You can do whatever you want, and you give no shits what other people think. That kind of freedom must be…intoxicating."

I almost laughed out loud at the irony. Do whatever I wanted? He had no idea. He envied me my "freedom" when I would trade it all for *one* person in his life.

Freedom is relative. We all have our burdens. I kept it at that.

"Maybe." Jordan rubbed a hand over his mouth. Neither of us paid any attention to the movie at all. "Do you know why I asked you to be my best man?"

I'm the only groomsman with more than half a brain cell.

His prep school friends were the two-legged equivalent of brainless slime mold. Rub two together and you wouldn't even get a spark of intelligence.

"No, and be nice," he admonished, but amusement glinted in his eyes. "You and I have been friends a long time, but I've known some of the other groomsmen longer than you. And God knows you're not a party planner in any sense of the word."

My eyebrows rose. That was an interesting explanation for a best man, but what did I know? I'd never been married.

"*But*," Jordan said. "Out of all my friends, I trust you the most. You've always been loyal, and you've always been honest, even when I don't want you to be." He laughed. "No one else had the guts to tell me that fall marketing plan I put together a few years ago was trash."

That's because they all have less than one brain cell, I deadpanned.

Jordan snorted. "No, seriously. I mean it. I know this whole best man thing is out of your comfort zone, so I appreciate you taking it seriously. I don't want to get all sentimental and shit because you'd hate that, but I'm almost glad that *thing* happened in college. If it hadn't, we might not be friends. Is that fucked up to say?"

The knots in my gut tightened. *No. I understand what you mean.*

"Good." He cleared his throat, the tips of his ears turning pink. "Now that we got the maudlin stuff out of the way, let's watch the damn movie. I want to know how they're going to break into that vault."

We lapsed into silence again.

I faced forward, but my brain was spinning.

It didn't escape my notice that Jordan never answered my question about whether he loved Ayana. My gut told me he didn't, but for whatever reason—either pressure from his family or the optics of canceling a high-profile wedding this close to the date— he was adamant about marrying her.

That didn't explain why Ayana had said yes to his proposal, but this wasn't the time to press him. Jordan had made it clear he didn't want to talk about it anymore. Pushing him would only make him dig his heels in more.

I watched the images onscreen without really seeing them.

My loyalty to Jordan had been a given since the day he wired me five hundred thousand dollars, no questions asked. The money had kept the Brotherhood at bay while I worked out a longer-term solution with them.

However, nothing had truly tested that loyalty until Ayana. The thought of standing next to Jordan at the altar while she walked down the aisle toward *him* made me want to light the entire fucking church on fire.

So the question was, did my loyalty to him outweigh my desire for her?

My head pounded. I still tasted her phantom sweetness. Still felt her soft lips parting eagerly beneath mine.

I reached for another drink and swallowed, but the taste lingered.

Haunting me.

After three hours of nonsensical action scenes and shooting the shit, I excused myself and walked home from Jordan's house. It was only a ten-minute walk, and the neighborhood's layout provided little cover for hitmen. I also wore my standard Kevlar-reinforced clothing and carried a concealed gun and knives.

A small part of me secretly hoped the Brotherhood would try and ambush me. I needed to vent my frustrations. Plus, once they made a move, I could retaliate instead of dealing with this insufferable holding pattern.

I hated waiting, but I couldn't go on the offensive yet because Roman was tied up on official business (or so he said). I needed his intel and help to launch a proper attack.

Meanwhile, my bugs in Emmanuelle's office had proved useless. Unless she was talking in code, it was all bullshit about model fees and bookings. I didn't expect her to discuss too much sensitive information at work, but if I had to listen to one more conversation about florals versus plaids, I was going to cut my ears off.

I'd put a tail on her in case that would be more helpful. So far, nothing.

Long story short: I was dead in the water on all fronts, and it put me in a real bad mood.

I made it halfway home when a scratching noise caught my attention. I tensed and instinctively reached for my gun, my gaze sweeping my surroundings until it landed on the source of the noise.

A tiny, mangy gray cat glared at me from atop the closed lid of a recycling bin. I didn't see a collar or other signs it belonged to someone, so it was probably a stray.

I relaxed but glared back.

I never understood why people were so infatuated with their pets. I didn't have anything against them in theory, but I didn't see the appeal of opening my house up to creatures who were smelly, needy, and almost certain to die before their owner.

That being said, the cat reminded me of Ayana's kitten mug, only less cute and more feral. It almost made me soften toward the thing.

Thunder rumbled overhead. The cat hissed, seemingly taking great offense at my audacity to walk past its makeshift playground without proper deference.

Any soft feelings I might've had vanished. I was close to letting out a snarl when I realized I was arguing with a fucking *cat*.

Christ. What was wrong with me today? If the Brotherhood was watching me, they were probably laughing their asses off.

I pulled myself together and walked away, the cat's suspicious stare burning into my back.

When I reached my house, I went straight to my office, where I tried to get some work done. It was Saturday, but I'd neglected a mountain of official paperwork during the week.

I managed to get through half a dozen documents before lightning streaked outside the window. The rumbles of thunder grew louder and more frequent.

For some reason, my mind flashed to an image of that stupid gray cat huddled under the sparse leaves of a tree. There wasn't much shelter in the area for stray animals. The little pest was going to get drenched.

Not that I cared. It wasn't my problem.

I refocused on my computer.

A minute later, the skies opened up. Rain splattered the windows in thick, unforgiving sheets. Another crash of thunder rocked the house, and a needle of unease pierced my skin.

The cat really did bear an uncanny resemblance to Ayana's mug, and it was both sad and impressive that such a small thing had lasted this long on the streets without protection. Annoying or not, it was a survivor.

I glanced outside the window. It was raining so hard I couldn't see the sky outside.

My teeth ground together. *Dammit.*

I pushed back my chair and went to my room. I tossed a black hoodie over my shirt, grabbed an umbrella, and stalked outside. I was instantly hit with a spray of icy water and strong gusts of wind.

I really hated myself sometimes.

I retraced my steps to where I'd seen the cat. It'd disappeared from the top of the recycling bin. A quick search of the area didn't turn up anything besides a promotional flyer for a women's clothing boutique.

I was ready to call it quits when a tuft of gray caught my eye. The cat was huddled deep within a bush, shivering. I would've never seen it if it weren't for its tail sticking out.

It let out a half-hearted hiss when I reached for it, but it didn't make another sound of protest after I picked it up.

Not so tough now, are you? I silently said.

It curled up tight against my chest and continued to shiver.

Thankfully, it was a short walk home. I'd hoped to sneak in without anyone noticing, but as luck would have it, I ran into Jeremiah in the foyer. His eyebrows shot up at the sight of me with a cat in my arms.

"Would you like me to take care of your guest, sir?" He wisely refrained from additional commentary.

I shook my head. It was bad enough that I'd brought the mangy thing home. I wasn't going to foist it off on my staff.

I headed to the kitchen, wrapped the cat in a towel, and placed it on the floor. From what I could glimpse, I guessed it was a male.

You're not a guest. I don't want you here. I only brought you in because you remind me of Ayana.

If he heard my unwelcoming thoughts, he didn't show it. His face peeked out from the makeshift blanket, his eyes narrowing at his new surroundings.

He was probably hungry, but I didn't have cat food. What the hell else did cats eat anyway?

After a quick Google search, I set out a bowl of water and some canned tuna. The ungrateful thing didn't even spare me a thank-you meow before he dove in.

An annoyed grumble worked its way up my throat.

Someone giggled behind me. I whirled around to find one of the maids grinning at me and the cat.

I scowled. Her smile immediately fell, and she squeaked out a "Sorry" before hurrying off.

I stayed and glared at the feline intruder again, unsure what to do after he finished eating. Toss him back out on the street once the rain stopped? Bring it to a shelter for adoption?

This entire situation was so out of character, I was at a loss.

I was saved from stewing in my indecision when my phone buzzed. A cool shock of surprise filled my lungs, followed by a streak of heat.

It was Ayana.

AYANA

Hi

Three chat bubbles popped up, disappeared, then popped up again.

AYANA

Are you busy right now?

I stared at the texts. They were our first written messages to each other. We'd talked in person, but conversations were consigned to the vaults of memory. These were concrete. Definable.

I savored the moment before I answered.

My team's code didn't allow me to message first, but I could reply without consequences.

No. I'm not.

AYANA

Would you be able to meet here within the next hour or so?

She sent me the address of a hotel on Madison.

AYANA

> We need to talk.

The kiss. We couldn't avoid it forever.

I rubbed a thumb over my mouth and made a split-second decision.

> I'll be there in thirty.

CHAPTER 26

Ayana

IN MY DEFENSE, I WAS A LITTLE BUZZED.

Okay, it wasn't really a defense, but it explained my courage in messaging Vuk first when I'd been eyeing my phone all week, waiting for him to call or text.

It was a little pathetic, but it was also exhilarating. He was the first guy I liked enough to *care* whether he called. I'd finally entered the club of people who gushed and obsessed over their crushes. It made me feel normal.

My alcohol ban had flown out the window that morning when I joined Maya for bottomless mimosas at brunch. We hadn't talked about Vuk, but seeing how unapologetic and badass she was made me want to say fuck it and take matters into my own hands.

I'd left brunch, booked a suite at the nearest hotel, and waffled for hours before I finally texted Vuk. I was currently wearing a hole in the carpet while I waited for him to arrive.

The wedding was in two weeks. My family was set to arrive in a few days, which meant this was my last weekend to myself until the ceremony.

It was now or never.

There was a heavy knock on the door.

I paused, my breath stalling in my lungs. Another knock snapped me out of my frozen state, and I counted to three to calm my nerves before I opened the door. It didn't work.

The sight of Vuk's frame filling the doorway sent those nerves into hyperdrive again. He wore a black sweatshirt and black pants, and droplets of rain peppered his skin. It was the most casual outfit I'd ever seen him wear.

I liked it even more than the tuxedo. It was more *him*.

"Hi." I hated how breathless I sounded.

"Hi."

A soft smile touched my mouth.

It was stupid, but I collected his words the way I collected perfumes and shoes. They glinted like precious stones in the sand, proof that he trusted me enough to communicate with me openly when he didn't have to. He simply chose to.

"Come in." I opened the door wider and stepped to the side. "I'm sorry for the last-minute, um, invitation." I couldn't think of a better word. "Did you eat already? The hotel supposedly has great room service."

My rambling melted beneath Vuk's visible amusement.

You said you wanted to talk. About what?

"Anything." Really, I wanted to talk about our kiss, but it seemed uncouth to jump straight into a thorny subject when he'd just arrived.

I walked over to the table by the window and poured a glass of water. It gave me something to do with my hands.

"So," I said lightly. "Attended any bingo nights lately?"

Vuk gave me sardonic look like, *Really? That's* what you want to talk about?

Which was fair, but it was the first topic that popped in my head. I was still fifty-fifty on whether he was lying about the bingo.

No. I figured I'd give the seniors a break from losing.

"Wow. Beating a bunch of eighty-year-olds must be thrilling."

Winning is winning.

Of course he would say that.

"Would you bring me to a game sometime?" I asked. "I haven't played bingo in forever."

Are you asking because you really want to play or because you don't believe I do?

"Both."

A hint of a smile pulled on his lips. *Good. Never take anything anyone says at face value.*

I shook my head. "That's a sad way to go through life."

Maybe. But it might also save your life.

Vuk came up beside me. I wordlessly handed him the water. He took it, his fingers brushing mine in the lightest of touches.

I felt it all the way in my bones.

I studied his profile. It was carved out of stone, its chiseled planes and remote coldness a convincing mask for the world. Every once in a while, that coldness lifted and offered a glimpse of the man underneath.

It happened more often than it used to. He'd shared more of himself with me than I'd ever expected, but there was still so much I didn't know. His past, his fears, his hopes and dreams.

Our physical attraction to each other wasn't a question. It was the emotional part I craved. He'd been there for me during some of my worst days this year, and I wanted to offer the same shelter for him.

Trust was a two-way street.

My gaze skimmed past his burn marks to meet his eyes. He was already watching me.

Vuk set the water back on the table. *Ask me.*

My gaze snapped to his. "About?"

What everyone wants to know. I'll answer.

My heart thumped. There was only one question at the top of everyone's mind when it came to him.

I searched his face, trying to gauge whether he was really okay discussing the issue or if he was simply humoring me.

But Vuk was Vuk. He wouldn't offer if he didn't mean it.

"What happened?" I asked quietly.

The story behind his scars was a mystery to the general public. Jordan refused to talk about it, and no one dared ask Vuk directly. Rumors ranged from the realistic (it was an accident that got out of hand) to the fantastical (Vuk was a former CIA member who'd been captured and tortured by enemy forces).

I suspected the truth fell somewhere in between.

Gray light slanted through the windows and painted his face with shadows. He didn't respond for a long moment. When he did, he spoke haltingly, his voice rough. "I had an...encounter with some old acquaintances after graduation. It left me with these." He gestured at his face and neck and paused again.

I waited patiently.

"I was celebrating with my brother the night after my graduation ceremony," he finally continued. "Lazar hadn't gone to college. He'd never been interested in school, but he was damn proud of my achievement. We were at home, drinking, when they broke into the house. I had something they wanted. I refused to tell them where it was—if I did, they would've killed us anyway. So they tied my brother up and tortured him."

Horror smothered me, and I sucked in a sharp breath.

Vuk recounted the events with clinical detachment, but an ember of deep-seated rage glittered in his eyes.

"I fought them off the best I could, but they had the element of surprise. They set fire to the house to cover their tracks. By the time I overpowered them, it was too late. The fire spread fast, and just like that, it was over. My house, gone. All my personal belongings, gone. My brother..." His throat flexed. "Gone."

His expression remained stoic, but I heard the anguish in his words.

My chest cleaved in half. "Vuk," I breathed, too stunned to formulate a proper response.

I'd assumed his brother had died of disease or an accident. Never in my wildest dreams would I have guessed the truth. The sheer brutality of it was unthinkable.

"The only reason I survived was because I left him." Vuk's tone was bleak. "I tried to save him, but he got trapped by a fallen beam. I couldn't free him. He said it was too late for him, but I still had a chance of surviving. He told me he'd never forgive me if I stayed. So I left him to burn."

It was obvious he was still beating himself up over that decision. I didn't blame him. Guilt had a way of outpacing everything else, even logic. *Especially* logic.

"It wasn't your fault," I said. "If you hadn't left, both of you would've been trapped."

I couldn't bring myself to say "died." The thought of never meeting Vuk—of him not even *existing* anymore—made my lungs squeeze.

He swallowed again. "Perhaps."

"What happened to your...acquaintances?" I asked. He said he'd overpowered them. What did that mean?

Vuk's expression didn't flicker. "Justice found them."

It was a callback to our earlier conversation at Valhalla.

Wentworth vanished. Do you happen to know anything about that?"

No. But I imagine justice found him.

Goosebumps coated my arms and shoulders. He wasn't talking about the police.

I didn't ask him what his idea of justice was; I didn't want to know.

I placed my hand on his without thinking. He glanced down, his shoulders tightening, before he let out a small breath and gradually relaxed again.

"Thank you for telling me," I said softly. "I know it's not easy."

It sounded like a platitude, but I meant every word. Our relationship had undergone several shifts over the months, but this was the biggest one so far.

He'd opened up willingly of his own accord, and if that wasn't a sign of trust, I didn't know what was.

It meant more to me than any gift could.

I've never told anyone the details of what happened before. Not Jordan. Not my staff. Vuk switched back to signing before he added in a low voice, "Just you."

Warmth unspooled in my chest. "Why me?"

"Ayana." My name sounded like a prayer and a curse on his lips. "You know why."

The air shifted. His words wiped away the melancholy and replaced it with agonizing awareness.

The mutual knowledge of our kiss bloomed between us, sweet and aching. I'd watched enough movies to know affairs were supposed to be passionate things, filled with fire and impulse. There'd been plenty of that at Valhalla.

But this? This was an entirely different form of intimacy.

Vuk was so close I could see every detail of his scars. His shoulders blocked out the rest of the room, and I had the heady sense that nothing existed outside this corner of space.

It was just him and me. His presence filled every molecule of air and lit me up from the inside out. It was like I'd been in hibernation and his proximity was the switch I needed to come alive again.

My pulse beat frantically at the base of my throat.

This was how I was *supposed* to feel toward my fiancé, not his best friend. But when it came to Vuk, I'd abandoned "supposed to" long ago.

I reached up and gently touched the burns encircling his throat. The thick, raised skin seared into my fingertips.

He said his brother had been the one who'd been tortured, but the pattern of the burns told me he'd left out crucial details of the story—like how someone had wrapped a rope around his neck and set it on fire.

Vuk must've escaped soon enough that it didn't cause permanent vocal damage, but the evidence of what'd happened was clear.

"Does this hurt?" My question was a whisper in the silence.

Vuk's jaw tightened. He shook his head.

I trailed my fingers up his neck and over the line of his jaw.

His eyes were aloof, but his throat moved with a visible swallow when I reached the scar next to his mouth.

I brushed my thumb over the puckered skin. "What about this?" I asked softly.

Another, slower shake of his head.

Other than my voice and the drumbeat of my heart, the air was so taut, a mere breeze could snap it in half.

The drumbeat grew louder.

I kept my eyes on his as I leaned in and slowly, gently kissed the corner of his mouth. My lips lingered on the scar, and I wished I could wipe away the pain and hurt that came with it.

I didn't have that power. This was all I had to give—the possibility of creating new memories to replace painful ones.

A shudder ran through his body.

I leaned back. My gaze remained locked on his as I reached for my engagement ring and slid it, inch by inch, off my finger.

It hit the carpet with a soft thud.

Darkness swallowed Vuk's eyes.

He didn't move. He didn't touch me. But his hands curled, ever so slightly, into loose fists when I slipped my cardigan off my shoulders.

It drifted to the ground and landed on top of the ring, obscuring it from view.

I was left in nothing but a short, silky dress. No shoes, no sweater, no diamond.

My heartbeat was so loud it drowned out everything else.

There were a thousand reasons why I shouldn't do this, but they all paled in comparison to the reason I *should*. Being with him was the first thing that'd brought me true joy in a long, long time. If I didn't take this leap, I would never forgive myself.

If that meant I was selfish, then so be it.

"Don't." Vuk's voice was ragged.

Don't. He'd told me that before, and I believed him as much then as I did now.

The evidence was in the way he looked at me—like it physically hurt him to lay eyes on me, but he couldn't bear to look away because that would hurt even more.

I called his bluff. "Then leave."

He stayed.

Lightning cracked outside. The glass was cool against my back, but I was burning up.

"You don't know what you're asking for, *srce moje*." His voice was lethally soft.

Srce moje. I didn't know what it meant, but the sound of it pooled inside me with languid warmth.

"You told me once to stop saying sorry," I breathed. "I will if you stop telling me what I should want."

"And what is it that you want?" A dark edge slid beneath his words.

More goosebumps erupted. A flame pulsed low in my stomach, hot and heavy with need.

I'd lost my words when he asked me a similar question at Valhalla. They flowed easily from me now.

"You," I said. Unapologetic, unabashed. "I want you."

Whatever thread of control he held on to snapped.

Vuk moved so swiftly I didn't have time to draw another breath before I was pinned between the window and the hard, unyielding muscles of his body. His mouth claimed mine, and I parted eagerly for him, drunk on his taste and clean, dizzying scent.

My hips canted up to press shamelessly against his arousal. His fingers dug into my hair; my hands gripped his shoulders. Urgent breaths panted between us, fanning the liquid fire in my veins.

I didn't care where we were or who saw or what happened after. This kiss was a revelation, at once brutal and worshiping, and I couldn't get enough.

Vuk nipped my bottom lip. The sharp sting throbbed in my core. "What else do you want? Do you want me to fuck you, Ayana?"

Oh God. The dirty roughness of his words poured pure lust on an already raging fire. Wetness pooled between my thighs, and I nodded, my mouth too dry for words to pass.

He groaned and said a thick word in Serbian before he grasped the hem of my dress and shoved it up around my waist. My head fell back, and I let out a small whimper when his fingers found the drenched evidence of my need.

"Say it," he commanded.

"I want you to fuck me." I gasped when he pressed against my core. Pleasure raced through my blood, drowning me in heat.

There was no room for coyness. I was too hungry for something to sate the hollow, aching space between my legs.

"Look at how wet you are." He pushed my underwear aside and rubbed his thumb over my slick, swollen clit. "So fucking greedy for my cock, *srce moje*."

A desperate sound wrenched from my throat. I tried to grind against him, but he forced my hips to still with one hand while he teased me with the other. Rubbing, stroking, *killing* me with alternating featherlight caresses and merciless touches.

Pressure built, then abated, then built again in an endless cycle of edging. I wasn't wet anymore; I was soaked. My juices dripped down my thighs and clung to my skin, and I probably looked like a mess. Legs parted, hair undone, the picture of wanton abandon.

"Please." My hips bucked again, but I couldn't find enough friction to end the torment. "Vuk, *please*."

He groaned. "Open your mouth." A trace of strain edged his otherwise controlled voice.

My mind was so hazy, I obeyed without protest. A moment later, he pushed two drenched fingers into my mouth. The sweet, tangy taste of my arousal flooded my taste buds.

I let out a muffled cry of shock. My skin flushed hot with embarrassment, but beneath that was something else—a darker kind of desire. A craving for more.

"Do you taste that, *srce moje?*" Vuk's eyes burned into mine. "That's the taste of your need for *me*. Not anyone else. *Me*." He pushed his fingers deeper. I choked, my eyes welling with tears. "You're mine, Ayana. *I teško onom ko pokuša da mi te uzme*."

He withdrew his hand and reached down. I groaned when he finally, *finally* slid two fingers inside me. They were still wet from my spit.

It'd been so long since I'd had sex that even two fingers was a stretch, but the initial discomfort soon melted into mind-bending pleasure.

I clenched around him, desperate for *more*. He wrapped his other hand around my throat, using it as leverage while he finger fucked me into a trembling, sobbing mess. Every thrust in made me see stars; every drag out made my head spin. I was so wet that obscene squelches echoed through the room with each brutal thrust.

My juices ran down my thighs with abandon, but I was flying so high I barely noticed. I'd never experienced such exquisite uninhibitedness. Never trusted anyone enough to let them see me like this or let *myself* go this fully.

It was intoxicating.

Vuk squeezed my throat, gentle enough not to hurt but hard enough to make me moan. He was the only thing holding me up at this point; my limbs were useless, and my brain was mush.

Even so, I had enough presence of mind left to gasp when he slowly slid a third finger inside.

"Oh my God." I panted at the renewed stretch. "That's too—I can't...oh, *fuck*." The squeal when he buried all three digits knuckle deep inside me couldn't have possibly come from my mouth.

It was too needy when I was already stuffed so full I could hardly breathe. I squirmed. The sensations from the resulting friction destroyed any lingering protests I might've had. A fresh whimper escaped, even needier than the last.

"Yes, you can," Vuk said calmly. If I didn't know better, I would've thought him unaffected, but his desire was clear in the pale pink flush decorating his cheekbones and the dark tenor of his voice.

"Look at how you're gushing all over my hand." He lowered his mouth next to my ear. "Do you wish it was my cock fucking you so deeply, hmm?" He withdrew and thrust all three fingers into me again. Hard. I cried out and clawed at his shoulders, silently pleading for more. "Do you want me to push you up against this window and take you from behind for the entire city to see?"

"Yes, yes, *yes!*" I sobbed and chanted in sinful prayer. "*Please.*"

"Listen to you." Vuk's mouth skimmed down my throat. He paused at the curve of my neck and sank his teeth into the tender flesh, marking me. Claiming me as his. The act shouldn't have turned me on as much as it did. "You sound so pretty when you're begging me to make you come."

It was too much.

His touch, his mark, his filthy words—they formed a fireball low in my belly, and my orgasm detonated. I convulsed around him, my cry of release sharp and keening. The rush of pleasure was so intense, the world seemed to collapse beneath its weight. I collapsed with it as my mind and body fractured into a kaleidoscope of sensations.

Wave after wave buffeted me. I was a thousand pieces of confetti fluttering in the wind until the tide finally eased, and I slowly drifted back to earth.

I slumped against the window, my breaths ragged.

Vuk pressed a kiss to the top of my head, released my throat, and pulled his fingers out of me with a slick *pop*. He dropped his forehead to mine, his breaths equally unsteady. His steel-hard erection pressed against my stomach.

"You didn't..."

"Come?" I heard the ghost of a smile in his voice. "No."

"I think we can take care of that." I was still swimming in the languorous aftermath of my orgasm. Emboldened, I reached for his belt buckle, but he stopped me with a hand around my wrist.

I looked up, confused. A trickle of trepidation seeped through my chest at his serious expression.

"Call off the wedding." Soft desperation ran beneath his otherwise cool command.

My stomach dropped.

The mention of the wedding wiped away my post-coital warmth. A chill swept in and tore through my lungs.

"I can't," I whispered. The words tasted bitter on my tongue.

Vuk's expression flattened, and the chill intensified. "You can't, or you won't?"

I shook my head, emotion tangling in my throat. "You don't understand."

How could I explain my situation to him? I was already in too deep. The wedding was in *two weeks*. As much as I wanted Vuk, I couldn't leave Jordan high and dry like that. I'd signed a contract, I'd made a promise, and I owed him.

But...maybe there was a way I could be with Jordan in public and Vuk in private.

Vuk dropped my wrist and stepped back. He signed his response. ***Then help me understand.***

He'd turned aloof again. Remote. How had the situation changed so fast? His visit was a roller coaster of emotions, and I couldn't keep up.

I straightened and fixed myself up while I tried to gather my thoughts into some semblance of coherence.

"I..." I faltered.

I couldn't tell him about my arrangement with Jordan. It was Jordan's secret more than mine, and I wasn't going to share it without his permission.

Even if I went back on my word and canceled the wedding, what good would that do? I'd need Vuk's help to get out of my contract with Beaumont, which meant I'd be trading one debt for another.

I trusted Vuk. He would help me, and I didn't believe he would hold that assistance over my head. But it would still be a power imbalance, and I refused to ask someone else to swoop in and take care of my problems. That was what had landed me with Beaumont in the first place.

At least with Jordan, it was a mutually beneficial agreement. He needed me as much as I needed him.

I had to solve my dilemma on my own. I owed myself that much.

"Jordan and I have an understanding," I finally said. "We're not in love with each other, but we agreed we could…see other people…" I trailed off again at the storm gathering in Vuk's eyes.

"If you're not in love, then why the fuck are you getting married?" he asked.

I released a shaky breath. "I can't tell you, but there *is* a reason. I promise."

I hated this. I knew we'd have to have this conversation eventually, but it was even harder than I'd imagined.

The worst part was, I understood where Vuk was coming from. If I were in his place, I'd be confused and pissed too.

I was the one who went to him after the Wentworth incident. I all but asked him to kiss me at Valhalla, and I'd invited him to a *hotel* before my wedding. Of course he thought I would call things off with Jordan.

Guilt shimmered beneath a slick coat of misery.

I'd allowed myself to be selfish for once, but that was the thing about doing what you wanted—the high didn't prepare you for the inevitable crash.

"So you're talking about an affair." Vuk's voice went soft again. This time, there was no gentleness, only derision. "Is that why you asked me here? To see if I fucked good enough for you to keep me on the side while you live out your high society dreams with Jordan?"

"No!" Tears stung my eyes. "That's not why. I want *you*."

"But you won't leave Jordan."

"I can't," I repeated brokenly.

A tear escaped and slid down my cheek. Vuk tracked it with his eyes, his jaw hardening into steel.

Beneath his icy demeanor was something worse than derision: *hurt*. And I was the one who put it there.

Grief cinched my chest. I couldn't draw in enough air to battle the overwhelming tide of self-loathing, so I stood there, my face wet with regret, while Vuk's head dipped toward mine again.

"There's one thing you should know about me, Ayana," he said, his breath grazing my ear. "I. Don't. Share."

Then he was gone.

The door slammed, and I was left all alone in the cold again.

CHAPTER 27

THE MORNING OF JORDAN AND AYANA'S WEDDING
dawned bright and crisp. Mid-seventies, clear blue skies,
golden sun.

It was a cruel twist of fate that the worst day of my life also
happened to be one of the most beautiful days New York had seen
all year.

I stared out the window, my teeth grinding. Behind me, Jordan
and the rest of the groomsmen relaxed and prepped themselves for
the upcoming ceremony. It was only an hour away.

An invisible iron band wrapped around my throat and
squeezed. I wanted to throw them all off the fucking balcony.

Call off the wedding.

I can't.

Two weeks had passed since I met Ayana in her hotel suite,
and those two words had imprinted themselves on my brain.

I can't.

Why the fuck not? What was so goddamn important that it
was worth throwing her life away on a marriage to a man she
didn't love and who didn't love her back?

The mystery ate away at me over the weeks and turned my mood so foul no one except Jordan dared step foot near me.

I would've pressed Jordan about the issue again, but I couldn't bear to talk to him unless I had to—both out of resentment for his part in the situation and self-loathing for what I did.

Even now, Ayana's moans echoed in my ears. Walking away from her when she'd been in tears had almost killed me, but I couldn't stay. I also couldn't get a clear answer out of Jordan unless I told him what happened, and that would affect Ayana's relationship with him as much as it would mine.

So here we were. An hour away from Armageddon.

The pressure in my chest ballooned and nearly suffocated me.

"Vuk." Jordan's voice brought my attention back to him. "You ready? It's almost go time."

I turned. The sight of him in his wedding finery made my eye twitch.

The other groomsmen had disappeared. I hadn't noticed them leave, and I couldn't care less where they went.

It's a big day.

We were staying at a luxury hotel near the church where the ceremony would be held. There were less than fifty people invited to the actual wedding—mostly members of Jordan's and Ayana's families and their closest friends.

The bridal suite was located two floors above us. Ayana was there at this very moment, preparing to wed another man.

A coppery taste filled my mouth. I hadn't trusted myself to talk to her since our hotel rendezvous. I'd spent the past two weeks trying to find a way out of this mess, but short of kidnapping her, my hands were tied.

And I had thought about the kidnapping angle. Multiple times. If it weren't for the Brotherhood and the other shit ruining my life, I would've even considered it seriously.

"We should be all set." Jordan seemed oblivious to my inner turmoil. "We need to head down soon to mingle with the guests before the ceremony. T-minus one hour until—"

"You don't have to marry her." My words slipped out and landed in a vat of pin-drop silence.

Jordan gaped at me. I couldn't tell whether he was more shocked by my declaration or the fact I was talking.

I'd communicated verbally with him on and off since my brother died, but I hadn't said a word after he announced his engagement to Ayana.

He finally closed his mouth. "What are you talking about?"

"If you don't love her," I said, "you don't have to marry her."

This was my last-ditch attempt to solve things the cordial way. I owed him that much.

But as I looked at him, in his custom tuxedo and fucking boutonnière, I burned with so much envy I almost choked on it.

I wanted to rip that boutonnière off his lapel.

I wanted to demand he tell me why he insisted on going through with this sham of a wedding.

I wanted to march upstairs, grab Ayana, and claim her so thoroughly in front of every damn person in the building, there'd be no doubt left in anyone's mind that she was mine. *Only* mine.

A small part of me had been tempted to take her up on her offer of an affair. God knew I craved her enough that I'd take any piece of her I could get.

However, the larger part of me had won out. Not because of morals or my friendship with Jordan, but because I was too fucking selfish to share.

When I said I wanted her, I wanted *all* of her. Every smile, every tear, every sigh and moan. She consumed me, body and soul, and I refused to settle for anything less in return.

"Jesus. Not this again." Jordan's incredulous laugh shook with a hint of nerves. "Who says I don't love her?"

"Do you?"

He stared at me. A minute ticked by, and it was in that moment that I saw the pieces fall into place for him.

I knew him well, but he knew me too. Sometimes, I forgot that.

He finally understood. Why I was invested in his feelings for Ayana, why I chose to talk about this topic today of all days...It crystallized into a glint in his eyes.

"Vuk." He painted my name with half horror, half realization.

I jerked my head away and stared out the window again. The seething jealousy inside me reached a full boil. If I kept looking at him, I was going to do something I'd regret.

Jordan came up beside me and looked out at the bustling streets below. A line of cabs crawled past the hotel like an army of yellow ants. "How long?"

I didn't bother denying what he now knew. We'd reached a point where lies served no further purpose. "Long enough."

From the moment I heard her laugh on that damn TV program years ago, I'd been a goner. She'd been a new model at the time, but there was something about the way she talked and carried herself that sank its claws into me and refused to let go.

She'd radiated authenticity, and she had the type of smile that made me want to smile too—and I fucking hated smiling.

I thought my reaction had been a fluke. I was still growing Markovic Holdings, and I'd had neither the time nor desire to obsess over a woman I didn't know.

But I couldn't stop thinking about her, so I purposely attended the same event as her one night to prove she couldn't be that captivating in person. Anyone could manufacture a goddess onscreen; selling that lie in real life was harder.

I'd been right. She hadn't been the same; she'd been better.

Brighter, lovelier, *realer*. I hadn't approached her, but I'd watched and listened.

After that night, I'd tracked all her appearances and consumed all her interviews. Every new detail I uncovered, from her college study abroad pictures in Ireland to her strange love of knitting, drew me deeper under her thrall. Even after her rise to fame, she maintained that same authenticity.

She was a splash of color in my world of gray, and before I knew it, I was ensnared. There was no way out.

Then Jordan told me about their engagement, and I'd been slowly dying since.

"You never said anything." His voice was quiet. "We were engaged for a year and a half, and you didn't say a damn thing. Now you're telling me to cancel an hour before my wedding?" A twinge of anger mingled with his disbelief.

I faced him. I'd betrayed him in more ways than one, but he hadn't been honest with me either. "I didn't tell you because I thought your feelings for her were real. Are they?"

"It doesn't matter."

"Yes, it *fucking* does!" My calm snapped. Frustration boiled up inside me, thirsting for a release. "Tell me the truth. No more lies. *Why* are you marrying her?"

Jordan's eyes flashed. He opened his mouth as if to argue, but then his shoulders slumped, and he seemed to deflate before my eyes.

A long silence passed before he spoke again. "You know my grandmother's sick. What you don't know is that she put a condition in her will. If I don't marry by the end of next year, I'll forfeit my inheritance. All of it." He scrubbed a hand over his face. "It's not just the money, Vuk. It's also the company. My family legacy. She'll give it all away unless I marry."

Christ. Orla Ford was a force to be reckoned with, but that was extreme even for her.

"I'm her only grandchild. Her only heir. And she would rather end the Ford legacy than pass it on unless I did what she wanted. So I came up with a plan." Jordan took a deep breath. "I asked Ayana if she would be open to a marriage of convenience. She plays the part of my wife for five years in exchange for ten million dollars. She said yes, and, well…" He gestured at himself. "Here we are."

My head spun.

This entire time, their relationship had been fake. I thought they'd entered it with the best intentions and realized along the way that they didn't have romantic feelings for each other, but this was beyond imagining.

"Why didn't you find someone you actually wanted to marry? You had years," I said.

"Because I'll never find that person." Jordan gave me a thin smile. "I'm not interested in romantic relationships. Never have been, never will be."

It took a beat for me to understand what he was saying. Once I did, I expelled a sharp breath.

I should've known. It explained Jordan's blasé attitude toward dating and sex and his unwillingness to enter a long-term relationship. He often seemed more invested in what he was having for dinner than courting a partner.

Now I knew why.

"Yeah," he said when realization dawned on my face. "So you understand why a marriage to someone I like platonically was the best-case scenario for me. Ayana and I have been friends for years. She is…the least worst option."

The least worst option.

My blood bubbled. She deserved to be the *best* option. In fact, there were no other options; there was only her.

Learning the reason behind their marriage didn't dampen my determination; it only strengthened it.

This was about money, and I had money in spades.

"I'll wire you the hundred twenty million."

Jordan's eyes snapped to mine. "What?"

"That's how much your inheritance is worth." My mind was already spinning with next steps. We needed to wrap this up quickly so we could call off the wedding. The guests would be baffled, but I was confident we could concoct a believable story for why Jordan and Ayana were no longer getting married. Couples got cold feet all the time. "One hundred and twenty million dollars. If you cancel the wedding, you'll have the full amount in your account by tomorrow morning."

My accountant would have my head, and I'd have to pull some strings to wire such a large sum overnight.

I didn't care. I would pay triple the amount if I had to.

Ayana was worth it.

Instead of expressing relief, Jordan's face darkened. "I'm not taking your money. Did you miss the part about the company? It's about more than a hundred twenty mil. I am *not* going to be the Ford who loses the family legacy."

"I'm sure we can find a way to help you maintain ownership of the company."

Hell, I'd buy the fucking thing and gift it to him. The shareholders would put up a fuss, but I'd give them a number they couldn't refuse.

"*We* aren't doing anything," Jordan snapped. "*I'm* getting married, and that's the end of it."

Anger outpaced disbelief. Why was he being so difficult when my solution was clearly the best option for all parties involved? "You don't even want to be married!"

"Maybe not, but I'm doing what I have to do." His knuckles whitened. "I'm not a charity case, Vuk. You may have hundreds of millions to throw around, but I don't need you to save the day like you're fucking Superman."

A new realization set in.

This wasn't about the company. Not entirely. This was about pride and ego. He couldn't stand to take money from someone else when he was supposed to be the golden kid.

I didn't blame him. If I were in his situation, I'd chafe at my offer too. I hated pity.

But his pride was also the only thing standing between me and Ayana, and that was unacceptable.

"It's not charity." I kept my voice as controlled as possible so I didn't snap at him.

"Then what is it? Payback for the money I lent you in college?" Jordan shook his head. "You wouldn't even be here if I hadn't saved your life, would you?"

I fell silent.

I'd grown to enjoy his company over the years, and I did value him as a friend, but it was true. If he hadn't saved my life, we would've never forged a friendship. Even if we had, I wouldn't have put in the effort to keep it after college.

"I don't mind that part. It is what it is," he said. "But how much is our friendship really worth when you didn't even tell me you were in love with Ayana all this time?"

I instinctively flinched. In love?

What I felt for her was fascination. Preoccupation. Obsession so deep I couldn't breathe sometimes.

But love? I didn't even know what that meant.

"We both kept secrets," I growled. "You let me believe this was a love match, and you didn't say a word about why you don't do relationships. So who's really tarnishing the value of our friendship?"

"I had reasons for that." Jordan's face flushed. "I didn't figure out why I wasn't...interested in sex and romance until two years ago. I just thought I hadn't met the right person yet. And if my grandmother found out about my arrangement with Ayana, that would be the fucking end. You know she has eyes and ears everywhere."

"Including with me?"

He looked away. "I couldn't risk it. Ayana and I agreed not to tell *anyone*. Not our families. Not our best friends. There was too much at stake."

I gritted my teeth, torn between the urge to shake him and sympathize with him.

I didn't have time for either. The clock ticked toward the half hour, and we needed to end this once and for all.

"Take the money, Jordan," I said.

His expression hardened. "No. I understand you have feelings for Ayana, but you can't get everything you want. If you truly wanted her, you would've said something sooner. You wouldn't have waited until the last minute."

I was struck by the bitterness in his tone until it hit me.

When we first met, Jordan had the upper hand in almost every way. He'd been the rich, popular, good-looking legacy kid whose family had attended Thayer for generations. He sailed through school knowing he had the world at his fingertips after he graduated.

I'd been the outsider, the scholarship student who worked alone and took side jobs to pay for his expenses.

Fast forward thirteen years, and I was worth multitudes more than he was. I had more power, more status, and more influence. It must be a jarring turn of events for him.

Jordan had never displayed open resentment toward my success, but that didn't mean it didn't exist.

Once again, it was pride and ego. Even the best people in the world were susceptible to it.

"You're right." I swallowed past the knot in my throat. "But

I'm asking you now. Don't do this." It was the closest I'd ever come to begging.

I had other options. I could tell his grandmother about the arrangement or lock him in this room and steal Ayana away. I could *force* him to do what I wanted at gunpoint.

But I would never exercise those options. Not with him. There were some lines even I wouldn't cross.

Jordan's throat bobbed. "It's too late," he said quietly. "I'm sorry."

He didn't ask what that meant for my best man role or our friendship. He simply left.

The door shut behind him. The minute hand swept past the half hour mark, and its soft tick was what sent me over the edge.

I swept my arm across a table of glasses in rage and watched them crash to the floor. The explosive shatter did nothing to alleviate the burn in my chest.

I'd tried to reason with Jordan, but I couldn't watch Ayana marry someone else.

I needed to talk to her. I needed…fuck. I needed *her*. I shouldn't have walked away from her at the hotel. I should've stayed and worked it out somehow. Convinced her that this arrangement with Jordan wasn't worth it.

Regret twisted inside me.

I checked the clock again. I still had a little time before the ceremony started.

I strode out into the hall and toward the elevators, my pulse pumping with adrenaline. I made it halfway when my burner phone rang. It was the one I used specifically to communicate with Roman.

Dammit. His was the one call I couldn't afford to ignore.

"What?" I resumed my walk toward the elevators.

"We have a problem."

Mental alarm bells clanged at his grim tone. "What kind of problem?"

"Our friend has reprioritized."

Translation: the distractions that'd kept the Brotherhood factions at bay had cleared up.

"Is he coming home?" In other words, were they actively targeting me again?

"Yes." Roman sounded tense. "I suspect he's...unhappy with me. I'm out in the cold in regards to details."

I swallowed a curse. The development couldn't have come at a worse time. "When?"

"I'm not sure, but it'll be soon. Knowing him, he'll choose a time when your guard is down and you're least able to retaliate."

My guard was never down. Even now, I scanned the hall, my ears cocked for the slightest hint of trouble. As for retaliation, the only times I couldn't really fight back were when I was asleep or...

My blood turned to ice. The gears in my head whirred and landed on one inevitable conclusion.

Fuck.

I hung up without a word and immediately called Sean from my other phone. He picked up on the first ring.

I bypassed the pleasantries. "The wedding has been compromised."

After a millisecond of audible shock, he recovered and immediately snapped into professional mode. Thank God I'd had the foresight to bring three of my men to the wedding despite the Fords' protests.

"Understood," he said. He hung up.

I checked my watch. The ceremony started in ten minutes, which meant Jordan and the guests were already inside. Ayana would be nearby.

I hoped I was wrong, but my gut screamed otherwise.

The Brotherhood wasn't operating by their old rules anymore. The fire at the Vault proved that. It didn't matter that this was a high-profile wedding when they usually operated in the shadows. And my absence from the church wouldn't deter them; it would embolden them to use people I cared about to get to me.

They'd done it before.

My heart crawled into my throat; I felt like I was going to be sick.

The elevator arrived. I jabbed at the button for the lobby, my body wired with so much tension I might explode before I got out.

Twenty floors.

Nineteen.

Eighteen.

When I finally arrived on the ground floor, I abandoned all pretenses and broke into a flat-out run. I ignored the passing shouts and curses.

Adrenaline fueled my pace, but that didn't stop an ominous feeling from spreading in my chest.

Please don't let me be too late.

CHAPTER 28

Ayana

"ARE YOU OKAY, AYANIYE?" MY MOTHER ASKED. Combining the first one or two syllables of a person's name with the suffix -iye was a common Ethiopian endearment, but she hadn't called me Ayaniye since I was a teenager. It unleashed a painful wave of nostalgia. "You look a little tense."

"I'm fine. Just pre-wedding jitters." I smiled, hoping she couldn't see past the perky mask I'd put on since she arrived in New York.

We were waiting for our cue to enter the church. My bridesmaids were already lined up for their walk down the aisle, but my mother had stayed with me instead of sitting with the rest of my family. My father stood a respectful distance away, giving us space for our last mother-daughter talk before I officially became a married woman.

Married.

My stomach pitched at the thought.

I looked the part. I was dressed in a stunning gown spun with delicate floral lace and flowy tulle. My makeup was perfect; my hair was pinned half up, half down, and adorned with pearls, courtesy of Kim. I'd accessorized with my mother's heirloom gold-and-diamond earrings.

It was the world's most beautiful cage.

"Good." My mother squeezed my hand, a touch of worry in her eyes. She'd aged in the years since I left home. Gray streaked her hair, and fine lines fanned from the corners of her eyes. But her skin remained a smooth, unblemished brown, and her eyes were bright with knowing as she studied me. "It's a big day. All your father and I want is for you to be happy."

Was this standard pre-wedding advice, or did she know something was wrong? I thought I'd done a good job of pretending, but never underestimate a mother's intuition.

"I know." I squeezed her hand back even as tears crowded my throat.

I wanted to fall into her arms and let her soothe my troubles like I was a kid again. Back then, things had been easy. There'd been no contracts, predatory agents, or complicated feelings toward best men. My parents had shielded me from the worst of the world.

I banished the thought of Vuk as quickly as it arose.

I would not let him *or* my feelings for him ruin this. I'd chosen this path; it was time to walk it. Once I was free from Beaumont, this would all be worth it.

Orchestral music swelled. The bridesmaids entered the church, and my father beckoned me. It was almost time.

"How did you know Dad was the one?" The question spilled out in a rush.

I wasn't sure what prompted it. I'd taken my parents' love for granted my entire life. They'd met at the restaurant where they both worked decades ago—my father as a line cook, my mother as a waitress. They quickly fell in love, and she was the one who'd encouraged him to open his own restaurant after their old employer retired.

"I can't explain it. I just knew," my mother admitted. "It's not a checkbox of qualities, *mamaye*. It's a feeling." She placed a gentle palm against my cheek. "I know that's not very helpful, but when in doubt, trust yourself. Your heart always knows, even if your head doesn't."

I smiled and tried to breathe through the blossoming ache in my chest.

Call off the wedding.

I can't.

The flash of hurt in Vuk's eyes resurfaced in my mind. I forced it aside.

Listening to my heart was nice in theory, but this was the real world. I didn't have the luxury of idealism.

The doors opened again. My mother went in first. Then I took my teary-eyed father's arm, and we walked down the aisle.

I felt like I was disassociating as I put one foot in front of the other. The faces of family and friends blurred when I passed them, and I couldn't feel anything except the painful thumps of my heart.

Jordan stood at the altar, his expression taut. His mouth was fixed in a semi-convincing smile of a groom in love.

The groomsmen were lined up next to him—including the best man.

Don't look.

But I had to.

My eyes slid from Jordan to the man beside him. I stumbled, and a wave of soft gasps rippled through the crowd before I quickly found my footing again.

"Everything alright, *mare?*" my father asked out of the corner of his mouth.

"Yes," I lied.

It wasn't. Because standing in the best man's spot, his

expression happy but a little confused, was Jordan's cousin. Vuk was nowhere in sight.

Part of me was relieved I wouldn't have to face him when I said my vows; another, larger part of me crumpled at his absence.

I'd counted on seeing him again today, despite the way we'd left things. I craved his presence the way an addict craved their next fix, and it'd been two weeks since I last had mine.

Perhaps it was irrational, but his absence made me feel like I would never see him again. Like our hotel room tryst had been my last chance to hold on to him, and he'd slipped through my fingers without me noticing.

Fresh tears stung my eyes.

I shouldn't have let Vuk leave. I should've...I don't know, done *something*. Explained myself better. Brainstormed ways we could make a relationship work. Called Jordan and asked him whether I could tell Vuk about our arrangement.

At the very least, I should've reached out in the weeks after and stolen a few more moments with him.

Now it was too late.

I managed to reach the altar without falling apart. I blinked back my tears and smiled harder as my father officially gave me away.

"You look beautiful," Jordan said. Up close, his eyes were bloodshot, like he'd been crying, drinking, or both.

"Thank you." I hesitated. Should I ask about Vuk? Was his absence the reason Jordan looked so miserable?

Before I could make a decision, the minister began the ceremony, and the church fell silent.

Jordan and I faced forward. I tried to focus on the minister's words instead of the growing hollow in my chest.

"Dearly beloved, we are gathered here today to witness the union of Jordan Ford and Ayana—"

The doors banged open, interrupting his speech.

I whirled around. For a brief, shining moment, I expected to see Vuk stride in and object to our marriage.

Instead, three men in dark suits marched inside, their faces grim. I recognized the one in front as Sean, Vuk's head of security.

Confused murmurs filled the air. Jordan's grandmother rose, her frail health no match for her fury as "outsiders" ruined her grandson's long-anticipated wedding. My father stood and stepped forward, only for my mother to pull him back.

"What are you doing? What's the meaning of this?" Jordan demanded when Sean neared.

"I'm sorry for the disruption, sir, but you have to evacuate the church. Now," the security chief said. His men were already ushering the baffled guests up and out of their seats.

"The hell I do. Where's Vuk? Did he put you up to this?" Jordan's face reddened. "Of all the—"

"Sir, please." Sean sounded strained. "The wedding has been compromised. You have to leave now, or you'll be in danger."

I glimpsed the gun at his hip. My mouth dried.

What was going on? The church was compromised by whom? Why had Vuk sent his team instead of showing up himself?

Jordan was still arguing with Sean, who looked like he was a second away from throwing him over his shoulder and forcibly carrying him out. His men had succeeded in herding most of the guests toward the exit.

I was about to interject and tell Jordan we should go outside and regroup when three things happened at once in seemingly slow motion.

The pianist rose from his bench and drew out a gun. The minister grabbed Jordan, and a familiar tall, dark figure sprinted into the church toward us.

Vuk. Panic suffused his face.

My ears rang. Time sped up again, and the next minute happened so quickly, I couldn't keep track of it all.

The pianist swung his gun toward Vuk, one of Vuk's men tackled him from behind before he could get off a shot, and the minister swung Jordan around, using him as a shield against Sean's drawn weapon.

The pianist managed to free himself from the bodyguard. He took aim again, this time at the altar—straight toward me.

A gunshot rang out.

My body turned cold with terror. I should duck, run, do anything except stand there frozen, but I was too slow and the bullet was too—

A large body tackled me to the ground as more gunshots ripped through the air. The taste of copper filled my mouth. Fresh screams erupted, something heavy crashed, and then...

Quiet.

I lay there, my mind so disassociated from the carnage that I couldn't wrap it around what just happened.

I was breathing, maybe. I couldn't tell. Everything was numb.

Vuk braced his arms on either side of me. His body covered mine so completely, I couldn't see past his protective shield to the ceiling above. He said something, but his voice sounded like it was coming from underwater. It was too muffled for me to understand.

Instead, I turned my head to the side.

My stomach heaved, and another scream shattered the silence. It took several beats for me to realize the terrifying sound came from me.

Because lying unconscious next to me in a pool of blood, his skin whiter than death, was Jordan.

CHAPTER 29

Vuk

BLOOD STAINED MY HANDS.

The thick, red liquid dripped from my fingers, painting the floor with sins past and present.

Charred flesh. Screams. The resigned determination in Lazar's eyes when he urged me to leave, and the heart-stopping moment when a bullet streaked through the air toward the altar.

In both cases, I'd had a split second to make my choice. Now Lazar was dead, and Jordan was…

"Sir." The word floated beneath my pounding heartbeat. The walls closed in; the acrid scent of smoke tainted my nostrils. *Drip, drip, drip,* went the blood. "Sir!"

My head snapped up to see Sean staring at me, his face wreathed in concern.

The sight of him slowly brought the world back into focus.

I wasn't at the church. There wasn't a fire, and no one was pointing a gun at me. When I looked at my hands, they were clean—literally, at least. Not a drop of blood marred the polished wooden floor.

It was the day after the church attack, and we were in the

living room of my secondary house in Westchester. We were safe—for now.

Not at all of us, a voice whispered in my head.

An image of Jordan's deathly still body swam before my eyes. Guilt settled thick on the back of my tongue, but I swallowed it and forced my pulse to return to normal.

What? I was on edge. We all were.

"Confirming the Kidanes are settled in on the second floor. It took some convincing, but they've agreed to return to D.C. on Monday," Sean said. "We've placed additional security at Ayana's building as well as around the Fords' house and the hospital. We told them it was to hold off the press, and they bought it." He hesitated. "We've also taken care of the perpetrators from the wedding. All but one were eliminated."

All but one, I repeated.

So there was still a culprit on the loose. Running, breathing, *living* when he should've been six feet under with a bullet between his eyes.

"He escaped in the chaos after Jordan got shot." Sean's face was impassive, but I detected a bitter seed of guilt. He'd had his hands full fighting the fake minister, who'd turned out to be a Brotherhood member in disguise, but he still blamed himself for not saving Jordan in time. "We have every informant and half the surveillance cameras in the city looking for him. We'll find him."

The memory of Jordan lying unconscious in his own blood resurfaced again, sharp and biting. It was overlaid by an image of Ayana's terror-stricken face and the sound of her scream.

Something cold and insidious stirred in my gut.

I took back my earlier sentiment. A bullet was too good for the last Brother.

When you do, leave him to me.

Sean nodded.

There'd been four assassins in total—the minister, the pianist, and two drivers who'd been waiting outside as backup. My team surmised that their primary objective had been to take me out while I was performing my best man duties and my guard was down. In case that failed, they would take Jordan as bait or, as a last resort, eliminate him in order to throw me off my game. Make me act on impulse instead of strategy and commit mistakes that they could then exploit.

It was a decent enough plan. Too bad for them they'd failed.

The other Brothers had died before I could get my hands on them, but once we found the last one, I was going to make it hurt.

Until then, I had other things to take care of.

I finally asked the question I'd been avoiding all morning. *How's Jordan?*

I'd gone with him to the hospital, but I couldn't stay since I'd had to formulate a battle plan with Sean. A full day had passed since then. Anything could've happened.

My chest tightened until Sean spoke again.

"He's still in critical condition," he said. "He's unconscious, but his vitals are stable."

I released a long breath. That was good. Unconscious was better than dead.

Still, it was a minuscule island of relief amidst a sea of guilt. This all happened because of me. I was the reason the Brotherhood showed up. I was the reason Jordan was shot, and Ayana almost died in the crossfire.

In that crucial moment, I could've saved one or the other. I chose Ayana. Now Jordan was in a coma with no prognosis as to when he'd wake up. The press was having a field day, and the Fords were, understandably, inconsolable.

My team quickly spun a cover story about how the attack had been part of a larger gang turf war. The minister and pianist were members of rival gangs. It was ridiculous, but it was more believable than the truth. Everyone bought it.

Thank you. I dismissed Sean. He was about to leave when I added, *It wasn't your fault. You performed admirably yesterday.*

No one on our side had died, and Sean had done the best he could with the time and information he had.

He swallowed. "Thank you, sir."

Get some rest.

He wouldn't rest until the last Brother was caught. Complacency wasn't in his DNA, but gratitude flickered over his mouth anyway.

He left, and I took the stairs to the second floor. I stopped outside Ayana's room, listening for the murmur of voices. I heard none.

Her family must be giving her space. Ayana had gone into shock after the shooting. Otherwise, she was physically unhurt, but they'd stayed by her side all day yesterday.

A pit opened in my stomach. The past day had been so chaotic I hadn't had a chance to really talk to her. I also wanted to give her time with her family. This would be our first face-to-face conversation since I brought her to Westchester.

After a beat of hesitation, I knocked on the door and waited for her soft "Come in" before I opened it.

I walked in. The curtains were drawn, but a trickle of late-afternoon sunlight leaked through the edges and cast a pale glow on the floor.

Ayana sat on her bed, dressed in an oversized T-shirt and sweats. I'd had my team bring some clothes and toiletries for her last night. Shadows of exhaustion smudged her eyes, and her dark hair tumbled past her shoulders in natural curls.

I closed the door behind me and sat next to her. *Have you eaten?*

I yearned to touch her, but what did I know about consolation? What business did I have comforting her when I was the one responsible for her distress? My skin was clean, but my hands were bloody.

"A little. I'm not that hungry." She wasn't in shock anymore, but I could tell she was still processing yesterday's events. She drew her knees to her chest, her face vulnerable. "Is Jordan still…"

Unconscious. But he's stable. He'll pull through.

I tried to look reassuring. I wasn't so confident about the last part, but he had to survive. There was no other option.

I hadn't wanted the wedding to happen. Hell, I'd been on my way to stop it before I got Roman's call. That didn't mean I wanted Jordan dead or injured.

If he never woke up, our last conversation would've been one of anger.

Regret punched through my chest, making my ribs tremble. I set my jaw and forced the ache aside. I didn't have time to dwell on what-ifs right now. My top priorities were making sure everyone was safe and hunting down the last Brother.

Ayana expelled a shaky sigh of relief.

She'd wanted to stay at the hospital with Jordan; I'd insisted we leave after an hour. I hated saying no to her, but even with my men standing guard, it was too dangerous.

The Kidanes had believed me when I said the "gang members" were neutralized, but I'd had to tell them the rest of the gang might be looking to eliminate witnesses in order to get them to Westchester.

The Brotherhood likely needed time to regroup after their failure yesterday, but I wasn't taking any chances.

My team is escorting your family back to D.C. on Monday. You should join them. Get some breathing room.

I'd checked in with Roman last night. He was still in the dark about the Brotherhood's next plans for me, but he said both factions were closing ranks. They were congregated in New York, and their presence along the rest of the coast was sparse.

I would feel a hell of a lot better if Ayana was out of the city until we caught the last Brother and interrogated him.

"No." Her jaw set with determination. "I promised my parents I would stay with them next weekend, but I'm not running away before that. Not while Jordan is in the hospital and all *this* is happening." She gestured at her phone. Every few minutes, it lit up with a new notification. She must be inundated with calls and texts from everyone with even the smallest connection to her.

"I just...I need time alone. You can stay," Ayana said when I moved to leave. "I meant I need time away from all the hovering and questions. I know my family means well, but I can't think when they're constantly checking in on me." She offered a wobbly smile. "You're different."

Because I rarely talk?

"Because you always know how to make me feel better." Her smile faded, and emotion glistened in her eyes. "Can you hold me?" she asked, her voice small. "Just for a little bit."

Fuck. My heart cracked straight down the middle.

I didn't say a word. I simply gathered her in my arms while she curled into a ball against my chest. She didn't cry, but she felt so fragile and vulnerable I wanted to go out and annihilate anyone who dared to even *think* about hurting her.

We sat in silence for minutes or perhaps hours. This was my first time truly holding her since I left the hotel. What happened then seemed so inconsequential compared to yesterday, especially after Jordan's admission of truth, but we had to acknowledge it eventually.

"I'm sorry for what happened in the hotel." It was as if Ayana had read my mind. "I was sending mixed signals, and I didn't mean to imply that you...that I wanted to marry Jordan in public and hide you away in private."

My heartbeats tied into an uncomfortable knot in my throat. "I know."

The thought had passed through my mind. She was the beauty, and I was the beast. What person would look at us and think I was worthy of her in any way? But Ayana wasn't that shallow. She judged people on their character, not their appearance. I wasn't exactly an upstanding citizen, but for some reason, she seemed to find my presence appealing.

"Jordan told me about your arrangement," I said, my voice low.

She raised her head and pulled back, her eyes widening with surprise.

"We fought over it. I told him I'd wire him the total sum of his inheritance if he called off the wedding. He refused." I swallowed. "That was why I wasn't at the church at first. I couldn't bear to see you marry him. I was on my way to stop the ceremony somehow when I received a tip that the wedding was compromised."

A glossy sheen brightened Ayana's eyes. "I wanted to tell you. But Jordan…"

"I know," I said again.

A trickle of my earlier regret seeped through the cracks in the box I'd locked it in. I wished I could turn back time and do yesterday over.

Ayana inhaled a shuddering breath. I kept my arms around her as silence descended again.

Now that I knew about her arrangement, where did that leave us? She was technically still engaged to Jordan. If and when he awoke, would they carry on with the wedding like nothing had happened? His grandmother's health slipped more and more every day, and yesterday's attack couldn't have helped.

Also, how fucked was I for thinking about these things when Jordan was in a coma? I really was a bastard.

"You said you received a tip." Ayana's voice was quiet. "Who were those people at the church? And don't say they were part of rival gangs. Tell me the truth. I deserve that much."

I suppressed a flinch.

My knee-jerk instinct was to give her a partial version of the truth. She didn't know about my fucked-up past or the many lines I'd crossed, and I wanted to keep it that way. I wished I was the man she saw when she looked at me—someone who was less flawed and worthier of her trust.

But Ayana was right. She deserved the whole truth. My past affected her directly, and if I wanted to protect her, I had to let her know what we were up against.

"They were members of the Brotherhood," I said. "It's an organization of professional contract killers. Extremely elite, extremely secretive. They operate out of the East Coast and have been responsible for thousands of deaths over the years."

Ayana paused as if to give me time to admit I was joking. When I didn't, she pulled away, her face stark with disbelief. "A secret organization of hitmen? Are you messing with me?"

I shook my head. "I know it sounds unbelievable, but assassins do exist outside of Hollywood. Powerful people don't like getting their hands dirty. They need organizations like the Brotherhood to take care of their more...delicate problems for them."

She sat frozen for a moment. "That's...okay. Okay. Hitmen. Got it." She closed her eyes and took a deep breath. When she opened them again, they were sharp with inquisitiveness. "This Brotherhood. They were after you."

"Yes," I said simply.

"Because you've hired them before, and things went wrong?"

"Because I used to be one of them."

My admission rang with painful clarity. I hadn't talked about my involvement with the Brotherhood in years. Besides Jordan and Lazar, Sean was the only other person who knew.

These conversations were never easy, but telling Ayana was the hardest of all. She belonged in a world where weddings were happy occasions and assassins didn't exist. She didn't deserve to have her innocence stripped away by my sordid past.

Her lips parted. She rocked back on the bed, seemingly too stunned to respond.

"I told you my brother hadn't gone to college," I said. "What I didn't tell you was that he worked at a casino in Maryland instead. D.C. insiders went there to gamble and make backroom deals, and one of them ended up being a Brotherhood target. My brother witnessed the hit. He escaped before they killed him too, but he knew he was a loose end and they might come after him again. He told me what happened, so I tracked the Brotherhood down and offered them a deal."

Ayana looked dazed. "You tracked them down? How?"

"I was my brother's twin." I smiled humorlessly at her jolt of shock. "I used myself as bait, and it worked. I didn't know about the Brotherhood then, but based on what Lazar told me, I correctly assumed the person who carried out the hit was a professional. I was also fortunate enough to have skills that organizations like theirs find useful."

Few people knew I had a twin. Lazar and I came into the world together, grew up together, and almost died together. He'd been the one person I trusted implicitly. Losing him had been worse than losing a limb.

That was why I didn't talk about him or have pictures of him on display. It was painful enough looking at myself in the mirror. Every time I faced my reflection, I was reminded of my losses—my brother, and the person I used to be.

"I majored in chemistry," I continued. "But I was interested in more practical applications outside the classroom. I was at Thayer on scholarship, and to earn money on the side, I created… substances that I then sold through intermediaries. Their effects varied. Some helped students concentrate when they had an exam;

others helped them relax or feel good. They weren't lethal or addictive, but they were highly profitable, and I developed a reputation amongst certain circles in D.C." Those days seemed like a lifetime ago. "The Brotherhood had heard of me, and as luck would have it, they were looking for a chemist at the time."

"To make drugs?" Ayana ventured.

"To make poisons."

She fisted the comforter, her knuckles tightening. Her eyes were huge, dark, and unreadable.

Her opinion of me had undoubtedly, irrevocably changed. Barbs prickled my throat, but it was too late to change course. I had to finish the story.

"I offered to join them if they left my brother alone. They agreed—*if* I put up half a million dollars upfront as insurance. If I didn't, the deal was off, and they'd kill both of us."

Realization sparked in Ayana's eyes. "That's the money Jordan lent you."

The mention of Jordan made my gut twist again. If it weren't for me, he would've never been in danger. He would be conscious. Healthy. *Safe.*

"Yes," I said. "I worked for the Brotherhood for two years. Most of their targets weren't good people. They were corrupt politicians, drug lords, sex offenders—or so they told me. I didn't question them too much. It was easier to do what I did if I thought the targets deserved it."

In hindsight, I'd been naive to believe my poisons were only used on those who "deserved it." The Brotherhood prayed at the altar of cold, hard cash. They would kill anyone if the price was high enough.

"But I couldn't stay with them forever," I said. "That wasn't the life I wanted, and the more I learned about them, the less I wanted to be part of that world. I had to get out. There was only one problem: the only way anyone left the Brotherhood was through official retirement, which the leadership had to sign off on, or in a body bag. I was too valuable for them to willingly let me go, so I needed leverage to *force* them to release me."

I could see the wheels turning in Ayana's head. "That's what they were looking for when they broke into your house."

Beautiful and smart. A woman after my own heart.

"Yes," I confirmed. "I got my hands on the leadership's ledger. It included a full list of Brotherhood members, their hits, their aliases, and who hired them. It was fully encrypted, of course. It would've taken me years to crack the code, so I didn't bother. I simply threatened to send it to rival organizations."

Fortunately for me, the leadership at the time had been overly paranoid about their members' loyalty (hence the ledger) and overly confident about their security measures.

I still had the ledger, but it was outdated and useless as leverage after so many years.

"Even if their rivals couldn't hack into it, the existence and possible discovery of such an item would've been devastating," I said. "In their field of work, discretion and word of mouth is paramount. If their clients found out their darkest secret was proven *in writing*, no one would ever hire them again. The organization would implode. With the threat of the ledger hanging over their head, they agreed to let me leave. But then…"

"They went back on their word and came after you," Ayana finished.

I gave a short nod. I left out what I did to the Brothers after Lazar died. She didn't ever need to see that side of me.

She blew out a huge breath. She appeared overwhelmed by the onslaught of information, which was understandable. It was a lot to take in, but it was better to rip the Band-Aids off all at once rather than drag it out.

Nevertheless, my skin drew tight over my bones. Every heartbeat felt like it might be my last.

I was used to being in control. Money and power meant authority was always at my fingertips, ready to be deployed. But I couldn't control the way Ayana reacted to my confessions.

She had the power to kill me with a single word, and she didn't even know it.

"That all happened so long ago," she said. "Why are they coming after you now?"

My shoulders relaxed an inch. She wasn't running screaming from the room—yet.

"Internal politics. Old leadership is gone, and people are fighting for the top spot." My mouth twisted. "I've been the ultimate thorn in their side. Killing me would cement the new guard's power."

Except the new guard wasn't as smart as the old one. They were sloppier, less disciplined. Yesterday's mess proved it.

The old Brotherhood would've *never* tried to pull off a hit or a fucking kidnapping at such a public, high-profile event. They were either desperate, or they were so caught up in beating the other side that they weren't strategizing properly.

I could use both those things to my advantage.

I was meeting Roman soon to debrief. He'd gained a smidge of my trust after yesterday's intel. If he hadn't tipped me off, the wedding would've been a bigger disaster than it already was.

"I see," Ayana said. It was impossible to gauge the feelings behind her neutral tone. "Thank you for telling me."

I felt the need to clarify. "I haven't been involved in that world for a long time. If they hadn't come looking for me, I would've happily left them in the past."

I wasn't a good man, but I wasn't *that* man anymore. Not unless I had to be.

"You mean you don't want to return to your life as a secret poison master for a deadly organization?" Ayana's mouth quirked up a fraction at the corners, and a tingle of relief loosened the vise around my chest.

I hadn't scared her off.

"People change, and you were forced into your position. I don't blame you for that. But all of *this*..." She gestured around the room. "It's a lot to process. I need time. I just...just give me some time to think, okay?"

It was a reasonable request.

Space would be good for both of us. With the escaped Brother on the loose and Jordan's life hanging in the balance, there was too much uncertainty for us to do anything except wait and see where the pieces fell.

Still, my stomach sank at the thought of leaving her.

"Okay." I stood, hiding my disappointment. "I'll let you get some rest. It's been a long day."

I was halfway out the door when she stopped me. "Vuk."

I turned.

Ayana's face softened. "Thank you for holding me."

A thick, foreign sensation invaded my chest. It was so warm, it was almost uncomfortable. I had no words to describe it, so I responded with the simple truth.

"Always."

CHAPTER 30

Ayana

"WHAT HAPPENED WAS A TRAGEDY. I SINCERELY HOPE Jordan wakes up soon. His death would be a great loss for the fashion world." Emmanuelle's voice oozed with fake sincerity over the phone. "That being said, it's been almost a month since your last job, darling. The people are impatient."

By people, do you mean you? I bit back my snarky response and stared out the window. It was the perfect fall afternoon. I should be outside, enjoying the sunshine, but I was holed up in my apartment. I'd barely left since I returned home on Tuesday against Vuk's strident objections. I couldn't stay in the suburbs forever. I needed a sense of normalcy.

"There's no better distraction than work," Emmanuelle continued. "Sage Studios is thrilled with the denim campaign. We should lean more into the commercial angle. You've done enough editorials this year, and commercial pays more."

I barely heard her. My mind was back in Westchester, listening to Vuk disclose his past.

Hitmen. Murder. Poison.

I felt like someone had plucked me out of my life and dropped me in the middle of a Nate Reynolds thriller.

I struggled to wrap my head around it days later. My family had reluctantly returned to D.C. after reassurances from both Vuk and the police that the "gangs" had been taken care of, and I was safe. I didn't want to know how Vuk got the NYPD to go along with his cover story.

I'd promised my family I would visit this weekend after I checked in on Jordan and finished some "work." So far, the only work I'd done was knitting half a blanket and reorganizing my perfume collection.

"Ayana!" Emmanuelle's silken voice grew fangs. "Are you listening to me?"

"Yes." She usually intimidated me, but I'd survived a church shootout and *professional assassins* last week. A pissy agency head was the least of my worries. My patience snapped. "I'm listening, but unfortunately, I won't be able to accept any new jobs at this time. As you so kindly mentioned, my fiancé is in a *coma*. He got shot at our wedding six days ago. Six. Days. I need time to grieve and heal, so unless you want me to show up and break down on set, I suggest we table any discussions of new campaigns until after the holidays."

Emmanuelle sucked in an audible breath. I doubted anyone had spoken to her like that in years. "You—"

"But since we're on the subject of work," I said, interrupting her. "I would appreciate it if you paid me for all the shoots I *have* done over the past twelve months. I'd like the money before the end of the calendar year. I've sent multiple emails to Hank and accounting, and I've only received a quarter of what I'm owed. As a businesswoman yourself, I'm sure you understand why that's unacceptable. Now, if you'll excuse me, I have some personal matters to attend to. Thank you for checking in."

I hung up on a spluttering Emmanuelle and tossed my phone on the couch, my heart jackrabbiting.

Oh. My. God.

I brought my hand to my mouth. *What did I do?*

Emmanuelle Beaumont was one of the most powerful women in fashion. If she blacklisted you, your career was over. If she dropped you from her agency, your career was over. If she…well, you get the idea.

I wouldn't have dared talk to her the way I had a month ago. However, near-death experiences had a way of putting things into perspective. My career was important, but it wasn't more important than standing up for myself. If I died tomorrow, what would I be prouder of—winning Model of the Year or knowing I'd fought for what was right?

I dropped my hand. Little bubbles of exhilaration dodged the barbed nerves in my stomach.

I might regret it later, but fuck, it felt good to put Emmanuelle in her place. I only wished I could've seen her face.

That phone call was the first time I'd felt any sense of control since the wedding, and I was going to ride that high for as long as I could.

Newly energized, I picked up my knitting needles and half-finished blanket. Liya always made fun of me for my "old lady hobby," but the mindless repetition of the movements boosted my serotonin like nothing else.

I was just getting into the groove again when my phone rang.

I frowned. It was the front desk. They rarely called unless I had a guest, and I wasn't expecting anyone.

I picked up. "Hello?"

"Good afternoon, Ms. Kidane," the concierge said. "There's a Maya Singh here to see you. Shall I let her up?"

Surprise washed away my confusion. "Thank you. Yes, please."

Maya had never been to my apartment before. What was she doing here on a Thursday during work hours?

My question was answered a few minutes later, when I opened the door to her knock and found her standing in the hall with a white bakery bag in hand.

"I'm so sorry. I didn't mean to drop by unannounced," she said as I ushered her in and led her to the kitchen. She sounded a little embarrassed. "But—and I'm fully aware this makes me sound like a stalker—I remember you said you lived in this building. I was already in the area, and I figured you could use a pick-me-up." She set the white bag on the kitchen island. "Ginger chai cookies from my favorite bakery. They're basically heaven in a box."

"Don't be sorry. This was a pleasant surprise, and you had me at ginger chai," I said with a smile. "Thank you. This was so thoughtful."

"Anytime." Maya drew her bottom lip between her teeth. She studied me, her brow creased with concern. "How are you feeling?"

After the wedding debacle hit the news, she'd checked in on me via text, but this was our first time discussing it in person.

"About how you'd expect." I removed two cookies from the bag and offered her one. She accepted it but didn't take a bite. "I'm feeling a little better now that things have calmed down. The press has moved on, but Jordan is still in a coma. I should be by his side more. Instead, I'm here."

Guilt gnawed at my stomach.

Engagement or not, Jordan was my friend. He was an innocent in all this, and I would give anything for him to wake up again.

My diamond ring glittered on my left hand. A real fiancée would stay by his side. She wouldn't be hiding at home, knitting and trying not to think about a certain man with a voice like rough velvet and arms that felt like home.

When Vuk held me that day in the bedroom, I felt like I'd

finally reached shelter after a long walk through a storm. Warm, comforted, *safe*.

It didn't make sense given everything he told me. He should be the most dangerous person I knew, and maybe he was. But not for me.

"Don't beat yourself up too much," Maya said. "We all handle trauma in different ways. You've been through a lot too, and camping out by his bedside won't change things. He has the best doctors in the city working on him. He's in good hands."

She spoke with such authority, I almost believed her. No wonder her father put her in charge of his company's entire sales and marketing department. She was naturally persuasive.

"Let's hope," I said with a half-hearted smile.

It was strange, talking to someone I'd met only a month ago, but there was something about Maya that made her so easy to confide in.

"Enough morbid talk." I brushed the crumbs from my hands before I reached for a second cookie. "Tell me what you've been up to. I could use some fun gossip."

I didn't need to ask twice. Maya launched into her plans for her upcoming birthday party and interspersed it with notes about how it'll make "Sebastian's Monte Carlo blowout look like child's play." I assumed she was referring to Sebastian Laurent. She brought him up a lot for someone she claimed to hate.

"Shit. I'm going to be late," she said after she mentioned, *again*, how she couldn't wait to see Sebastian's face when he realized she'd one-upped him on the party front. She frowned at her watch. "I wish I could stay longer, but I have a meeting in twenty minutes."

"It's okay. I have the rest of the cookies to keep me company." I nudged the half-empty bag. "These are *divine*."

"I know, right? They're so good, I'm kind of mad we aren't

the ones who manufacture them." Maya threw on her scarf again and hesitated. "If you need anything, text me. I mean it. I know we met not too long ago, but I don't bring just anyone ginger chai cookies, you know."

A genuine smile blossomed across my face. "I will. Thank you. And remember, your birthday party is for *you*. Not Sebastian."

"It's not for him. It's for beating him." Maya huffed. "Anyway, I really have to run, or my father will kill me. Talk later!"

She hurried out.

After she left, I finished the rest of the cookies and returned to the couch. My phone kept buzzing with notifications. It was incredible how many acquaintances crawled out of the woodwork when they heard you were involved in a tragedy.

Some of those messages were probably important. I'd avoided my inbox like it was contagious all week. Sloane had called me on Monday, more as a friend than a publicist. She'd escaped outside by the time the shooting started, but I could tell she was shaken by what happened. Now that she'd had time to regroup, she was likely in full PR mode.

Honestly, I didn't care about the press. The public's interest in the church attack was already fading. The news organizations and Internet would do what they do. I couldn't control them; I could only control my reaction.

My gaze drifted to the window again.

It really was a beautiful day. Why was I inside when I should be out there? I hadn't survived a brush with death to sit on my couch and knit all day.

But every time I pictured myself leaving the building, I heard the echo of gunshots. The sickly metallic scent of blood clogged my nostrils, and I became painfully aware of the fact that had Vuk been a second too slow, or I'd moved an inch too far to the left, I would be dead.

Every corner hid an assassin waiting to finish the job; every rooftop bristled with snipers tracking me in their scopes.

It wasn't rational, but fear rarely was.

I bit my lip. Vuk was giving me space like I'd asked him to, and my incredulity over his story was starting to fade. Most people would flee from him considering he used to, you know, *concoct poisons* for an organization of professional killers.

I saw things differently. Like me, he'd been caught in a situation with no other way out. He hadn't taken pleasure in what he did. It was an act of loyalty and survival, not malice.

Did I think he always kept to the right side of the law? No. I didn't know what he'd done to Wentworth, but I bet it wouldn't please the courts. He didn't kill him though, and the law wasn't always right either. Look at how many innocents had been jailed, or how many violent offenders had walked free.

Vuk's morals blurred the lines between black and white, but they always bent toward justice.

Either that, or you're twisting yourself into knots trying to justify his actions because you like him, and he saved your life.

Fine. So what if I was? That didn't make my justifications any less true.

I closed my eyes, remembering the solid strength of his body covering mine. He'd literally thrown himself in front of a bullet for me.

I would always be grateful to him for that, but a chill slipped beneath my skin at the thought of Vuk getting hurt. He was smart, powerful, and capable, but he wasn't invincible. He was flesh and blood like the rest of us, and he could've died saving me.

The chill sank deeper, frosting my bones and lungs.

During the shootout, I'd been the proverbial damsel in distress. I never wanted to feel that helpless again. I wanted to go outside and protect *myself* if I needed to.

The kernels of a plan formed in my head. Before I could talk myself out of it, I grabbed my coat, put on my favorite pair of heels, and left my house for the first time in two days.

CHAPTER 31

Vuk

"IT COULD'VE BEEN WORSE, ALL THINGS CONSIDERED."
Roman sat across from me, his expression bored. He'd healed
from the bullet I put through his shoulder, but his movements were
careful as we went over the events of the past week.

"Jordan is in a coma," I said flatly.

"But he's not dead." The other man gave me a cool smile. "I
held up my end of the deal. I gave you all the information I had at
the time—which puts me in a dangerous position, by the way. If
Shepherd so much as suspects I was the one who leaked advance
notice of the hit, he'd put an unofficial bounty on my head. Again."

He said it like that was my problem. I was grateful for his
heads-up, but it was up to him to be careful.

It was Thursday, almost a week after the wedding disaster.
Roman and I were meeting at the same warehouse where we'd
kept Wentworth, who had since wisely disappeared to an island
in the Caribbean.

My team was still hunting the escaped Brother, but we were
getting close. Someone matching his description had been spotted
on a traffic camera near Philadelphia.

"It's time for you to put your money where your mouth is," Roman said. "Move against Shepherd while my intel is still good. I can't guarantee he won't change tactics and hideouts if and when he finds out I've been double-crossing him."

Between his "business" commitments and the wedding, I'd been playing defense since Roman and I struck our deal. He promised me info I could use for an ambush that would wipe out Shepherd and his inner circle, but I still didn't fully trust him.

The wedding intel could've been a Trojan horse that he used to gain my trust before springing a trap. I needed more assurances.

"You're going to find the last Brother from the church first," I said. "Once you do, you'll deliver him to me, alive and whole. After that, we can talk."

Roman's jaw hardened. "That's bullshit and you know it. I don't have time to play pet hunter for you when I'm also at risk of being hunted."

"No?" I lifted a brow. "Perhaps I can strike a deal with Shepherd instead. My immunity and one member on the run in exchange for a traitor. I wonder who they'll choose."

If the Brotherhood worshiped money, they *despised* traitors. Internal warfare was one thing; conspiring with outsiders was another. Before Roman, only one person in the organization's hundred-year history had been foolish enough to try the latter. His death had been so horrific, no one stepped out of line for decades.

Roman leaned forward. His eyes glittered in the dark. "Don't threaten me, Markovic," he said softly. "We may be on the same side when it comes to the Brothers, but that doesn't mean I won't gut you like a fucking fish if you try to double-cross me."

The irony of him warning me against a double-cross.

My mouth curved. "You can try."

The air stretched taut. Water from a leaky pipe dripped in the corner. Every thud of a droplet hitting concrete echoed in the vast warehouse, and the silence thrummed with the kind of stillness that only existed before a predator pounced.

Neither Roman nor I moved.

Finally, after several tense heartbeats, he blinked. He leaned back again. "You think you're so damn clever, but you made a rookie mistake." A vicious sort of satisfaction tinged his words. "Ayana."

I wasn't an impulsive person. I operated rationally, strategized every move, and considered all my options before I acted.

Ayana was the only exception. Hearing her name come out of *his* mouth, confirming he was aware of her existence and possibly how important she was to me, sent every fucking fiber of my being into fight mode.

It made sense that Roman knew who she was. She'd been the fucking bride at the wedding. But there was a difference between knowing something theoretically and hearing it out loud.

The only reason he brought her up was because he'd added her as a pawn in his game, and if he so much as touched a *hair* on her head...

Crimson splashed across my vision. My adrenaline spiked, and the taste of copper filled my mouth. I shot up from my seat, ready to lunge for Roman until his gloating smile stopped me in my tracks.

"That's what I thought," he said when I stilled. I fisted my hands on the table, my pulse pounding. "You gave yourself away when you saved her. Vuk Markovic almost taking a bullet for someone else? Please." Dark humor laced his soft laugh. "You showed you cared, which means you're vulnerable. You have a weakness. If you don't think the Brotherhood will exploit that weakness any way they can, then you've grown naive."

Ice snaked down my spine. "They don't involve civilians in their business."

It was a hollow reply. The hit at the wedding proved that

wasn't true. Hell, they'd already bent their rules when they killed my brother, though that'd been an ambiguous case since they'd already planned to kill him before I struck my deal with them.

An argument could be made that Jordan was an obvious target because we had an established friendship. My public attachment to Ayana was much looser.

But Roman was right. I'd shown my hand when I saved her, and with the escaped Brother on the loose, I had a witness. Even if I didn't, my reaction just now proved Roman's suspicions were correct.

My heart crashed against my ribcage. *Fuck.*

"In the olden days, they didn't," Roman said. "As you might've guessed, we're in a new era. It's chaos. The old rules no longer apply, so you can threaten me if you want. But if you lose me, you lose your only in. Even out in the cold, I can do more for you than you can do on your own." He smiled. "Think about that the next time you threaten me."

I unclenched my fists and retook my seat. The urge to shoot that smile off his face consumed me, but I couldn't afford to lose my cool again.

"Like I said, I'll take care of your problem after you take care of mine," I said. "I'm not going to spread my team thin by ambushing Shepherd when we have a wild card on the streets. That's a sure way to fail."

Roman's mouth tightened. A moment later, he inclined his head in silent acceptance.

"One more thing." Something about this situation had been nagging at me for weeks. "How are the factions financing their ops? Rumors of the civil war have made their way through the underworld. Business is down, but weapons and logistics on the scale they're operating at cost money. They must've gone through most, if not all, of the organization's coffers by now. So where is the cash flowing in from?"

"I don't know the details. I'm not their fucking CFO," Roman said. "Don't underestimate the ability of professional killers to find money and clients when they need them. Someone somewhere always wants someone else dead."

"You seem to always be light on the details."

"You seem to always be heavy on the asks without giving anything in return."

We glared at each other, but a rustle of noise quickly snuffed out the tension.

Less than a second later, we were out of our seats, our guns drawn and aimed in the direction of the noise. Our reaction was so swift, we didn't even have time to blink.

A furry gray creature slithered out of the shadows.

What the fuck?

I watched, stunned, as Shadow stretched and yawned. He appeared unfazed by our guns as he padded over, jumped onto an empty chair, and curled up lazily on the seat like it was his throne. A silver collar with the serpentine Markovic crest gleamed around his neck.

Most Serbian families didn't have crests, but I'd had it designed years ago as a symbol of legacy. In hindsight, I shouldn't have put it on a pet collar.

"You brought your fucking cat?" Roman asked with disbelief.

"He's not my cat, and I didn't bring him," I growled.

I glowered at the insufferable creature. I'd had every intention of tossing him back on the street after the rainstorm, but my staff had cried and protested until I gave in. Apparently, petting a fluffy little monster was soothing to some people. God knew why.

Much to my displeasure, everyone had insisted I give said monster a name. He had an uncanny ability to sneak around and blend into the shadows, hence his new moniker. If Shadow were a person, he'd make a killer CIA agent, as evidenced by how he'd managed to follow me here without me knowing. He must've hidden in the back of my car.

As it was, he was a huge pain in my ass. I couldn't wait for the day when everyone tired of him so I could drop him off at the nearest shelter.

Shadow flicked his tail back and forth as if to taunt me. *They'll never tire of me*, I imagined him saying. *That's why they bought me this collar.*

Bastard.

I'd bought him that collar. Quite unwillingly, I might add. The staff had huffed and sighed until I had the collar made just to shut them up.

Roman lowered his gun. He stared at Shadow for an extra beat like he expected the Egyptian Mau to morph into a human assassin. When he didn't, he lowered his gun and shook his head.

"We've wasted enough time," he said. "I'll see what I can find out about the last Brother. You start putting together a strategy for the ambush. And Markovic? Remember. If Shepherd finds out what we've been up to, we're both fucked."

I didn't linger at the warehouse after Roman left.

I was tempted to leave Shadow there, but at the last minute, I grabbed his smug ass from the chair and took him home. I suppose Jeremiah and the rest of the staff wouldn't believe me if I told them Shadow "ran off" on his own. He'd gotten a little too used to his comfy new surroundings and fancy tuna. My butler was waiting for me in the foyer when I returned.

"Good afternoon, sir. You have a guest," he said. "Ms. Kidane is waiting for you in the living room."

I stopped short. I dumped an indignant Shadow on the ground before responding. *How long has she been here?*

"About ten minutes."

Why didn't you call me?

"Well, sir," Jeremiah said, his face placid. "I assumed a phone call wouldn't magically evaporate traffic." He reached down to pick up Shadow. "However, you'll be pleased to know we've taken excellent care of Ms. Kidane. We served her the custom-blended tea you like so much. She's a big fan."

I ignored his pointed tone. Any other day, I would've called him out for giving me lip, but I'd kept Ayana waiting long enough.

I strode across the house to the living room. The initial knot in my throat gradually unraveled into a tangle of anticipation.

I'd respected her wishes and given her space after our talk in Westchester. The bodyguard I'd stationed at her building told me she hadn't left her apartment since returning home, so the fact she was here meant she'd made up her mind about something.

If she didn't want anything to do with me, she wouldn't be here. She could've texted to say my past was too much for her and she never wanted to see me again, or she could've ghosted me altogether.

Her presence was a good sign. Right?

Ayana stood when I entered the room. Gone were the sweats and old T-shirt; in their place was an orange silk top, jeans, and heels. Gold earrings peeked out from behind lush curls.

A smile ghosted my mouth. I didn't care what she wore; she could throw on a potato sack and still blow every woman in the city out of the water. But she loved fashion, and it was nice to see her back in fighting form.

"Hi." She tucked a curl behind her ear. "I hope you don't mind me dropping by. I should've called first, but it was a, um, last-minute thing."

You can come by any time you want. I paused, my mind flashing to Roman's warning. *Fuck.* If the Brotherhood was watching,

Ayana's visit would bolster the notion that she was my weakness. It was too late to change that, so I shelved the worry for later. *I didn't expect to hear from you so soon.*

"Because of what you told me?"

I pressed my lips together and nodded.

Ayana opened her mouth. Then her gaze slid past me, and her eyes widened. "I didn't know you had a cat."

I whipped around in time to see Shadow trot into the room like he owned it. He ignored me and went straight to Ayana. He rubbed his head against her leg and purred when she bent to scratch him behind the ears.

"He's not my cat." I was getting tired of repeating myself.

Ayana picked him up and cuddled him close to her chest. "What's his name?"

"Shadow," I said, my tone sour.

Shadow stared straight at me while he nuzzled her breast. He let out a small meow, which she interpreted as a sign of affection and I interpreted as a big, fat *fuck you*.

My molars ground together, but Ayana's next words pushed my thoughts of animal murder to the back burner.

"I've had time to think about what you said." Her expression sobered. "I'll be honest. I was...taken aback at first. And afraid. Not of you, but of the situation and the world I suddenly found myself in. I've seen plenty of questionable things in the fashion industry, but they're nothing compared to hitmen and murder and torture." She took a deep breath. "I can't say those things don't make me uneasy, but you had a good reason for doing what you did. If I'd been in your shoes, and joining the Brotherhood was the only way I could save my family, I would've done the same."

The knot in my throat untangled fully, but it still took a moment to find my words. "Meaning?"

I didn't care what other people thought about me, but Ayana

wasn't "other people." She was the only one whose opinion mattered.

"Meaning if you think you've scared me off, you haven't." Ayana gave me a half-shy, half-mischievous smile. "You're stuck with me, Markovic."

That foreign warmth prickled my chest again. A weight slid off my shoulders, and the ensuing lightness was so disorienting I almost stumbled.

"Strong words, *srce*," I said softly.

Shadow yowled, but even he couldn't ruin this moment.

It was the closest to happiness I'd ever been.

"They're the truth." Ayana hugged Shadow closer to her chest and bit her lip. "But I have a confession. That's not the only reason I'm here."

I raised my eyebrows.

"I want to learn how to protect myself," she said. "I've taken self-defense classes, but they're not much use against guns. If I find myself in danger again, I don't want to rely on someone else to save me."

"When you say 'protect yourself'...what do you have in mind?"

Ayana met my wary gaze with a sure one of her own. "I want you to teach me how to shoot."

CHAPTER 32

Ayana

TO MY SURPRISE, VUK DIDN'T SHUT DOWN MY SUGGES-tion. In fact, he seemed to embrace it, though he refused to give me details about when and where the lessons would start. He just said "after D.C."

I wasn't a fan of guns or violence in general, but with people like the Brotherhood running around trying to kill those close to me, I couldn't stick my head in the sand.

Vuk had a point about D.C., though. I was scheduled to take the train home the following day, so I didn't have time to do anything except pack and visit the salon after I left his house. I liked to style my hair in low-maintenance box braids when I traveled, even if it was a short trip, and Kim did them faster and better than anyone else I knew.

However, when Vuk found out I was taking the train, he insisted on driving me to D.C. himself "for safety reasons," which was how I found myself going on a road trip with Vuk freaking Markovic.

"I love that you brought your cat." I petted Shadow and smiled when he thumped his tail against my thigh.

"He's a temporary guest, and I didn't bring him," Vuk said in

296 I ANA HUANG

a long-suffering tone. "He's a stowaway. I didn't notice him hiding in the back until we stopped for gas." He scowled at the sleepy feline. Shadow was curled up in my lap, oblivious to his owner's irritation.

I stifled a laugh at Vuk's endearing grouchiness.

"I would've noticed him earlier," he added, "if you hadn't packed your entire closet for the weekend. I can barely see past the mountain of luggage in the rearview mirror."

"It's not my entire closet," I said. "It's only one-eighth of it."

Three suitcases, one duffel, and one vanity case was the bare minimum. Did he *know* how much space shoes took up?

"That's...terrifying." Despite his words, a little smile tugged at the corner of his mouth.

My indignation melted into an answering smile. Maybe it was his company, the comfort of petting a cute cat, or the prospect of seeing my family again, but this was the lightest I'd felt all week.

My trauma from last Friday's attack was nowhere close to healed. I probably needed extensive therapy to deal with what had happened, and Jordan's fate remained in limbo. The Brotherhood remained an ominous specter in the background. But people needed hope in the darkest of times, and spiraling into a pit of worry wasn't going to help anyone.

I reached for my phone and changed the music to something more upbeat. I was the DJ for our trip, and Vuk seemed content to let me fiddle with the Spotify stations as I saw fit.

"Is this your first trip out of town this year? Besides San Francisco," I amended. "I feel like you never go on vacation."

"No, and I don't have time for vacation."

"Everyone has time for vacation."

"Not me."

"Then what were your other trips for?"

"Business."

God, he could be infuriating. "That's boring."

Vuk slid a sideways glance at me. "Says the girl who flies from photoshoot to photoshoot around the world. When was the last time *you* went on vacation?"

"That's not the same." I smoothed a hand over Shadow's fur. "I build in vacation days around the photoshoot when I can. For example, after I did that perfume campaign for Chanel, I stayed in Provence and took four days off."

"But you still flew there for work. You wouldn't have been in Provence if you weren't required to be there."

I opened my mouth, then shut it. *Dammit.* He had a point.

Travel was one of my favorite parts of modeling, but it would be nice to go somewhere I didn't have to worry about work at all.

"Fine," I said after I'd regrouped. "If you *did* have time for vacation, where would you go?"

Vuk's brows drew together in thought. I loved that about him. When he wasn't intentionally pushing my buttons with blasé answers, he considered every question with the same gravity a CEO considered an important business decision. It didn't matter how silly the question was.

He made me feel seen, but he made me feel heard too.

"Somewhere cold," he mused. "I like the mountains and snow. Fewer people there."

"Why am I not surprised?" I teased. "I'm a warm weather girl. Give me a beach and fruity drinks with little umbrellas in them any day."

"A beach is fine if it's deserted."

"What do you have against people?"

Vuk gave me a sardonic look. *Right.* Stupid question. People had shot at him, killed his brother, and tried to kill him too. That wasn't counting all the strangers who gawked at his scars like he was a zoo animal. No wonder he hated leaving the house.

"Never mind. Deserted beach or deserted mountain. Noted." My teeth dug into my bottom lip. There was another question I wanted to ask, but...*Screw it*. We had over an hour left on our drive, and I was finally comfortable enough to broach a topic that had been on my mind for a while. "After my bachelorette, you started talking to me verbally. What changed that night?"

"Besides the fact that you tried to kiss me?" Vuk's cool drawl brought a flush of heat to my neck and chest.

"Besides that," I said.

I didn't care how Vuk expressed himself as long as he was comfortable. Verbal or ASL, what mattered most was how he felt. However, he'd only used ASL with me until I tried to kiss him. I thought that was a one-off due to his shock, but we'd been having verbal conversations almost exclusively for weeks.

He didn't even talk this much with Jordan, and Jordan had known him before the fire.

"It felt right," Vuk said simply. "You're the only person I talk to this much besides Willow."

Something green hissed through my veins. "Who's Willow?" The name sounded familiar. I pictured some leggy, faceless beauty and frowned.

"My former assistant."

"Hmm. How old is she?" I asked casually.

Vuk glanced at me, one eyebrow cocked. "She was my mother's best friend, so she's in her fifties. She took me in after my parents died. She retired earlier this year and moved to Oregon. We don't talk as much as we used to given the distance, but I'm planning to visit her in a few months."

"Oh." Now that he mentioned it, I vaguely remembered a frighteningly competent older woman who'd been at his side at my engagement party.

Dark amusement coasted through his gaze. "Jealous, *srce moje*?"

"Yeah, right." Heat singed my cheeks. "Well, I'm honored to be one of the two chosen ones. Really." Sincerity softened the last word.

A quick smile flashed over Vuk's mouth before it disappeared. He returned his attention to the highway. After a short pause, he asked, "Did Jordan tell you why I stopped speaking?"

I shook my head. "He said it wasn't his story to tell."

"He would say that." A twinge of melancholy colored Vuk's voice. Despite our easy conversation, Jordan's current condition never strayed far from our minds.

There was another, longer pause before Vuk spoke again. "The night Lazar died was the night everything changed. One of the Brothers who broke into my house tried to choke me with a rope. When that didn't work, he set the end of the rope on fire. I managed to free myself in time, but the incident left me with this." He gestured at his neck. "The doctors said it was a miracle my vocal cords weren't destroyed. Even so, it took a lot of surgeries and voice therapy before I could talk normally again. For months, it hurt to say a single word, so I didn't. I let people think it was a random break-in gone wrong. Jordan knew I was involved with a shady crowd, but even he didn't know the extent of what happened."

The music segued into a new song. I turned it off, my heart in my throat. I'd guessed something like that had happened to give him his scars, but the truth was even worse than I'd imagined.

"I got used to not speaking," Vuk said without taking his eyes off the road. The hint of emotion behind his words betrayed his stoic expression. "I learned ASL and used that to communicate instead. But even after I healed, I'd feel a phantom pain when I talked. It reminded me too much of that night. Injuries aside, I was also pissed at the world and myself. I only left my house if I had to for work. Being quiet was…easier. Preference became habit, and habit became the new normal."

A deep ache formed behind my ribcage.

He'd been so young then. The guilt and loneliness must've been unbearable. His twin brother had died, and he couldn't tell anyone what really happened. He'd had to live in a world of half-truths.

I didn't have personal experience with hitmen or murder, but I understood what it was like to feel alone in a crowd. To hold secrets close to my chest, and to be surrounded by people yet have no one to confide in.

"Sometimes I have no choice but to speak," Vuk said. "Those situations are rare. I don't like wasting my words on people unless…"

My heart rate picked up. "Unless?"

"Unless they're special to me." His eyes remained on the road, but his voice was softer than I'd ever heard it.

My breath stalled in my lungs. Honeyed warmth curled through me, its silken tendrils soothing the ache that had blossomed earlier.

I couldn't find the right words to describe the sentiment, so I reached for his hand instead. It rested on the center console between us, and his skin was warm and rough when I laced my fingers through his.

Vuk's hand tensed. After a moment, it relaxed again, and he tentatively curled his fingers around mine.

We stayed like that for the rest of the ride.

Vuk

We arrived at the Kidane home close to dinnertime. Rush hour traffic had slowed us down, and I would've been more worried about the Brotherhood somehow ambushing us from a nearby car had I not taken my fully armored Range Rover.

Bulletproof glass, Kevlar-reinforced interior, puncture-proof tires, blast-protected flooring—I didn't leave anything to chance.

Luckily, we made it to Ayana's parents' house without incident. I helped carry her luggage to the door, where they were already waiting with anxious expressions.

My palm tingled from Ayana's touch. My chest was still tight—from recounting the aftermath of the fire or her tender response, I wasn't sure. Either way, the weekend had barely started, and I was already out of my depth.

Abel and Saba Kidane cooed over Shadow and fussed over their daughter, demanding to know whether she'd eaten lunch and if she'd been getting enough sleep. Her father shook my hand in greeting while her mother turned to me.

"Vuk." A warm smile eased the worry lines around her eyes. "Thank you so much for driving Ayana down and for...everything. You didn't have to do any of this."

I'd had two of my men drive them home on Monday. They were still in D.C., keeping an eye on things until I arrived.

Tears glistened in Saba's eyes. Her husband placed a hand on her shoulder, and she wiped them away with an embarrassed expression.

"You'll have to excuse me," she said. "I'm normally not this emotional, but if you hadn't been at the church—if you'd been a few minutes late—we wouldn't...I wouldn't..."

Heat curled around my ears. I glanced at Ayana in a silent plea for help. I appreciated her mother's sentiment, but I hated when people thanked me, and I had no clue what to do with tears.

"Mom, I'm okay," Ayana said gently. "Let's not dwell on the past."

"She's right. No need to torture ourselves with what-ifs," her father declared. "Let's get them inside. It's chilly out."

"You're right." Saba cleared her throat and stepped aside

so her husband and I could move Ayana's overstuffed suitcases into the entryway. If that was only an eighth of Ayana's closet, I couldn't imagine what her full collection looked like. "Vuk, Ayana mentioned you're driving her back as well. Where are you staying for the weekend?"

Ayana said her entire family learned ASL after one of her aunts lost her hearing, so I signed my response.

I booked a hotel nearby.

Saba looked appalled. "A hotel? Nonsense. You saved my daughter's life, and you drove her all this way. You'll stay with us. We have a guest room upstairs, and you'll join us for dinner. Aaron and Liya are coming by as well."

"*Mom.*" Ayana sounded embarrassed. "Vuk probably has dinner plans already. Don't strong-arm him into staying."

"Dinner plans where? What restaurant meal compares to a homemade one?" the elder Kidane countered. "And I say that as a restaurant owner." She faced me again. "You're staying with us. We'll get the guest room ready."

I was the CEO of a multibillion-dollar corporation and a former member of an assassins' organization, but even I knew better than to argue with a determined mother.

Thank you. I'd love to stay.

My previous dinner plans had consisted of takeout and working on my laptop. I wasn't sorry to see them go.

"I'm sorry," Ayana muttered as we walked deeper into the house. "Once my mom sets her mind on something, there's no arguing with her."

Sounds like someone else I know.

My mouth twitched when she elbowed me in the ribs. I liked talking to Ayana when we were alone, but I preferred to use ASL when we were in earshot of other people.

The Kidanes lived in a cozy two-story house on the border

between D.C. and Maryland. It was decorated in the same bright colors as Ayana's apartment, and there were photos of their children and grandchildren everywhere.

Three full shelves in the living room were dedicated to various blue ribbons, academic trophies, and athletic medals. Framed magazine covers decorated the walls—there was Ayana posing for *Vogue*, Ayana smiling in *Harper's Bazaar*, Ayana smoldering for *Cosmopolitan*. Pictures of her sister at her pinning ceremony for nursing graduates lined the mantel next to behind-the-scenes shots of her brother in the kitchen.

It was a house filled with love. I hadn't experienced that in years, but I was glad Ayana had such a strong support system at home. Whatever bullshit happened in New York, at least her family had her back.

Saba gave me a full tour while Ayana unpacked and Abel prepared dinner. It ended at the guest room.

"Dinner will be ready in an hour or so," she said. "The bathroom is across the hall. Fresh towels are in the closet next to it." The sound of the doorbell interrupted her. "That must be Liya or Aaron. Excuse me."

I thanked her again. She left, and I tossed my duffel bag on the chair in the corner. The room was small but well-appointed. A navy comforter covered the bed; a hand-knotted rug adorned the floor. There was an armchair in the corner with an intricately woven cotton blanket draped over it. It wasn't as luxurious as the penthouse suite I'd booked at the Ritz, but this was the house where Ayana had grown up. That was better than any five-star amenity.

I unpacked, showered, and changed. I texted my team to let them know I was staying with the Kidanes while Shadow stole into my room and sniffed through my duffel like I was hiding tuna from him in there.

Get out.

He ignored my silent missive, slinked across the room, and parked himself right in the middle of my bed.

Fucker.

I swallowed my grumble and went downstairs. Laughter drifted over from the kitchen, and the entire house smelled like mouthwatering spices and simmering meat.

I made a mental note to figure out food and litter for Shadow.

"Perfect timing," Saba said when I entered the dining room. "Dinner is just about ready."

How can I help?

I couldn't cook for shit, but I could set the table.

"Absolutely not." Her tone was firm. "You're a guest. Sit. We'll bring the food out."

Two children—one boy, one girl—raced past her, shrieking. They couldn't be older than five or six. Liya came up behind them with a frown.

"What did I say about running in the house?" she called out. "Put your toys away and remember to wash your hands before dinner!"

Their only response was an indulgent "Yes, Mom" followed by more laughter and a high-pitched "Kitty!"

Shadow must've wandered downstairs. That cat went anywhere and everywhere.

Liya shook her head. "Hi, Vuk," she said on her way back to the kitchen. "Good to see you again."

I nodded in greeting. She'd escaped the church attack unscathed. I didn't know how she felt on the inside, but outwardly, she'd reacted the calmest to last week's events. According to Ayana, Liya was an ER nurse, so she was used to seeing messed-up stuff.

"I should've warned you. It's a bit of a zoo on Friday nights." Ayana's voice sounded behind me.

I turned, my muscles loosening at the sight of her. She'd also changed into a more comfortable outfit. The red sweater and jeans complemented her dark brown skin perfectly.

I don't mind.

"I thought you hated people?" She arched a teasing brow.

I shrugged. *Some people. Not all.*

Her smile dazzled, and I grew warm all over.

Dinner started soon after. There were ten of us in total—me, Ayana, her parents, her siblings and their spouses, plus Liya's two children. Shadow ignored the bowl Saba set out for him and sat at the kids' feet, basking in their attention instead.

As promised, the food was delicious. There was a tomato salad with onions, jalapeños, and a light lemony dressing; fried fish; spicy beef stew, and bread. Ayana's mother had been right. Nothing beat a home-cooked meal.

"So, Vuk," Aaron said halfway through dinner. "What is it that you do again?"

I run an alcohol company.

He whistled. "It must do pretty well. Your car is sick."

Either he was the world's best actor, or he really didn't know who I was. It wasn't that far-fetched. Few people outside New York and the business world paid close attention to CEOs.

It does okay.

"He's being modest," Ayana interjected. She sat next to me, so close I caught a whiff of her perfume every time she moved. "His company is the largest in its industry. He started it when he was twenty-three and built it from there." A note of pride rang through her voice.

The tips of my ears grew warm again.

I wasn't used to people praising me without angling for something in return. It was...unsettling, but not unpleasant.

Everyone at the table looked at me, even the children.

"Damn," Aaron said. Liya glared at him, and he winced. "Don't say that word," he told the kids before facing me again. "Any chance I can take a look at your car after dinner?"

Be my guest.

"Don't let him behind the wheel though," Abel said. "I remember when he drove my car straight over a curb two days after getting his license."

"Dad." Aaron crossed his arms while the rest of the table laughed. "When are you going to let that go?"

"When I grow old, and my memory fails me."

More laughter and lighthearted ribbing. Aaron rolled his eyes, but a smile lurked at the corners of his mouth.

"My brother had to do all the household chores for *months* after as punishment," Ayana whispered to me. "Liya and I were secretly hoping he'd nick the car again so we wouldn't have to do any more dishes before college."

I smirked at the image of her and her sister conspiring against their older sibling.

Dinner continued in the same vein, with Ayana's family teasing each other and asking me genuine questions about my life and work. Nobody brought up the ruined wedding or its aftermath.

We'd spent the past week dwelling on it, and I suspected everyone needed a mental health break. No one wanted to ruin the relaxed atmosphere with a heavy topic.

No one stared at my scars or asked me about them either, not even the children. By the time we finished the main course, I'd relaxed enough to lower my guard a bit.

"So. Did Ayana tell you about our game night?" her father asked over coffee and tiramisu.

I shook my head.

"It slipped my mind," Ayana admitted. "We have a board or card game night the last Friday of every month. It's been a family tradition since I was a kid. Obviously, I haven't been able to participate since I moved, but it's a lot of fun. Don't feel like you need to join though," she added hastily. "You can if you want, but it's been a long day. I totally understand if you'd rather get some rest instead."

The tiniest bit of amusement rose at her flustered ramble. *I'd love to join.*

She gave me a small smile, which I almost returned until I caught her mother staring at us with a speculative gleam in her eyes.

I flattened my mouth into a straight line and finished my water.

A lively debate ensued over which game to play.

"I vote for Monopoly," Ayana said.

"Boring. We always play Monopoly," Aaron said. "How about Exploding Kittens?"

Shadow's ears pricked up. He raised his head and pinned Ayana's brother with a death glare. His tail swished against the floor.

"Maybe not." Aaron moved his foot a little farther from the plotting cat.

"If only we had bingo cards," Ayana said mischievously. "Vuk is the bingo king."

I knocked a warning knee against hers under the table and earned myself a giggle. The sweet, silvery sound reverberated through me.

In the end, we settled on Pictionary. Ayana and I ended up on the same team as her mother, her brother, and her nephew. After an hour and a half of heated competition, the other team squeaked out a narrow win.

Normally, I'd take the loss as further evidence I should avoid team activities. I could only rely on myself to win.

But I liked the Kidanes, and I'd enjoyed watching Ayana celebrate each point with a little dance so much that losing didn't seem like that big a deal.

"Thanks for indulging them," she said after her siblings left and her parents turned in for the night. We lingered in the living room, the lamps casting a warm amber glow over the scene. "They're super into game night."

"It was more fun than reviewing security briefs," I said.

"But not better than bingo."

"What is your obsession with bingo?"

"Um, I'm not the obsessed one." Ayana huffed. "You're the one who plays at senior centers."

"And you're the one who keeps bringing it up."

"Only because you refuse to confirm or deny whether you were joking about playing."

"If I was, you'd feel pretty silly for ragging on me about it, wouldn't you?"

"You—" She pressed her lips together. Their tiny quiver detracted from her stern expression, but her tone was lofty when she said, "You know what, it's too late for me to argue with you about this. Good night."

My own lips curved. "Good night, Ayana."

The set of her mouth softened. It was so late that no sounds disturbed the night, but I could see her pulse fluttering at the base of her throat.

She pushed a braid behind her ear. Opened her mouth. Closed it.

The next beat of silence lasted just long enough for me to picture pulling her close and slanting my mouth over hers. I was full from dinner, but I could drink in the sweetness of her kiss forever and never be sated.

It was a fucked-up thought, considering she was still engaged to Jordan, and he was still in the hospital. But my desires were dark and selfish, and I never claimed otherwise.

Her lips parted like she could hear my obsessive thoughts. For a split second, I thought she would kiss me first.

Then she blinked and gave a small shake of her head. "I'll see you in the morning," she said, a little too huskily.

She disappeared up the stairs. I waited until she turned the corner before I released a long, slow breath.

I glanced around the living room. Shadow was curled up asleep on the couch. The Pictionary box remained on the table, its scattered pieces waiting to be collected come morning.

Tonight had been my first taste of normal since my brother died. The Kidanes weren't my family, but they reminded me of what I missed most: warmth. Belonging. The simple pleasure of life.

I took in the quiet scene for one more moment before I turned off the light and went upstairs.

CHAPTER 33

Ayana

MY MOTHER WAS RIGHT. A WEEKEND AT HOME, surrounded by family, was just what the doctor ordered.

The next morning, after my first restful night's sleep in a week, I joined Aaron and my parents at their restaurant while Vuk met up with his security team for a debrief.

I used to help out in the kitchen after school, and I quickly settled back into the comforting rhythm of putting in orders and packing to go bags. The mundane tasks were so far removed from the fashion world and threat of assassins that they were almost therapeutic.

"I told you, you don't need to do this," my mother said. "You should be relaxing. Go to a spa. Go shopping. Have fun."

I shook my head. "I can do that in New York. I'd rather be here." I placed two sets of utensils in a brown paper bag. "I've missed this place."

"If she wants to work, let her work," Aaron said as he passed by with a bowl of stew. "We could use the help, and she's been lazing around in the big city for too long. It's time she remembers what *real* labor looks like."

He laughed when I swatted his arm.

Our mother shook her head. She was smiling, but an inkling of worry darkened her eyes when she looked at me.

My family had avoided talking about the wedding or Jordan so far. I assumed they were worried I'd slide off the deep end or something if they brought those topics up. They didn't know about my arrangement with Jordan, so in their eyes, I was a devastated fiancée who was putting on a brave face for the world.

I mean, I *was* devastated and putting on a brave face—but not as much as I would be if I were in love with him. In fact, there'd been moments yesterday when he'd slipped my mind entirely, like when I was teasing Vuk about bingo and we said goodnight. If I'd stayed a second longer, I might've kissed him.

Just one more brick to add to my house of guilt.

Fortunately, the restaurant was so busy, I didn't have time to dwell on it. It wasn't fancy, but it'd garnered a cult following over the years. Every celebrity who visited D.C. usually dropped by for a meal.

Autographed photos of high-profile guests covered the dining room's Wall of Fame. They featured everyone from movie star Nate Reynolds to British soccer phenom Asher Donovan to Queen Bridget of Eldorra, who'd been a regular here during her student days at Thayer University.

"So," my mother said during our lunch break, which we took at a table set against the Wall. "What's going on with you and Vuk?"

I almost choked on my water. I should've guessed she was just waiting for the right moment to pounce.

"I don't know what you mean." I schooled my face into a neutral expression.

"Ayana, you may be an adult now, but you're still my daughter. I know you better than anyone." Her tone gentled. "We don't have to talk about this now if you don't want to. It's been a heavy week. But I saw the way you looked at him last night. You seemed…happy. I haven't seen you laugh like that in a long time."

I stared at my vegetable bowl. The bricks kept piling up in my stomach. "I shouldn't be happy. Jordan is in the hospital."

My engagement ring glinted on my finger. I didn't know how to navigate the post-wedding world. Should I act more like a fiancée or a concerned friend? If Jordan stayed in a coma indefinitely, should I tell people about our arrangement, or should I return the ring and let them think I was a cold-hearted bitch for ditching my fiancé when things got tough?

"Joy doesn't require the absence of grief," my mother said. "We have the capacity to hold both at the same time. That's part of the human experience." She paused and waited for a server to pass. The dining room was so loud, no one paid us any mind except for a group of teenage girls who seemed to recognize me. They kept looking over and trying to take discreet photos on their phones.

"I don't want you to take what I'm about to ask in the wrong way," my mother said after the server was gone. "I'm your mother, and I'll never judge you. So tell me the truth. Is there a part of you, however small, that's…relieved the wedding didn't go through?"

The floor opened beneath my feet. I plummeted, my stomach free-falling with nauseating speed. I opened my mouth, but no words came out.

Was I that transparent? I'd been home for less than a day, and my mother had already clocked the real reason behind my guilt. She was right; I *was* relieved I hadn't had to marry Jordan.

Logic and loyalty had refused to let me call off the wedding on my own, but if the universe intervened, that was a sign, wasn't it? I would've never wanted the wedding to end the way it had, but now that it was done—or at least postponed—I felt more at ease.

The ball wasn't in my court anymore. All I had to do was wait.

"Would I be a terrible person if I said yes?" I asked in a small voice.

"No." My mother squeezed my hand, her voice unexpectedly fierce. "We can't control our feelings. Whether it's envy, bitterness, or, yes, relief, we've all felt things we were ashamed to feel. But it's our actions that matter most. You weren't the one who instigated the shootout or put Jordan in a coma. You mourned what happened as much as anyone else. So give yourself grace for the part of you that's human. You are *allowed to feel* however you feel."

I swallowed the emotion burning in my throat. "How did you know?"

"I'm your mother. It's my job to know." Her eyes crinkled with a sad smile. "You never seemed *quite* as excited as brides usually are in the lead-up to the wedding. When you asked me how I knew your father was the one, it clicked. I saw your face before you walked down the aisle, Ayaniye. That wasn't the face of a woman in love."

"No." My voice grew smaller. "It wasn't."

"Were you ever in love with him?"

I gave a slow shake of my head.

"Then why marry him?" A crease formed between my mother's brows.

"It's complicated."

For the umpteenth time, I debated telling her about my arrangement with Jordan. Given what happened, he probably wouldn't be upset about me breaking our "tell no one" rule if and when he woke up.

Even so, I couldn't place that burden on her. If I said it was to help a friend, she'd say no true friend would put me in such an uncomfortable position. If I said it was for money, she'd ask what I needed the money for. I already made a comfortable living as a model, and shopping habits aside, I wasn't that materialistic.

But if I told her I wanted to leave Beaumont, that'd lead to more questions until she eventually found out how much they mistreated me. I'd successfully pretended I was living the glam life in New York because on the surface, I was, and I didn't see my family in person often enough for them to notice the cracks. If she discovered how unhappy I was, that would crush her. She worried enough about me living in the city on my own.

Most of all, I didn't want my family to know I'd rushed into the Beaumont contract for them. They'd never forgive themselves.

"More complicated than your relationship with Vuk?" my mother asked shrewdly, bringing my attention back to the present.

I let out a rueful laugh. "I don't know. They're pretty close on the complication meter." I shredded my injera into little doughy strips. I loved my father's cooking, but I wasn't hungry anymore. "If you suspected I didn't love Jordan, why didn't you say anything?"

She was quiet for several beats. "I should've," she finally said. "But I think I didn't want it to be true. On paper, Jordan is a *good* match for you. He's kind, successful, and wealthy. You were already friends, and he could give you a good life. He's every mother's dream son-in-law, and I desperately wanted to believe you were happy with him. I told myself I was overthinking things. That was my fault."

"It wasn't," I said. "Even if you'd said something, I probably would've gone ahead with the wedding. Like I said, my reasons for marrying him are…"

"Complicated?"

I nodded.

"Are you in trouble?"

"No," I hedged. "Not really." If I stayed with Beaumont, I wouldn't be in trouble, per se. Not the way she meant it.

"Will you tell me what those complications are?"

"I can't, but I have everything under control." Sort of. Not really. But she didn't need to know that. "Let's talk about something else, okay?"

"Alright, alright." My mother tsked. "I can tell when I've reached my limits. But if you *do* find yourself in trouble, you must tell me. We're your family. That's what we're here for."

"I know, Mom. I will."

If I weren't grappling with last week's traumatic events, she never would've let me off the hook so easily. Once my mother sniffed out problems in her children's lives, she was like a dog with a bone.

Unfortunately, she segued straight from Jordan into another uncomfortable topic. "Back to Vuk. That man jumped in front of a bullet for you," she said a little too casually. "It was quite a save."

"Hmm." I chewed a mouthful of vegetables so I wouldn't have to reply.

"I googled him," she said. "He has a very impressive background. It seems like he's single too."

My cheeks flamed. I swallowed and said, "Mother, please." I pointed to the diamond still on my finger. "Love or not, I'm still engaged. Remember?"

"I didn't say you weren't." My mother was the picture of innocence. "All I'm saying is, when Jordan wakes up—and he *will* wake up; I feel it in my gut—you can sort out your...complications. After that, who knows?" She took a demure sip of water. "The world is your oyster."

I winced. "Please don't ever say something like that again. It's super cringe and cliché."

She laughed. "As a parent, you get used to being cringe." Her eyes slid past me. They lit with a twinkle of mischief. "Speak of the devil. Here he comes."

I whirled around. Vuk entered, his imposing presence sucking up all the oxygen in the air. Sean followed on his heels, dressed in a similar T-shirt and jeans as his boss. Several diners stopped eating to stare at them as they made their way over to me.

I'd invited Vuk to check out the restaurant, but I hadn't expected him to come. And that skip in my heart when I saw him? Totally normal.

His mouth tipped up when our eyes met.

My lips curved in return before I remembered my mother was watching. I turned back to find a knowing smile on her face.

I pointedly ignored it and took another bite of salad, my heart still fluttering.

Totally. Normal.

Vuk

I hadn't planned on visiting the Kidanes' restaurant. Ayana needed time alone with her family, and I had a thousand and one things on my plate.

But my morning debrief with my team had passed quickly, and I couldn't focus on the mundane shit I had to do for Markovic Holdings. It wasn't anything important—just some paperwork that needed to be signed. I also called the hospital for my daily check in on Jordan. He was still unconscious, but his vitals had improved and his injuries were healing well. That was something, at least.

Sean, who'd driven down that morning to personally update me on the manhunt, convinced me to "take a break." I suspected he just wanted to try out the Kidanes' food, but I let him talk me into the detour anyway.

He'd worked his ass off on the Brotherhood stuff the past

month. We hadn't found the escaped Brother yet, but we were making steady progress. He deserved a break too.

While he introduced himself to Saba and claimed an empty table nearby, I took a seat across from Ayana. The lunch rush appeared to be dying down, so I felt a little less bad about intruding on their work time.

"Where's Shadow?" she asked.

At the hotel, pestering my team.

She smiled. She was dressed in a plain black T-shirt and jeans that coincidentally matched my outfit for the day, and she'd wrapped a blue-and-gold silk headscarf around her braids.

"You hungry? Let me get you something to eat." She rose halfway out of her seat before her mother pushed her back down with a firm hand on her shoulder.

"Nonsense," Saba said. "I'll get it. You keep Vuk company. Sean will eat with me."

She winked at Ayana before she disappeared into the kitchen. She returned minutes later with plates of injera bread and beef tibs. She moved her own food to Sean's table, leaving me alone with her daughter.

"So...this is the family restaurant," Ayana said. She swept her arm around the dining room. "What do you think?"

It's perfect. I meant it. I didn't need fancy china or white-glove service to appreciate good food. The restaurant's unassuming decor and earthy homeyness matched its owners perfectly.

Ayana's smile widened. "Thanks. We're really proud of it. It's a small space, but my parents prefer it that way. They've had plenty of opportunities to expand. Someone from the Laurent Restaurant Group even offered to franchise it last year, but they declined. They said more locations wouldn't matter if the soul isn't there."

Smart choice. Franchises can be hit or miss. The Laurents were royalty in the culinary scene, but more money didn't mean better quality. If the Kidanes sold to them, they would become just another notch in the Laurents' already-crowded belt. *You said your brother will take over after your parents retire?*

Ayana nodded. "That was the plan from day one. Liya and I have no interest in running a restaurant, and Aaron is the best cook out of all of us, anyway. We helped out in the back when we were teens, but that was it."

Are you happy with modeling? She'd stumbled into the career after being scouted, and she'd achieved extraordinary success since then, but that didn't mean anything. Plenty of successful people were miserable in their jobs.

The sparkle in her eyes dimmed a bit. "To an extent," she said cautiously, lowering her voice. "Like I said, I love fashion. I grew up idolizing Iman and Beverly Johnson and Pat Cleveland. If all I had to do was show up in front of a camera or the runway, then yes, I'd be very happy. But I wasn't prepared for the business side of things or the types of people who try to take advantage of you in the industry. It's jarring."

You mean people like agents?

I still didn't have anything concrete on Emmanuelle. It frustrated the hell out of me. At this point, I almost hoped my original instincts were wrong. If they weren't, that meant I was slipping—or she was that good.

Ayana's face clouded. "Yes." She tilted her head, her eyes narrowing. "Hank has been strangely accommodating since he surprised me at my place. I know I took most of the month off for the wedding, but still. Normally, he'd be breathing down my neck about me 'slacking off on the job.' You wouldn't happen to know anything about that, would you?"

I shrugged and washed down my food with water. *Maybe he figured out being an asshole will come back to bite him in the ass. You could've sued him for his surveillance stunt.*

My team had debugged all her devices, which meant he had to know she was onto him. Ayana didn't want to confront him about it until she was ready to leave the agency for good, but the more I thought about it, the more I wish I'd stabbed him all the way with the knife.

"Yeah." Ayana grimaced. "I can't believe he…" She trailed off and glanced back over her shoulder. Her mother was engaged in lively conversation with Sean, but she clearly didn't want the other woman to know about her troubles with Beaumont. "Anyway, I'm glad that all got sorted out."

For now. Once I wasn't busy with the Brotherhood, I was going to pay Hank Carson another visit. His actions couldn't go unpunished.

However, I kept that plan to myself. No need to involve Ayana in the less savory parts of my business.

"What are your plans for the rest of the day?" she asked.

"The team and I were going to take him out for drinks," Sean said before I could answer. Saba had left to take care of a customer, and he'd obviously been eavesdropping. "He turned the big three-five today."

I could've strangled him.

Ayana's eyes rounded. "It's your birthday?"

Technically. I followed up my reluctant response with a glare at Sean, who was too busy scarfing down a second helping of beef to notice.

He was the consummate professional at work, but put him in front of a plate of food and he lost all decorum.

"Oh my God!" Ayana slapped her hands on the table. "We have to celebrate."

I fought a grimace. *I'm not big on celebrations.* I hated birthdays. They reminded me that Lazar was no longer around to celebrate with me.

The gradual dimming of Ayana's smile told me she'd just come to the same conclusion.

"Celebrate what?" Her mother returned in time to hear the tail end of our conversation.

"It's Vuk's birthday." Ayana tucked a braid behind her ear. "But he wants to keep it low-key, so we—"

"Nonsense." Saba planted her hands on her hips. "Birthdays are special. You shouldn't be spending them inside. In fact…" She pursed her lips. "Ayana, why don't you show Vuk around the city? I'm sure he'd love to see more of D.C."

That's not—

"Mom, he doesn't want—"

"It's settled, then," Saba said, ignoring our protests. "But first, I have something for you."

Thank you, but it's really not—

She vanished into the kitchen.

Necessary, I finished.

Ayana groaned. "I'm so, so sorry," she said. "There's no stopping my mom once she sets her mind to something. If you don't want to celebrate, we totally don't have to. We can just walk around and pretend it's *not* your birthday. I don't want you to feel…bad." She stumbled over the last word.

A sliver of amusement loosened the fist around my heart. I tried to forget about my birthday whenever possible, but she was so endearingly worried, it made the occasion feel more bearable.

Don't worry about it. I'll be okay.

The kitchen doors swung open. Saba came out carrying more plates and a bottle of golden orange liquid.

"Baklava and our signature honey wine," she announced. "I won't subject you to a *happy birthday* song, but I insist you try our dessert before you leave."

I didn't argue.

Sean and I cleared out our plates in record time. When he tried to join me and Ayana as we got up to leave, Saba stopped him with a pointed arch of her brow.

"Never mind. I'll stay and, uh, review our security plans," he said. "I'll let you know if anything pressing comes up."

I smirked at the sight of my former Special Ops security chief being brought to heel by a woman half his size and twice his age.

Tell the guys I'll pick up Shadow later. I paused, then added, *Make sure they don't give him any fucking milk. Cats are lactose intolerant.*

This time, Sean was the one who smirked. "Got it." He gave me a two-finger salute. "Have fun, boss."

CHAPTER 34

Ayana

RETURNING TO D.C. WAS LIKE SLIPPING ON A COMFY old pair of pajamas. No matter how long I'd been away, the city was so easy and familiar, I didn't have to think about where I was going or how.

The Brotherhood, Jordan, Beaumont...they all melted beneath the sunshine and maple-scented breeze.

Vuk let me set the itinerary. Since he'd visited the city before, I skipped the touristy spots and took him to my favorite hidden gems.

Our first stop was Apollo Hill Books, a charming bookstore stuffed to the brim with new and vintage titles alike. We didn't buy anything, but I loved browsing the aisles and breathing in the crisp scent of books. Afterward, I took him to Crumble and Bake (not a hidden gem, but they had the best cupcakes) and a cool interactive spy museum.

"You would make a good spy," I said after we left the museum. "You have that whole dark, brooding thing going on."

Vuk's mouth twitched. "You think spies are dark and brooding?"

"Aren't they?"

"Usually no. The point is to blend in. They're usually unassuming, like him…" He nodded at a plain-faced man wearing a blue sweater and glasses. "Or her." The "her" in question was an elderly woman with curly gray hair and a pink crocheted cardigan.

"I guess," I said doubtfully. "But I like the dark and brooding thing better."

We meandered through the cobblestone streets of Georgetown. The late-afternoon sun slanted against the quaint storefronts, and my usual brisk Manhattan pace had slowed to an easy saunter. Vuk walked quietly beside me, his expression pensive.

I'd avoided mentioning his birthday since we left the restaurant. It hadn't occurred to me that it might be a sensitive topic until he flinched at my celebration suggestion. Lazar was his twin, which meant they'd shared the same birthday. The reminder of his brother's absence must be incredibly painful, which was why I was determined to fill today with happy memories instead.

"Oh, I *love* this place," I said when we passed a familiar white storefront. Dozens of beautiful glass bottles gleamed in the window display. "It's one of my favorite shops."

"Let's go in."

"But it's a perfumery." I could shop for perfumes and shoes all day, but this was Vuk's day, not mine.

"I'm aware." He placed a hand on the small of my back and guided me firmly into the shop.

His palm burned through my wool coat. When he removed his hand, the imprint of his touch lingered, and little sparks of electricity buzzed through my veins.

I was so flustered I almost didn't hear the sales associate greet us.

"Welcome. Can I help you find anything?" Her tone was polite, but I caught her side-eyeing Vuk's scars. Her lip curled into a small grimace.

Blood rushed to my face. I glared at her, and she quickly averted her gaze.

"No, thank you," I said curtly. "We're just looking."

Vuk raised his brows when I grabbed his arm and dragged him to the back, far away from the rude associate.

Didn't she know it was impolite to stare? If she *had* to stare, then she should've at least had the decency not to make a disgusted face.

I'm used to it. Vuk examined a shelf of essential oils, his face impassive.

"What?" I tried to breathe through my silent fuming. In the grand scheme of things, a stranger's judgment fell way down on the priority list of problems, but for some reason, her reaction to Vuk rankled me.

The staring. I'm used to it. He picked up a sandalwood oil, read the label, and put it back.

The fact that he'd noticed the associate's behavior infuriated me all over again. "That doesn't mean it's right. It's—" I stopped myself. Did I really want to spend this time complaining about someone who didn't matter? It would only make Vuk feel bad.

I forced another breath and changed the topic. "Anyway, I used to come here all the time," I said. That associate had definitely *not* been an employee back then. "Everyone knew me by name, and they were nice enough to let me sample a ton of fragrances even though I didn't have the money to buy most of them." I smiled at the memory. "I told you I majored in chemistry too, right? Well, I was fascinated by the science of scents. How humans process smell, the interplay of different notes, the way the same perfume can smell different on different people depending on their individual body chemistry. If I hadn't become a model, I might've gone into perfumery, but now, I settle for collecting fragrances instead."

Vuk had stopped browsing the shelves and was listening

intently. *I think I saw the collection when I was at your apartment. It was in the living room.*

"Those were the empty bottles. I keep the pretty ones on display," I admitted. "The real collection is in my closet. My sister makes fun of me for it. She says there's no way I can use them all in my lifetime, and that's probably true. But I don't collect them to wear. I collect them to...remember, I guess. Some people buy postcards or T-shirts as souvenirs; I buy perfumes. Lemon verbena for the Amalfi Coast, green tea and rose for Japan, lavender for Provence. A different scent for a different memory. That's why I only buy them for places I love."

I ran my fingers along the smooth wood shelves. The older I got, the more susceptible I became to nostalgia. One whiff of a familiar scent, and I was instantly transported back to a certain place and time.

I'd tried to explain it to Liya once, but she didn't really get it. She was a visual person, so photos and videos meant more to her than the rich aroma of our mother's coffee or the spices and herbs peppering our father's kitchen.

"Did you know smell is more closely tied to memory than any other sense because of the brain's anatomy?" I rarely got a chance to talk about this particular hobby, and the words spilled out without thought. "Touch, taste, sight, hearing—those all pass through the thalamus first before they're relayed to the relevant parts of the brain. But scents bypass the thalamus and go straight to the olfactory bulb, which is directly connected to the amygdala and hippocampus. It's why..." I trailed off, my face heating. It was his birthday, and here I was, going on and on about *my* hobby. "Sorry. I'm nerding out."

It's okay. I like hearing you nerd out. A smile ghosted Vuk's mouth. *What was the last perfume you bought?*

He seemed genuinely interested.

I cast my mind back to my last purchase. "Snow and pine,"

I said. "Finland. I did a photo shoot for Stella Alonso's winter collection there last year. I didn't have enough free time to stay and explore after, so I didn't get to see the Northern Lights, but the mountains were so beautiful I had to get a souvenir."

We dallied at the shop for a while longer until our stomachs rumbled. We were about to leave when an idea sparked in my head.

"Can you wait for me outside?" I asked. "It's gotten so crowded in here, and I have to use the restroom."

I pretended to head to the restroom until Vuk was gone. Once I was sure he couldn't see me, I doubled back and grabbed what I was looking for. I made sure to bypass the rude sales associate from earlier when I paid.

I walked out a few minutes later, shopping bag in hand. Vuk looked up from his phone, his eyebrows arching again when I thrust the bag at him.

"This is for you," I chirped. "It's a thank-you present. For saving my life."

He stared at the bag like it was a viper waiting to strike. *You didn't have to get me anything.*

"I wanted to. It's nothing fancy, but the scent reminded me of you."

He still didn't take the bag.

A twinge of doubt set in. Had I made a mistake? Should I have left it alone and not gotten him anything at all? I'd framed it as a thank-you gift instead of a birthday gift, but maybe presents in general were a trigger for him too.

"If you don't like cologne, I can return it," I said uncertainly. "Don't feel like you have to—"

No. I want it. Vuk swiftly removed the bag from my grasp.

I bit back a smile. "Open it."

He did, his expression wary. The sleek black bottle with silver engraving matched his majority-black wardrobe perfectly. It'd caught my eye when we were browsing, and the scent notes were perfect for him too.

I pointed them out on the packaging. "Soft woods for the mountains, which you said you liked. A hint of rum because you run a liquor and spirits company. Vanilla, for warmth and comfort." *Which is what you mean to me.* I was too shy to say the last part out loud, so I hoped he picked up on my underlying meaning.

Vuk turned the bottle over his hand. He didn't say anything.

"I wasn't sure what types of scents you liked, so I guessed." I shifted my weight from foot to foot. The sun was unbearably warm against my skin. "You totally don't have to wear it. I just thought it would be nice for special occasions. I don't think you smell bad or anything."

For the love of God, stop talking. When I was nervous, I rambled, and I was rambling a lot.

Vuk's small smile left my insecurities in the dust. I'd forgotten how beautiful he was when he let his guard down. His whole face softened, making him look years younger than he was.

Noted. He placed the cologne back in the bag.

"Thank you, *srce*," he said. "I love it."

I smiled back, my giddiness taking flight. "You're welcome."

We resumed our walk. We were both hungry, and Vuk didn't want anything fancy, so we stopped at the nearest fast casual restaurant for pizza (him) and a veggie burger (me).

"What does *srce* or *srce moje* mean?" I asked toward the end of our meal. "You keep calling me that."

Vuk finished his slice without answering.

"Hello?" I waved my hand in front of his face. "Earth to Vuk."

He swallowed and wiped his mouth. ***It's better if you don't know.***

"Is it something embarrassing? You're not calling me, like, little rat or something, are you?"

Vuk smirked but didn't confirm or deny.

"I could just look it up," I said. "Once I figure out how to spell it."

So look it up.

I let out a frustrated growl. "For someone who can be so thoughtful, you can also be a real asshole."

He shrugged. *I never said I was a good person.*

"I didn't say you weren't a good person. I said you're an asshole." My words lacked any real bite, but I thought I'd give him a taste of his own medicine. "*Ahya.*"

His eyes narrowed. *What does that mean?*

I took a demure sip of water and smiled. "Look it up."

That was when it happened. He laughed. *Again.*

It was only my second time ever hearing him laugh—fully and unabashedly, with his eyes crinkling at the corners and his teeth flashing white against his face.

The sight and sound were so captivating, my ability to breathe ceased to exist.

Unfortunately, his laughter also drew the attention of a nearby table of college students, who ruined the moment with their stage whispers.

"Is that who I think it is? Oh my God, it *is*. That's Ayana Kidane."

"The model? Oh my God, you're right. What's she doing with *him*?"

"Maybe he's really rich. Pretty girls date ugly guys all the time for money."

"Hmm, I wouldn't say he's ugly. It's just those scars…"

"Yeah, they're pretty gross."

"But isn't she engaged to that Jordan Ford guy? I remember reading an article about that in *Mode de Vie*."

"Hello? Where have you been? Some gang shot up their wedding and—"

I'd had enough. I hadn't confronted the sales associate earlier, but this group's audacity was more than I could take.

I spun toward them and experienced a vicious stab of satisfaction when they fell silent, their faces red.

Yeah, I could hear you, assholes.

"The next time you talk shit about people, have the courtesy not to do it within earshot," I snapped. I didn't care if I ended up on some celebrity gossip forum for being "rude" or "a bitch." They deserved it. "His scars are a sign of character, but your actions are a sign that you lack basic common decency. If I were you, I'd have a harder time looking in the mirror than anyone else here. It's not him who's 'ugly'—it's you."

I shoved my chair back and stood. I belatedly remembered I hadn't finished my burger, but it was too late.

"Come on," I told a bemused-looking Vuk. "Let's go. I've lost my appetite."

He didn't argue.

The table of stunned collegiates stared at us, their mouths hanging open in four identical Os.

On our way out, I "accidentally" knocked one of their sodas into their lap. It was petty, but I'd be damned if it didn't feel good.

CHAPTER 35

Ayana

VUK WAS LAUGHING AGAIN. THIS TIME, I WAS LESS charmed than the first two instances.

"It's not funny." I crossed my arms, still heated from our dinner encounter. "They were so rude. Who does that? It's not like our tables were that far from each other. They *had* to know we would hear them."

"They're college students. They're lost in their own world." Vuk was surprisingly calm. "I told you, I'm used to the stares and whispers. Their insults don't come close to the worst thing people have said about me."

"Which is what?" I was too curious not to ask.

He shook his head, the remnants of a smile playing on his lips.

We were walking home from the restaurant since Vuk had left his car at my parents' house that morning. We'd been Ubering all day. It was a thirty-five-minute trek, but the weather was beautiful, and I needed to cool off.

"I didn't think you had an insulting bone in your body," he said. "You're full of surprises, Ayana Kidane."

"Only when I'm fired up. It doesn't happen often. I'm as

non-confrontational as they come," I admitted. But I had my limits.

We made a right onto my parents' street. A strange tug of sadness pulled at my gut. I wasn't ready for the night to be over yet. It was the first time I'd felt carefree in ages. Even though we were staying in the same house, and Vuk would be there in the morning, it wouldn't be the same. Tonight held a special kind of magic.

"That's weird," I said when we arrived at the house. The windows were dark, and it was eerily quiet. "They should be home by now."

An irrational streak of fear raced through me. Had the Brotherhood followed us to D.C.? Were my parents locked up in a dingy basement while Vuk and I had been eating and shopping our way through the city? Or was it something more mundane but equally insidious, like a car accident or mugging gone wrong?

Vuk tensed beside me. I wasn't the only one whose thoughts were running wild.

I was about to call my mom and check in on her when she texted me with eerily perfect timing. I swear, she had a magical sixth sense.

MOM

I forgot to tell you earlier. Your uncle got us last-minute tickets to the Kennedy Center tonight. Don't wait up for us.

MOM

I hope you had a good time with Vuk. Remember to lock up before you go to bed.

I breathed a sigh of relief. *Thank God.*

"Everything okay?" Vuk asked.

"Yep." I fished my keys out of my bag and opened the door. "My parents are at the Kennedy Center. They won't be home until late."

Vuk relaxed. He didn't say anything else as we stepped into the entryway and removed our shoes.

I wasn't used to the house being this quiet. My parents didn't go out often, and the rooms were usually filled with the rumble of my father's voice or the background noise of the television. The stillness was disconcerting.

Vuk removed his jacket and hung it on the brass tree by the door. I did the same. Our arms grazed, and a tiny electric thrill sparked at the base of my spine.

If he felt the same, I couldn't tell. The silence seemed to swallow our earlier camaraderie, twisting it into something heavier. More significant.

"Well, this is it," I said. "I hope you had a good time today and that it wasn't too, um, terrible. I know my mom kind of forced you to spend the day with me."

I winced. *Great job, Ayana. You really have a way with words.*

"It wasn't...terrible." Vuk placed an amused emphasis on the end of his sentence. Fire blazed across my face. "It was nice to have a distraction. You're better company than Sean and my men."

"I'm flattered." We walked toward the stairs, our steps falling easily into sync. A teasing edge slid into my voice. "Is that what I am? A distraction?"

"Among other things."

I stumbled over the edge of a rug. I caught myself before Vuk noticed—hopefully—but the fire spread from my cheeks down to my neck and chest. A thousand velvety flutters disrupted my heartbeat.

Among other things.

Our day together had been perfectly platonic. We hadn't

kissed, held hands, or exchanged sexual innuendos; we'd simply been two friends enjoying each other's company.

But now that we were alone, away from the bustle of the city and the company of crowds, a latent spark of awareness flared to life.

The wooden steps creaked beneath our combined weight. The staircase was so narrow we couldn't move without bumping into each other.

My heart slowed beneath the weight of our proximity. He towered to my left; the wall hemmed me in on the right. Yet his body seemed even more solid and immovable than stone.

Vuk's hand brushed mine when we reached the second-floor landing. The hairs on my nape prickled. It was an innocent touch, but the promise of something more danced in the air.

We stopped outside my bedroom. It was so quiet I could count the thuds of every heartbeat.

"Thanks for letting me drag you around the city today," I said. "Happy birthday and, um, good night."

The *birthday* part slipped out before I could stop it. *Shit*. I winced again, hoping I hadn't ruined the night with my slip-up.

Fortunately, Vuk didn't appear upset by the reminder. He dipped his chin, his face inscrutable in the darkness. "Good night."

A beat passed. He didn't move, and my pulse skyrocketed. This was it. He was going to—

Walk away and disappear into the guest room.

My chest deflated when the door shut behind him. I followed suit, kicking my door closed and flopping onto my bed with a sigh.

"I'm such an idiot," I muttered.

I turned my head to check the time. It was only a quarter to nine. In hindsight, I could've suggested we stay downstairs and play a game or something, but it was too late for that. If I sought him out now, it would be too obvious.

Like buying him freaking cologne isn't obvious. That was the type of gift you received from a girlfriend, not a friend—a friend who happened to possess intimate knowledge of the way his kisses tasted and his touches felt.

A full-body flush consumed me. I'd done a good job of pushing our hotel room tryst to the back of my mind given everything that'd happened since then, but the memory resurfaced with sudden, staggering intensity.

The hand curled around my throat. The weight of his body pinning mine against the glass. The—

A knock startled me out of my filthy reminiscence.

I bolted upright, my heart rate accelerating again. Heaviness gathered between my thighs.

I stared at the door, frozen, until another knock brought my feet to the floor and across the room.

Obviously, it was Vuk. It couldn't be anyone else, but that didn't stop a sliver of pleasant surprise from piercing my chest when I flung open the door and found him standing a foot away.

Like me, he hadn't changed out of the outfit he'd worn all day. A black T-shirt stretched across the width of his shoulders; black pants hinted at the solid muscles underneath. Piercing blue eyes glided over my face with a tingle of heat.

"There's three hours left of my birthday." Soft, so soft the words were a shadow of a whisper.

I merely nodded in return.

I couldn't speak. I could barely breathe. The air was so thick I was afraid any errant noise on my part would send it crumbling to pieces around us.

"I was about to go to sleep when I realized I forgot something." His tone was impassive, but his eyes—his eyes burned so hot and *deep*, I felt it in my bones.

My toes curled. The heaviness between my thighs throbbed, and I scrounged up a reply from somewhere in my throat. "What's that?"

My breathless response earned me a dark smile. I was acutely aware of how flimsy the physical barrier between us was—nothing more than a few inches of space and even fewer heartbeats, closable with one decisive step.

"This." That rough, single word was my only warning before he gripped the back of my neck and smashed that barrier to smithereens.

His lips claimed mine, and my mind blanked, the commanding pressure of his kiss dragging me under to a place where oxygen didn't exist. My blood turned to molten lava, but my nipples pebbled like I'd plunged headfirst into a lake of ice. The contrast of hot and cold set off a series of mini fireworks across my skin.

Vuk's tongue thrust into my mouth, parting my lips and coaxing a moan from my throat. I gasped, and the world snapped back into hyperfocus.

I was no longer underwater; I was in my childhood bedroom, clinging desperately to Vuk for strength while he systematically and expertly obliterated my defenses. He kissed me like a man starved, like he could drink me in for eternity and not be sated. I thrilled at his possessive hold on my neck, and if he weren't holding me up, I would've melted to the floor in a puddle of need.

"More," I breathed. I tugged at the bottom of his shirt, and he obliged. He pulled back to yank the shirt over his head with one hand before he brought me close again.

He tasted like ice and sin—a combination so intoxicating, I barely noticed when or how the rest of our clothes ended up on the floor.

His skin was hot against mine. I pressed tight against him, loving the way my soft skin molded to the hard planes of his body. Somewhere in the recesses of my mind, I possessed a hazy recollection of reasons why we shouldn't be doing this. I was sure they were good reasons. Great ones, even. But they didn't hold a candle to the desperate, clawing *need* inside me.

What happened in the hotel room had been a tease, a taste of what could happen if we let ourselves cross the line we'd so carefully toed.

Well, that line had been annihilated. Demolished by every secret shared, every look exchanged, and every touch stolen, not only today but every other day for the past two months.

I didn't care if this was wrong. How could something be wrong when it felt so right? And when I was with Vuk, it *always* felt right, like a sweater that fit perfectly on the first try or a puzzle piece that slotted into place with little effort.

This was where I wanted to be. He was who I wanted to be with.

The air was heavy with our pants and sighs. My head spun, but when he reached for the light switch, I had enough presence of mind to stop him.

We hadn't come this far to sneak around in the dark.

"No." My voice was so husky it barely sounded like mine. "I want to see you."

Vuk stilled. After a long moment, he dropped his hand so it rested by his side, and the urgency of our kiss dissolved into something more languid.

His throat flexed when I dropped my eyes from his face to his torso, soaking him in.

Appreciation hummed in my veins. I didn't care what strangers or society dictated. Vuk Markovic was *beautiful*.

I didn't mean the type of beautiful you saw on social media or movie screens—men with gym-chiseled abs and spray-tanned skin, their features nipped and tucked and sculpted into such uniform perfection that they all started to look the same.

His was a raw, primal beauty, free of pretension and vanity. At six foot five, he eclipsed me by a solid seven inches. Thick bands of muscle corded his arms and legs; a light dusting of hair trailed over his chest and past his navel. An old bullet wound and knife scar pitted the skin on his lower left abdomen. They weren't as stark as the scars on his neck and face, but they were vicious all the same.

His body was a portrait of the life he'd lived—hard, sometimes brutal, but so strong and imposing there was no questioning his raw power. Every scar and every burn was a testament to the trials he'd survived so he could be *here*, living and breathing and looking like a god of war before he rode off to battle.

Pure magnificence.

I met his gaze again. It was weighted with the tiniest hint of trepidation, like he was waiting for me to run and scream or recoil with disgust.

That trepidation melted into a flare of surprise when I slowly sank to my knees before him.

His lips parted, but I shook my head before he could say a word.

"It's your birthday," I said in a low voice. He'd mentioned the occasion when he showed up at my door, so I assumed it was okay to bring it up now. "Just relax..." My hands glided up his thighs. "And let me take care of this for you."

On the ground, with my knees digging into the carpet and his heated stare burning into my skin, I was eye level with the evidence of his arousal.

It was as gorgeous and intimidating as the rest of him. Long, thick, and so hard I could see the veins pulsing along its straining length. Pre-cum dripped freely from its swollen head.

My mouth watered. When I looked up at him again, his face had darkened with pure lust.

Without taking my eyes off his, I leaned forward and dragged my tongue across his slit. His nostrils flared, but he didn't make a sound as I licked up every drop of pre-cum before engulfing the tip in my mouth. I grasped the base of his cock with both hands and swirled my tongue around the head, moaning at the salty, masculine taste of him.

I sucked and licked my way down his length, getting him all nice and wet before I took as much of him down my throat as possible. I choked, my eyes welling with tears, but I didn't let that deter me as I quickly settled into a rhythm. I squeezed and twisted my hands in opposite directions, enjoying the way his cock pulsed while my head bobbed up and down with greedy slurps.

My gurgles and moans mixed with the sloppy choking sounds of his cock hitting the back of my throat. I was on fire, drowning in the taste and heat of him. My clit pulsed with such urgency I almost reached down to touch myself, but I didn't want to let go of him. Not when a strong hand came down on the back of my head and Vuk finally uttered a deep, guttural groan.

"*Fuck*," he hissed, and every nerve ending sparked like live wires in the rain.

I loved his taste, loved the way his girth stretched my throat and filled it so completely I could hardly breathe, but hearing someone so controlled lose it because of *me* sent my hormones into overdrive.

Triumph and lust pooled between my legs.

I sucked harder, my cheeks hollowing. Instead of easing the ache with my fingers, I spread my legs and leaned forward, trying to grind against the floor. The need for friction burned through me like a lit match.

"Look at you, trying to come." Vuk grabbed my head and pushed himself deeper down my throat. "You like choking on my cock that much? Hmm?"

My whimpered reply turned into a muffled squeal when he pulled out only to slam in again. He started slow at first, but soon he was face fucking me hard enough to make tears spill down my cheeks.

I couldn't take it anymore. I dropped one hand and frantically rubbed my clit while the other pinched and rolled my nipple between my fingers. I was so turned on I could feel my arousal slicking my thighs, and every thrust sent a new zap of pleasure through my body.

"God, look at you." Vuk groaned. "You take my cock so well, don't you? I can see it bulging your throat. So *fucking* needy."

Yes, yes, *yes*.

His filthy words poured straight through me like bourbon. I moaned again, my fingers working faster. My clit was so swollen and sensitive, I might die if I didn't come soon, but I didn't want to finish before he did.

He was close. His thrusts were becoming erratic, and I redoubled my efforts until he cursed loudly and thick, hot jets of cum flooded my mouth.

My orgasm hit me at the exact same time. I cried out, my body shuddering. Cum leaked from the corners of my mouth, and I choked a bit before I swallowed the rest of it eagerly. The mixture of his taste and the white-hot waves of sensation almost pushed me toward a second breaking point.

I pulled back to catch my breath. I must have looked like a mess, covered in sweat and drool and cum, but I didn't care. I reached for him again to clean him up. I only made it halfway before he lifted me to my feet and tossed me on the bed as easily as someone tossing a rag doll.

"You've had your fun." The dark glint in his eyes made my thighs clench. "It's my turn."

I opened my mouth, but whatever I'd planned to say died the instant his lips latched onto my still-tender clit.

"Fuck!" I was the one cursing this time. Cursing and screaming and sobbing as he ate me out with the same single-minded determination that had earned him his title as one of the most powerful men in the world.

He was ruthless, his mouth and fingers and tongue working in tandem to bring me to the edge of delirium and back again. Over and over, harder and harder, until he pulled me apart and put me together so many times I lost count.

Somewhere between one sea of pleasure and the next, I heard the rip of foil. A second later, the head of his cock nudged my entrance.

I was humiliatingly drenched, but he was so big, and it'd been so long, that his initial push made me tense with discomfort.

"Breathe, *srce*," Vuk murmured, his voice surprisingly gentle considering the brutal orgasms he'd wrung out of me. "You can take it."

He was only halfway in. I felt like I'd already reached my limits, but I gritted my teeth and tried to relax as he sank deeper inside me.

"That's it." He groaned. "Your cunt is so fucking wet. It's *begging* me to stretch it."

And he did. Inch by inch, his girth threatened to split me in half as it spread me wide and penetrated me deep. I didn't think it was possible, but eventually, my pussy swallowed the full length of his cock.

A shudder rippled from my head to my toes. I was stuffed so full I couldn't think straight, and the noises that came out of my mouth sounded barely human when Vuk started moving.

Long, easy strokes morphed into faster, harder ones, and pleasure eventually eclipsed pain as he set a punishing rhythm. He fucked me to the hilt, his balls slapping against my skin. Sweat and sex soaked the air. I cried and bucked, too delirious to do anything except give in to my body's basest needs.

My nails clawed at him hard enough to draw blood. Instead of deterring him, it only made him more feral. His teeth closed around my nipple and tugged. Hard.

The sharp sting wrenched another cry from my throat. The helpless sound was still hanging in the air when he flipped me over and pounded me harder. The headboard banged against the wall, and my body trembled and shook with each forceful thrust.

My arms were weak, and my elbows finally bucked when he hit a spot that made me see stars. I collapsed face first onto the bed. Vuk took advantage of the new angle and lifted my hips higher. The pillow muffled my screams when he drove in so deep it felt like he would come out of my throat.

The sex was raw and animalistic and blissfully, mind-bendingly wonderful.

The past few years, I'd spent more nights with my vibrator than a man. I hadn't minded. My previous sexual encounters were satisfactory but nothing to write home about, and at least I didn't have to make small talk with my vibrator before it got me off.

But this? This unraveled parts of me I hadn't known existed.

"Oh, God. *Yes*!" I moaned when Vuk reached around to play with my clit.

"You didn't think you could take it earlier, but look at you now," he mocked. "Such a greedy little cunt. Stuffed tight with every inch of my cock and it still wants more."

His filthy words washed through me, burrowing past any pretenses of decency to awaken the darkest parts of me. He was wrong; I wasn't greedy. I was insatiable.

"Yes, please," I whimpered. "I want more. I need—*oh God*—I need you to fuck me—"

My pleas devolved into a strangled cry when he gave me exactly what I was asking for and more. If he'd been rough before, he was merciless now, and it took only a minute before my orgasm hit with blinding intensity.

One second, I was on my hands and knees, taking him deep. The next, I was splintering into a thousand jagged pieces that floated and whirled through the air like flakes of snow in a winter storm. My pussy clenched and spasmed. I screamed over and over as each wave of pleasure hit me, but he kept going.

Vuk turned me over and crushed his mouth to mine. The possessive urgency of his kiss set me off again, and I came around his cock for the umpteenth time that night. Third? Fourth? Fifth? I'd lost count. They all rolled into each other, undulating as one giant sea of sensation.

Eventually—right when I was at the brink of begging him to stop, to have mercy and let me breathe because if I came one more time I might actually die—he came with a guttural cry.

He collapsed next to me, his breaths ragged. My mind was still short-circuiting from the rush of endorphins, and I was too dazed to do anything except lie there when he got up a minute later.

I heard the door open and close. Vuk returned soon after with a glass of water. *Huh.* So he'd put on his pants before going downstairs. How'd I miss that?

"How do you have enough energy left to walk?" I mumbled. "That's not normal."

I was exhausted, and I wasn't even the one who'd put in the most work.

His low chuckle made me smile. He sat beside me and brought the glass to my lips. "Open."

I obeyed. He tilted the glass so cool, crisp water flowed down my throat. Once he was satisfied that I'd been properly hydrated, he picked me up without asking and carried me to the bathroom.

I was hoping we could check shower sex off my bucket list. To my deep disappointment, Vuk shook his head and tucked my hair into a shower cap before he gave us both a quick but thorough rinse instead.

"Next time, *srce*, or you won't be able to walk in the morning."

"I'm pretty sure it's too late for that," I sulked.

He laughed again, the sound filled with amusement and pure male satisfaction.

He dried us off and carried me back to bed. I mustered enough energy to tie my hair down with a silk scarf before I slid beneath the covers and sighed, lazy with contentment. There were a hundred things we needed to talk about after tonight, but they could wait until tomorrow. I was too happy and sated to allow anything to burst my current bubble.

Vuk slid into bed next to me. He pulled me close to him, and I allowed myself one indulgent stretch before I curled into his embrace.

Maybe it was a good thing he'd said no to more sex. The shower had sapped me of my remaining energy, and I couldn't...I couldn't...

My eyes drifted closed. The last thing I felt was a soft kiss on the top of my head before sleep claimed me, and everything went dark.

CHAPTER 36

Vuk

I STAYED AWAKE LONG AFTER AYANA FELL ASLEEP.

I held her close, savoring her warmth and breathing in the scent of her. It wasn't perfume or shampoo; it was something uniquely *her*, and it was enthralling. If I could go back to the perfumery and bottle it up, I would.

I closed my eyes, basking in the moment. Our problems lurked outside the door, waiting to pounce, but I'd dreamed of this for too fucking long to let them ruin my glimmer of happiness.

It wasn't just the sex; it was everything. The walk through the city, the conversations, seeing her relaxed and in her element as she rambled adorably about perfume. The cologne she bought me wasn't the most expensive or most extravagant gift I'd ever received, but it was the most thoughtful.

Vanilla, for warmth and comfort.

I'd picked up on her meaning without her having to say it. The idea of anyone finding me warm and comforting was laughable, but she made me feel like I could be the person she thought I was. With her, I came the closest to feeling normal.

His scars are a sign of character, but your actions are a sign that you lack any common decency.

Pressure expanded in my chest. An image of Ayana's fierce scowl played behind my eyes. I was used to people's stares and whispers. I didn't need her to stand up for me, but the fact that she had made my insides twist.

Somehow, she'd turned my most dreaded day of the year into a memory I would cherish.

I turned my head and took in her slumbering form. Her brow was smoothed, and the tiniest hint of a smile pulled at her mouth. A spill of moonlight softened her features, gilding her cheekbones and making her skin glow. She looked so beautiful and peaceful, I wanted to etch this version of her into my brain forever.

I skimmed my fingertips over the curve of her shoulder. The digital numbers on her alarm clock flipped to one a.m. sharp. I should really leave.

Reluctance tugged at my gut.

I wished I could stay in her room all night, but I didn't want her parents to catch me sneaking out in the morning. That would lead to too many questions, especially for Ayana. Plus, I needed to grab some shuteye. It'd been a long day.

I allowed myself another minute by her side before I pressed a soft kiss to her forehead and gently extricated myself from her arms. I slipped out of bed and returned to the guest room, where I finally crashed.

I managed to get a solid three hours of sleep until an insistent ringing startled me awake.

I groaned, but I sat up and swiped my phone off the night-stand with minimal dawdling.

The sight of Sean's name instantly wiped away my grogginess. He wouldn't call this late unless it was an emergency. Hell, he wouldn't call, period; we usually communicated by text.

I picked up. He didn't wait for a greeting before he said, "We got him."

My heartbeats crashed together. I sat up straight, my mouth filled with the sudden taste of adrenaline.

"We followed the tip from your friend," Sean said, anticipating my question. Roman had messaged me yesterday morning, telling me to double down on the Philly search. He hadn't promised anything, but he'd pointed out a few neighborhoods that Shepherd's faction was particularly fond of. "Bruce and Mav nabbed him in his hotel. No witnesses. They're bringing him back to the warehouse, but it's only a matter of time before the Brotherhood realizes he's been compromised. Once they do, they'll flip everything he had his hands in. Any intel we squeeze out of him will be useless."

My mind whirred. He was right. Our captive was only useful if Shepherd didn't know we had him.

"What's our window?" I asked. I'd spoken verbally to Sean before, though those occasions were rare.

A primitive, feral part of me didn't give a shit if the intel was worthless. I simply wanted to make the bastard pay.

Blood for blood. That was my moral code. It'd served me well all those years ago, when my revenge campaign against the Brotherhood left such a mark, they'd steered clear of me for over a decade.

But I wasn't a lone operator hellbent on vengeance anymore. I had a business. I had employees. Most importantly, I had Ayana. I couldn't afford any rash decisions that'd jeopardize her safety.

"Forty-eight hours max," Sean said. "Twenty-four, to be on the safe side. I assume he has a check-in protocol. For most organizations, those are usually every twelve to twenty-four hours. When someone misses more than two check-ins, they go on high alert."

I cursed. That meant I needed to return to New York ASAP. Ayana was staying in D.C. through Monday, and I couldn't tell her the real reason I was leaving early. She knew about the

Brotherhood, but I'd planned on keeping the dirtier side of my business far, far away from her.

"We'll leave immediately," I decided. "Have the current team stay here to keep an eye on Ayana and drive her and Shadow back to the city on Monday. I'll pick you up in thirty."

"Understood."

I hung up, changed, and repacked my duffel. It didn't take long; I hadn't brought much with me.

I wrote two notes, one for Ayana and one for her parents. The house was dead silent, and my careful footsteps barely made any noise against the thick hallway carpet.

I stopped outside Ayana's door. Our blissful, lust-soaked session earlier already seemed like a lifetime ago.

Fuck. I was glad my team caught the Brother, but I wished I could have *one* full night to myself before reality intruded. The afterglow from my time with Ayana had barely faded before Sean called.

My fingers curled around the edge of her note. After a heartbeat of hesitation, I slid the folded paper under her door instead of waking her up.

If I saw her, I'd be too tempted to stay. I'd talk myself into thinking an extra hour or two with her in my arms wouldn't make a difference when they could very well be the difference between taking down Shepherd's faction and not.

I cast one last glance at her door before I went downstairs. I placed the note for her parents on the coffee table. It thanked them for their hospitality and apologized for leaving without saying goodbye in person. Hopefully, they wouldn't be too upset about me slipping out in the middle of the night.

When I shut their front door behind me and locked it with the spare key they kept under the flowerpot—*note to self: remind Ayana to tell her parents to keep that key in a safer, less obvious place*—not a single person in the house stirred.

———

After I picked up Sean at the hotel, we made it to Brooklyn in record time. The lack of late-night/early-morning traffic shaved almost an hour off our drive.

By the time we arrived at the warehouse, a pale orange tinge was barely creeping into the sky, and I'd pushed all thoughts of the Kidanes aside in favor of work. I'd worry about Ayana later; right now, I needed to focus.

Sean and I bypassed the storage room and headed for the basement, where the two men we'd sent to Philly were waiting for us beside a custom steel door. The storage room worked for the likes of Wentworth, but members of the Brotherhood were another matter.

Mav and Bruce greeted us with deferential nods.

"We knocked him out with a tranquilizer," Mav said. "He's just coming around now."

"Good." Sean glanced at me.

I'll handle this myself. This was my fight, not theirs.

No one argued.

I opened the door and walked in. The basement was even more bare bones than the rest of the warehouse. Stone walls, stone floor, minimal furnishings save for a table along the wall, a tarp on the floor, and a chair in the middle.

The man currently tied to the chair had a bag over his head. His chest rose and fell with steady breaths. Alive and whole, just like I wanted.

My steps were silent in the soundproofed room. His breathing pattern didn't change, though a hint of tension crept into his neck and shoulders. His alias was Dexter—a cheeky play on the TV serial killer of the same name.

I removed the bag from his head.

Brown eyes stared up at me from behind wire-framed

spectacles. Salt-and-pepper hair and the leather elbow patches on his tweed jacket formed the image of a mild-mannered professor.

Like I said, if you hate someone enough to kill them, have the balls to do it up close and personal.

"Dex." My smile lacked any trace of warmth. "Good to see you again."

CHAPTER 37

Ayana

I AWOKE TO AN EMPTY BED.

The sheets were rumpled from last night's activities, but Vuk's side of the mattress was cold. He must've slipped out after I'd fallen asleep.

It was a smart move. My parents were early risers, and they were right down the hall. I wouldn't want them to see him coming out of my childhood bedroom, reeking of sex.

I swung my legs over the side of the bed and stretched. The delicious soreness between my legs eased my irrational sting of disappointment at finding Vuk gone.

Last night had been incredible. There was no other word to describe it. The whole *day* had been incredible—minus our run-in with the jerks at dinner—but seeing Vuk fully lower his guard and lose control wasn't something I'd ever forget.

My toes curled at the memory of his cock filling my throat and his guttural cry when he came. Our bodies had fit so perfectly, so naturally, that I couldn't imagine doing the things we did with anyone else.

He'd ruined me for other men.

I am so fucked. Literally and figuratively. Even so, my cheeks ached with a smile.

It was Sunday, so my parents were home. The restaurant didn't open until noon today, and I could hear the sizzle of turkey bacon and smell the coffee from downstairs.

I threw on cashmere sweats and was about to join them in the kitchen when a folded white square by the door caught my eye. My name was scrawled across the top in Vuk's familiar handwriting.

I picked up the note and opened it.

THERE'S A WORK EMERGENCY IN NEW YORK. I HAD TO LEAVE IMMEDIATELY, BUT I DIDN'T WANT TO WAKE YOU. MY TEAM WILL DRIVE YOU BACK ON MONDAY. UNTIL THEN, ENJOY YOUR TIME WITH YOUR FAMILY. I'LL SEE YOU BACK IN THE CITY. P.S. I'LL MAKE IT UP TO YOU. I PROMISE.

I stared at the bold, blocky letters, my emotions swinging from pleasure to dismay and back again.

It was the weekend. What kind of emergency required the CEO to race back immediately? Then again, Markovic Holdings was a multibillion-dollar company with thousands of employees. A number of things could go wrong at any time. I didn't think Vuk was lying; logically, it made sense.

Emotionally, however, I experienced another pang of disappointment. Insecurity scuttled through my veins. We'd slept together for the first time only for him to leave in the middle of the night. I didn't even get a chance to say goodbye.

Yeah, that didn't feel great. At all.

But…he'd left a note. A lengthy one, by his standards. Its contents might sound stiff to someone who didn't know him, but if he wasn't sincere, he would've disappeared with three words maximum—or, most likely, no note at all.

I'll make it up to you. I promise.

A fresh wave of warmth washed away my insecurities. I trusted Vuk. He wasn't the type to play games. If he said he had an emergency, he had an emergency.

I tucked the note into my handbag. After I washed up and made myself presentable, I wandered downstairs. My father was reading the Sunday paper while my mother puttered around the kitchen.

"Good morning," I said. "How was the Kennedy Center?"

"Oh, it was wonderful. We should really go there more often." My mother's eyes twinkled. "How was your day with Vuk?"

"Good." I fought a blush and avoided her eyes. I swear she could read my mind sometimes.

"Here. Sit." She gestured at the table. "We saved some breakfast for you. You don't want it to get cold."

She didn't have to ask twice. I was famished.

I sat across from my father and dug into a plate of eggs, hold the bacon. Despite the fashion industry's exacting and oftentimes toxic weight standards, I refused to starve myself. I worked out five times a week and usually ate a healthy, well-balanced diet, but after yesterday's binge with Vuk, I had to be careful about not overdoing my indulgences.

I asked my parents more questions about the Kennedy Center before my father set his paper aside.

He regarded me with an assessing look. "So," he said. "Vuk's gone."

"He had to go back to New York. Work emergency." I took a sip of my mother's signature shai blend (not to be mistaken with chai). It was like comfort in a mug. "I missed this." I sighed. "Thanks, Mom."

She smiled. "I'll pack a few extra bags for you to bring home."

"Yes, I know," my father said, bringing the conversation back to Vuk's absence. "He left us a note."

My heart skipped with pleasant surprise. Of course he had. He was so damn thoughtful when he wanted to be.

"A very nice one," my mother interjected.

"Yes, yes." My father waved his hand in the air. "He's an interesting man. He seems very...dedicated to you, Ayana."

I shifted beneath his shrewd gaze. "Well, he's a good person."

"I'm sure he is. If it weren't for him, who knows what might've happened at the church?"

"Abel, please. She just woke up." My mother cut him off with a warning stare. "Let's save the interrogation for later."

"Or never," I added. "We could save the interrogation for never."

"I'm not interrogating her. I've asked one rhetorical question," my father grumbled, but his face softened. "I just want what's best for you, Ayaniye. I'm not saying Vuk is a bad person or has malicious intentions. I like him, but he's not the only man in the picture." He cast a pointed glance at my left hand—my *bare* left hand. My breath hitched. *Shit.* I'd forgotten to put my ring back on before I came downstairs. "He saved your life. Strong...feelings are normal. But feelings are malleable; integrity isn't. We do not entangle ourselves in new ties before the old ones are broken."

The eggs churned in my stomach. I pushed my plate aside, my throat too thick to swallow any more food.

Last night with Vuk had seemed natural. Inevitable. It hadn't been a lurid one-night stand we jumped into because we couldn't control our hormones; it'd been the culmination of months of increasing intimacy, both physical and emotional.

But in the light of day, with my father's words echoing in my ears and my ring sitting upstairs, all I felt was shame.

"That's enough." My mother shushed him and switched to

Amharic. "Listen to you. Our daughter is finally home after a terrible tragedy, and you ambush her at breakfast. What kind of example are *you* setting?"

"It's not an ambush, Saba. It's a gentle reminder."

"We have different definitions of 'gentle.'"

While my parents argued, I downed the rest of my tea, hoping it would soothe my nausea.

It didn't.

My father meant well. He wasn't aware of my situation with Jordan, and he (hopefully) had no idea about the recent, er, carnal shift in my relationship with Vuk. My mother was my comfort; my father was my guiding star. He was the one I counted on to steer me in the right direction when I was lost, and he was right.

If I wanted to pursue things with Vuk, I needed to officially end things with Jordan first. But how could I do that when—

My phone rang.

In hindsight, the timing was so fortuitous it couldn't have been anything other than a sign from the universe—a giant, blinking neon sign with all the bells and whistles.

But in that moment, the shock of the call was so great I couldn't do anything except sit and listen.

After I received the short update, I hung up.

My parents had stopped bickering and were staring at me with varying shades of curiosity and concern.

"Who was it? What happened?" my mother asked.

"It's Jordan." My pulse raced. "He's awake."

Everything happened quickly after that.

I insisted on returning to New York immediately to visit Jordan, and I rebuffed my parents' attempts to join me. I appreciated the sentiment, but I didn't know what condition he was in.

Too many people could be overwhelming. Plus, my parents were getting older; long drives were hard on their bodies.

After a whirlwind packing session and promises to update them as soon as I could, I met Vuk's security team outside. Jake and Peter were the ones who'd escorted my parents home after the church attack.

Vuk had left their numbers on the back of my note. When I called and explained the situation, they'd agreed to drive me to the hospital as long as Sean cleared it.

The security chief must've said yes, because less than an hour after I received the call from Jordan's mother, we were speeding back to Manhattan in an armored black Suburban. Shadow was curled up next to me in the backseat, sleeping.

My thoughts were a mess the entire time. Relief camped out next to anxiety, turning my emotions into a battlefield.

I was thrilled Jordan was awake, but last night remained fresh on my mind. Could people see it? When I walked into the hospital, would his family spot the stain of unfaithfulness marring my skin? How could I tell him I wanted to break our arrangement when he'd just escaped the jaws of death? If I did tell him, should I do it immediately or wait?

And Vuk—did he know his friend was conscious? Was he already at Jordan's side, waiting for me to arrive, or was his emergency so dire he was completely off the grid?

A geyser of hypothetical questions spewed forth and clogged my mind. I wanted to text Vuk, but my overloaded brain couldn't handle any more information.

A dull ache formed at the base of my skull. I closed my eyes and forced myself to take several deep breaths.

One. Two. Three.

By the time we entered New York City limits, I'd successfully calmed my thrashing heart. There was no point working myself into a frenzy over hypotheticals. What mattered most right now was Jordan. Everything else could wait.

We arrived at the hospital. Peter accompanied me to Jordan's room while Jake parked the car. He stopped a respectful distance away while I greeted Jordan's father. He stood in the hall, his shirt wrinkled and his hair mussed. Exhaustion lined his face.

"How's he doing?" I asked quietly. I'd only met Richard Ford a few times in group settings. He divorced Jordan's mother years ago, and he spent most of his time golfing in Scotland or sailing around the Caribbean.

"As well as can be expected," Richard said. "Margot's with him right now." Margot was Jordan's mother.

"What about Orla?" I was surprised his grandmother wasn't here too. She'd basically raised Jordan while his mother was busy with her string of lovers and his father was off traveling the world.

"She was here when he woke up, but she can't exert herself too much for too long." Richard pushed his hands into his pockets. "She fell on Friday. We moved her into a suite down the hall."

My guilt compounded. I wasn't close with Jordan's family, but he cared about them, and I cared about *him*. Rationally, I couldn't have known about his grandmother's fall unless the Fords told me, which they hadn't. Still, I couldn't help agonizing over the fact I'd been playing Pictionary on Friday while Orla was in the hospital.

The door opened, and Margot stepped out.

We exchanged a cool greeting before I walked around her and entered Jordan's room.

His mother was the Ford who liked me the least. I wasn't sure why, but the feeling was mutual. She was about as warm and fuzzy as a frozen porcupine.

Despite their dysfunction, the Fords had splurged on the best recovery suite for their son. With its state-of-the-art TV and chic decor, it looked more like a hotel than a hospital room, but I ignored the fancy trappings and focused on the man smiling at me. It was a weak smile, but it was a smile nonetheless.

"Hey, MOTY," Jordan said.

"I've told you that is not a cute nickname." I approached his bedside, my heart clenching at how pale and thin he looked. But he was alive, conscious, and coherent. That was what mattered. "If you think it is, I'm calling the doctor to check your brain."

His laugh rattled in his lungs. He coughed before saying, "My mother told me you were in D.C. You didn't have to rush back up the same day. I'm alive, not dying."

"Of course I did." I squeezed his hand. "What did you think I was going to do instead? Laze around my parents' house while you watched daytime TV in the hospital by yourself?"

"I hate daytime TV."

"Exactly."

Jordan laughed again, but the sound soon faded beneath his sober expression. "How've you been?"

"I've been okay." *Better than I should've been considering you were in here.* I swallowed past a knot in my throat. "I should ask you that question. When I saw you at the church after—after what happened, I thought…"

"I know. Me too," he said quietly. He released my hand and swiped his over his face. "What a wild fucking day. I heard it was some sort of gang turf war gone wrong?"

"Something like that."

Jordan had to know about the Brotherhood if he'd lent Vuk the money to pay them off, but I wasn't sure *how* much he knew. It wasn't my secret, so I didn't feel comfortable correcting him. The truth was up to Vuk to disclose or hide.

"Of all the weddings in all the world, it had to be ours," he said humorlessly. "If that isn't a sign from the universe, I don't know what is."

Indeed. I wasn't a very superstitious person, but it was hard not to take your fiancé of convenience nearly dying at the altar personally.

My engagement ring winked beneath the fluorescent lights. I'd remembered to put it on again before I left, and the weight of it felt like a dozen boulders strapped to my finger.

I shouldn't force Jordan into a hard conversation after he just woke up, but it wasn't fair to drag things out when I'd already made up my mind. I'd shoved my pre-wedding feelings aside for the sake of practicality, and look where that got us.

If I'd listened to my heart and called off the ceremony instead of trying to push through it, we wouldn't have been at the church, and Jordan wouldn't have gotten shot.

Concrete sludge poured into my stomach. I forced my mind off my escalating nerves and onto the task at hand. "Actually, since we're on the subject, I have something to tell you."

"Wait. Let me go first. Please." Jordan took a deep breath. "I'd hoped to have this conversation later, when I was out of the hospital and we'd had more time to…process, but we've always been honest with each other, right?"

The sludge solidified into granite. "Right." I managed a feeble smile. *I am so going to hell.*

"So." He coughed again. "We made our pact almost two years ago. At the time, it seemed like the right thing to do. We'd both get what we wanted. Marriage didn't seem so bad when we were already friends, and people would finally stop asking me when I'd settle down. I thought it would be like having a roommate, you know? Totally doable. But the closer we got to the wedding, the more I got…I don't know. Not cold feet. But *doubts*. Small ones. Easy to brush off. Who cared if I had to pretend to be in love for five years? People in our circle do that all the time. Who cared if my family didn't *really* know me? They're not around much anyway. Then something happened before the ceremony that almost made me rethink things, but I didn't. Because of pride, ego, saving face. Whatever." This time, his laugh was laced with bitterness. "I got shot an hour later. Like I said, the universe isn't subtle. I should've listened to my gut in the first place."

His words whirled through my brain. It sounded like…but no, he couldn't…but what if…

"What are you saying?" I held a bracing breath against his reply.

Jordan swallowed. "I'm saying, I want to call off our arrangement."

The breath expelled in one huge rush, leaving me lightheaded.

"I'm sorry for leaving you in the lurch like this." His eyes pled with mine. "I'll still pay you for your time. We never got married, but you spent the past eighteen months pretending to be my fiancée. That's worth something. It won't be five million—I don't have that much liquidity to spare—but it'll be at least one mil. I hope that's—"

"Jordan." I placed a hand on his shoulder, stopping him mid-ramble. My heart pounded so hard I half expected it to burst out of my chest and perform a happy jig right there in the middle of the hospital. "Stop. I'm not mad at you, and you don't owe me anything. In fact, I…well, I was going to tell you that I wanted to end the arrangement too."

His mouth parted. "Seriously?"

I nodded.

"Fuck." He dropped back against his pillow. "I should've let you go first and saved myself that speech. I…" Another cough interrupted him mid-sentence. "I need some water after all that."

A giggle climbed up my throat. I tried to tamp it down, but once it was on the move, there was no stopping it. It spilled out in a burst of laughter, and after a shocked beat, Jordan started laughing too.

I doubled over, tears of mirth blurring my vision. Jordan's shoulders shook so hard his bed squeaked. The room reverberated with the sounds of our relief as the dark cloud over my head finally evaporated.

Other problems like Beaumont and the Brotherhood lurked at the fringes, but I allowed myself to enjoy this moment for now.

When our laughter finally faded, I brought Jordan a bottle of water from the room's mini fridge and tried to sort through our next steps. I wasn't too worried about announcing our "split." The wedding attack gave us a springboard for breaking up, and Sloane and the Fords' PR team could iron out the finer details.

I was more worried about the tangible consequences for Jordan. "What'll happen to your inheritance?" I asked.

Uncertainty swallowed the remainder of his humor. "I don't know, but I almost died, Ayana. That really makes a man reevaluate his priorities. When the bullet hit me—before I lost consciousness—I wasn't thinking about money. I was thinking about the life I'd lived and the regrets I had. I would've died without telling my family the truth. That was my biggest regret of all." Jordan's mouth thinned. "My grandmother's not doing well. I mean, she hasn't been for a while, but hopefully our breakup doesn't send her to an even earlier grave."

I reached down and squeezed his hand again. I wished I could do more to help, but this was Jordan's fight. He had to face it on his own.

"She values honesty, so there's that. But I don't know how she'll react to the...revelation about me or our previous arrangement." He blew out a sigh. "I guess the worst that can happen is she disinherits me, which isn't as bad as dying. Losing the company would hurt more than the money, but at least I wouldn't have to hide who I really am anymore."

"Don't count her out yet. Your grandmother is a reasonable

person. She might surprise you," I said. Orla Ford was a lot of things, but close-minded wasn't one of them.

"Maybe." Jordan fixed me with a shrewd stare. "What about you? What's your reason for wanting to end the arrangement?"

"Um, well..." He wouldn't care that Vuk and I got together, but it seemed tacky to tell him we'd been fooling around while he'd been lying here unconscious.

"It's Vuk, isn't it?"

For someone who'd woken up from a week-long coma just hours ago, he was surprisingly observant.

I supposed he already knew Vuk had feelings for me since Vuk had asked him to call off the wedding, but he didn't know if those feelings were reciprocated—until now.

"Yes," I admitted. "He told me about your argument before the ceremony, and he was in D.C. with me. He left this morning for a work emergency, but we...I mean..."

"It's okay," Jordan said. "You don't have to tell me. I know. I see it written all over your face."

"I'm sorry," I said miserably. "Even if you and I weren't truly dating, it was wrong of us to carry on behind your back. It happened once before the ceremony. In the beginning of October. And also...this weekend. Before we officially ended our arrangement." Flags of shame scorched my cheekbones.

"I don't need to know the details, but we did say affairs were allowed in our marriage as long as they were discreet," Jordan conceded, his tone dry. "What happened between you two was just an iteration of that. I admit, it would've been a little weird for you to get with a close friend—it makes things messier—but I'm not angry at either of you for what you did. I'm more upset that you didn't tell me earlier." He shook his head. "Then again, I kept my doubts to myself too, so I guess we both had our secrets."

"I guess we did." I smiled sadly. We'd wasted so much time

when we should've been honest from the start, but some things were only clear in hindsight. "Hopefully, that's all behind us now."

"Hopefully." Jordan's energy was flagging. His eyes drooped, and his breaths turned shallow. This was a lot to put him through so soon after regaining consciousness, but he waved me off when I tried to get him to lie down again. "About Vuk. He's not perfect, but when he cares about someone—*truly* cares about them—he'll go to the ends of the earth for them. Remember that the next time he pisses you off because that's sure to happen."

Fresh laughter bubbled in my throat. "Oh, I know. Trust me." I glanced at my phone. No new texts or calls yet. "Does he know you're awake?"

"Who knows? My mother said she called him, but it went straight to voicemail. That bastard." Jordan sighed. "I return from the dead and he doesn't even have the courtesy to greet me with a 'welcome back' balloon."

"If it makes you feel better, he's more the type to bring a handle of vodka."

"True." Jordan's eyes fluttered like he was struggling to keep them open.

It was time for me to leave.

"Get some rest. We'll talk later." I slid the diamond off my finger and pressed it gently into his palm. His hand curled around it as I leaned down and kissed his cheek. "It was a pleasure being your fiancée, Jordan Ford."

His smile held all the nostalgia of our long friendship. "Back at you, Ayana Kidane."

His parents were already gone when I exited his room.

I took the elevator to the lobby and walked out into the sunshine, feeling lighter than I had in years.

CHAPTER 38

Vuk

DEXTER, ALSO KNOWN AS BONE MAN. AGE: FORTY-ONE. KILL count: fifty-plus, making him one of the Brotherhood's most prolific killers.

He hadn't changed much over the years. Same eyes, same glasses, same shitty attitude as he smirked at me.

"Markovic." His soft, almost high-pitched voice was deceptively gentle. "Still alive, I see. What a shame."

I ignored the bait and walked over to the table. A range of instruments glinted atop the wooden surface. I selected the pliers—something easy to start us off.

When I turned, Dexter's face was placid, but I caught the split-second flick of his eyes to the table.

He knew exactly what each and every instrument was for. He hadn't earned the nickname Bone Man for nothing.

Most hitmen liked clean kills. He was the one clients called for…messier jobs.

"Attacking during the wedding was a mistake," I said softly. I untied one of his hands from the chair and, without ceremony, ripped his thumbnail off with the pliers.

A lesser man would've screamed; Dexter simply gritted his teeth, his muscles tensing. Blood splashed onto the tarp.

"I thought I made myself clear years ago." I took a second nail and earned a flinch. It was a boring start to our session, but warmups were important. "If you're going to come for me…" I leaned down to look him straight in the eye as I removed the third nail with cruel, agonizing slowness. "Don't fucking miss."

His first scream came at nail number five.

Here was the thing about hitmen: they weren't used to being prey. Sure, some of them came from Special Ops backgrounds, and some were tougher than others, but in the end, everyone broke. It was just a matter of time.

Unfortunately, our time together was limited. I had a handful of hours to get the information I needed out of him, which meant I needed to speed things up. I couldn't toy with him forever.

Luckily, I'd always hated Dexter. I resorted to extreme violence when it was necessary, but he relished brutality for brutality's sake. A little psychopath dressed up as a professor. If he didn't have the Brotherhood to control his urges, he'd be an indiscriminate serial killer.

He wasn't part of the old leadership or the group that broke into my house, which was the only reason he'd survived my purge all those years ago. But he shot Jordan, and he almost hit Ayana. He'd signed his long-overdue death warrant a week ago.

After I rid him of all ten nails, I tossed the pliers aside and got to work. I had plenty of tools at my disposal, and if I was put off by his screams or the amount of blood soaking the tarp, I only had to picture Jordan lying on the ground, his eyes wide open. I heard Ayana's scream and felt her tremble as she went into shock. I tasted the cold, metallic fear that inundated me whenever I thought about how close she'd come to getting a bullet in her heart.

I remembered, and I felt, and I *raged*.

Every ounce of guilt, fury, shame, and helplessness I'd felt over the past week—hell, the past *year*—funneled through my veins and into my bloodthirstiness.

The world didn't exist outside this room. D.C. was a distant memory; Ayana a pinprick of light above the surface, too far for me to reach here in the depths of my depravity.

My veins pulsed. The dormant monster inside me clawed its way out, shredding recollections of smiles and perfumes and late-afternoon walks in the sun.

This was it. Beneath the suits and guise of respectability, this was who I am. I took my pounds of flesh from my enemies, and I didn't feel a speck of remorse about it.

"When's the next hit, Dex?"

We were hours into our session. He was unrecognizable, his face a crimson pulp of bruises and flesh. Several teeth littered the floor next to his nails.

"Fuck you," he slurred.

So there was still a bit of fight left in him.

He'd given up what he knew about the current state of the Brotherhood's finances, safe houses, and internal workings, but he hadn't budged on their immediate future plans—yet.

"Tell me or don't. You'll die either way. But we can make this relatively quick…" I tossed the drill aside and picked up a handsaw. "Or we can do this the hard way."

Dexter's breath bubbled with panic. The handsaw was his favorite toy. He knew exactly how creative its users could get.

He watched me approach, his eyes losing their spark of defiance. He hadn't pledged undying loyalty to the Brotherhood. They were merely an employer, and his refusal to give me what I wanted was rooted in pride and spite, nothing else.

Luckily, pride and spite didn't compare to the merciless teeth of pain.

It took less than fifteen minutes for the saw to achieve its objective.

Dexter gave up Shepherd, and I gave him the (relatively) quick death I'd promised.

I pressed my gun to his head and pulled the trigger. Crimson mist spattered my skin. His body slumped, and it was over.

I stood in the resulting silence, my skin sticky with blood. Carnage and gore piled around me in a scene that would make the strongest stomachs heave, but I felt detached from the whole thing.

This. This was why the Brotherhood had left me alone for all these years. They were professional killers, but when I locked onto a target, I was vicious. Pitiless.

Adrenaline continued to pump, and the stench of death choked my lungs. I should leave and let my men clean this mess up, but I didn't.

My body was here, but my mind was hundreds of miles and years away. Thirteen years ago, to be exact, when I'd systematically hunted and destroyed those responsible for my brother's death.

The arrogance of the Brotherhood's old leadership proved to be their downfall. They didn't think one man could possibly pose a threat, but vengeance had a way of turning ordinary people into monsters. I'd quietly studied their kill methods during my years with them, and when the time came, I adapted them for my own use.

I went into hiding after the fire. I used my knowledge of their tricks and capabilities to evade them while I formulated my plan. Once I was fully healed, I tracked the leaders down over the course of a year. The ones who broke into my house were mere foot soldiers; it was the people at the top who really needed to pay.

I found them in their homes, in their cars, and at the day

jobs they worked to keep up pretenses. When they sent their best after me, I killed them too, and I made sure their deaths were so gruesome it dissuaded others from hunting me.

Eventually, the leadership's ranks dwindled to the point that they offered a truce. They would forget about the ledger, and I would end my revenge campaign. I'd gotten my pound of flesh and more. As long as we stayed out of each other's way, we could coexist in uneasy peace.

I'd agreed. I'd made my point, and decimating the Brotherhood wouldn't bring Lazar back. It was either let them go or spend the rest of my life looking over my shoulder.

Now here we were, back to square one. Them hunting me; me exacting my vengeance. The circle of life and death went on.

Spots flickered in front of my vision. I blinked, and the world slowly came back in bits and pieces.

Dexter. The warehouse. New York.

Clarity set in at the same time my murderous haze dissipated.

Twelve hours ago, I'd held Ayana in my arms. Touched her with the same hands that'd tortured and ended a man's life. Kissed her with the same mouth that'd pressed for *more*—more intel, more screams—while I broke another human into a shell of who they used to be.

What would she say if she knew what I was truly capable of?

The coppery scent of blood thickened. Bile rose in my throat, and I turned abruptly, eager to cast Dexter behind me.

When I exited the basement, Sean was waiting for me. He must've sent Bruce and Mav upstairs to man the exits.

"I assume it went well," he said. He didn't flinch at my splattered clothing. He had his fair share of skeletons in the closet; my actions wouldn't faze him in the slightest.

I gave a terse nod. I shared the info I'd gleaned and tasked Sean with confirming its veracity. There was a slim chance Dexter had fed me bad intel, though most of it matched Roman's. The details that didn't were the ones Roman didn't know.

We had to move fast. According to Dexter, Shepherd's faction was planning another hit before the end of the month. No witnesses or public events this time—it would be targeted directly at me. That was all he knew.

I believed him; Shepherd wouldn't share his entire strategy with underlings. Luckily, Dexter had given me the location of his primary war room and weapons stash. If we preemptively destroyed those or, better yet, killed Shepherd, we could end the Brotherhood's civil war and get them off my fucking ass.

"I'll double-check the intel and have someone recon their war room," Sean said. "But we're already stretched thin, and this is going to take all our resources. Do you want us to pull back on Emmanuelle until we hit Shepherd?"

I'd kept my tail on the Beaumont agency head, but months of reconnaissance had turned up nothing. My gut told me I shouldn't dismiss her—there was something there—but I couldn't make the pieces fit yet. Given the circumstances, I had to prioritize.

I nodded again, giving Sean the go-ahead to consolidate our resources.

I left him, Mav, and Bruce to dispose of Dexter while I cleaned up, changed in the bathroom, and tossed my old clothes into an incinerator. It wasn't much, but at least I didn't look like I'd walked off a horror movie set anymore.

I waited until I was half an hour out from the warehouse before I turned on my phone. Missed calls and text messages flooded my screen.

My heart stopped. At first, I thought something had happened to Ayana, or Jordan had died, but a quick scan of the messages proved otherwise.

A cool shock of air burned my lungs.

He was awake.

He hadn't died because of me.

He was awake.

CHAPTER 39

Vuk

JORDAN WAS ASLEEP WHEN I ARRIVED, SO I WAITED BY his side until his eyes finally cracked open. The nurses had protested before they found out who I was and how much money I donated to the hospital every year. After that, they left me alone.

Fortunately, Jordan woke up not long after, so I wasn't stuck staring at him from an uncomfortable plastic chair all day.

He blinked up at me, his eyes bleary. "Jesus," he said. "Creep much? I know you missed me, but you don't have to watch me sleep like you're Edward fucking Cullen."

I ignored the pop of relief in my chest and snorted. *Talking shit the minute you wake up. Typical.*

"How would you know? You weren't here the minute I woke up," he retorted. "It's been hours. I was beginning to think you'd fucked off and forgotten about me."

Anyone ever tell you you're needy as hell?

"Yeah. You."

We stared at each other for a taut moment before we broke out into grins. Well, he grinned, and I sort of smiled.

I leaned forward and clasped him in a hug—our first in years.

I wasn't a hugger by nature, but fuck, it felt good to see him back in form.

The heart monitor had beeped steadily the entire time I was here, but I hadn't been convinced Jordan wasn't actually dead until he opened his big mouth.

I gave him one last thump on the back before I pulled away. My smile faded. Despite his wisecracks, he was pale and gaunt after a week in the hospital—a week he'd spent here because of me.

I'd gotten him shot, *and* I'd slept with his fiancée while he'd been out cold. Engagement of convenience or not, it was still a shitty thing to do.

I was going to rot in hell. That had already been a given, but my recent actions really put me in the red.

The weight of our last conversation ballooned between us. We'd both said things we shouldn't have, but time and a near-death experience had smoothed the jagged edges of our anger.

I'm glad you're okay. I settled for the obvious before we jumped into the inevitable.

"Me too." Jordan gave me a half smile. "The doctors said it was touch and go there for a bit, but you can't get rid of me that easily." He hesitated. "What happened to the shooters?"

I took care of them.

Jordan knew about the Brotherhood in the vaguest terms. I'd told him enough to explain why I needed the money in college, but he never grasped the full extent of what they did or my involvement with them.

I planned on keeping it that way. I refused to drag him into the seedy underbelly of my life.

"You took care of them," he repeated. "Do I want to know how?"

I shrugged.

"Right." His grimace told me he had his suspicions, but he'd rather not confirm them. "Ayana came by this morning. She told me about you two."

My eyes flew to his.

"Don't worry. I'm not pissed or anything," he said with a wry smile. "We had a long talk. It was…helpful, so I'll tell you the same thing I told her. Getting shot really made me reevaluate my priorities. Like, if it didn't involve the risk of death, I'd recommend everyone try it because the clarity you get is unmatched." His joking tone fell away with his next words. "I don't want to pretend to be someone I'm not anymore, Vuk, and I definitely don't want what happened before the ceremony to come between us."

This time, I was the one who grimaced. We had to talk about what happened eventually, but I looked forward to it about as much as I looked forward to a root canal with no anesthesia.

"I was blindsided by, you know, the whole Ayana thing." Jordan sighed, and a pang of guilt prickled my skin. "You should've told me earlier, Vuk. All those months we were engaged, you never said a thing. I made you take her to California for our cake tasting, for Christ's sake."

It wasn't relevant at the time. Because I thought they'd been in love and that I could bury my obsession beneath avoidance. What a fool I'd been.

"It was relevant enough for you to try to buy me out an hour before the wedding. One hundred and twenty million dollars. That's a hell of a commitment," Jordan countered. "I was angry you'd kept such a big secret from me. I felt like an idiot, pushing you two together all the time when you…" He sighed again and rubbed a hand over the back of his neck. "Anyway, it doesn't matter. The truth is out. The real question is, what happens now?"

A rock pressed right against my ribs.

He said he didn't want to pretend anymore. Did that mean…I didn't dare hope…

KING OF ENVY | 373

"I'm tempted to keep you in suspense, but fuck it." Jordan reached for something in his bedside drawer. When he uncurled his hand, a familiar diamond glittered in the cradle of his palm. "I ended things with Ayana. Officially."

My breath exploded out of me in a rush. The boulder collapsed, dragging a heavy ball of dread and anxiety away with it.

He'd ended things with Ayana. No engagement. No wedding. No sneaking around behind Jordan's back. They were both single and *free*.

If I weren't sitting, I might've floated to the ceiling like Mary fucking Poppins.

"It was a long time coming. We made the pact so long ago, and neither of us was into it when the ceremony rolled around. We'd just invested too much into the sham to call it off at the last minute," Jordan said. "I admit my ego also got in the way. No one wants to feel like a charity case, and it felt like you were just throwing money at me to make me go away. Like an amount that was such a big deal to me was nothing to you."

A thread of guilt tethered me back to earth.

That wasn't my intention, but I know I wasn't particularly tactful during our conversation. I hesitated. *I asked Ayana to call off the wedding a few weeks before the ceremony. She refused. Up until the last minute, I thought I could respect both your wishes and bear it anyway. Pretend it wouldn't kill me inside to see her get married to someone else. But I couldn't. In that last hour before the ceremony, I panicked, and when you told me about the arrangement, I thought I saw a clear way out. I wasn't thinking about anything except stopping the wedding. That was my fault. I'm...sorry.*

I wasn't big on sharing my feelings or apologizing. I did what I did because I felt like it, and no one dared say a thing.

But this situation with Jordan and Ayana was different. They both deserved more from me.

"Jesus." Jordan gawked at me. "I don't think I've seen you express so many words at once, ever. Not even in college."

I snorted *Don't get used to it. I've almost reached my word quota for the year.*

"Good thing the year's almost over, huh?" He tossed a small smile my way. "I appreciate the apology, and I accept. I'm sorry too, for letting my ego dictate my actions. I shouldn't have tried to push through the wedding. It wasn't fair to any of us. So." Jordan cleared his throat. "I guess there's no need for a long, drawn-out *thing* now that we've both apologized, right? We're cool?"

My mouth tipped up. *Yes, as long as you put that ring away. I never want to see the damn thing again.*

"Hey, this 'damn thing' cost a shit-ton of money." But Jordan did as I asked.

When do you go home?

"The doctors want to monitor me for a few days. After that, I'm outta here." He glanced at the door, his expression clouding. "Once I'm home, I'm going to tell my family everything. I'm dreading it, but maybe they'll go easy on me considering I almost died. My grandmother is the one I'm most worried about. She fell on Friday, and that's on top of her diagnosis. I hope our conversation doesn't make things worse."

I didn't know what to say. I didn't have experience with this sort of thing. When I was worried, I liked to hole myself up at home and shut out the rest of the world. I assumed that wasn't what Jordan wanted.

It'll all work out in the end. What a stupid platitude, but people liked hearing it.

Jordan eyed me. "Words of comfort from Vuk Markovic?" he joked. "Ayana's influence, I presume."

The only ones you'll get from me. You want to talk more? Get a real therapist.

"You're such an asshole," he said with a laugh.

We shot the shit for a while longer before a nurse came by to say visiting hours were over.

I left, my body buzzing with relief. He was okay, and we were okay.

For years, I'd thought Jordan and I didn't have much in common except for our history. I hadn't realized until now that we did share one important trait: loyalty. Hell, he was more loyal than I was, given the whole Ayana situation, and I'd taken it for granted. I wouldn't do so again.

I'd cleaned up before I visited Jordan, but I took a real, thorough shower when I went home. I scrubbed myself raw, determined to wash away the stain of that morning's events. Dexter deserved what he got, but I took no inherent pleasure in what I'd done.

It was only when I was squeaky clean and changed into a fresh set of clothes that I called Ayana.

She picked up on the second ring. "Hey." Her warm voice trickled right through my chest. "Did you take care of your work emergency?"

"For the most part." I sat at my desk and stared at my dark computer screen. "I just came back from seeing Jordan. He told me you two ended things."

There was an audible hitch of breath, followed by a cautious, "We did."

"Good." One word encompassed a world of emotion.

Ayana was back in the city. I wasn't thrilled about that—she was a little too close for comfort given the Brotherhood developments—but she and Jordan were over, which meant there was nothing stopping us from being together.

My worries about the Brotherhood were the only thing keeping me from going to her apartment right now. We'd been apart for less than a day, and I already missed her. It was pathetic.

Unfortunately, I had to deal with Shepherd first. Once he was out of the way, I could take all the time in the world to be with her.

"I have to tie up some loose ends for this work project over the next few days," I said. "But if you'd still like shooting lessons, meet me at the Valhalla Club on Friday. Six p.m. Wear something comfortable."

"It's a date." Ayana paused. "That is, I mean—"

"It's a date."

I could practically hear her smile over the phone. "Then I won't keep you much longer since you have work. I'll see you on Friday. Good night."

A strange warmth rippled through my veins. "Good night, *srce*."

My phone call with Ayana was my last moment of peace before I snapped into work mode.

It took Sean less than eight hours to confirm Dexter's intel. It took us another twelve to formulate and prep a strategy that was as fast, nimble, and effective as it could be given our limited time and resources.

In an ideal world, we'd have more than two days to carry out a hit against elite assassins. Unfortunately, grabbing Dexter had tipped our hand. Shepherd was spooked, and if we didn't move soon, he'd go underground before we could nab him.

I wasn't going to drag this out any longer than necessary. I wanted the Brotherhood problem behind me, once and for all. After Shepherd died, Roman would rally the troops and take out the other faction. He already had a plan; he just needed my resources to pull it off. Once that happened, he'd take control of the Brotherhood, and he swore he would perform a blood oath that would prevent the organization from coming after me ever again.

The plan required a lot of trust in someone who was inherently untrustworthy. Unfortunately, I had no better options. It was either go along with Roman or look over my shoulder and wage war against the Brothers for God knew how long. I couldn't allow that to happen now that they'd broken their old code and were going after civilians.

User 02: *T-minus five minutes*.

My pulse raced at Roman's encrypted message. I nodded at Sean, who ordered the rest of the team to get ready.

It was Wednesday night. D-Day. I had twelve people on my team, not including myself. Half of whom were here with me. That was Team A. Team B waited less than five minutes away in case we needed backup.

Shepherd's primary safe house occupied the end of a cul-de-sac in Jersey, about a forty-minute drive from the city. My recon team had been staking him out since Monday and reported a spike in activity over the past few days. He was moving equipment, which confirmed my decision to strike fast before he abandoned this outpost.

I'd anonymously hired a local actor to invite the other residents on the street to a free "exclusive dining experience" at one of New York's most famous restaurants. The meal was worth over a thousand dollars per person, and getting reservations was usually impossible. The actor framed it as a special giveaway to celebrate the restaurant's one-year anniversary. The offer was too good for anyone to turn down, so the street was empty tonight save for us.

Team A was set up at the house closest to Shepherd's. We were able to slip in and set up after Roman drew the faction leader out of his safe house with some bullshit excuse. Thankfully, there were no other members present.

Now, Shepherd and Roman were minutes from returning, and the tension was so thick I could slice it with a knife. I was downstairs with Sean, Mav, and Bruce. The others were upstairs.

I wondered what the house's real owners would think if they saw seven men staked out in their living room and bedrooms, bristling with weapons and computers. Probably not anything good.

If everything went according to plan, we wouldn't need to use our weapons, but it never hurt to be prepared.

A black SUV pulled onto the street and parked in front of the safe house. I tensed. Beside me, Sean did the same.

A man with silver hair stepped out, his lean frame and stern expression belying his casual clothing. Roman followed soon after. He didn't spare our house a single glance.

My team and I were well hidden in the shadows. Nevertheless, I waited with bated breath for the moment Shepherd turned and saw us trying to ambush him.

The moment never came.

He and Roman entered the house. Our computer feeds flickered to life, displaying black-and-white images of the two men inside. The timer we'd wired to the front door started ticking down.

Five minutes.

Shepherd and Roman stopped in the dining room. They exchanged words, their expressions calm. Unfortunately, we didn't have time to set up an audio feed, so I couldn't hear what they were saying.

Four minutes.

Roman gestured at the exit, his expression still calm. He walked toward the exit, but Shepherd grabbed him before he made it two steps.

"Fuck," Sean whispered.

My heart rate sped up. The plan was for Roman to ensure

Shepherd made it into the house and *stayed* there until the explosives went off. He had a five-minute window to get out himself, or he'd be blown to bits along with the faction leader.

Three minutes.

Roman must've been convincing enough to get Shepherd to leave the house with him when the other man was already suspicious about Dexter's disappearance. However, Roman's sudden attempt to leave had obviously raised some red flags because Shepherd's face twisted into a scowl.

Two minutes.

Shepherd dropped Roman's arm. With a snakelike movement so fast I could barely track it, he pulled out his gun and pressed it straight to Roman's temple.

"Shit." Mav this time. "That fucker's toast."

"At least he's making sure Shepherd's inside while the house blows," Bruce said. "That's something."

No one responded.

One minute.

My pulse ticked in time with the final countdown. A messy tangle of emotions knotted in my gut.

I didn't like Roman. Barely trusted him when I didn't have to. Would've happily shot him dead that day in my office if he hadn't saved himself by the skin of his teeth.

Traitors were traitors, and even if he was on my side, his actions left a bad taste in my mouth.

However, he'd also provided invaluable help and intel in my fight against the Brotherhood. Did he have selfish motives? Yes. But he hadn't steered me wrong yet, which was honestly more than I'd expected from him.

I glanced at the timer. Thirty seconds left.

We'd raced against time to wire Shepherd's house with explosives on the lower and upper floors. Their range was limited to the house and part of the yard, but they were powerful enough to decimate anyone within that radius.

We'd explored subtler options, including a sniper or poison, but they left too much to chance. Sometimes, brute force was the only way to go.

Onscreen, Roman was talking. Whatever he said was enough to keep Shepherd from pulling the trigger. That was a mistake.

In a move even quicker than Shepherd's, Roman twisted the other man's arm and knocked the gun across the room.

Twenty seconds.

Roman didn't bother to look back at the faction leader. He sprinted for the exit. Shepherd ran after him, his expression almost feral.

Ten seconds.

Bruce and Mav straightened. My heart thundered.

Five.

Roman was almost at the door when Shepherd grabbed the tail of his shirt. Panic spread across Roman's face.

Four.

He turned and found enough leverage to slam his knee into the other man's groin. Shepherd doubled over.

Three.

Roman managed to free himself and fling open the door.

Two.

He raced across the yard and—

BOOM.

The explosion sent him flying into the street. Flames burst out from the windows and lit up the night sky.

My team and I were prepared with protective hearing devices, but the blast was still so loud, it rocked the house and rattled my bones.

Team A immediately spilled into the night to deal with the

aftermath and make sure Shepherd was dead. One of them pulled a soot-covered and annoyed-looking Roman off the pavement.

I stayed inside the house. I stared at the flames dancing less than two dozen feet away. They were beautiful, which made them more insidious. The acrid scent of smoke seeped through the bolted windows and into my lungs.

Burnt flesh. A whole body of it. Would Shepherd's corpse look like my brother's? Did he die in as much pain as Lazar, or was his an undeservedly quick and merciful death?

"Vuk." Sean's quiet voice brought me out of my spiral.

He'd anticipated the effect the fire might have on me; I'd insisted on coming anyway. I wouldn't have my men risk their lives if I wasn't willing to do the same.

I smoothed my expression and turned to my security chief. He'd been communicating with the team via his earpiece.

"All clear," he said. "Shepherd was the only person in the house. The guys have his body. He's dead."

Dead.

Shepherd was dead. Our rushed plan had somehow gone off without a hitch.

I stared out the window again.

My team had gotten the flames under control. Roman had disappeared, as expected. We'd intercepted the emergency phone lines so no first responders would interrupt us, but it was still prudent to leave the scene as quickly and cleanly as possible.

When investigators finally looked into the explosion, they'd find planted evidence of a half-truth—a criminal leader taken out by his adversaries. Law enforcement never put too much effort into bringing a killer of killers to justice. Soon, the case would be relegated to the back of a drawer, never to be touched again.

Shepherd was dead.

The revelation cycled through my mind again. I expected to feel relief, but the boulder on my shoulders didn't budge.

Roman's near-death aside, the ease with which we'd taken out one of the Brotherhood's faction leaders seemed anti-climactic. *Too* anti-climactic. We hadn't even called in Team B.

Was it really that easy? Was the new generation so sloppy, they'd fall victim to a hastily constructed scheme?

We had an inside source and the element of surprise on our side (sort of), which might explain our success.

Still, as my men and I tied up our loose ends and left, I couldn't quite shake the feeling that my troubles weren't over yet.

CHAPTER 40

Ayana

I WAITED ON PINS AND NEEDLES ALL WEEK TO SEE VUK AGAIN.

During that time, I shopped, knitted, watched TV, and declined a booking for next month. I'd expected Emmanuelle to retaliate in some way after I told her off, but she'd been quiet since our phone call. Hank was the one who'd sent me the campaign opportunity, but I wasn't mentally prepared to go back to work yet.

He'd been upset, but he was the last thing on my mind when I arrived at the Valhalla Club's indoor shooting range on Friday.

The facility looked like something out of a high-stakes spy thriller. Light gray stone floors, Kevlar-covered walls, fourteen state-of-the-art target lanes separated by custom-designed dividers that funneled firearm sounds down range, thereby reducing the decibel level in the stalls. According to the crisp black info sheet at the entrance, the range also boasted a gun-smoke-removing air filtration system and a virtual reality bay, whatever that meant.

Despite its high-end, high-tech trappings, it was completely empty save for Vuk and me. I was ten minutes early, but he was already waiting for me when I arrived.

Black shirt, black pants, black buzz cut. He looked the same as always, but my stomach cartwheeled like this was our first meeting ever.

I hadn't seen him since D.C.

Six days. It felt like a lifetime.

A smile teased his lips when he saw me. "That's your idea of a comfortable outfit?"

I'd opted for an ultra-soft cashmere dress and knee-high Christian Louboutin stiletto boots. I'd slicked my hair back into a bun and accessorized with a pair of simple gold studs. I didn't want my jewelry to get caught on anything.

I shrugged, not seeing the problem. "I'm comfortable in heels and dresses."

I'd been wearing stilettos since I was a teenager. At this point, I could run a marathon in them.

Vuk shook his head, but his grin widened a fraction of an inch.

"Did you take care of business?" I asked.

"Yes." His eyes tracked me as I walked toward him, my hips swaying in a more casual rendition of my runway strut. A flare of heat swallowed the humor in his gaze.

"Did it go the way you wanted?"

"Yes."

"Good." I came to a stop inches from him. The scent of vanilla, soft woods, and a hint of rum swirled in my lungs. He was wearing the cologne I'd bought him for his birthday. I breathed it in and suppressed a schoolgirl-giddy smile. "I wouldn't expect anything less."

"Good to know." Amusement leaked into his eyes again, tempered by apology. "I'm sorry again for sneaking out in the middle of the night. The issue was…urgent."

"It's okay." I stepped closer. My chest brushed his, and his breath hitched. "I know a way you can make it up to me."

"Yeah?" His eyes grew hooded. "How?"

I leaned forward, my lips tickling his ear. "By teaching me how to shoot."

His laugh followed me all the way to the shooting stall.

I grinned. I liked messing with him, and I liked hearing him laugh even more.

Since it was my first time at a shooting range, Vuk started by explaining safety procedures and giving me a rundown of how things worked—how to hang targets, when to take breaks, what to do when something went wrong, so on and so forth. Once he walked me through the full process, we put on our safety gear and got started.

Vuk stood behind me and adjusted my form. "Hold it half an inch higher. Bend your left elbow and turn your left side toward the target." His hand was rough and warm, his instructions cool and precise. "Just like that. Good."

The soft breath of his praise ghosted the back of my neck.

My belly clenched. This shouldn't be so hot, but his proximity and the confident, capable way he manipulated my body into the exact position he wanted it in made desire pulse between my thighs.

I forced the lusty thought aside. The last thing I wanted was to be distracted while I held a literal gun in my hands.

Once Vuk was satisfied with my form, he stepped aside. I pulled the trigger, and...missed my target. I also missed the next one, and the one after that. Between the kickback and my nerves, shooting was a lot harder than Nate Reynolds made it look in his action thrillers.

To be fair, I hit some parts of the target, just not the parts I *wanted* to hit. Its knee and forearm were peppered with holes when I was aiming for the heart.

I was so embarrassed I almost called it quits halfway, but quitting was worse than failing. So I stuck it out until my last shot came within several inches of the heart. It wasn't great, but it was preferable to shooting the knee again.

"Better." Vuk had been surprisingly patient throughout my many misses, and he smiled now at my pout. "You'll get the hang of it."

"I hope so. Otherwise, I'm as liable to shoot myself as I am anyone else," I grumbled.

Despite my dismal performance, I felt a small flutter of pride. I wasn't planning on actually shooting anyone—guns still made me nervous, and there was a difference between firing at an inanimate object versus a flesh-and-blood person—but the simple act of learning how made me feel safer. More in control.

In a world where organizations like the Brotherhood existed, every advantage counted.

After our lesson ended, I freshened up in the bathroom and met up with Vuk again in the waiting area. We left the range together, our steps falling easily into sync.

"I told you I could shoot in heels," I quipped.

"Maybe you would've hit the target if you were in something else," Vuk said.

I gasped and swatted his arm as we stopped in front of a gilded elevator. He smirked, his eyes dancing with mischief.

Despite his absolute disrespect toward my beloved footwear, I loved this teasing, light-hearted side of him. Whatever he'd accomplished at work had wiped away some of the stress lines around his mouth. They weren't gone completely, but they were noticeably softer.

I wondered if his "work" had anything to do with the Brotherhood. I didn't want to ruin the mood by asking, so I kept my curiosity to myself for now. If he wasn't worried, I wasn't worried.

The elevator had a biometric pad in place of a button. Vuk

pressed his thumb against the pad. There was a beeping sound accompanied by flashing yellow lights. Two seconds later, the lights blinked a solid green, and the doors slid open.

See? Spy thriller shit.

"Fancy," I said, taking in the elevator's shiny mirrors and plush red carpet. I wasn't sure where he was taking me, but I was happy to follow along for now.

"The managing director title has its perks," Vuk said. "This is the private elevator to my office. No one can access it without my fingerprint."

The doors closed, and he pressed the button for the fourth floor.

"So this is completely private," I said. "No one can accidentally walk in?"

He shook his head.

I was still riding an adrenaline high from the range, and I remembered the heat of his body when he'd stood behind me. His control, his precision, his commanding tone when he told me what to do and how to do it.

My skin buzzed. I reached forward and pressed the emergency stop button before modesty could talk me out of it. The elevator shuddered to a halt.

Vuk's brows rose.

"I realized we never properly greeted each other." I licked my lips. My throat was drier than parchment. "Today's our first time seeing each other since Jordan and I broke things off. I'm not engaged anymore."

It was like I'd tossed a lit match into a pool of gasoline. Sparks flared to life in the tiny elevator, and Vuk's gaze darkened at the edges.

"No. You're not." If he were anyone else, the softness of his words would've sent me running. As it was, they only fanned the flame flickering in my core.

Nevertheless, I took an instinctive step back when he closed the distance between us. I hit the wooden rail, and Vuk placed his hands on either side of me, caging me in.

"There are no cameras in here," he murmured, his lips skimming along my jaw. "I can do whatever I want to you…" He nipped my earlobe hard enough to make me whimper. "And no one will know a thing."

My nipples hardened, and I didn't bother to hold back a moan when his hand slid under my dress.

"Good," I panted.

Vuk groaned. He pulled me in for a rough kiss and I returned it eagerly, my fingers digging into his shoulders while he picked me up and set me on the rail.

It wasn't wide enough to hold me without support, so I wrapped my legs around his waist and deliberately arched against him. The thick, hard press of his erection against my clit elicited another, needier moan.

There was no engagement hanging over our heads anymore. Nothing to prevent us from giving and taking as much as we wanted, and God, I *wanted* him. So much so that I could barely breathe.

Vuk's kiss grew more insistent as he pushed my dress up around my waist. Cool air grazed my inner thighs. The contrast between that and his body heat made my head swim.

He trailed his fingers along the seam of my underwear and slipped them past the flimsy silk.

"Soaked already." He tsked like he was disappointed at my shamelessness. "You've been dreaming about getting fucked all week, haven't you?"

I was growing wetter by the minute, but I couldn't resist a little cheek. "Not all week. You fucked me on Saturday."

It was only Friday, six days later.

Vuk laughed, the sound edged with dark amusement. "No,

srce. That wasn't fucking." He withdrew his fingers and, before I could register what was happening, slapped my pussy with his hand. The shocking sting of his palm against my clit made me squeal. My vision hazed; arousal gushed and ruined my already drenched underwear. "This is."

CHAPTER 41

Vuk

AYANA'S NEEDY CRY WAS MY UNDOING. SHE WAS *dripping* after I slapped her pussy, and I didn't bother to hold back when I hooked my fingers in her underwear again. I tore it off with one sharp yank and tossed the shredded material on the floor.

I'd been on edge all day. All damn week, if I were being honest. The ambush on Shepherd had monopolized my time and energy, which meant I hadn't seen her in days.

I'd survived decades without her, but now that I had her in my life, I couldn't imagine living in her absence.

I needed to see her.

Touch her.

Taste her.

Fill myself up with her so thoroughly that she was forever etched into my soul.

"Tell me." I pushed a finger inside her. She was so wet it slid in without resistance. "Did you ever kiss Jordan during your engagement?"

Ayana's breath stuttered. She rolled her hips, trying to grind against my hand without falling off the narrow rail. "Are you really asking me about another guy right now?"

I pushed deeper inside her, hitting a spot that made her gasp. "Answer me." My tone was hard and unyielding.

She was soaking my hand. I hungered to give her what she silently begged me for until she gushed all over me, but I held back. *Not yet.*

After years of waiting and wanting, she was finally mine. *Only* mine. And I was going to savor every goddamn second of it.

"Yes." Ayana swallowed. "A few times."

My thumb pressed against her clit hard enough to elicit an involuntary jerk. Her hips bucked again. "How many times is 'a few?'" I asked darkly.

"I'm—I'm not sure." A desperate mewl escaped when I withdrew my finger.

"Guess." I delivered another slap to her pussy. Her clit throbbed against my palm, and the sweet, musky scent of her arousal thickened in the air.

Fuck, she was wet. My cock pulsed with need.

"Four," she sobbed. "We kissed four times."

"Good." I brushed a stray wisp of hair from her face and brought my mouth next to her ear. "Because that's how many times I'm going to fuck your brains out in this elevator, *srce*. I'm going to make you come so fucking hard you won't remember your own name after, much less how often you've kissed another man."

She shuddered. The hard points of her nipples poked through her dress.

She wasn't wearing a bra.

The knowledge sent a rush of white-hot desire to my groin. My cock was so hard it hurt, and I couldn't hold back any longer.

I pushed Ayana's legs wider with my knee and retrieved a condom from my pocket. I only had one on me, so I had to be creative about those four orgasms, but I was sure I'd think of something.

Once I sheathed myself, I wasted no time plunging inside her. I tugged at the zipper of her dress until the material sagged around her waist, baring her breasts. I lowered my head and feasted on her nipples while I pounded her and drank in the sweet sound of her screams and moans.

The wet, obscene sounds of flesh slapping against flesh filled the elevator. This was the only thing that existed. Being with her enthralled me completely, and I was possessed by the need to drive every other thought out of her mind. To consume her as much as she consumed me.

I closed my teeth around her nipple and tugged. She convulsed around my cock with a gasp. I was so deep inside her I didn't know where I ended and she began, and it still wasn't enough.

I raised my head and kissed her again, drinking in her taste. Her desire. Her passion.

I wasn't used to losing control. Whether in business or sex, I always kept a tight rein on emotions. I approached every negotiating table with the upper hand because I never wanted the deal as much as the other side did. I could easily walk away and not think twice about it.

But with Ayana, there was no walking away. No negotiation. She was *mine*, and I would die before I lost her.

"*Vuk.*" She cried out, her heels digging into my back. She was as ferocious in her lust as I was, and I fucking loved it. Seeing her at the shooting range had been the hottest thing I'd ever encountered—not because of the weapons or those sexy yet impractical heels, but because of her strength and determination. When she wanted something, she went after it. When she failed, she picked herself up and tried again.

There was nothing in the world sexier than that.

"Say my name again," I growled.

"Vuk." Ayana's head fell back against the wall. Her chest heaved with shallow breaths. "Please."

"Please what?"

"Please fuck me harder. I want—I need to—*oh God!*" Her cry ripped through me when I thrust into her with fierce abandon. She was shaking, her screams melting into a sob as she buried her face in my neck and rode out the waves of her orgasm.

"Count it." I slowed my thrusts, not wanting to come too soon. We had so many more orgasms to go. "Count how many times you come for me, *srce*."

"One." She whined in protest when I pulled out of her and set her on the floor.

"Bend over and grab the rail," I commanded.

She obeyed without hesitation. My cock throbbed again at the luscious sight of her spread wide and soaked from me. The aftermath of her first orgasm slicked her thighs. Her panties were a shredded mess on the floor, and her dress was bunched around her waist, but those boots…fuck. The sleek black leather molded to every curve of her legs, and the heels were sharp enough to kill.

The most beautiful woman in the world, bent over half-naked and wearing the sexiest shoes I'd ever seen. I almost blew my load right then and there.

I gritted my teeth and counted to three. Once I'd regained sufficient control, I lined the tip of my cock against her pussy again.

"You like it when I fuck you hard, don't you?" I squeezed her ass with both hands.

Ayana nodded frantically, her body quivering with anticipation.

I gave her exactly what she asked for. I leaned forward and closed one hand around her throat, using it as leverage so I could fuck her faster, harder, *deeper*. Sweat coated our skin. The scent of sex drenched the velvet-paneled walls, turning the elegant elevator into a depraved den of sin.

It didn't take long for Ayana to come apart again. Her back bowed, and her pussy spasmed, milking my cock in a hungry search for more.

Shit. I closed my eyes, the pleasure almost too much to bear. "Count," I ordered. The sound of my taut voice restored some semblance of restraint.

"Two," she sobbed.

I pulled out again, turned her around, and sank to my knees. My entire body pulsated with lust. I needed more time to cool down, so I coaxed her third orgasm out another way.

I started slowly, bathing her sensitized clit with long, slow sweeps of my tongue until the throes of her orgasm abated. When her breathing steadied, I intensified my efforts, licking and sucking with single-minded intensity until I had her writhing against my face.

Ayana grabbed the back of my head and pressed my face tighter to her body. "Right there! *There.* Oh *fuck*!"

I hooked one of her legs over my shoulder so I could dive deeper. I thrust my tongue inside her, and it took her less than two seconds to flood my mouth with her sweet juices.

She tasted so fucking good, I couldn't let any of it go to waste. I held her firmly in place until I'd lapped up every single drop. When I finally rose to my feet, my face glistening with the reward of my efforts, she was nearly incoherent.

"Three." Her throaty rasp shot straight to my groin. "I can't take anymore," she pleaded when I lifted her up and wrapped her legs around my waist. "Vu—*ungh*." She groaned when I slowly impaled her on my cock.

"Yes, you can," I said calmly. "You can take all of it, sweetheart." I pushed deeper until I was buried balls deep inside her.

"One more." I placed a tender kiss on her lips. "Let's make it count."

And we did.

By my second thrust, Ayana had forgotten her protests and was riding me with abandon. I held her while she bounced up and down my cock, wringing every ounce of pleasure from both of us until I couldn't take it anymore.

My balls tightened, and I hissed out a curse. I shifted my weight so I could reach down and play with her clit. I dug my thumb against the swollen nub, urging her toward—

Ayana cried out for the umpteenth time that day. Lights exploded behind my eyes. My loud grunt mingled with the sounds of her ecstasy as we fell apart together, our bodies pressed into one trembling, sweat-soaked embrace.

Whereas the climb had been exquisite agony, the comedown was soft, almost peaceful. We held each other long after our breathing returned to normal, each too lost in our own world to risk pulling away first.

"Four," Ayana whispered.

"Four what?" I asked against her neck.

"What?"

"What are you counting, Ayana?"

"I don't know." She sounded dazed. "I can't really think properly right now."

Her skin muffled the sound of my chuckle. I lifted my head and set her gently on her feet. "Come on, sweetheart. Let's get you cleaned up."

She was a wreck, but she was still so gorgeous she took my breath away.

I restarted the elevator and picked up her ruined underwear from the ground. When we arrived at my office, I cleaned us both off with a long, hot shower.

"Thank God for private elevators," Ayana said after. "And private bathrooms." She sank onto the bed with a drowsy sigh. She was practically swimming in my bathrobe.

I smiled. "Like I said, being the MD has its perks."

My office at Valhalla was really a suite of rooms that included the actual office, a sitting area, an en suite bathroom, and even a bedroom with a view of the landscaped grounds. I rarely used it, but it came in handy today.

"I hope you don't mind, but I sent your dress down for dry cleaning while you were, uh, busy," I said. Ayana had stayed in the bathroom after our shower and spent quite a while on her after-shower beauty routine. "It'll be ready in a few hours. In the meantime, you can choose a new outfit from the closet."

The last word barely left my mouth before she bounded to her feet and beelined to the walk-in wardrobe. "Do you always keep women's clothes in your office?" she teased. She threw open the doors, her face lighting up at the wealth of options awaiting her.

I grunted. "They're for you. I called the club's in-house stylist and had her bring up some options while you were in the bathroom."

"You didn't have to do that." But Ayana was already deep in the closet, her voice muffled by layers of silk and cashmere. She reappeared a minute later with wide eyes and a silky gold dress in hand. "Vuk. This is a ten-thousand-dollar dress."

"Yes." When she continued to gape at me, my brows furrowed. "Too cheap?"

"Too *expensive*." She rubbed the material between her fingers. "This designer only makes ten of each dress. It's not something you throw on while you're waiting for your dry cleaning."

Ten of each dress sounded like a stupid business decision, but I kept that to myself.

"It's just a dress, *srce*," I said, amused. "Unless you don't like it, in which case I can have someone bring more options."

"No." Ayana clutched the dress to her chest. "This is perfect. Don't you dare take it from me."

"You're the supermodel. I thought you'd be used to ten-thousand-dollar dresses," I teased.

"Listen, that stuff is for the runway. I love a good exclusive piece, but I don't walk around in couture every day. That's just asking to get robbed." She took off her bathrobe and slipped into the dress. It fit her perfectly.

"If someone tries to rob you, shoot them," I said. "But try to hit *them* and not an innocent bystander."

I laughed when she pinned me with a playful glare. She threw a wadded-up piece of tissue paper at me. I easily caught it with one hand.

"What are you doing next Friday?" I asked.

"It's Maya's birthday. She's throwing a big party to celebrate." Ayana came over and sat next to me on the bed. "You're invited too. You should come."

The only Maya I knew was Maya Singh. I liked her well enough, but I hated birthday parties.

I made a noncommittal noise. "Maybe."

"Why? What's going on next Friday?" Ayana asked.

"I was planning on making D.C. up to you then, but we can push it to the Friday after next."

"Um." I felt the heat pouring off her cheeks. "I thought that was what the elevator was for."

"I like to be thorough in my apologies."

Another smile surfaced at her flustered expression. I didn't have more sex planned for my "official" apology—though I certainly wouldn't be opposed to the idea—but a knock on the outer office door interrupted our conversation before I could clarify.

A notification popped up on my phone, reminding me of my scheduled appointment. Shit. I'd forgotten all about it.

"Excuse me. I have a quick meeting I need to take, but make yourself at home," I said. "I'll be back soon."

"Don't worry," Ayana reassured me. "I'll keep myself entertained."

I left the bedroom and closed the door behind me. Dominic Davenport strode in right as I sank into the seat behind my desk.

"You wanted to see me." He took the chair opposite mine and leaned back, his expression cool. In his custom-tailored suit and perfectly knotted tie, he was the picture of a Wall Street titan.

He also didn't insist on small talk. I liked that about him.

I wrote my reply on a sheet of paper. *I need you to trace a money trail for me.*

Shepherd was dead, and Roman had pinned the safe house explosion on the other faction. He was currently consolidating Shepherd's followers under his leadership. It was all going according to plan, but there was one other thing that had been bugging me.

Dexter had provided some meager details about the source of the Brotherhood's funding, but I wanted to know exactly who was funneling money into the organization when they weren't taking on new contracts.

Roman would shit a brick if he ever found out I was involving his brother in our scheme, but when it came to the financial world, no one was more powerful or resourceful than Dominic.

Dominic's eyes glinted. "You want a favor."

I rarely asked for favors. I hated owing other people, but sometimes, it was necessary.

I nodded.

He smiled. "Consider it done."

CHAPTER 42

Ayana

AS EXPECTED, MAYA WENT ALL OUT FOR HER BIRTHDAY gala. It was held at a private event space downtown, and the theme was the Seven Deadly Sins. There were party stations for each of the sins, including a lavish buffet for Gluttony, eye-popping burlesque performances for Lust, and custom massages and facials for Sloth.

I'd convinced Vuk to make an obligatory appearance, but we were coming separately since I got ready with Maya beforehand.

> **VUK**
> I'm on my way. Be there soon.

> **VUK**
> I can't wait to see you.

He followed up his text with an excited cat meme. I giggled and responded with a similarly excited minion meme.

I never thought there'd be a day when I would exchange silly memes with Vuk Markovic, but here we were. It started after I left the Valhalla Club last Friday. I'd sent him a stupid, gushy thank-you meme—for the shooting lessons, *not* the admittedly mind-blowing sex—and he'd shocked me by responding in kind. Since then, it'd been a nonstop volley of images, GIFs, and the occasional social media video.

I was sure he was doing it to indulge me since I would've bet my entire shoe and perfume collection on him not being a meme guy, but that only made it more endearing.

I was still grinning when I looked up from my phone and saw Maya beelining toward me, champagne flute in hand. We'd split when we arrived since she had so many people to say hi to, but she appeared frazzled as she came up beside me.

"Please save me," she said. "My mother invited a *blind date* for me. Can you believe that? He's been trying to dance with me for the past twenty minutes, and I'm over it."

I followed her not-so-subtle grimace to where a handsome man with a neatly trimmed beard was staring at her with a longing expression.

I laughed. "Hey, he's good-looking and he seems taken with you. There are worse things in the world."

"He also has the personality of wet cardboard. No, thanks. Besides, it's my birthday. I want to flit around, not settle down. Look at me." Maya gestured to her outfit. She was clad in a stunning, floor-length orange gown that complemented her brown skin perfectly. She'd styled her thick black hair into an intricate twist, and a pair of diamond showstoppers grazed her delicate shoulders. "This was not meant for a blind date."

"True," I acknowledged.

"Anyway, forget about him. Are you having fun? Where's Vuk?"

The news about my "split" with Jordan broke last weekend, around the time I told her about my relationship development with Vuk. Jordan and I had released a joint statement that'd been cleared by both our PR teams.

Canceling wedding plans was easy; dealing with the aftermath was harder, especially when I'd been seen with my ex-fiancé's best man before the breakup was publicly official. Throw in the wedding attack and Jordan's recent coma and it was all very scandalous. Maya took the news in stride, but the city's rumor mill was in overdrive.

I didn't care. I was finally happy, and I wasn't going to let a few whispers ruin that.

"He's on his way," I said. "This party is wild. I saw Indira and Riley K. doing shots with Asher Donovan and his girlfriend at the bar."

I swear, half of Manhattan, Hollywood, and London society was in attendance.

"Oh yeah, that tracks." Maya grinned. "Also, can I just say those earrings look *stunning* on you? Wherever did you get them?"

"Thank you. I believe they're from your closet."

"They are, aren't they?" She sipped her drink. "Damn, I have good taste."

We collapsed into giggles. I'd grown closer to her over the course of six weeks than I had with people I'd known for six years. Friendship wasn't always about history; when two people clicked, they clicked. End of story.

The emerald-and-diamond earrings she'd lent me *were* stunning, though. I'd leaned into the sin of Envy for the night, choosing an emerald satin gown with a slit up the thigh and the most exquisite gold heels. The earrings matched beautifully.

Maya was about to say something else when her laughter died. She stared past me, her eyes narrowing. I didn't have to turn to guess which guest inspired such immediate contempt.

"Sebastian." Her voice dripped with ice.

The French billionaire joined us, looking as handsome and perfectly tousled as ever. "Maya." A smirk accompanied his smooth drawl. "Surprised to see you had time to plan a birthday party this year. Don't you have a marketing department to run to the ground?"

"We've increased our profit margins by thirty percent this past quarter. What have you done?" Maya arched a well-groomed brow. "Open the same type of boring, soulless restaurant you always do and irritate everyone you work with in the process?"

"Those 'boring, soulless' restaurants have earned more Michelin stars than there are hits in your latest product line, so I understand why you'd be bitter." Sebastian glanced around the party. "Seven Deadly Sins. Cute."

"You—"

"Ayana, good to see you." He interrupted her reply and faced me. "You look lovely." He sounded sincere.

"Thank you," I said, torn between good manners and loyalty to my friend. I settled somewhere in between. "Which sin are you?"

Most of the guests chose to dress up as one of the seven sins. Sebastian wore a white shirt, charcoal pants, and suspenders. The top button of his shirt was undone, adding to his rakish appeal. He and Kai Young were the only people I'd ever seen successfully pull off suspenders in real life.

"None. I'm sinless." His mischievous smile sharpened when he faced Maya again. "I'm not a big fan of party themes, unfortunately. They're a little tacky, but if anyone can make a brave attempt at classing them up, it's you, Sal." He raised his glass in a mock toast, his eyes sliding past Maya toward someone at the bar. "Ah, I spot Kai. Perfect timing. We need to discuss my next cover story for *Gourmand*. Have fun. Oh, and happy birthday."

He walked away, leaving a steaming Maya in his wake. I swore I saw smoke pouring out of her ears.

"Breathe." I placed my hands on her shoulders. "You cannot murder a guest at your own birthday party."

"That's what you think," she growled. "I should've chosen a Murder Mystery theme and used *him* as the dead body. Bonus points for realism when I stab him with a butcher's knife. See if he finds themes tacky then."

"Okay. Enough champagne for you. We don't need alcohol fueling your violent fantasies." I eased the delicate flute out of her hand and placed it on a nearby table. "What was that about anyway? Why did he call you Sal?"

I'd interacted with Sebastian briefly on several occasions. He'd always been charming and gracious, which was why it was a shock to see him and Maya snipe at each other. It was like they turned into different people when the other was near.

"Nothing. He was just being a competitive asshole." A scowl fell over her pretty features. "He's been that way since we were teenagers."

"Were you classmates?

"Yes. We went to the same boarding school in Switzerland."

Of course they had.

"Sal is short for salutatorian." Maya's scowl deepened. "I got food poisoning right before my chem final and was wrecked the entire time. I could barely concentrate. I ended up getting an eighty-nine, which dragged down my whole average. That little weasel beat me to the valedictorian spot by a quarter of a grade point, and he never let me forget it."

"Ah." Thirteen years seemed like a long time to hold a grudge, but I supposed I would be upset too if someone was constantly rubbing my failure in my face. Being salutatorian wasn't a failure, but in Maya's eyes, it was.

"The only reason I invited him is because I wanted him to see all this firsthand. Don't let him fool you. He's just bitter he didn't think of this party theme first," Maya said. "His last bash was a blowout in Monaco. Like *that's* original."

"Not original at all," I said loyally.

"Exactly." She sighed. "Sorry to dump all this on you. You're supposed to be having fun, not listening to me whine."

"I don't mind." It was pretty amusing, though I'd never tell her that. In my experience, people who were that riled up about each other either ended up killing each other or falling in love. I had my suspicions about which category Maya and Sebastian belonged to, but I valued my life too much to voice them out loud.

"Thanks." Maya's face softened into a smile. "I have to make the rounds again or my parents will complain I'm being a 'bad hostess.' Let's catch up later?"

"Sounds good."

She left. Vuk wasn't here yet, and I debated checking out the massage room when I heard my name.

"Ayana."

Cold slithered down my spine. "Emmanuelle."

I maintained a neutral expression as the agency head sauntered up to me. She was a vision in red. Red dress, red lipstick, red shoes.

"I didn't know you were friends with Maya Singh," she said.

I responded with a tight smile. This was our first conversation since our phone call, and I was half convinced she was planning to stab me in the eye with her heel.

"I hate to talk business during such a lovely party, but there are a few items I wanted to go over with you." Her smile lacked as much humor as mine. "I spotted you and figured this would be better than a phone call."

"I'm not taking any more bookings until the new year," I said.

The agency still hadn't paid me for the work I'd done, and while I did miss being in front of the camera, I needed a physical and mental break. With the holidays coming up soon, it seemed smart to wait and start with a clean slate in the new year.

Despite my protests, Jordan had paid me for the time I'd put into being his fiancée. It wasn't five million dollars, but it was enough money in the bank for a small safety net if I left Beaumont and they put up a fuss about it. It was also enough to cover my legal fees. I already had an appointment with my attorney to discuss potential next steps for breaking my contract.

I hadn't told Vuk about any of this yet. I wanted to figure things out on my own first. I couldn't always rely on other people to fix my problems for me.

"That's not what I wanted to talk about," Emmanuelle said. "You were right. It was wrong of us to slack on our payments to you. If you check your accounts, you'll see you've been paid in full as of this evening."

I rocked back on my heels. Out of everything I expected her to say, "you were right" ranked dead last. She never admitted she was wrong, which was why I digested her quasi-apology with a healthy dose of wariness. What did she have up her sleeve?

"I mean it." Emmanuelle gestured at my phone. "Check your account, Ayana."

I did, and there they were. Every missing payment from the past year—minus agency fees, of course.

"Thank you." I didn't lower my guard yet. There was a catch. There had to be.

"You're welcome." Emmanuelle finished her drink. "Now that that's settled, our business is concluded. You're officially terminated from the agency." She dropped the bombshell as casually as one might announce they were going out for lunch.

The music swirled around us. My stomach plunged as I gaped at her, sure I'd heard her wrong. "Excuse me? On what grounds?"

I wanted out from Beaumont, so this should be a blessing in disguise. But the shock of Emmanuelle dropping me in the middle of a birthday party with zero warning had me scrambling for answers.

Hank just sent me a booking days ago. Sure, I'd declined, but why would he do that if the agency was planning to drop me?

"Unprofessional conduct and intimidation by proxy," she said without batting an eye.

My jaw unhinged. "I didn't do any of that!"

"No? I remember our last phone call. While you were right about the payments, the way you communicated with me—the *president* and founder of the agency—was deeply unprofessional. As for intimidation by proxy, Hank told me what your new boyfriend did." Emmanuelle's eyes glittered. "Vuk Markovic barged into his apartment and assaulted him on your behalf. He threatened him with more physical harm if Hank didn't prioritize premium bookings for you over his other clients. His building's surveillance footage will back him up."

My ears buzzed. "Vuk would never do that."

Okay, the threatening part, maybe. But demanding that Hank prioritize bookings for me? Absolutely not. Not when he knew I didn't even like Hank and wanted to leave Beaumont.

"Hmm. Maybe not. Who knows? It's our word against yours." Emmanuelle shrugged. "Expect a lawsuit come Monday. Enjoy your booking fees while you have them, Ayana. Once the news breaks and the rest of the industry finds out about your behavior, I doubt you'll book anything except a sad photo campaign for local STD awareness." She raised her glass. "Cheers."

My feet stayed rooted to the floor while she swanned off. A lawsuit? Was she joking?

Be careful what you wish for. That's what my mother always said, and she was right.

I hated Beaumont, but I loved modeling. The beauty of movement, expression as art. I felt at home in front of a camera and on the runway, and I was *good* at it.

I'd achieved a great amount of success, but even the most

successful models weren't immune to being smeared and black-listed by the industry's powers that be. It was all politics, which I was terrible at navigating. What would I do if I couldn't model anymore?

My stomach bubbled with acid.

Someone touched my shoulder. I whirled around, my knee-jerk instinct to flee evaporating when I saw Vuk's concerned frown.

What's wrong?

"Emmanuelle's here. We talked, and she—she dropped me from the agency." I summarized the rest of our conversation, watching Vuk's face grow darker and darker until it resembled a thundercloud ready to burst. "Is it true? What she said about Hank?"

I didn't believe a word out of Emmanuelle's mouth, but I had to be sure.

I didn't tell him to play favorites; I warned him about the way he treated you that day he showed up to your apartment unannounced. Vuk's jaw turned to granite. *The grounds for a lawsuit are bullshit. My lawyers will destroy it in seconds, especially since we have evidence Hank was secretly surveilling you.*

"It's not about the legal standing for their case," I said. "It's about the optics. Emmanuelle doesn't care if she wins or loses the lawsuit. She just wants to drag my name through the mud and ruin my career."

History was littered with examples of famous women who were brought down by smear campaigns. Even if they hadn't done anything wrong, the *illusion* that they had was enough for people to turn on them.

Emmanuelle was doing all this because what, I talked back to her? Asked her to give me something that rightfully belonged to me?

A dash of fire swallowed my nausea. Despite my personal feelings toward Beaumont, I'd been nothing but professional over the years. I was their highest-earning model, and I never even talked bad about them to other models. Now, Emmanuelle was trying to ruin me because I'd bruised her ego. What gave her the fucking right?

"I need to tell Sloane. She's here somewhere," I said, formulating a plan on the spot. "Emmanuelle said the lawsuit will drop on Monday. We need to get ahead of it. I also need to talk to my accountant and hire—"

Ayana. Vuk placed his hand on my shoulder again. *Breathe. We're going to get through this. Emmanuelle fucking Beaumont will NOT ruin you. I'll die before I let that happen.*

Streaks of emotion burned through my panic.

We're going to get through this. Not I. *We*.

I was struck again by the strange sensation of having someone by my side, fighting with me. The shield to my sword, or the sword to my shield—whichever one worked in the situation. I wasn't going into battle alone, and that simple fact was enough to steady my breathing.

I might not have wanted other people to solve my problems for me, but I wasn't naive enough to think I could take on Beaumont without Vuk's help.

"Thank you." I swallowed. "I'm sorry about ambushing you with bad news the minute you walked through the door. Parties are usually more fun. I promise."

I doubt it. Vuk glanced at the burlesque performance. His mouth twisted into a grimace. *Talking to you about anything, even bad news, is definitely the highlight of this party for me.*

I laughed. I ignored the stares of other partygoers and laced my fingers with his, determined to show him a good time despite the Beaumont-shaped cloud hanging over our heads.

I pulled him toward the bar, the pressure in my chest easing with each step. Vuk was right. We were going to get through this.

As long as we were together, we could get through anything.

CHAPTER 43

Vuk

EMMANUELLE HAD SOME FUCKING BALLS.

It was Saturday, the afternoon after Maya's party, and I was still seething at the agency head's audacity to not only drop Ayana with no warning, but to do so in the middle of one of the biggest social events of the season.

It didn't matter that Ayana was planning to leave Beaumont anyway. It was the principle of the matter.

Once I was through with Emmanuelle, she'd be lucky to have a business card left, much less a thriving agency.

I hadn't thought she was bold or stupid enough to go up against me—and she had to know that by targeting Ayana, she was also targeting me—but she'd been clever in the way she framed her accusations. I'd give her that. By accusing me of "intimidating" Hank on Ayana's behalf, she'd essentially tied my hands. I couldn't do anything outside the legal scope of things without bolstering her claims.

It took everything in me not to find Hank and deal with him personally, but that would be playing right into their hands, so I let Sloane and my lawyers handle the situation. For now.

Meanwhile, I had another problem to deal with.

"You told me you could handle the other faction once Shepherd was out of the picture." I leveled a cold stare at the man across the table. "Now you're asking for my help again?"

"I said I *might* be able to handle them," Roman corrected. "They've proved more resilient than I gave them credit for. Plus, Shepherd's death has had…ripple effects. It's complicated."

We were meeting in the Brooklyn warehouse again. I wasn't concerned about Roman knowing the location since I didn't have anything of value here; it was merely a private place to handle unofficial business.

But Roman refused to tell me who the other faction leader was, claiming he didn't want to give up all his bargaining chips until he got what he wanted, and I was tired of his vague explanations.

I'd killed Shepherd and held up my end of the deal. Now he wanted me to provide manpower and resources to take out this other faction leader as well?

"You know," I said softly. Lethally. "If I didn't know better, I'd think you were giving me the runaround."

"Think what you like, but you won't find peace until I'm in control of the Brotherhood, and I can't get control until the other faction leader is dead. Plus, I have to deal with…other issues outside the organization." Roman's jaw flexed. Judging by his haunted expression, I assumed he meant the "they" he'd referred to in the note he left for me a lifetime ago. He said it was someone he'd crossed paths with while he'd been hiding from the Brothers.

I didn't care. His past wasn't my concern; his ability to restrain the Brotherhood was.

"The other faction has gone underground since Shepherd's death, but they're still gunning for you," Roman said. "They haven't made a move yet because they're waiting for the wedding fallout to subside. But unless you want to drag this fight out for weeks or even months, I suggest we lure them out so we can take them on our terms."

"And how do you suggest we do that?"

"By using bait."

Silence descended. What did we have that...

No. I tensed. Surely Roman wasn't idiotic enough to suggest what I thought he was suggesting.

His next words proved that he was, in fact, that idiotic. "We can't use you since they're not dumb. They won't go after you directly without careful thought, and we don't want them to be careful. We want them to be reckless. Now, the people close to you...that's another matter." He rapped his knuckles on the table. "Your relationship with Ayana is basically public knowledge now. They know you care about her, and she's a model. They won't think for a second that she can—"

The click of a gun stopped him short.

In the heartbeat between him uttering her name and now, I'd surged to my feet and leaned across the table.

I pressed the butt of my Glock under his chin, forcing his eyes up to meet mine. "If you go near Ayana or involve her in this in any way," I said, my voice so cold and quiet the air steamed with small white puffs, "I will make you *wish* I'd blown your head off."

What I'd done to Dexter wouldn't compare to what I'd do to anyone who knowingly put Ayana in harm's way.

Roman's eyes sparked with defiance. "This is exactly what I'm talking about," he said with a sneer. "The sentimentality. The emotional reactions. They're going to get you and, worse, *me* killed. She's fucking with your judgment, Markovic. Threaten me if you want, but my plan is a logical one, and you know it."

My teeth ground together.

My feelings for Ayana did cloud my judgment. Even when I'd been planning my attack against Shepherd, I was thinking about how I just wanted to get it over with so I could spend more time with her.

But I didn't care that Ayana was a distraction. She was *my* distraction, the only one I wanted. Roman could talk shit all he wanted; I drew the line at using her as bait. There was no world in which I'd ask her to put herself at risk for me.

"If you don't want to involve her, fine. But think about it," Roman drawled, unfazed by the gun aimed at him. "Are you willing to give up your life for a relationship that won't last? And don't kid yourself because it *won't* last. Not when Ayana finds out who you really are."

My grip strangled the gun. "She knows."

"Does she?" His tone turned mocking. "Does she know what you did to Dexter? What you did to the Brotherhood's leaders all those years ago? I'm talking gory details, Markovic. Maybe she's aware that you were part of the organization and that you've done illegal things in the past or even the present, but is she fully cognizant of what you're capable of? Because there's a long leap between 'illegal' and cutting a guy to pieces, even if he deserved it. Most people would find the latter...unconscionable."

My stomach congealed. All the blood in my body seemed to be sloshing in my ears, the liquid ripples a nauseating background for the brutal truth behind Roman's words. He'd ripped my worst fears out from the recesses of my mind and turned intangible nightmares into concrete words.

Would Ayana stay with me if she discovered what I was *truly* capable of? The whisper of cold against my neck teased at the answer.

I never wanted to find out.

"Like I said." Roman pushed his chair back and stood, heedless of my threats. "Think about it."

He walked away, leaving me alone in the silence.

CHAPTER 44

Ayana

WHEN I WAS STRESSED, I KNITTED.

Since last Friday, I'd completed a pair of mittens, a hat, and half a blanket, which was an extraordinary number of items considering I was still a novice and it'd only been a week.

The lawsuit had officially dropped on Monday, and the past few days had been a whirlwind of calls, meetings, and brainstorm sessions with Sloane and Vuk's lawyers (now my lawyers). The industry's whisper network was ablaze, and while the news wasn't big enough to hit the mainstream yet, the fashion gossip blogs were salivating for details. At Sloane's urging, I'd deleted my social media apps off my phone and stayed off the Internet.

Everyone was waiting with bated breath to see what would happen. The lawyers' consensus was that the charges were bullshit, but we all knew that. Emmanuelle simply wanted to seed doubt in people's minds and make my name synonymous with scandal and unprofessionalism, even if it wasn't true. Sloane agreed and was on top of it.

I trusted her. Nevertheless, I needed a distraction, so I

knitted and convinced Vuk to give me a second shooting lesson. Apparently, picturing Emmanuelle did wonders for my aim, because I'd pretended the target was her and hit it right in the face. It'd been deeply satisfying.

My most anticipated distraction, however, was tonight. It was the night that was supposed to officially make up for Vuk leaving me in D.C., and I could hardly contain my curiosity.

Do you ever wear anything except heels? Vuk asked as Sean whisked us uptown in an armored SUV. I thought the armored car was overkill, but I wasn't a security expert.

He hadn't mentioned the Brotherhood since the wedding attack, and I was increasingly convinced he'd left D.C. to deal with them without telling me. But he was here and he was alive, so that was a good thing, right?

"Rarely. Are you complaining?" I crossed my legs, purposely showing off their curves. I suppressed a smile when Vuk's gaze heated.

He'd told me to dress casually, which I *had*. A cashmere sweater and tailored pants were casual. I'd even selected my oldest pair of pointy-toed pumps instead of something from next season.

Not complaining. Merely questioning your definition of the word "casual."

"My definition is perfectly valid, and if you're going to question my fashion choices, have the balls to do so out loud," I said.

Vuk's eyes crinkled at the corners. His rich laughter warmed my stomach, and I saw Sean gape at us in the rearview mirror before he caught himself. He faced forward again, but I thought I saw his mouth curve before he did.

Vuk had tried to explain his role to me once, but it went over my head. Sean was Vuk's security chief, but he was also a bodyguard and a driver? I thought a former Special Ops soldier would have better things to do than ferry us around on a date night, but maybe not.

Ten minutes later, we pulled up to a plain red brick building on a quiet street. I squinted at the gleam of silver letters over the entrance.

"The Greenberg Senior Citizen Center?" I frowned. Why would Vuk take me to...*oh my God*. The pieces clicked, and my eyes flew to his face. "You didn't. Are you serious?"

He shrugged. The spark of boyish mischief in his eyes made me grin almost as much as his laugh.

Sean told us he'd wait for us outside, and we entered the center to a delighted greeting.

"Vuk!" The plump, pleasant-faced woman behind the reception desk beamed when she saw us. "It's good to see you again. It's been too long. And you brought a girl! It's about time. Aren't you just beautiful, dear? Well, don't let me keep you. Go on ahead. It's about to start."

The other staff members we passed on our way to wherever Vuk was taking me greeted him with equally warm hellos.

Eventually, we stopped at a pair of blue double doors. He opened them, and we entered what appeared to be a community room. Round tables dotted the space. Residents occupied most of the chairs, colorful plastic chips in hand. Several squinted at sheets of paper in front of them. At the front of the room, a dark-haired woman with a microphone stood next to a professional bingo ball dispenser.

It was bingo night at the senior center, and Vuk had finally answered my question about whether or not he was joking about his love for the game.

My chest felt like it would burst.

We took a seat at an empty table in the back. Several residents waved to Vuk, and a male nurse in scrubs handed us our chips and bingo cards.

"I can't believe it." I tried to wrap my head around this

confirmed new side of Vuk, the bingo lover. It was like finding out the governor of New York spent his free time playing with Barbies, or a mob boss had a side gig performing clown tricks at children's birthday parties. "You need to give me the backstory on this. When did you start coming here? How—"

Shh. Later. He studied his bingo card, his brow furrowed in concentration. *The game's about to start.*

My mouth snapped shut.

Over the course of the next hour, two things became clear: 1) Vuk Markovic was *really* into the game. Like, he refused to talk at all while it was happening, and 2) he was competitive as hell. It was a game of chance, but I was convinced he'd wrestle Lady Luck to the ground for victory's sake if he could.

I hadn't played since my fifth-grade Spanish teacher used the game to teach us vocabulary words, but I had a surprisingly great time. X'ing out squares on my card was quite therapeutic.

"B24!" the caller announced. She'd barely finished speaking before Vuk shoved a sheet of paper in the air. It said *BINGO!* in big black letters.

"And we have a winner!" the caller said amidst a cacophony of groans. "Let's break for intermission. The next game will start in ten minutes."

"Goddammit." A white-haired woman at a neighboring table banged her fist against her armrest. "That's the third time in a row I've lost!"

"Shut up, Fran," the man next to her said. He had a hunched back and a raspy voice. He looked like he was at least ninety. "You used to swindle tourists with rigged card games in the park. This is karma."

Fran cackled but didn't deny the accusation. "Only people I swindled were those stupid enough to fall for it."

Fran and Tom, Vuk said in response to my curious glance.

I guess he was okay with talking now that the game was over. *They're dating.*

Oh! Well, good for them.

"I see. Congratulations. You beat a room full of seniors," I teased. "You must be proud."

I told you. Vuk appeared quite pleased with himself. *I always win.*

"Uh-huh." I rolled my eyes, but I was smiling. "Tell me. When did the big, bad Vuk Markovic first enter the thrilling world of competitive bingo?"

Big and bad, huh? He looked even cockier than he had a second ago.

I kicked him playfully under the table.

He laughed, but he gave me a serious response a moment later.

A few years ago, I was trying to close a big deal with a subsidiary. The father of the CEO at the time was a resident here. He loved Friday bingo nights, so the CEO tried to play with him at least once a month. We were down to the wire in negotiations, and Friday night was his last night in the city before he left on a long trip to Asia. I offered to close out our negotiations here.

I tilted my head. "You negotiated a multimillion-dollar deal with another Fortune 500 CEO at a senior center bingo night?" I asked doubtfully.

Vuk smirked. *It's not any better or worse than closing deals on a golf course or over dinner.*

Okay, valid.

His father passed soon after the deal closed, but I enjoyed our bingo night so much that I came back the next week, and the week after that. Like I said, it's nice to unwind with something that doesn't require much thought or strategy.

"The center lets you play even though you don't have family here?"

Vuk just looked at me.

"Right." I shook my head. Did anyone ever say no to him?

*Some staff members were wary at first, but they got used to seeing me here. I also donate a lot of money to them every year, and I paid for a professional bingo setup. I think...*He was quiet for a moment. *My father would've liked it. Not the nursing home part, but the fun and camaraderie. He loved playing games, especially with strangers. He used to sit in the park and challenge passersby to checkers or chess. He almost always won.*

My heart twisted. "You must miss him very much," I said softly.

It was Vuk's first time discussing his parents. I read somewhere that both of them died of different illnesses a while ago.

It's been years. I got used to his absence. Despite his efforts to hide it, I caught a glimpse of pain in Vuk's eyes.

He obviously didn't want to talk about his family anymore, but I felt compelled to share something equal in return.

I toyed with the edge of my bingo card, debating, before I said, "My father's the reason I signed with Beaumont. When Hank scouted me, my family was going through a tough time. The restaurant hadn't quite taken off yet, and my father's hand got injured in a kitchen accident. It was...horrific. He needed extensive surgery and physical rehab after. His insurance only covered a fraction of the costs; we had to pay the rest out of pocket or forgo rehab altogether. But the doctors warned us that if he skipped rehab, he might never regain full use of his hand. He wouldn't be able to cook like he used to."

Memories collided with the ghost of helplessness. Vuk listened, his eyes never straying from my face.

"He already gave up one of his dreams," I said. "He'd studied engineering in Ethiopia, but once he immigrated to the U.S., his degree was worthless. So he turned to his second love, cooking. If he lost that too…it would've devastated him. We *had* to make it work." I ripped off a corner of the bingo card. "Liya and I were both in school at the time. My mother and Aaron worked at the restaurant, and it was all they could do to keep it afloat in my father's absence. We tried our best, but we didn't have enough money to cover the medical bills. Not even close. When Hank came along and offered me this glamorous modeling career, it seemed too good to be true."

I'd been right. It *was* too good to be true. The career had worked out, but at what cost?

I should've stopped there—I doubted Vuk wanted to hear the whole, sordid tale—but now that the floodgates had opened, I couldn't prevent the rest of the words from pouring out.

"He said they'd offer a bonus if I signed with Beaumont. The bonus alone was enough to pay for months of rehab. They also paid for my headshots, transport to casting calls, everything I needed to get started. I'd heard of Beaumont, and all my research suggested they were a legit agency. One of the best, in fact. Plus, I was so desperate to help with the bills that I didn't review the contract as thoroughly as I should've. I saw a few red flags, but Hank assured me they were standard for the industry, and we didn't have money for a lawyer. So I signed with them. It wasn't until years later that I realized how predatory the contract really was. Plus all those headshots and costs they so 'generously' covered for me? They took those out of my paycheck. Even when I started getting bookings, I was in debt to them for two years."

I'd been so naive to think they'd paid those costs as an invest-ment in my career. Beaumont never did something out of the goodness of their hearts.

"Things changed when Jordan chose me to be the face of Jacob Ford. That was my breakout campaign, and I was booked solid after that," I said. "But even after I got out of debt with Beaumont,

I had issues with late payments and random fees. I would've left ages ago, but my contract also included a clause that held me liable for a significant amount of money if I tried to terminate without 'just cause' as determined by *them*. The penalty would've wiped out my savings, and I was also scared Emmanuelle would blacklist me if I left on bad terms." I let out a humorless laugh. "I guess I should've done it anyway since I ended up in pretty much the same place I was trying to avoid."

She's not going to blacklist you. Vuk finally spoke. Intermission was drawing to a close, but he didn't seem so concerned with the game anymore. *You have more power than you think. Don't let her intimidate you.*

"I'll try," I said with a weak smile. "I told my parents Beaumont and I parted ways, but I kind of...glossed over the details." Hopefully, they never found out the ugly truth. "If the lawsuit news hits the major outlets—"

It won't. I'll take care of it.

If Vuk were anyone else, I'd call bullshit, but he exuded such confident authority, he could tell me he'd bring down the moon and I'd believe him.

"Thank you. For sharing this with me..." I gestured around the community room. "And for listening."

His face softened. *Anytime.*

Our gazes broke apart when the dark-haired woman called the next game into session, but the warmth from our conversation lingered.

It was funny how talking about the hard things with Vuk always made me feel better afterward, not worse.

We stayed at the center for another hour. Neither of us felt like going out after bingo night officially wrapped, so Vuk had Sean drive us to my apartment. He walked me upstairs while his security chief waited in the car.

"You should come in," I said. "For a nightcap."

"If I come in, I won't leave, *srce*."

"I'm okay with that," I said shyly.

We hadn't had the "so what are we?" conversation yet, and he'd never stayed over at my place. But there was no better time to start than now, right?

To my disappointment, Vuk shook his head. "As much as I'd love to spend the night with you, I have a meeting with Singapore in half an hour. It's about our expansion there. I've already pushed it back once; the board will kill me if I postpone again." He gave me a rueful smile. "I've been neglecting the company. Lots of distractions lately."

I raised my eyebrows. "Are you calling me a distraction again?"

A shadow passed over his face, but it disappeared before I could say anything. "The best kind." He leaned down and gave me a lingering kiss. "I'll see you Tuesday?"

That was the date of our next shooting lesson.

I nodded. We said good night, and he waited until I safely entered my apartment before he left. I heard his footsteps fade as I slumped against the door, my lips still tingling from his kiss. I couldn't suppress a huge grin.

Even though he couldn't stay over, tonight had been incredible. Seeing a new side of Vuk and hearing him open up about his family, even a little, was better than any fancy date or expensive gift.

I basked in the afterglow for a minute longer. Then I turned on the lights, tossed my bag on the couch, and was about to head for the shower when the hairs on my nape prickled.

Something was wrong. I felt it in my gut.

The warmth evaporated from my skin. My pulse accelerated, and I almost unlocked the front door so I could easily escape into the hall if needed. But what if there were intruders outside, waiting for me to do just that?

Instead, I pulled up Vuk's number. I kept my thumb over the call button while I listened for strange noises.

Dead silence.

Nevertheless, I crept into the kitchen and grabbed a knife. I inched my way through the apartment, my heart racing. A quick check of the closets, bedroom, bathroom, and even under the sink revealed nothing out of the ordinary. The windows were closed, and everything was where I'd left it.

I released a slow, shaky breath that gradually turned into a laugh. I was fine. I was simply being paranoid.

I returned the knife to the kitchen and went back to the living room to grab my water bottle. It was halfway out of my purse when a manila envelope caught my eye. It sat on the coffee table amidst a pile of magazines, knitting needles, and a legal pad filled with notes from my last call with Sloane. It blended in with the mess, which was why I'd missed it earlier.

My heart picked up speed again. I stared at it, frozen.

There was no return address or text on the envelope. It was perfectly innocuous.

It was also proof that someone had been inside my apartment because it *definitely* hadn't been there when I left.

I edged toward the table and picked up the envelope with a trembling hand. Whoever left this was gone, but that didn't stop an army of ants from crawling over my skin.

I wanted to run downstairs and open it in the safety of company or toss it in the trash and pretend I never saw it.

But I didn't.

I retrieved its contents and—

My stomach lurched. I gagged, the remnants of dinner surging up my throat as I stared at the images in horror.

They were photos. Bloody, gruesome photos of a man's mutilated corpse. He was so mangled, he looked like something out of a slasher movie.

There was a note clipped to one of the photos. It contained one sentence typed out in neat black font.

It's time you found out exactly the type of man Vuk Markovic really is.

CHAPTER 45

Vuk

I SPENT MY WEEKEND KNEE-DEEP IN PAPERWORK AND calls. Amidst all the Brotherhood and Emmanuelle drama, I actually did have a company to run. My staff had kept things flowing while I'd been busy with other priorities, but if I didn't buckle down before the holidays, I'd have a mutiny on my hands.

However, all thoughts of product launches and fiscal reports evaporated when Dominic emailed me Monday afternoon.

Subject: Done

The email contained no text, only an attachment. After the prerequisite cybersecurity checks, I downloaded the folder and opened the files.

My pulse thundered as I read through the documents. My team was good, but tracing money trails wasn't in their wheelhouse. It was in Dominic's.

I'd given him Shepherd's old safe house address. He was able to take that grain of information and chase it all the way to the end.

The intricate web of aliases and shell companies would've taken normal forensic accountants years to untangle, but Dominic's team wasn't normal; they were the best of the best. Plus, the favor

I'd promised him provided strong incentive for him to find what I was looking for within my given timeframe.

Say what you will about the man, but he got the job done.

I skipped past the unnecessary details and zeroed in on the name at the end of the trail.

The breath vanished from my lungs, and I smiled.

Bingo.

After I found out what I needed to know, I saved Dominic's files to a secure location and deleted his original email. I kept my revelation to myself for now. I had to be strategic about how I used the information, which meant I couldn't rush into action yet—no matter how much I wanted to.

The next afternoon, I went to the Valhalla Club for my shooting lesson with Ayana. She'd been strangely distant since Friday night. She hadn't texted me as frequently as she usually did, and when I reached out, she replied with uncharacteristically terse answers. She said she was simply stressed about the Emmanuelle situation, but I suspected there was something she wasn't telling me.

"You're early," I said. I'd arrived fifteen minutes before our scheduled lesson, but Ayana was already waiting in our usual stall. She normally didn't bring any accessories with her, but today, she carried a giant tote slung over her shoulder.

I kissed her hello. She returned it with noticeable hesitation.

"Everything okay?" I asked with a frown.

"Yes. No." Ayana's fingers strangled her bag strap.

I waited, a cold sensation creeping into my gut. This wasn't like her. Even when she was upset, she was never this aloof.

"After we said goodbye on Friday, I went into my apartment and…" She took a deep breath. "Someone broke in while I was out. They left something for me."

My reaction was so visceral, my head snapped up before her words fully registered. Blood rushed to my ears, and a sudden snarl of pure, icy panic exploded in my chest.

"Are you hurt? What did they leave you? Why didn't you call me?" I fired the questions one after another, like bullets from a loaded gun.

Fuck the Singapore meeting. I should've gone in with her and made sure everything was okay before I left. Shepherd might be dead, but the other faction was still out there.

It was a rare oversight on my part. I should've known better. Hell, I should've gone with my initial instinct and kept a twenty-four-hour guard at her building even after Shepherd died. Ayana would've hated it, and my team was already overworked, but it would've been worth it.

Now, someone had broken into her apartment, and I hadn't been there.

Regret serrated my stomach.

"I'm fine," Ayana reassured me. "Don't freak out. They were already gone when I got home, and they didn't take anything. I also filed a police report and changed my locks. Someone is coming later this week to upgrade my security system."

"My team will do it today," I said. "This can't wait, and their upgrades will be better than anything on the market."

"No. I already have it all set." Ayana wore a strange expression. I was about to argue when she added, "The person who broke in left me this."

My regret flattened into dread. I watched, stomach twisting, as she retrieved a manila envelope from her bag and passed it to me. There was a slight shake in her hand.

I hesitated for a second before I took the envelope.

Opened it.

Retrieved the contents.

And felt every ounce of blood drain from my face.

My breath knotted in my throat. The shock of seeing those particular images crystallized into jagged little ice chips that stabbed deeper and deeper the longer I stared.

There were three photos in total, detailing what I'd done to Dexter in graphic, gruesome detail. My team had dumped his remains near a known Brotherhood hub as a warning. If taking Dexter had tipped my hand to Shepherd, I might as well have gone all out—there'd been no point trying to hide what I'd done.

The pictures were taken where we'd left him, which meant someone from the organization had been inside Ayana's house. There was no one else who would've had the means or motive.

My blood thundered in my ears. I dragged my eyes from the close up image of Dexter's mangled face to the note clipped on top.

It's time you found out exactly the type of man Vuk Markovic really is.

A sickening taste filled my mouth. Time slowed into an excruciating pace. Each second scrounged forth a different memory.

Jordan getting shot. My first night with Ayana. Sean's call telling me he'd found Dexter. The warehouse. Roman's taunt about Ayana leaving me if she ever found out what I was truly capable of.

That'd been just over a week ago. I couldn't think of another reason why someone would leave Ayana these photos besides wanting to break us up, and the timing was a little too convenient.

The images crumpled in my fist. If that weaselly bastard Roman had anything to do with this, I was going to gut him like a fish.

But first, I had to deal with the present.

When I finally looked up again, Ayana was staring at me with that same strange expression, like she was torn between painful hope and possibly throwing up.

Time returned to normal, but my blood remained frozen.

"Tell me the truth." She gestured at the photos, her voice trembling. "Did you do it?"

Ayana

It was silent enough to hear a pin drop.

Vuk stared at me, his knuckles white around the photos—the gut-churning, blood-soaked photos that had haunted my nightmares for the past four days and made all my food taste like cardboard.

They rested in the same hands that had held me. Touched me. Comforted me.

I couldn't imagine them being responsible for something as brutal as what'd happened to the man in the pictures. I didn't want to believe it. There had to be another explanation.

Someone had either left them as a sick joke, or they were trying to frame Vuk. While I'd suspected Vuk's idea of justice crossed the line of what was technically legal, I never thought he'd be capable of *that*. There was also a difference between suspecting something and seeing it laid out in macabre detail.

Tell me it's not true. Please. Tell me it's not true.

His response shattered my fragile tendril of hope.

"I did."

My stomach plunged over the side of a cliff and straight into the icy waters below. The cold consumed me as I blinked, trying to match the implication behind his words and his stoic expression. It was like someone had slammed a gate shut over his face and turned the man I knew into a stranger.

I did.

"Okay." What a stupid, inane reply, but I couldn't grasp the right word amongst the thousands swirling through my head. I couldn't breathe, couldn't think, couldn't do anything except stand there and watch my world crumble around me. "Do you…" Once again, the words escaped me.

"Do I regret it?" Of course Vuk understood what I was trying to say. He always did. "The only thing I regret, *srce*, is that I didn't have more time to work on him." There wasn't a single trace of remorse in his voice.

Saliva vaporized in my sandpapered throat. The room was spinning out of control, and I had nothing to hold on to except the tatters of what used to be.

Vuk swallowed the distance between us with two strides. He held the photos up. "This is the man who shot Jordan. The man who almost killed *you*. For that alone, he deserved worse than what he got." His voice was arctic, but his body was an inferno. Heat poured off him like a living, breathing reminder of his duality.

The businessman and the criminal.

The protector and the murderer.

The man who could kiss me so tenderly one day and kill so viciously the next.

"In my world, justice comes in one form: retribution." Vuk cupped my cheek, his touch unbearably gentle. "I told you I wasn't a good person, *srce*. You should've believed me."

I closed my eyes, trying to reject his words even as I savored the warmth of his palm against my skin. My breaths escaped me in tiny, gasping puffs.

I was hyperaware of how isolated we were. The shooting range was always empty besides us, and it was located at the very back of Valhalla.

If I screamed, would anyone hear me? If they did, would they come to my rescue?

My mind brushed aside the hypotheticals as they popped

up. Despite Vuk's admission and the evidence of his cruelty, I wasn't afraid. Anxious, yes. Stunned, definitely. But I didn't feel an ounce of the fear that'd engulfed me when I'd been alone with Wentworth or when I saw a bullet streaking toward me at the wedding.

No matter his crimes, I didn't believe for a second that he would hurt me.

"Look at me." Vuk's command wrenched my eyes open. His stare burned into mine, equal parts unyielding and desperate. "This is who I am, Ayana. What I did to the man in these photos doesn't compare to what I did to those responsible for my brother's death. If I had the chance to go back in time, I'd do it all again a hundred times over. *No one* harms the people I care about and walks away intact."

My vision blurred. Part of me wanted to scream. Why couldn't he lie and let me live in blissful ignorance? Why couldn't he give me leeway to pretend nothing had changed? Why did he have to be so crushingly honest when it meant we'd never be the same?

"I won't hurt you. Ever," Vuk said. "If you walk away right now and say you never want to see me again, I'll respect your wishes. But I can't pretend to be somebody I'm not. What's done is done, and if someone came after you tomorrow, I'd deal with them the same way I dealt with the shooter." His tone was hard. Ruthless. "It's in my DNA, *srce*. I can compromise, but I can't change the core of who I am. No matter how much I wish I could."

My heart splintered at the small crack I heard in his voice toward the end.

I understood his implicit question.

Would I stay, knowing the things he'd done and was capable of? Or would I walk away like he said I could and leave the darkness of his world behind?

The prospect of the latter tore through me in a blaze of pain, but it was chased by the phantom screams of a man I didn't and now would never know.

Crimson images flickered behind my eyes, and my stomach heaved for the dozenth time since Friday.

Do I stay, or do I leave?

"I..." Words stuck in my throat. A decision glimmered beneath the murky waters of indecision, but I couldn't reach it. If I tried, I would drown.

"I need time." A tear slipped down and scalded my cheek. "I just—I can't think right now. I need to be alone for a while so I can..." Unshed tears swallowed the rest of my sentence. "I just need to be alone," I repeated.

Vuk swallowed. Emotions battered at his stony facade. Fear, panic, desperation—they surfaced for a gasp of air before his face shuttered again.

He dropped his hand and stepped back.

A chill swept over my skin. I shivered, yearning to feel the warmth of his touch again even as the hole in my chest threatened to swallow me.

"Take as much time as you need," he said. "I'll be here."

His quiet promise was supposed to make me feel better, but it only made me feel worse. And when I walked away, my throat so tight it was impossible for me to squeeze another syllable out of it, I couldn't help but look back.

Vuk was standing exactly where I'd left him, his head and shoulders bowed.

We hadn't said goodbye, not yet, but I felt like a chasm had opened up between us all the same.

I sucked in a shuddering breath and faced forward again. *One foot in front of the other. That's it. You can do it.*

I walked through the halls of Valhalla like a ghost, corporeal yet lost. Somehow, I found my way to the exit, but I didn't know where to go from there.

The thought of returning to my empty apartment made me flinch. Despite what I'd said about upgrading my security, I was on edge knowing someone—most likely a member of the Brotherhood—had broken in so easily. Perhaps I should check into a hotel or ask Maya if I could impose on her for a few nights.

In an alternate reality, I would stay at Vuk's house, but that was no longer an option.

I swiped at my tears and took another deep breath. I could break down later, in private. Right now, I needed something, anything, to distract me.

I walked down the street from Valhalla and hailed a cab. I told the driver to drop me anywhere in SoHo. A walk would calm me down, and the neighborhood was crowded enough on a weekday afternoon to provide the illusion of safety.

Thirty minutes later, I exited the cab and ducked into a nearby café for tea. It wasn't my mother's shai, but it'd do in a pinch.

I let the drink's comforting warmth wash away the rest of my tears as I wandered through the streets. My nose was stuffy, and my head pounded the way it always did after I cried, but I was so emotionally exhausted I didn't even care if someone recognized me while I looked like shit.

Who cared about a potentially bad candid photo when my heart was being crushed?

It doesn't have to be this way. I could run back to Valhalla right now and throw myself into Vuk's arms. I could look the other way if and when he did what he did, and we could live happily ever after.

But a part of me would always know. I would always be on edge, and he would always feel my distance unless I found a way to reconcile my morality with my feelings toward him.

Whether or not that was possible remained to be seen.

"Ayana."

I paused at the familiar voice. It was one I hadn't heard in person in months.

Hank stood outside Beaumont's headquarters, a cigarette in hand. I'd been so preoccupied by my thoughts I hadn't realized I'd meandered straight to my old agency's offices.

I stiffened. My former agent looked the same as always, all slicked-back hair and spray-tanned skin. However, dark shadows smudged his eyes, and his hand trembled as he brought the cigarette to his mouth.

I remembered what Emmanuelle had said about Vuk threatening him. Perhaps I wasn't that good of a person after all because, while I couldn't stomach torture, the mental image of Hank cowering before Vuk gave me an immense sense of satisfaction.

"What do you want?" I asked.

He took a drag of his cigarette before he spoke again. "We never got the chance to say goodbye. Six years of partnership down the drain." Hank shook his head. "You really pissed Emmanuelle off."

"By asking for what I was *legally* due?" My grip tightened around my cup. "And when you say six years of partnership, you really mean six years of exploitation."

"Exploitation?" He scoffed. "You'd still be a nobody in D.C. if it weren't for me. I gave you a career. Fame. Money. Even if you take your agency fees into account, you've earned more with me than you ever would've doing…what? Toiling away in some chemistry lab somewhere?" Hank's eyes glinted. "You think you would've ever met men like Jordan Ford or Vuk Markovic if it weren't for me?"

"I never asked for any of those things," I snapped. Anger was good. Anger kept me from dwelling on the sharp pang of hearing

Vuk's name. "I just wanted enough money to pay my father's medical bills. I didn't want to be famous, and I definitely didn't want to be locked into your sham of a contract."

"Maybe not, but here we are." Hank gave me a thin smile. "At least you won't have to worry about your contract any longer. Just a lawsuit."

"The lawsuit is bullshit, and everyone knows it."

"Sure, but by the time it's over, you won't be the untarnished golden girl of fashion anymore, will you?" Hank stubbed out his cigarette. "Emmanuelle knows what she's doing. You may have Markovic on your side, but she's not someone you want to cross. Ever."

I suppressed a flinch at his second mention of Vuk. "I'm not afraid of her," I said. "Not anymore."

What else could she do to me that she hadn't already done?

"That's too bad." Something flickered in Hank's eyes. "I thought you were smarter than that."

Screw this. I'd wasted enough time on him. He wasn't my agent anymore, and I had no reason to indulge his attempts to get in my head.

I left without another glance, but his words followed me like a putrid scent.

Did Emmanuelle have something else up her sleeve or another motive to target me besides one semi-heated phone call? I'd been Beaumont's top-earning model, and she was a shrewd business-woman. Her decision to drop me didn't make practical sense.

Then again, ego had a way of making people act against their best interests. Two years ago, an up-and-coming fashion designer ignored his friends' advice and sank a million dollars of his own money into a last-minute event to spite his rival, who was hosting his own event that night. The whole thing had been a disaster, and the designer never recovered socially or financially.

So yes, I believed Emmanuelle was really that petty.

I turned the corner onto a side street. It was one of those empty lanes that served no real purpose other than as a conduit from one major thoroughfare to the next.

I spotted the gleam of a familiar café across the way. I was almost finished with my tea, so it was perfect timing. Instead of running around downtown, I was going to order another drink, park myself in a corner booth, and browse the latest posts from my favorite perfume blog. No emails, no texts, no checking social media, and *no* thinking about Vuk. Once I cleared my head, *then* I could decide what to do next.

Resolve quickened my steps, but I'd only made it halfway down the street when a sharp pain pierced my neck.

At first, I thought I'd been stung by a bee. My hand flew up to swat it away, and that was when the world tilted. My cup fell from my other hand and rolled across the ground. The lid popped off, and the remnants of my tea seeped into the concrete like a dark stain.

Tightness seized my lungs. I stumbled, my breaths coming out in short, shallow bursts. The last thing I heard was the slam of a car door before iron hands grabbed me, and the world went black.

CHAPTER 46

Vuk

I COULDN'T SLEEP, AND I COULDN'T WORK. SHOOTING HELD
no satisfaction when the range reminded me so much of Ayana, so
the day after she showed me the photos, and my world fell to pieces,
I did something I never did: I went to the boxing gym.

I could count on one hand the number of times I'd entered the
gym since I joined Valhalla. Boxing wasn't my sport of choice, but
when it came to venting frustrations, nothing beat an old-fashioned round in the ring.

"So, tell me," Dante said. "Who the hell pissed you off?"

I dodged his fist and countered with an uppercut. I didn't
answer his question.

It wasn't his first time trying to pry information out of me. I
was lucky Dante had been at the gym when I arrived so I didn't
have to look for a sparring partner, but I wasn't here to talk. If I
told someone what happened with Ayana, that would make it real,
and if it was real—if she was really gone for good—then I would
want to tear this building apart with my bare fucking hands.

I need to be alone for a while.

Her words clawed at my stomach, deeper than fear, deeper

than regret. They shredded me from the inside out, and there was nothing I could do to stop the bleeding.

I need to be alone for a while.

The echoes haunted me as doggedly as the sight of her tears. I should've known it would come to this. Some secrets couldn't stay buried forever, and mine were more egregious than most.

I could've lied, but that would've been a Band-Aid, not a solution. Ayana and I hadn't defined our relationship yet. If and when we did, I wanted her to know exactly what she was getting herself into.

No matter how much I wished I could be the good, gentle man she deserved, I couldn't. I was who I was, a monster forged by nature and circumstance. I couldn't destroy the darkness in me any more than a leopard could change its spots, and I would never apologize for exacting vengeance on those who deserved it.

But if she decided to walk away, then—

A fist collided with my jaw. My head snapped to the left, and the tang of liquid copper flooded my mouth. I spat it out, my ears ringing.

"You're distracted." Dante tsked. His eyes held a touch of amusement. "I don't suppose it has anything to do with a certain model I saw running out of the club yesterday."

A growl rumbled in my chest. I landed a direct jab, and he absorbed the hit with a pained grunt.

"I'll take that as a yes," he said.

I attacked again. I was beyond caring whether I won or lost at this point. I just needed to punch something, and Dante was as good a target as any.

Sweat poured down my face and into my eyes. My muscles were wound so tight, they felt like they were going to snap.

I need to be alone for a while.

That could be days, weeks, or months. It could be forever. The uncertainty of it all gnawed at me with poison-tipped teeth, as did the reason behind the Brotherhood's actions.

What did sending her those photos accomplish besides driving her away from me? Why would they care if we were together or not? If anything, they should want us closer—that would give them more leverage over me. Or maybe their goal was to throw me off-balance. Distract me with my relationship troubles so I would be more vulnerable to another attack.

My phone's telltale ring cut through the cacophony of my thoughts. I called a time-out so I could answer.

Normally, I'd ignore it and keep going, but it might be Ayana. It was unlikely, given less than twenty-four hours had passed since our last conversation, but a man could hope.

Unfortunately, it wasn't Ayana; it was Sean. And he was calling, which was never a good sign.

I picked it up, listened—and for the second time that week, my world exploded into pieces.

"How the *fuck* did this happen?" The snarl that tore out of my throat was positively feral.

Sean didn't flinch, but his grim expression betrayed his worry. "We sent one person to her building after you called me yesterday, but we don't have eyes on her when she's not home. As you instructed, we'd planned on keeping a full-time guard with her starting today, but it was already too late." His jaw tightened. "This was my oversight, and I take full responsibility."

We were at my office in Valhalla. I'd left the boxing gym and had Sean meet me here immediately after he called to tell me Ayana was missing.

Missing.

My stomach sloshed with acid.

The guard I'd stationed at Ayana's building alerted Sean this morning that she hadn't gone home last night, which was almost unheard of for her. A quick check with her friends revealed no one had heard from her since yesterday afternoon. She couldn't have gone on a trip, since she would've needed to go home after Valhalla to pack.

That was when Sean suspected something was amiss and called me.

Rage shimmered beneath a slick coat of panic. It'd been twenty-two hours since she was last seen, and I wanted to burn the city to the ground until I found her.

"We were able to access Valhalla's security footage and get the license plate of the cab she took after leaving the club," Sean said. "We tracked the driver down. He remembered her and said he dropped her off in SoHo. We pulled the surveillance footage from around her drop-off spot and saw her enter and exit a nearby café."

Despite Sean's earlier apology, I was clear-headed enough to recognize that what happened wasn't his fault; it was mine. I should've been on top of it. I should've made sure she was safe before I let her go, I should've warned her about the Brotherhood, I *should've should've should've*. And now, it might be too late.

A sour feeling spread through my stomach. "Were you able to trace her steps and find out where she was last seen?"

He hesitated. "To a point. I have the entire team working on it, but it's a lot of footage. That's assuming she went missing somewhere that *has* surveillance. A lot of businesses in the area don't have CCTV." Sean opened his encrypted laptop, which he'd set up on my desk. "However, we realized Beaumont's headquarters was a ten-minute walk from the café. Given her current complications with the agency, we checked the building's cameras just in case, and…" He pulled up a video.

The man onscreen faced away from the camera, but I'd

recognize that overly gelled hair and flashy Rolex anywhere. He was smoking a cigarette. A few seconds later, Ayana entered the frame. Her eyes appeared swollen, and she was holding a cardboard cup from the café.

A star-bright wave of pain blazed through me. *She's fine. She's okay.* She had to be.

The two appeared to have a heated discussion before Ayana walked off with a defiant expression.

"Unfortunately, there are no other surveillance cameras nearby, so we couldn't trace where she went afterward," Sean said. "But I have people manually checking the area in case she left any clues."

"Update me as soon as they find *anything*. Until then, bring Hank to me," I commanded. "Immediately."

"Done."

After Sean left, I paced my office and tried to control the nausea rising in my throat. I could control myself when I was giving orders and formulating plans, but with nothing else to do except wait, a yawning pit had opened in my stomach.

Ayana's conversation with Hank was the last time she'd been seen. According to the video's time stamp, that had been twenty-three hours ago. An eternity in my world.

There was a slim chance she'd willingly gone off the grid without stopping by her apartment to grab her stuff first, but my gut told me that wasn't the case.

She was in trouble, and if whoever took her harmed a single fucking hair on her head...

My heart hardened into black, pitiless ice as I stared at the grainy image of Hank onscreen.

God himself wouldn't be able to stop me from taking my revenge.

CHAPTER 47

Ayana

I SMELLED THE BLOOD BEFORE I OPENED MY EYES.

It reeked of metal and death, and the scent was so thick and pungent I couldn't draw a single breath without it choking my lungs. Every inhale felt like I was snorting copper straight into my nose. The phantom taste settled on the back of my tongue, and I had to fight the urge to gag.

My gut churned. I squeezed my eyes shut, terrified of the gory scene that awaited me when the smell of blood was so strong, but I couldn't stay in the dark forever. Not when someone had grabbed me off the street and taken me to...wherever I was.

They must've injected me with a sedative because a headache pounded behind my temple, and sensation was just starting to creep back into my arms and legs.

I braced myself and slowly opened my eyes. I blinked away the grogginess until the room came into gradual focus.

I was tied to a chair in the middle of a wide aisle. Rough rope bound my wrists behind the chair, and my feet were similarly shackled to the chair legs.

Dust motes swirled in the weak beams of sunlight slanting

through the room. It appeared to be a warehouse of sorts. Soaring ceilings, concrete floors, grimy windows perched high on bare walls. Shipping containers were stacked around me, obscuring my view of anything not in my direct vicinity.

And lying right in front of me, less than ten feet away, was a dead body.

Correction: *pieces* of a dead body. A torso, an arm, and…

My stomach rebelled. Bile sloshed up my throat, and I retched with a gagging sound.

I wanted to close my eyes again and pretend it wasn't there—pretend I was safe and warm in my bedroom, with my comforter pulled up around my chin and my favorite lavender aromatherapy candle burning on the nightstand—but I couldn't look away.

It was the photos from the envelope come to life, only this was a different man. I couldn't tell who it was. His face was turned the other way, which was a small blessing. I didn't think I could handle a pair of lifeless eyes staring at me while I awaited whatever horrible fate my abductors had planned for me.

I sat frozen in terror, convinced that whoever was responsible for the man's gruesome death would turn the corner and hack me to similar pieces. But several minutes passed, and other than the ragged gasps of my breaths, I couldn't hear a single sound.

Get a fucking hold of yourself. Hysteria won't help you. You need to think.

I silently counted to ten and eventually calmed my breaths enough to take stock of my surroundings.

There weren't many places in New York that could accommodate a warehouse of this size. Certainly none in Manhattan. Of course, we could be in another state entirely.

How long had I been out? Hours? Days? Long enough to spirit me away to a neighboring state like Pennsylvania or at least out of the city.

Judging by the slant and color of the light, it was late afternoon, nearing evening.

My mind whirred. I needed to get out of here while I could, but how?

I wiggled, testing the strength of my ties. The rope wasn't that thick, but the knots were killer. I didn't see my bag anywhere, nor did I see any sharp objects I could use to saw through the rope.

Frustration tunneled under my skin.

Breathe. Think.

I was alive, which meant my kidnappers had plans for me. If they'd wanted to kill me, they would've.

Whether I would prefer death over their plans was another matter.

Sickening images of what someone could do to a person besides kill them played through my head. My stomach sloshed again, and I forced a shaky inhale through my nose.

Panicking wasn't going to get me anywhere. I needed a clear head if I was going to get out of this. What would Vuk do?

Vuk. The thought of him twisted my heart into an agonizing knot. Our argument, if it could be called that, seemed like a lifetime ago even though it couldn't have been more than one or two days. I didn't know what was going to happen with our relationship, but I would give anything to see his face and hear his voice again. If I didn't, our last words to each other would've been in shock and anger—on my part, at least.

Regret formed a pit in my stomach. Until now, Vuk's world of hitmen and murder had seemed removed from real life. I'd known it existed, but even during the wedding attack and its aftermath, I'd been so numb that it hadn't fully registered. Vuk's men had stopped the attackers, and Jordan had survived despite being shot. The threat had been there, but it hadn't seemed *real*.

Not the way this did.

I glanced at the body again. I fought back another gag. Even if I made it out of here alive, I would never forget that sight.

It gave me a little more empathy for Vuk's actions. An eye for an eye wasn't always the best form of justice, but at least it was *a* form of justice.

Tears crowded my throat. If only he were here. If only I could tell him everything running through my mind.

But he wasn't, which meant it was up to me to get myself out of this mess. I refused to die without seeing him and telling him I...

I took another deep inhale and shook my head. *Focus, Ayana. One thing at a time.*

First order of business: figure out who I was dealing with. Who had the means and motive to kidnap me? Emmanuelle hated me, but she wasn't exactly the kidnapping type. She was more likely to cut you with words and blackmail. The only other people I could think of was the Brotherhood. They'd already ruined the wedding, and I wouldn't be surprised if they were trying to use me to get to Vuk.

If that was the case, I was fucked. There was no way I could take on professional killers.

But I had to try.

I wiggled in my seat, trying to loosen my bonds. Nothing.

Sweat gathered beneath my underarms and formed a thin film across my forehead and upper lip. My stomach growled. I hadn't eaten since the eggs and smoothie I'd gulped down before meeting Vuk at Valhalla. Maybe if I had, I'd have more energy to—

Footsteps broke the utter silence.

I froze. Acid lined my throat.

The footsteps got louder...

My heartbeats hammered in sync with their steady, ominous rhythm.

Louder...

I wriggled harder. Strategy fled as panic turned my movements frantic. Even if I got loose, I doubted I could outrun my abductor, but I was *not* going to sit here and wait for them to butcher me without a fight.

Louder...

Was I imagining things, or did the rope around my right ankle give a little? I put more weight on that side, trying to—

The footsteps stopped.

They were here.

I stilled. My pulse tried to claw its way out of my veins, and I steeled myself again to face my abductor.

I dragged my eyes up, over the dead body and up a pair of black-clad legs.

Up, up, up, all the way to a familiar face.

My breath condensed into icicles.

No.

CHAPTER 48

Vuk

"I DON'T KNOW WHERE SHE IS!" HANK BLUBBERED. "I swear! She happened to walk by while I was taking a smoke break. That's all. I had nothing to do with her disappearance or Emmanuelle dropping her. I—" His words devolved into gurgles when I tightened my grip around his throat.

His face turned purple, and his feet kicked futilely in the air.

I'd started interrogating him the minute Sean dumped him at my house an hour ago, and I was tired of his excuses. More than twenty-four hours had passed since Ayana was last seen; my patience, like my mercy, had run dry.

"Please." Hank gasped. "I can help. If you let me—I—" He choked again, his eyes bulging.

I was tempted to squeeze harder until this pathetic stain on humanity was no more, but he was the last person to have spoken with Ayana. Plus, he had an inside line to Beaumont, which might or might not come in handy, depending on how things played out. There was just too much fucking uncertainty at the moment.

I reluctantly released him. He doubled over, wheezing.

I'd moved from my office at Valhalla to the basement of my

house soon after Sean went to fetch him. It was a tertiary office I'd set up across from my makeshift rage room. I needed somewhere private to deal with Hank, and neither Valhalla nor my official company headquarters was the place.

"Look, I—I don't know what happened, but I saw what street she turned onto when she left," Hank said when he regained enough oxygen to speak properly again. "It was that…that side street with no shops. It leads to a bunch of cafés and stores. I know Ayana—I've been her agent for years. When she's stressed, she'll go to a coffee shop and sit there for *hours*. If you check the—"

"We did," Sean said coldly. He'd been watching us quietly from the corner. "She doesn't show up on the surveillance footage from any of those businesses."

Beads of sweat gleamed on Hank's upper lip. "Well, there are a lot of other…" He faltered at my glare. His eyes darted left and right, left and right before they finally met mine again. "Okay. You say she's been missing since yesterday afternoon, right? Well, I don't know if this is connected or helpful at all, but, um…"

"Spit it out," Sean growled.

"I haven't seen Emmanuelle since yesterday afternoon either," Hank blurted. "We had a meeting scheduled for this morning, and she didn't show up. That's not like her. I'm not—I'm not saying she's a kidnapper or anything, but the timing is weird, right? And I know she has it out for Ayana, so maybe she knows something?" His voice turned into a squeak at the end.

Sean and I exchanged glances.

Hank might be smarter than we gave him credit for because the same thought had initially crossed my mind, only I had information he didn't.

Thanks to Dominic, I knew for a fact that Emmanuelle Beaumont, née Élodie Beaumont, was involved with the Brotherhood. She was the sister of Stéphane Bouvier, also known as

Shepherd, no last name. The name of their tiny French hometown was what had tripped my alarms when I read her bio.

Shepherd and I had crossed paths briefly before my brother died. He'd joined the Brotherhood a month before I left, and he'd wanted to see my poison-making process. During that night in my lab, he'd made an offhand comment about his hometown.

It was a mistake on his part. The Brothers were trained never to share personal details, not even with each other, but he'd been too new and green to catch his slip-up. I hadn't paid much attention at the time, but I remembered looking it up out of curiosity and finding out there were only a thousand or so residents who lived there.

What were the odds of Emmanuelle and Shepherd *both* hailing from the same place without some sort of connection to each other?

My team couldn't make the connection because the only evidence of it was hidden deep in their finances, but Dominic's forensic accounting had finally confirmed my hunch. Emmanuelle was the one who'd kept Shepherd's faction afloat with money embezzled from her agency and her more lucrative but abhorrent side activities.

Dominic had found a string of large deposits that couldn't be attributed to her Beaumont salary or other sources. A deeper dive revealed an ugly underbelly to her work—specifically, a "sexual entertainment" ring that drew its "entertainers" from her own model base.

Beaumont's high-earning models were shielded from that side of the business, but the girls who'd been with the agency for years and hadn't earned enough for management's liking were coerced into working off their debts in other ways.

Dominic hadn't dived into who their clients were, but I bet it read like a who's who of the fashion industry and beyond. It would explain why Emmanuelle wielded so much power.

So yes, she had a direct link to the Brotherhood and motive for hurting Ayana. She also had extra motive to hurt me, considering I'd killed her brother, but she wasn't the one who'd taken Ayana. If she had, Enzo—the tail I'd put on her—would've told me, but he'd reported as normal all day.

I didn't know why Emmanuelle missed her meeting with Hank. Maybe she was as sick of him as I was.

Hank was blathering on about cafés again when Sean called me over. "Vuk." He tipped his head toward the door, indicating we needed to talk in private.

We left Hank in the room. We didn't have anything sensitive in there, so I wasn't worried.

"I got a call from my guys on the ground," Sean said once we were alone. "They found a to-go cup on the side street Hank mentioned. It matches the one Ayana was holding in the footage. They brought it back to our lab to dust for fingerprints. The problem is, the street is a blind zone. No cameras, hidden from view for most passersby. If someone parked a van at either end, no one would see what was happening."

Frustration chafed beneath my skin. *So it doesn't matter if the cup is hers. We'd know where they'd grabbed her, and that's it.*

"Maybe, maybe not." Sean pulled up a photo on his phone. In it, a silver button gleamed against dirty concrete. "They also found this on the ground near the cup. Maybe it fell off someone else who walked down the street that day, or it ended up there some other way. There's nothing to suggest it's tied to the Ayana situation, but the guys brought it back anyway. They ran its analysis first. No fingerprints, but they did find a trace of alluvial soil. Long Island in particular is covered with that stuff. It's a tenuous link, but…"

If they were to bring her somewhere, they'd choose somewhere secluded, where there's little chance of witnesses or cameras.

That ruled out most of Manhattan. Long Island, on the other hand, would be perfect.

Like Sean said, it was a tenuous link. The button could be from a random Long Islander who happened to be visiting the city. But it was a lead, and I was desperate enough to chase down any clue we found, no matter how small.

"Exactly," Sean said. "Long Island's a big place, but we'll sweep the more isolated areas first, especially those with abandoned warehouses."

I'm going to join you. I needed to do something. If I stayed inside the house for one more minute, I was going to lose it.

Sean didn't argue. "I'll let you know once we're ready to roll out. What do you want us to do with Hank?"

Lock him in there. I want to keep an eye on him. I doubted he had a hand in Ayana's disappearance, but I still didn't trust that little weasel.

While Sean went to make the necessary arrangements, I called Roman. It went straight to voicemail—again.

I hadn't been able to reach him since yesterday. He was a ghost in the wind, and I was growing more and more certain that he was involved in this shitstorm.

There was a ninety percent chance he was the one who'd sent Ayana those photos. Once I got my hands on him, I was going to—

My burner phone rang. *Speak of the devil.*

I picked up immediately. "Where the fuck have you been?"

"Sorry, but I don't exist at your whim," Roman snapped. "I've got my own shit going on. Now what's so important that you called me *twenty times* in the past two hours?"

I tamped down my questions about the photos and focused on the important topic at hand. I could kill him later; for now, I needed his help.

I gave him a quick summary of Ayana's disappearance, what

we'd found, and where we were at in our search. "Do you have any information about where the other faction operates? Any safe houses or hubs on Long Island?"

Roman was quiet for a long moment. "Maybe. I'd be surprised if they *didn't* have something on Long Island." More silence. I almost thought he'd hung up when he spoke again. "This other faction...there's something I need to tell you. In person."

"Is this important, or are you going to feed me more bullshit?"

I didn't have time to waste. Every minute counted in missing persons cases, and I'd already squandered too many.

"It's important. Trust me," he said. "In fact, it could help you get Ayana back."

That was all I needed to hear.

We set a time and location, and I hung up.

I stared at my phone, my throat thick with desperation. I tried not to imagine Ayana tied up somewhere, terrified and alone.

Hold on, baby. I'm coming.

CHAPTER 49

Ayana

"YOU LOOK SURPRISED," WENTWORTH DRAWLED. "NOT who you expected to see?"

I gaped at him, wondering if the sedative had really been a hallucinogen. That was the only explanation I could think of for why the former fashion photographer was pointing a gun at me in the middle of an empty warehouse.

I hadn't seen or heard from him since he tried to attack me at the Sage Studios shoot. Now here he was, looking a little worse for wear but very much alive.

His eyes glittered as he stared at me. His nose was crooked, like it'd healed the wrong way after being broken—I felt a pang of satisfaction at that—and his hair was longer. A blue cast wrapped around his right hand, which meant he was holding the gun in his less dominant left hand.

"You're a member of the Brotherhood?" I couldn't keep the disbelief out of my voice.

I doubted it. The prospect was more absurd than a mob boss being a secret party clown, but I needed to stall while I figured out how the hell I was going to get out of this.

Assassin or not, Wentworth held a personal vendetta against me. A man with a grudge and a gun was a dozen times worse than a detached professional.

"Not a member, no. But you could say we have a mutual acquaintance." Wentworth's smile sent chills down my neck. "They wanted Vuk, I wanted you. Luckily, you two are a package deal these days. I only wish I could've seen that asshole's face when he realized you were gone. He must've lost it." He sounded positively gleeful. "We were following you all day. He never noticed because he never left Valhalla. Lucky us."

I recognized that hyper, manic tone. He was high again.

Great. Like dealing with a vindictive, gun-wielding asshole wasn't enough; I had to deal with a vindictive, gun-wielding, coked-out-of-his-mind asshole.

I kept my gaze on his as I pressed my right ankle against my ties. The rope gave another fraction of an inch.

"Do you know what he did?" I froze when Wentworth came up next to me. His breath smelled like sickly sweet fruit and whiskey. It made me want to vomit. "He destroyed my hand. Smashed it with a hammer. I'll never be able to shoot again— not with a camera, anyway." He waved his gun in the air and laughed at his own joke. "All because I wanted a little kiss from *you*."

The cold metal of his gun pressed against my temple. Terror staled on my tongue, and I couldn't suppress a whimper.

"He didn't believe me when I said you were asking for it, but I've seen what you do in the name of 'modeling,'" Wentworth sneered. "You're half naked on a billboard in Times Square. If that isn't an open invitation, what is?"

Hot, eviscerating anger boiled up my spine. My skin flushed, and I bit my tongue so hard, I tasted blood. I wanted to lash out and tell him people like him were everything that was wrong with the world, and maybe Vuk should've smashed his mouth in instead. That way, he wouldn't be able to spew his vile poison.

Unfortunately, I couldn't antagonize him when I didn't have leverage. He wasn't rational. Who knew what he would do if I set him off?

I forced myself to swallow my acidic response and tipped my chin past him instead. *Ignore the bait. Keep him talking.* "The body. Who is that? Why did you kill him?"

Wentworth rolled his eyes. "No one important. He crossed the wrong person, and that's that. But I didn't kill him. I only wanted you." He smiled again. My skin crawled with the phantom legs of a thousand spiders. "If I had my way, we'd get reacquainted now, but they'll be very upset if I deviate from our plan. Besides, I want Vuk here to watch. It shouldn't be long before he finds us." My surge of hope was dashed by his next words. "The Brothers left him a nice clue on the street. He'll think he's onto something, but we'll be ready. Besides..." He gently traced the side of my face with his gun. "No matter how many people he brings as backup, it won't be enough." He stopped and jabbed the cold metal under my chin. "Because we have you, and he'll never jeopardize your life. Not even to save his own."

"You won't get away with it." I couldn't resist a reply. I had to keep talking, or I was going to throw up all over Wentworth's shoes. That probably wouldn't go over too well. "You'll never beat him. He's too smart."

"We'll see."

Wentworth's blasé attitude terrified me more than a raging temper tantrum. What trap did he and the Brothers have planned?

It doesn't matter. Vuk will get out of it. He has to.

He was invincible. Mortal, yes, but the idea of anything or anyone taking him down was unfathomable.

He was *not* going to die because of me. I refused to even entertain the possibility.

"I have to go. Lots of things to do, but I wanted to stop by and say hi," Wentworth said. "Enjoy your time alone while you can." He laughed again.

I held my breath until he disappeared into the darkening bowels of the warehouse. How many guards were here? What would Vuk be up against if and when he found me?

We have you, and he'll never jeopardize your life. Not even to save his own.

Tears scorched my throat.

Wentworth and his co-conspirators wouldn't kill me until Vuk was here. They needed me alive as leverage. But that didn't mean they couldn't do other things to me.

I had to free myself. If I couldn't escape, I could at least hide until I found a way to call for help. It was almost nighttime, and it was always easier to hide in the dark.

I scanned my surroundings again. I didn't see any cameras, and I was grateful they hadn't stationed a guard here to keep an eye on me. If I were Vuk, they'd have a dozen armed guards on me at all times. They must not have thought I posed enough of a threat to warrant more resources than some rope and a quickly fading sedative.

That was the upside of the "dumb model" stereotype. People constantly underestimated me.

I reexamined my situation. Trying to break free from the knots was impossible. Even if I got my right ankle out, it wouldn't help much. I needed to free my hands.

I looked around for the umpteenth time, desperately seeking a hairpin or anything I could use as a makeshift blade.

Nothing.

I was about to give up and try wiggling out of my ties again when my gaze fell on my shoes. As always, I was wearing heels—beautiful, spiky, four-inch stiletto heels. They weren't a knife or scissors, but they were sharp, and they could be deadly if utilized correctly. Even better, they were pumps, which meant I could slide out of them easily.

A plan took shape in my mind. It was a long shot, but it was better than nothing.

I only hoped I had time to execute it before Wentworth returned.

CHAPTER 50

Vuk

WE FOUND IT.

After three hours of searching, planning, and agonizing, we fucking found it—the warehouse where they'd taken Ayana.

My breath steamed in the chilly evening air as Sean, Bruce, Mav, and I observed the sprawling building from behind a low concrete wall. It was eerily similar to the one I'd bought in Brooklyn. It sat on a desolate lot of cracked concrete and spindly weeds, and there were no signs of life other than a rat that'd scuttled past our hiding place a minute earlier.

A black van was parked outside, and a weak golden light pierced the warehouse's grimy windows.

There was a five percent chance this was the wrong spot, but Ayana was inside. I *felt* it. Her proximity was a magnet pulling me toward the light, and adrenaline packed my blood, sharpening my senses as we waited for the right moment to strike.

"I told you." Roman's cool drawl brought four glares his way. "You owe me."

"We don't owe you anything," Sean growled. "We don't know for sure that she's in there."

His reconnaissance confirmed the presence of the Brotherhood, but he couldn't say for certain whether they had Ayana.

"She is. Once you rescue her, I'll take care of the rest." Roman's gaze met mine. "So don't fuck up."

My eyes narrowed. My finger twitched on the trigger of my gun, and the temperature dropped another ten degrees as I tried to corral the fury that rushed through me every time I looked at his face.

We'd met earlier like he'd asked. He'd had a lot to say—about Ayana's kidnapping, the other faction, and the truth behind some of the bullshit he'd fed me the past few months.

He was lucky I hadn't killed him. I came close several times, but he *had* provided crucial intel, even if it was information he should've told me long ago.

I also needed Roman for cover tonight. I'd only brought three of my men because walking into a direct gunfight with the Brotherhood was different than an ambush. I had no illusions about overpowering them the way we had Shepherd; this was going to be a nasty battle, and I wasn't going to lead my entire team to a slaughter.

Stealth also mattered more than manpower in this particular scenario. If I brought all twelve men, there was no way we could sneak in without alerting the Brothers. The more we caught them by surprise, the better.

Despite his faults, Roman was a valuable asset. He was a skilled shooter, and he operated well in the dark.

"It's the top of the hour." Sean's quiet voice tore our gazes away from each other.

His words brought a noticeable shift in the air. Bruce and Mav tensed, their faces hardening beneath the pale moonlight. Roman's smug amusement vanished, and lightning crackled along my skin. My previous surge of anger retreated in the face of cool, calm logic.

It was time.

Without another word, Sean, Roman, and I peeled away from the others and crept toward the warehouse. Bruce and Mav would stay behind as a cover force while we battled our way inside and rescued Ayana.

We stayed close to the shadows, our footsteps nearly silent. Fear, panic, worry—they all fell away as I locked in on the side exit. It loomed ahead, its rusted metal door beckoning like a siren's song.

My heart slowed to a painful rhythm.

I was well aware this could be a trap. I didn't believe for a second that Ayana's abductor had left something as obvious as a fucking button behind by accident, especially when the button didn't have fingerprints.

The new generation of Brothers was sloppier, but they weren't that sloppy. The button was meant to lead us here.

Even so, I had no choice but to take the bait. If I didn't, they'd resort to more extreme measures to get my attention—a severed finger, a video of Ayana being tortured. They might not kill her, but there were worse things than death.

The horror of those mental images hooked into my stomach and yanked. Ice spilled through my gut.

They haven't touched her yet. It's too soon. The chill spread into my chest. *It's too soon*, I repeated silently.

But I couldn't stop the images from replaying in my head. They were interspersed with memories from the past few months—Ayana laughing, Ayana teasing me about bingo, Ayana lighting up when she explained the science of smell.

She was the brightest part of my world. The thought of anyone or anything snuffing out her joy sent a streak of scarlet across my vision. My chest constricted.

I couldn't lose her. Not now. Not ever.

We'll find her. Even if I had to raze the city to the ground, I'd find her, and she'd be okay. She had to be.

Sean, Roman, and I reached the door without incident. As expected, it was locked, but a mini blowtorch quickly took care of the problem.

My hand hesitated on the handle. The hairs on my nape prickled. I envisioned a firing squad of assassins waiting on the other side, ready to riddle us with bullets.

No, that wasn't right. They wouldn't kill me so quickly. The same went for Roman when they found out he'd betrayed them. Sean was the only one who might be afforded a quick death.

Might, but wouldn't, because none of us were going to die.

Roman and Sean pressed themselves against the wall on either side of the door. I opened it, expertly maneuvering myself behind the door in case anyone lunged out of the darkness.

Silence.

Nevertheless, I kept my guard up as I inched inside and—

A volley of gunshots exploded in the night. A bullet hit the door by my ear. Metal pinged, and curses flew out as we scrambled to return fire.

Fuck! We'd mentally prepared for this, but that didn't stop my pulse from spiking to dangerous levels. Our Kevlar vests wouldn't stop us from getting shot in the head, and now that I'd opened the door, I had to monitor two fronts in case someone attacked from inside.

So far, nothing. All the shooters were outside, but that would change soon. I'd bet money on it.

"We'll take care of this!" Sean shouted. "*Go.*"

Another bullet embedded itself in the wall above his head. Roman swung around and fired at someone inside the van.

Glass shattered. Cries of pain and the thuds of falling bodies echoed around us. It was impossible to pinpoint where all the shooters were, and I heard the distinctive sound of Mav's yell in the distance. He was hurt.

Guilt flickered in my gut. I'd led my men here knowing there was a strong chance we would get ambushed. They'd understood the risks, but at the end of the day, this was my fight.

"Go!" Sean shouted again. Roman was still busy exchanging fire with the attackers in the van.

A bullet whizzed past us and grazed Sean's ear. He hissed and returned the favor. Another thud sounded in the distance, but the shots were coming from closer. The shooters were advancing.

His steely order snapped me out of my daze. It'd lasted less than two seconds, but every second counted.

Sean and Roman could take care of themselves. My number one priority was finding Ayana.

Sean covered me while I slipped inside the warehouse. He was trying to prevent the shooters from swarming me as long as he could.

The fact that they were attacking from outside wasn't good. It meant they had a trap waiting inside.

Eerie silence descended as I crept through the aisles. The deeper I went, the fainter the sounds from the fight outside became. The warehouse was enormous, and shipping containers towered all around me, providing ample ambush spots for the Brotherhood.

My caution meant I made painfully slow progress. I didn't know where Ayana was held, and there were over a dozen aisles in here. Eventually, however, I spotted a glimmer of light ahead. It was bright white, like the glow cast from a cell phone or a flashlight.

I highly doubt her abductors would've given her either of those things, which meant a Brother was nearby. If I quietly captured them, I could make them tell me where she was or at least what I was up against...unless *this* was the trap.

Practicality and desperation warred for dominance. If my old self could see me now, he'd berate me for my impulsiveness and idiocy. I was throwing the playbook out tonight, and I wasn't thinking as strategically as I should. Every rational decision was overshadowed by my need to get to Ayana as soon as possible.

That was what the Brotherhood was banking on, but I didn't have a choice. Thankfully, I had an ace up my sleeve. If that didn't work out...well, I was fucked.

I edged toward the light. I'd silenced my weapon before we left my house, but hopefully, I wouldn't have to use it at all. A knife was quicker and quieter, but a Glock made for better intimidation.

I almost reached the end of the aisle when the click of a gun sounded behind me. Before I could react, cold metal pressed against the side of my temple.

I stilled.

"Drop your gun."

Hot, angry flames blazed through me. I gritted my teeth, but I did as they asked. The gun clattered to the ground.

"Kick it away."

The flames swelled into a murderous inferno. I kicked the weapon aside. It skittered across the floor and came within centimeters of hitting a nearby shipping container.

A moment later, a familiar face came into view. Blood trickled from his forehead, but his eyes were cool and clear.

"So sorry about this," Roman said calmly. "But you'll have to come with me."

CHAPTER 51

Ayana

AFTER WHAT FELT LIKE HOURS, I SUCCESSFULLY GOT enough wiggle room around my right ankle to kick off my heel. It was a tiny achievement, but I felt like I'd successfully climbed Mount Everest.

My shirt and pants stuck to my skin with sweat. My lungs burned, and my arms and shoulders ached after countless hours of being bound.

But I wasn't done yet, and I had a new problem to solve. How was I going to reach my heel when my hands were tied?

I bit my lip. The stench of the dead body had worsened as the hours passed, but I'd grown numb to it. It was just another shitty aspect of an already shitty situation.

Thankfully, Wentworth hadn't returned yet, and none of my other abductors had shown their faces. After a minute of thinking, I held my breath and scooted as close to the shoe as possible. The scrape of chair legs against the floor was deafening in the silence, but no one came running to investigate the noise.

After I situated myself where I wanted, I eyed the shoe and

mentally calculated the angles. They weren't perfect, but they would have to do.

I braced myself and, instead of wiggling again, rocked my body from side to side. I threw as much of my weight toward the right side of my chair as possible, paused for breath, and did it all over again. It took half a dozen tries before gravity finally took hold and the chair tipped over.

I stifled a cry when my shoulder slammed against unyielding concrete. A shockwave of agony reverberated through my body, and I hoped to God I'd imagined that small crunch of bone.

I gritted my teeth against the pain and fumbled behind me for the heel. I grazed it a few times, but I couldn't quite get a hold of it. The bonds around my wrists were too tight, and I couldn't twist my head far enough to see behind me.

Come on. Come on. Come—there.

My fingers closed around the heel right as a burst of noise outside shattered the silence, and I dropped it again.

"*Fuck.*" I couldn't swallow a heated curse. I'd been *so close*, but my frustration died when I finally registered what the noise was.

Gunshots. Dozens of them.

My stomach cramped. I'd heard gunshots before, during my shooting lessons with Vuk. However, there was a difference between hearing them when you were in control of the weapon and hearing them when you were tied up and starving with a potentially fractured shoulder.

But...the Brothers wouldn't shoot at each other. The gunfire meant someone else was here. It meant *Vuk* might be here.

He'll think he's onto something, but we'll be ready. The memory of Wentworth's taunts grabbed my momentary elation and snapped it in half.

Even if Vuk *were* here, we weren't out of the woods. They'd been expecting him. All those gunshots...What if he—

No. I refused to think that way. I was going to be fucking delusional and imagine him shooting his way through the ambush, hopefully putting a bullet through Wentworth's smug mouth along the way.

The prospect of a rescue filled me with a fresh burst of energy. I searched for the heel with renewed determination and tried my best to ignore the growing fire in my shoulder. This time, it took me less than a minute to snag the shoe.

I shifted my body so I could wedge the stiletto into the knot tying my wrists together. It wasn't sharp enough to saw through rope, but it was thin enough to slip into the knot and hopefully loosen it if I leveraged it right.

It was a long shot, but it was all I had.

The sounds of gunfire abruptly ceased. *Shit.* I'd hoped the firefight would distract the Brothers long enough that they wouldn't check on me before I escaped.

What did the sudden silence mean? Who won? If Vuk was here somewhere, was he injured or dead?

Spots danced in front of my eyes. The room spun, and my efforts to loosen the knot weakened as images of Vuk's broken, bleeding body flashed through my head.

"Stop it," I whispered fiercely. "Get it together, Ayana." I couldn't afford to spiral over hypothetical scenarios. I needed to free myself *now*.

They were coming. It was only a matter of time.

I resumed my efforts, but my earlier burst of energy had waned. I paused after a few seconds and tried to catch my breath. The fire in my shoulder had dulled, but I wasn't sure if that was because it'd *actually* faded or if my adrenaline was blocking out important pain receptors.

I pushed the stiletto a little deeper into the knot. If I—

Footsteps. Two sets this time.

And they were close.

There was no way I'd free myself in time. If those footsteps belonged to my abductors, I was done. They'd know I was trying to escape and keep me under lock and key so I wouldn't come close to succeeding again.

The footsteps stopped in front of me.

Angry tears sprang to my eyes. So close. I'd been *so close* to loosening the knot.

There was nothing I could do about it now. Time was up, and "close" didn't count in situations like these.

My gut clenched. I blinked away my tears and forced my eyes up, up over black-clad legs and torsos until—

"Vuk." His name fell out on a breath of shock. My body buzzed. I blinked again, sure I was seeing things, but no. There he stood, tall and strong and *alive*.

An instinctive wave of relief slammed into me. I almost asked him to untie me before I realized I would never have to ask Vuk to do that. Under normal circumstances, I would already be in his arms, and he would've already come up with a plan to get us out of here.

My smile vanished as my hyperfocus on him faded, and the rest of the scene sharpened with painful clarity.

Vuk was staring at me, his face stark with guilt and horror. His hands were tied behind his back, and the man next to him had a gun pressed to his head. I'd never seen the second man before. Green eyes, dark hair, deceptively good-looking in a cruel, brutal way.

He took in my current position on the ground with no discernible emotion.

Before I could say anything else, another pair of footsteps sounded behind me.

Vuk's nostrils flared. He stared past me, his eyes burning so cold I felt their chill from a dozen feet away.

Wentworth came into view. Beside him was...

My stomach free fell. Again.

My breath exploded out of me in shock as the elegant blond surveyed the scene with amusement.

"I see everyone's here," Emmanuelle said. "Let's get started, shall we?"

CHAPTER 52

Vuk

I WAS GOING TO RIP THEM APART WITH MY BARE HANDS. *All* of them.

Wentworth, the slimy coward who'd climbed back out from under his rock now that he had someone to hide behind.

Emmanuelle, the evil bitch who'd masterminded all of this.

And Roman, that *fucking* asshole.

I tried to breathe through a cloud of impotent rage. The knife blade of retribution pressed under my skin, drawing blood. It bubbled and sparked, incandescent in its anger and waiting—just waiting—for the moment it could burst forth and turn its enemies to dust.

That moment would come. Until then…

My attention returned to Ayana. She lay on the ground, her arms and legs bound to a chair. Inexplicably, she held one of her shoes behind her back. Huge, wide eyes stared up at me, glossy with fear and pain.

She didn't appear seriously hurt, but she was scared, and that was enough for me to want to kill every single person responsible.

Outside, the sounds of gunfire had ceased. I had no idea

whether anyone from my team was still alive. I had to trust that they were. If they weren't...

I shoved the thought aside. *One thing at a time.* First, I had to figure out how to untie myself and deal with the trio in front of me.

"What? No snarky response?" Emmanuelle shook her head in mock disappointment when Ayana remained silent. If she was surprised by her old agency head's appearance, she didn't show it. "Ah, well, that's too bad."

"You said we could start. Can we start now?" Wentworth was practically bouncing on the balls of his feet. The fucker was high out of his mind. "Vuk's here."

Emmanuelle's mouth twisted for a brief moment before her expression smoothed again. She was dressed in a tailored blouse, pants, and heels. If it weren't for the gun in her hand, she could've passed for an executive on her way back from the office. Which, I supposed, she usually was.

"Patience, Wentworth," she said, her voice sharp.

He fell silent, his expression sulky. He also held a gun, but the hand I'd smashed was still wrapped in a cast. It gave me a vicious sense of satisfaction.

Emmanuelle walked over the mangled body parts rotting between me and Ayana. The warehouse's size had diffused its stench earlier, but the smell from up close was putrid.

She nudged the head with her foot so it rolled over.

I didn't allow a single twitch to mar my face—I wouldn't give her the pleasure of a reaction—but my stomach revolted at the familiar face.

Enzo, the newest member of my team. I'd hired him to tail Emmanuelle. He'd sent me updates all day, but the condition of his body suggested he'd been dead for at least twenty-four hours. She must've hacked into his phone and fed me the false information.

He'd joined the team a year ago. Now he was dead because of me. *Always because of me.*

"Did you think I wouldn't notice?" Emmanuelle said. "I knew he'd been tailing me for weeks the same way I knew you'd bugged my office. I admit, it took me longer to find the surveillance chip than I would've liked, but you are better at this than him. I'm almost offended you didn't send someone more experienced to keep an eye on me." She clicked her tongue. Her eyes slid past me and rested on Roman, who'd been silent this whole time. "Good job. He fell for the plan just like you said he would."

"He's predictable when it comes to her." Roman tipped his chin toward Ayana. He sounded bored. "It would be romantic if it wasn't so stupid."

Ayana's eyes blazed. She glared up at him like she was imagining tearing his entrails out, inch by inch.

"Enough chitchat. It really is time to get started." Emmanuelle waved her gun in Wentworth's direction. "Do what you must."

His face lit up. He approached Ayana and sat her upright again.

"Trying to escape with a high heel?" He laughed. "Cute, but it was never going to work." He reached for her top.

"Touch a hair on her head, and you'll regret it. I promise." My soft warning echoed in the vast space.

The thirst for vengeance pressed deeper inside me, making me bleed, bleed, bleed until a film of bloody crimson covered my vision.

Wentworth paused. Surprise lit up his face, followed by malicious delight. "So he speaks! Here I thought you were just a stupid brute."

Ayana opened her mouth, but I cut her off with a quick glance. I did not want that asshole's attention to return to her.

"What's the reason for this? Control of the Brotherhood? Or revenge for your brother?" I asked Emmanuelle. She was the one I needed to worry about, not some punk who was trying to act tough. "If you wanted me, you could've attacked me directly instead of doing all of this." I nodded at our surroundings.

"My brother?" Emmanuelle blinked, clearly surprised I'd connected the dots between her and Shepherd. She recovered a second later and laughed like I'd told a particularly funny joke over afternoon tea. "So. You found out about Stéphane—or Shepherd, as he called himself before he died—but no, this isn't about him. In fact, you did me a favor by killing him. He thought he was so smart and could take control after the old leadership died." She snorted. "But he always lacked vision. Strategy. That was how you were able to ambush him so easily. But he had the name recognition and manpower, which was how he'd stayed in the game for so long. Otherwise, I would've crushed him long ago."

Her words sank in. My gaze didn't waver from hers. "You're the other faction leader." It wasn't a question.

Emmanuelle's smile widened. "No, not a stupid brute at all," she said. Wentworth rolled his eyes, but he appeared to be so enraptured by our conversation he'd forgotten about Ayana—for now. "I've kept my identity hidden from all except my most loyal followers. No one ever suspects I'm a woman. Misogyny can be a useful tool if you know how to wield it." She closed the distance between us. "Roman was my cover. My figurehead. People thought he was the leader." She laughed again. "We sent him to infiltrate my brother's faction, and he did so admirably. Even convinced you to take out Shepherd for us."

She paused for a response. When I didn't give her one, she continued, looking slightly disappointed. "I initially didn't care whether we took you out or not. We'd agreed that whoever killed you would become the next leader, but I simply sat back and let Shepherd go after you. I knew he'd never beat you. It was only a matter of time before you got rid of him for me, and you did." Emmanuelle shrugged. "Control of the Brotherhood is an

472 | ANA HUANG

inevitability. Like I said, my brother had no vision. He wanted to keep things the same when the organization has the potential to be so much more than a group of for-hire killers. With its manpower, it could be an *empire*. Arms dealing. Money laundering. Nothing was impossible. But he never got that."

"Yet you funded him throughout this 'war' between the factions," I said coldly.

"Only a little bit." She wrinkled her nose. "I had to play the part of the good sister. He didn't know I was the other faction leader. That's how clueless he was. He told me a little too much about the Brothers even before the old leadership died. Shepherd always had a big mouth. I was able to slip in through him and see how things worked. I quietly built a following of members who shared my vision. Only a trusted few knew my real identity; the rest were drawn to what I promised, not who I was. If Shepherd had taken control, he would've run the Brotherhood into the ground. But you know..." She tapped her gun against my arm. "I would've left you alone if you hadn't stuck your nose where it didn't belong. I don't like leaving loose ends behind. Fortunately, Ayana turned out to be a useful distraction." Her smile returned. "I kept you both busy enough with the lawsuit while I set all this up, didn't I?"

"She had me plant the photos of what you did to that poor man in Ayana's apartment," Wentworth piped up. "Said it would throw you two into a tailspin, and it did. If she—"

"Shut up, Wentworth," Emmanuelle said without taking her eyes off me.

He quieted again, his mouth taking on a mulish set.

"He was very upset with what you did, Vuk," she murmured. "I promised him he could make you suffer if he helped me out with a few small tasks. I hope you don't mind. I simply must repay my debts if I want to start my empire on the right foot."

I was sick of this woman's voice. She was smarter than her brother, that much was true, but she was also like every other narcissistic megalomaniac out there—driven by the desire to flaunt her "accomplishments" and blinded by the need for validation from those they deemed worthy of bestowing it.

That was why she'd rambled on for so long when she could've easily shot us both and gotten this over with.

Sadly for her, she would never have my respect. Not a single ounce of it.

I leaned forward, looked her dead in the eyes, and spat in her face.

Wentworth's jaw dropped.

The saliva dripped off Emmanuelle's perfectly made-up face. A snarl destroyed her gloating calm, and she backhanded me with the gun so hard my ears rang. Pain exploded across my right cheek. I spat out a mouthful of blood and smiled.

That only enraged her more. Her eyes bulged, and she raised her arm as if to strike me again before she stopped. "Roman, step back. Wentworth, take care of Ayana," she ordered.

Roman removed the gun from my temple and stepped aside without a word. Terror seeped through the cracks of my fury when Wentworth reached for Ayana again.

"I was going to let you sit quietly and watch, but I see I was being too nice." Emmanuelle aimed her gun at my face and cocked the trigger.

"No!" Ayana screamed. She struggled wildly against her ropes, derailing Wentworth's efforts to get a solid hold on her. "Don't—"

The blast of a gunshot wiped out the rest of her words. My vision darkened; agony blazed as the bullet tore through flesh and bone and set off a thousand fires that ate away at my consciousness—but I was alive.

Emmanuelle had switched her target at the last minute and shot me in the thigh.

My teeth clenched so hard my jaw ached. My head swam, and my legs almost crumpled, but I forced myself to stay upright. I refused to fall to my knees in front of her.

"A taste of what'll come later." Emmanuelle wiped my spit off her chin, her eyes bright. "Next time, I'll aim for your fucking balls."

She turned her attention to Wentworth, who was watching the events unfold with rapt fascination. "I said *take care of her*," she growled. She swung her gaze back to me. "Let's see if you can take her pain as well as you take yours."

I snarled.

Wentworth pushed Ayana's top up, and my vision blacked out for an entirely different reason.

I was a rational person. I was calm, collected, and strategic. I didn't let emotions overshadow reason

But in that moment, I *didn't care*. I wanted his blood on my hands and his head on a fucking plate.

I lunged forward, heedless of my bound wrists or the hostile weapons surrounding me. Emmanuelle's gun snapped up. Behind her, Ayana shouted, the sound brimming with anger more than fear. She tried to headbutt Wentworth, but he easily ducked out of the way.

Emmanuelle aimed for my groin and—

A gray blur leapt from the top of a nearby shipping container and onto Wentworth's face. He screamed. His gun clattered to the floor while her shot went wide. It hit the spot where Roman had been standing.

The asshole was nowhere to be seen, but I didn't have time to dwell on where he went or when he'd slipped away.

Emmanuelle whirled in time to see the newcomer swipe its

claws across Wentworth's eyes with an angry hiss. He screamed again in obvious agony.

Shadow. That *fucking* cat.

I could kiss the damn thing.

Emmanuelle tried to shoot at him, but Wentworth was flailing around too much for her to get a clear shot. He tried to peel the cat off him, but Shadow clung on like a barnacle. The furry menace yowled, dug his claws deeper, and gouged the fuck out of Wentworth's eyes.

I took advantage of Emmanuelle's distraction and tackled her from behind. We hit the concrete with pained grunts. She attempted another shot, but I'd landed on top of her, and she didn't have enough leverage. The bullet pinged off a metal container, as did the next two after that.

Even with my hands tied, I could do some damage as long as I prevented her from shooting properly. I rolled over and pinned the arm holding her gun beneath my body weight. She struggled to free herself, but she was no match against two hundred-plus pounds of muscle and pure, unadulterated rage.

I threw my head back and slammed it into her face. Bone crunched and blood gushed.

Emmanuelle howled with anger. She reached down and jammed her nails into my bullet wound.

A hoarse shout tore from my throat. Dark spots crowded my vision. It wasn't just my leg; my entire body was on fire, bones and muscle crumbling to ash as excruciating torture hijacked all my senses. I would've passed out if not for the dim awareness that Ayana and Shadow were still here, and I needed to help them.

I scrounged up enough strength to headbutt Emmanuelle again. She gasped and gurgled, blood dripping down her chin. This time, she didn't recover so fast.

Wentworth's panicked shouts ceased. I lifted my head in time to see Shadow fly across the room. He hit one of the containers and dropped to the ground with a pained mewl.

Emmanuelle shoved at me. I was too weak and dizzy from blood loss to offer much resistance. She freed herself and scrambled to her feet.

"Time to end this," she hissed. She raised her gun again.

A shot blasted through the air.

I instinctively recoiled and braced myself for impact—but it never came.

Emmanuelle's mouth formed a surprised O. A small, perfect red dot blossomed between her eyes. Her lips moved as if she wanted to say something, but then she swayed and tilted to the side. The light in her eyes died before her body hit the ground.

Cool air eased some of my pain. I summoned my last reserves of energy and looked up.

Ayana had somehow freed herself from the chair. She stood there, Wentworth's gun clasped between her shaking hands. Her wide, unblinking eyes were locked on Emmanuelle's body.

Behind her, the photographer was trying to crawl away as inconspicuously as possible.

I'd deal with him later. Emmanuelle was dead, and Ayana was in shock, but this wasn't over. We needed to get out of here before backup came.

"Ayana, sweetheart, look at me."

She didn't move. She appeared to be transfixed by Emmanuelle's prone form.

"Ayana." My voice firmed. I was minutes away from losing consciousness, and I needed to get through to her before I did. "It's okay, *srce moje*. *Look* at me."

A shudder ran through her body. She wrenched her eyes away from her old agency head and focused on me instead.

Awareness gradually set in. She sucked in an audible breath

and ran over. She was still missing one shoe. It lay next to her chair amidst a tangle of rope.

"We don't have time," I said as she untied me. "I brought a few men with me, but I don't know if they're dead or alive. We have to leave in case other Brothers come."

"Okay." Her voice trembled. "Can you walk? Do you know where the exit is?"

She finally freed me from my ropes. I allowed myself a tiny sigh of relief before I replied. "I'll manage, and yes. But first…" I gently eased the gun from her hand. "There's one more thing we have to take care of."

Emmanuelle was right about one thing. No loose ends.

A feral hiss drew our attention to the other side of the aisle. Shadow had bounced back from his earlier injury, and he was pissed. He raced after Wentworth and grabbed the man's pant leg between his teeth. A vengeful slash against his ankles brought forth another howl.

I was tempted to let Shadow take care of him, but like I said, we didn't have time.

Ayana helped me to my feet. Despite the pain, I closed the distance between the other man and me with several heavy steps.

I'd let him go the first time. He wouldn't be so lucky the second time.

"Wait," Wentworth pleaded. His face was a bloodied mess. One eye was swollen half shut from his injuries, and his voice bubbled with panic. "Wait, if you let me go, I swear I—"

"I told you what would happen if you went near Ayana again." I pressed the gun against his forehead. He sobbed. The scent of urine filled the air. "But I forgot to mention another thing. Don't *touch* my fucking cat."

This time, the gunshot was accompanied by a spray of crimson mist and gore. Behind him, Shadow's tail thumped with satisfaction.

I preferred knives, but Wentworth didn't deserve a blade; he deserved an unremarkable death.

Ayana's mouth opened and closed. She appeared to be sliding into shock again.

"Markovic!" Roman rounded the corner, looking noticeably worse for wear. His shirt was ripped at the shoulder, and a nasty bruise blossomed over his left eye. His eyes were uncharacteristically frantic. "We gotta go. They wired this place to blow!"

We sprang into action. I couldn't move fast with an injured leg, but I tried my best. However, I made sure to grab Shadow and take him with us as we raced toward the exit.

Ayana and Roman wrapped their arms around me and helped me along.

"Sean and the others are waiting outside with the car," Roman said. *Thank fuck*. They were alive. "We took care of the other Brothers in here. There weren't many. Emmanuelle only brought her most loyal soldiers, and now they're all dead."

I didn't have enough energy to respond. My breaths weakened by the second, and we were only halfway to the exit.

A boom rocked the air. Heat billowed over us in waves. Shadows of roaring flames danced on the walls, and the unmistakable scent of burning flesh saturated the air.

"Fuck!" Roman cursed again.

I didn't have to look back to know that the flames were streaking toward us. That was the trap. Emmanuelle must've rigged the explosion to go off at a certain time, near flammable material. She would've left before it blew, and she would've made me die after living through my worst fear.

Fire. Smoke and death and heat. The sizzle of it against my skin. The scent of my own flesh melting off. The sight of my brother's body charred beyond recognition.

I stumbled. My knees hit the ground; the walls closed in.

Somewhere high above me, or far from me—I wasn't sure—I heard Roman shout. Ayana shouted back. Then the noises dulled to a low, steady roar so the only sound that broke through was the frantic *thump thump thump* of my heart.

The heat was intensifying. It didn't have to touch us—we were so flammable it only needed to come near us to guarantee instant death.

That was why I should run. Leave. Escape. *I should I should I should* but I couldn't move and the memories and the smell and—

Strong hands grabbed me. Roman.

The world was a blur as he half-dragged, half-carried me toward the exit.

Roman.

This was all his fucking fault. This was *his* plan.

He'd told me Emmanuelle was the other faction leader and that she was working with Wentworth. He said the photographer and another Brother were the ones who'd grabbed Ayana off the street. After months of lies about him not having insights into the other faction, he'd finally told me the truth.

Emmanuelle had thought he was loyal to her, and he'd convinced her it was her idea to send him to me as a double agent. She had no idea we were really conspiring against her and not the other way around.

In order to guarantee I got to Ayana safely, Roman had pretended to betray me. We had to make it convincing, hence the bound hands. While my men engaged the rest of the Brothers, we would bide our time until the right moment. Once Emmanuelle and Wentworth were sufficiently distracted, Roman would free me with a quick slice of the ropes and give me back my weapon (which he'd tucked into his waistband) so we could take on the pair and rescue Ayana together.

He couldn't shoot either one of them before freeing me first.

The risk of the other attacking him while he was busy with the first was too great. He needed my cover.

It was a shitty plan, which made sense because it ended up going to shit. We hadn't foreseen Emmanuelle shooting my leg first, though I suppose that was my fault for spitting in her face after she baited me.

I should've kept my calm. I should've—I should've—

Fresh air slammed into me. The scent of roasting flesh faded as I gasped in a breath, and the world returned in splotches of color and movement.

Roman had somehow managed to carry us to safety.

Us. Ayana.

I searched for her in the dark. Roman was doubled over next to me, his chest heaving. Shadow sat at my feet, his small face worried while Sean and Bruce rushed toward me from the car. I didn't see Mav; I also didn't see Ayana.

"Where is she?" I demanded. I grabbed Roman's shoulders and shook him. "*Where is she?*"

"I don't know," he gasped. "She said I should take you and go ahead since you were injured. I thought she was right behind us." He lifted his head and looked around. "*Fuck*. I—where are you going?"

I was already halfway back across the lot.

I didn't know where I found the strength. A second ago, I would've sworn I didn't have any left. But if Ayana wasn't out here, then she was in there, and I hadn't come all this way to let her die. I *refused* to let her die.

"Sir! Vuk!" Sean's panicked voice grew closer. He grabbed me. I shook him off. "You can't go in there! The fire is already…" He kept talking, but his protests blended into one long, continued whine of noise.

My ears buzzed; my heart pounded so hard, I might throw up.

My wound was bleeding out, but I barely felt the sticky warmth dripping down my leg. My pain was nothing compared to the sheer, blinding terror of what I might find inside.

Ayana trapped. Injured. Dead.

Roman said she was right behind us. The only reason she wouldn't have followed us out was—

No. She was alive. She had to be.

If she was gone from this earth, I would feel it. I would *know* because I would be dead too.

Somehow, I made it back to the warehouse. Sean gave up trying to convince me and followed me inside.

Boiling heat and fetid scents engulfed us. Due to the warehouse's sheer size, the fire hadn't reached us yet, but it was close. Too close.

Sean gagged while I stared at the flames, my feet rooted to the ground. The smell reminded me so much of *that* night. Past and present blurred together as images of my brother's charred corpse flashed through my head.

If you don't move, the same thing's going to happen to Ayana.

The thought spurred me into action again because *fuck* that. Nothing was going to happen to her. Not while I lived and breathed.

My pyrophobia retreated to a distant corner of my mind as I searched frantically for her amidst the smoke and shadows. It was impossible to see clearly. Where—

"There!" Sean shouted. He pointed to a figure on the ground about fifty feet away.

I was already moving. *Sprinting* as fast as my injured leg would allow. It was the same strength that allowed mothers to lift cars off their child and other superhuman feats. I barely felt the gunshot wound or heard Sean behind me.

Every cell of my body, every ounce of my attention, was locked in on Ayana's motionless form.

When I got closer, I was relieved to see she was breathing, albeit shallowly. She was already weak and exhausted after a full day of captivity; she must've passed out from the smoke inhalation.

"It's okay, baby." It was my turn to lift her up and wrap an arm around her. She didn't wake up. "I'm going to get you out of here."

I staggered with her toward the exit. The flames were closing in. Their greedy fingers grasped at our backs, hungry for more flesh to devour.

Sean met me halfway. He draped Ayana's other arm around his neck and together, we half-ran, half-dragged her across the remaining two dozen feet, through the door, and into the night air. We made it a quarter of the way across the parking lot before the fire swallowed metal and concrete whole.

The warehouse erupted behind us, fully ablaze.

Someone took Ayana; someone else pulled me toward the car.

I was aware people were talking, and things were moving, but I couldn't make sense or shape of them.

Their voices fell away, and the last thing I saw before darkness claimed me was the orange glow of fire painted across the night sky.

CHAPTER 53

Ayana

SMOKE INHALATION. A SPRAINED SHOULDER. BRUISES
and cuts all over. Oh, and someone's death on my hands plus
trauma for life unless—or even if—I got a *really* good therapist.

But I was alive.

We were alive. The people who mattered, anyway. Emmanuelle,
Wentworth, and the rest of their co-conspirators could rot in hell
for all I cared.

In the grand scheme of things, it could've been worse.

Still, my nerves were shot as I approached Vuk's room. Sean
and Jeremiah conferred quietly outside.

"Ayana." Jeremiah saw me first. Worry filled his eyes. "You
shouldn't be out of bed."

"If I stay in bed any longer, I'll fuse with the mattress," I said
with a weak smile. It'd been three days since my rescue, and all
I'd done in between doctor's visits was eat, sleep, and watch bad
reality TV. I'd spoken to Vuk twice, but there was so much chaos
after my kidnapping and Emmanuelle's death that we hadn't had
time for a proper conversation. "Is he awake?"

"Yes. You'll be happy to hear he's been terrorizing everyone,"

Sean said. "Almost bit the doctor's head off when he said he couldn't see you this morning. The only reason the man's still alive is because he said you were sleeping and that Vuk shouldn't disturb your rest."

I laughed. "I am glad to hear that. At least he's back to form."

I left Sean and Jeremiah to their conversation and entered Vuk's room. He was sitting up in bed, his face set in a frown while a nurse checked his vitals. She excused herself when she saw me and sped out.

"I heard you've been terrorizing your doctors again," I teased, taking a seat by his bedside.

"Not terrorizing. Supervising—which I wouldn't have to do if they did their job properly. It's been days. There's no reason to keep me cooped up in here like I'm dying," Vuk grumbled, but his frown softened when I gently touched his leg. A nonstick bandage protected the gunshot wound on his thigh; smaller bandages covered various cuts and bruises across his body.

The doctors had assured me the gunshot wound would heal and that, with the proper rest and rehab, Vuk would walk properly again in a few months to a year. He was lucky; the bullet had made a clean exit and missed his major arteries.

Still, the sight of him bruised and injured made my eyes burn.

I would never forget his involuntary flinch when the bullet tore through his thigh, or the terror that'd smothered me when Emmanuelle aimed her gun at him the second time.

I couldn't even remember my thought process in that moment. I only remembered freeing myself while Shadow distracted Wentworth and Vuk tried to subdue Emmanuelle—I'd quietly worked on my knots the whole time they were talking, and it'd paid off.

I remembered grabbing Wentworth's gun before he could retrieve it.

And I remembered lifting it and shooting Emmanuelle right between the eyes.

If I hadn't, she would've killed Vuk. That'd been my only thought, so I hadn't hesitated, hadn't even really aimed. I just…did it.

I killed someone.

My hand trembled. I moved to pull away, but Vuk's hand covered mine a moment later, trapping it between his leg and his solid, comforting touch.

"It's a surface wound. Don't worry, *srce*. I've endured worse," he said. Only Vuk would call a bullet to the leg a "surface wound." "Now I have another scar to add to my collection."

I didn't laugh. "That's not funny. You could've *died*. You could've…I would've…" My throat closed. The burn in my eyes intensified, and a tiny trickle scorched my cheek. "I can't believe you agreed to that *stupid* plan by that Roland guy—"

"Roman." Vuk's mouth twitched.

"Whatever. It was a terrible plan, and he could've gotten you killed, and then what would I have done?" The tears were flowing fast and free now.

He'd explained the plan when I came to see him the morning after our escape. Apparently, Roland—I mean, Roman—was a Brotherhood member who'd been secretly helping him this whole time. He'd saved Sean from getting killed when he slipped away during the Vuk and Emmanuelle confrontation. Apparently, Sean had been overpowered by the other Brothers until Roman went back to check on him and get more backup. Roman had also carried Vuk to safety after I insisted they go ahead.

None of that meant his plan wasn't stupid.

"It wasn't the best plan, but it worked out in the end. I'm okay," Vuk said tenderly. He curled his fingers around mine. "I'm more worried about you."

I swiped at my tears. "I'm fine. The doctor said my shoulder will heal in a few weeks."

Vuk's team took us straight to his house after we escaped. He had a private medical wing set up to treat his members' injuries as well as two private doctors on call. Apparently, they never went to the hospital for "work-related" injuries—too much paperwork and too much hassle.

Vuk's doctors were the best of the best, and I trusted them.

"I'm not talking about your injuries, *srce*," Vuk said. He examined me, his brow furrowing. "If you want to speak to someone about what happened, I know a therapist. Mira. She helped me after my brother died, although I never saw her regularly. She's good."

I managed a smile. "If you say she's good, she must be fantastic." He didn't dole out compliments easily. "I might take you up on that after everything settles." I let out a sniffling laugh. "She's going to be so sick of me in a few months."

I had a *lot* to talk about in therapy.

I didn't regret killing Emmanuelle. It was her or Vuk, and even if she weren't evil, I would choose him. Every time.

When he told me about Roman's plan, he also revealed the truth about her side activities and what she'd coerced some of the agency's girls to do. I was still reeling from the revelation.

Her involvement with the Brotherhood was shocking enough, but the fact that Emmanuelle Beaumont—the polished former supermodel and industry legend—had run what was basically a high-end prostitution ring boggled my mind.

Vuk's team had anonymously leaked that information the night after the fire, along with the news about her and Wentworth's deaths. The cover-up story was that Emmanuelle and Wentworth were lovers, and they were killed by a vengeful ex-client of hers that she'd tried to blackmail.

He'd sent the proof of her wrongdoings to all the major outlets, and it sparked an absolute media firestorm. The FBI had already taken over Beaumont's offices and frozen its accounts while it investigated. Emmanuelle's old lawsuit against me was dead and buried. No one even remembered it.

My parents had freaked out when they heard, and they freaked out even more when I told them I'd sprained my shoulder in a gym accident. My mother wanted to come up and take care of me until I was fully healed, but I'd quickly shot her down. That would be too close for comfort.

There was no way I could tell my parents the truth about my kidnapping or what I did. They would lock me up and never let me out of their sight again—if they didn't keel over from shock first. They said Emmanuelle's death was karma, not knowing their daughter was the one who'd delivered it.

Maybe it was karma, but Emmanuelle had still been a person. A living, breathing person whose life I snuffed out with one pull of the trigger.

The thud of her body hitting the ground echoed in my ears. When I closed my eyes, I saw the hole in her forehead and the surprise on her face.

Her blood would forever stain my hands, but it was a worthwhile tradeoff for me, Vuk, and all the girls she'd terrorized.

"I'll give you Mira's contact information," Vuk said. "It's there whenever you're ready."

"Thank you," I said quietly. "Have you heard from Roman?"

"Not since yesterday. He's busy consolidating what's left of the Brotherhood now that Shepherd and Emmanuelle are both dead, but he's their new leader now, just like he wanted." Vuk's tone was dry. "He swore a blood oath that the Brothers wouldn't come after me anymore. An oath taken by the leader applies to all the members. New rules."

My heart beat faster. "Does that mean you're free? You don't have to worry about them anymore?"

He nodded.

A sweet headiness filled my veins to bursting. No more Brotherhood. No more hitmen and kidnappings and murder—maybe.

The specter of our last conversation pulled me back to earth as quickly as I'd floated off it. I couldn't believe that'd been less than a week ago. A lifetime had passed since then, but some issues remained unresolved.

I still hadn't answered Vuk's implicit question: could I be with someone who'd proved he was capable of murder, torture, and other crimes? No matter how much I yearned to be with him, was the chasm between our moralities too wide for us to bridge in the long term?

But that was the thing. I wasn't sure the chasm was as wide as I'd originally thought. I'd witnessed him shoot Wentworth point blank without hesitation, yet I'd done the same to Emmanuelle. Part of me had even wished I'd killed Wentworth myself, but I was glad I hadn't. Taking one life was enough; taking two would've been too much for me to cope with, no matter how justified I was.

Seeing him crawl away like the pathetic coward he was in his last moments on earth had been satisfaction enough. A small death for a small man. It was what he deserved.

Vuk had a greater capacity for death than I did, but we were driven by the same desire: to protect the people we loved.

"Do you remember our conversation at the range? Before, um, everything that happened?" I asked. Vuk's expression clouded. His throat bobbed, and he responded with a short nod. "Well, I made a decision. That is, I, um, have an answer."

This wasn't my most eloquent moment, but I'd never had to say these things to someone before.

Vuk's hand tensed over mine, but he didn't pull away, and neither did I.

"There was a moment in the warehouse—*several* moments— when I thought, this is it. We're going to die, and I'd never get the chance to say what I wanted to say. To tell you how much you meant to me." I swallowed. "I knew that you had a different concept of justice than most people, but when I saw those photos, I couldn't reconcile the different sides of you. There's the you who walked around D.C. with me and took me to bingo night and indulged my family even when they were being totally nosy and annoying," I said with a teary laugh. "Then there's the you I saw in the warehouse. The one who could kill and maim without remorse."

The room was silent save for my voice and the rhythm of Vuk's breaths. He didn't speak. He simply watched me, his eyes dark with unidentifiable emotion.

"My knee-jerk instinct was to run away because how could I be with someone who had that much blood on their hands? But then I realized I was thinking in terms of my old life, the one that existed before I knew about the Brotherhood and Emmanuelle's atrocities and everything else that came to light," I said. "I was sheltered, and I had a predetermined view of right and wrong based on the life I'd lived up to that point. But the world is bigger and darker than that, and we can't always play by the rules when the other side has none. The wedding attack opened my eyes, but the warehouse was the tipping point. Sometimes, we have to break our own rules to survive. I mean, look at me. I shot Emmanuelle."

This time, my laugh contained a hint of hysteria. More than that, though, it held empathy. I saw exactly where Vuk was coming from.

"What I'm trying to say is, I understand the reasoning behind your actions," I said. "I don't think violence is the answer to every problem. Most of the time, it's not. But I understand that it's sometimes necessary. You did what you had to do for the people you care about, and I would've done the same. I don't regret shooting Emmanuelle because it saved your life. And if someone had hurt my family—if they'd taken my niece or nephew and hurt them—I can't say that I wouldn't have wanted them to suffer for what they did."

I took a deep breath. Vuk still hadn't said a word, so I rambled on, rushing to get my next words out before I lost my nerve. "When I thought you were going to die, everything else stopped mattering—the Brotherhood, the photos, your utter lack of appreciation for my shoe collection." A breath of amusement escaped him, and I allowed myself to smile before I continued. "All that mattered was *you* because I want to be with you." He continued to stare at me. No reply. "That's, um, my answer," I said in case I hadn't been clear. "To your question from Valhalla the day I got kidnapped? Well, you didn't actually ask a question, but I understood what you meant. And as long as you don't go around, like, stabbing people who give you a parking ticket, I—"

Vuk finally moved. He grabbed me and crushed the rest of my ramble with a kiss, his mouth hot and urgent. I melted. My hands slid over his shoulders as I returned his kiss with equal fervor, letting the taste and feel of him sweep me away until I was breathless.

He was alive. It finally, truly sank in. He was alive, and we could be together, no holds barred. No engagement, no secrets, no Brotherhood hanging over our heads.

If Vuk hadn't been holding me, I would've floated straight off the ground.

"So, no stabbing parking attendants," he said when we broke for air minutes or possibly hours later. I heard the smile in his voice. "Any other conditions I should know about before we make this official?"

"Um." *Just kiss me again. Immediately.* But he was right. We should lay out our ground rules first. "Basically everything that falls under the same category. No gratuitous violence unless it's extremely justified. As in, Emmanuelle-and- Wentworth-level justified."

"But non-gratuitous violence is okay?" Vuk laughed when I gave him a disapproving look. "I'm joking, *srce*. I know what you mean." He gave me another, softer kiss. "A compromise then. No gratuitous violence without proper justification."

"Thank you."

"Can I threaten someone if they disrespect you?"

I thought about it. "Yes."

"Good." His breath whispered over my skin. "*Nisam sklon kompromisima, srce, ali za tebe bih pristao i na hiljadu njih.*"

I waited for a translation that never came. "You're going to make me look that up too, aren't you?"

Vuk flashed a cocky grin. "If you give me a kiss, I'll tell you what I said after."

He didn't have to ask twice.

I leaned forward and brushed my lips across his. My mouth lingered, savoring the moment before I pulled away.

"Okay, Markovic, pay up," I said. "What did you say?"

"I'm not usually a compromise person, *srce*, but for you, I'd agree to a thousand compromises if you asked."

Was it possible for a person to dissolve from a single sentence? Because I was certain that was what was happening. There was no other explanation for my weakening limbs or the spill of honeyed liquid oozing through my veins.

"And yet, you won't translate *srce*," I breathed, trying to restore some semblance of control to my emotions.

"You know what it means," Vuk said, his voice tender again.

I did. I'd finally looked it up, but even if I hadn't, I heard the sentiment every time he uttered it.

Srce moje. My heart.

I kissed him again, even more urgently this time. His palm slid over my hip and up the curve of my waist. My skin flushed, and electricity crackled up my spine.

"Wait. You're still hurt," I protested half-heartedly. "The doctor said—"

"Fuck what the doctor said." Vuk nuzzled my neck. "I pay him, so my orders supersede his."

"I don't think that's…" He kissed a particularly sensitive part of my throat. I moaned, my protests fading.

I slid my hands over his shoulders, eager to—

A loud *meow* interrupted our makeout session. I startled, and we parted just in time for Shadow to jump onto the bed and plop himself right on Vuk's chest.

Despite Shadow's exceedingly poor timing, I couldn't help but giggle at the scowl on Vuk's face.

"Get out," he ordered. "We're busy."

Shadow ignored him and stretched with a lazy yawn. He nudged Vuk's chin with his nose before he made himself comfortable again on his owner's chest.

After his life-saving turn in the warehouse, he'd returned to a flurry of cuddles and doting from everyone on Vuk's staff. Fortunately, he hadn't been injured when Wentworth threw him, and he seemed to have taken his newfound hero status in stride. Shadow entered every room like he owned it—just like someone else I knew.

"You are the biggest pain in my ass," Vuk grumbled. He scratched Shadow behind the ears. The cat purred, his tail swishing back and forth like the world's most content windshield wiper. "But I was right. You are a survivor."

"Did you ever figure out how he followed you to the warehouse?" I asked. I pet Shadow with a smile. His purring intensified. God, he was too cute.

I assumed he'd stowed away in Vuk's car again, but I had no

idea how he'd gotten from the car to the site of the warehouse action without anyone noticing him.

"No. He goes where and when he pleases. I don't even know how he got into this room since the door is closed." Vuk shook his head. "Cockblocked by a cat. Unbelievable."

"Oh, let him have his moment. We'll have plenty of alone time later now that we're official and all," I teased. My tone softened. "Plus, you saved my life. Again."

I'd been unconscious during the last part of the night, but knowing Vuk had run in to find me despite his past trauma with fire...

A fist squeezed my heart.

"No, *srce*," Vuk said. "You saved mine."

"Roland—Roman—was the one who carried you out."

"I'm not talking about the warehouse."

My breath fluttered in my lungs. His voice was warm, meaningful, and if I hadn't melted before, I was definitely a puddle of goo now.

I didn't need to ask him what he meant. Like so much of our relationship, some things were felt rather than heard.

Shadow meowed again as Vuk and I exchanged knowing, secretive smiles. We didn't have to say anything else, and despite my injuries and trauma, I'd never felt happier than in that moment.

Like my mother said, joy didn't require the absence of grief, and happiness wasn't always found in the big moments. More often than not, they existed in small pockets of time like these—in a room with an adorable cat, the man I loved, and the knowledge that he loved me back.

CHAPTER 54

Vuk

ONCE THE TRUTH CAME OUT ABOUT EMMANUELLE, the rest of the pieces fell into place. By the time the holidays rolled around, and the city was blanketed in snow and festive window displays, Beaumont had been effectively dismantled. The FBI arrested all the agents who'd been complicit in her dealings and repossessed the company offices.

That left its former models agent-less, though that was a good thing in most cases. I paid off all of the models' existing debts so they could start over with a clean slate. If they wanted to leave the industry and go home, I bought them first-class tickets and supplied them with a year's worth of living expenses. If they wanted to stay, I had my lawyers review their new contracts to ensure they were fair. I also paid for counseling and medical services for those who'd been forced to participate in Emmanuelle's illicit activities.

I didn't know any of the models except for Indira (whose success had shielded her from Beaumont's ugly side), but they all deserved better than what they got.

Unfortunately, and somewhat shockingly, Hank wasn't one of the complicit agents. He had, however, been found guilty of invasion of privacy and the unlawful surveillance of Ayana and several other models. I may or may not have leaned on the prosecutors to pursue the maximum prison sentence, and I may or may not have asked the warden to make Hank's time in there a little more unpleasant.

I also set up Enzo's family with enough money for life. It wouldn't bring him back, nor did it fully assuage my guilt over his death, but it was the least I could do.

Meanwhile, Ayana had decided to go freelance. She didn't want another agent; she wanted full control over her own career and finances. She planned on hiring an assistant in the new year to help manage her calendar and bookings.

Ironically, the months she'd taken off from work had turned her into the industry's hottest commodity. Everyone wanted to book her, and she had jobs lined up through the end of next year.

We were currently at an event for Stella Alonso, a fashion designer she'd worked with since she was a new model. She was hosting a holiday preview at the Vault, and the club swarmed with dozens of guests.

"It's good to see you back on the circuit." Stella gave my girlfriend a warm smile. She was even taller than Ayana, with curly dark hair and green eyes that matched the emeralds around her neck. She also happened to be married to Sean's old boss, Christian Harper. "We missed you in the European shows this year."

"It's been a wild fall," Ayana admitted. "But I'm happy to be back. I can't wait for the fall/winter shows."

"Same. Between you and me…" Stella's voice dropped to a conspiratorial whisper. "I always thought you were too good for Beaumont. Emmanuelle gave me the creeps. I wouldn't be surprised if we found out she killed someone too."

Good instincts. No wonder Harper married her.

496 | ANA HUANG

"Anyway, enough morbid talk for the night. Let's meet up for lunch after the new year. I'd love to catch up," Stella said. "Now if you'll excuse me, I have to make sure my husband isn't wreaking havoc in my absence. When Christian's bored, things tend to...go awry."

"I understand what you mean." Ayana gave me a pointed stare.

I returned it with an innocent expression. I'd behaved perfectly this month—except maybe for that time I "accidentally" pushed a guy into an indoor pool for staring at her ass too long. The guy had been undressing her with his eyes in front of everyone at an industry event.

How was I supposed to know he couldn't swim? He'd survived in the end. Some Good Samaritan had fished him out like a wet rat.

"It was nice to meet you, Vuk," Stella said.

I inclined my head in a *likewise* motion.

You missed this, didn't you? I asked after Stella left.

It was the week before Christmas. We'd spent most of our post-escape weeks at my house or her apartment, lost in a daze of sex and food and sleep. We'd shut out the rest of the world in favor of each other. It was enough for me, but Ayana was a more social creature than I was, and I wanted her to have an opportunity to shine now that Beaumont was out of the picture.

"I did," she admitted. "Don't get me wrong. I loved spending time with you, but it's nice to see some familiar faces again. There are snakes in the industry, but there are good people too. Speaking of which..." She trailed off and looked past me with a grin.

I turned and immediately snorted. *Did you go to the islands, or did you fall into a vat of bronzing oil somewhere?*

"Hilarious," Jordan said, rolling his eyes. He'd gone to St. Bart's over the weekend, and he was at least five shades tanner than before he'd left. "You should think about doing either of those things sometime, or people will mistake you for a corpse."

That was fine with me. I'd rather roll around on a mat of poison ivy than willingly bake on a hot beach surrounded by sweaty strangers. Whoever invented the concept of sunbathing must've been a masochist.

"Did you get everything sorted out?" Ayana asked. "How's your grandmother?"

Jordan's face sobered. Orla went into hospice at the beginning of the month. She'd held on longer than the doctors expected, but her time was near. Everyone had mentally prepared for it and were getting her affairs in order.

That was why Jordan had gone to St. Bart's—to officially hand over her villa there to its new owners. Save for her Rhode Island home, Orla wanted to divest herself of all her real estate holdings before she died and donate the proceeds to charity.

"She's the same. Always tired now, but she has some fire left in her. She was the one who insisted I go down to the islands instead of letting her lawyers handle it." He gave us a sad smile. "The old dragon can't stand to have us all hovering over her."

He used the term "old dragon" affectionately. Jordan had grown even closer to his grandmother after Thanksgiving, when he'd officially told his family that he was aromantic and asexual. He also never planned to marry, and he didn't want biological children.

His father hadn't been present (though he'd apparently been indifferent when he found out), and his mother had broken down about never having grandchildren, but Orla had taken the news in stride. She hadn't questioned him or tried to convince him he was "wrong." She'd simply changed her will so Jordan would keep his inheritance.

"People are who they are," she'd said. "They shouldn't be punished for it."

All that time, Jordan had been terrified of telling his

grandmother—even going so far as to attempt a marriage of convenience—and she'd turned out to be the most understanding one of all.

"Anyway, I heard you guys were coming, so I swung by to see you and say hi to Stella," he said. "But I have to leave soon. I'm heading to Rhode Island tonight. I think I'll stay there until...well, you know."

"We know." Ayana enveloped him in a hug. "I know it's family-only there these days, but tell Orla we're thinking of her, okay?"

Call us if you need anything, I added.

Jordan responded with another sad smile. "I will."

We chatted for another few minutes before he excused himself so he could make his flight.

No one had paid our trio any more attention than usual. People had gotten used to our new normal, and the scandalous whispers that'd circulated about Ayana and I dating so soon after they broke off their engagement had died once everyone realized we were all on truly good terms.

"I'm glad he's spending Christmas with Orla," Ayana said, looking wistful. "I hope she's at peace."

It's Orla Ford. She'll be fine no matter what.

She was a tough woman. Death would have to drag her kicking and screaming through its door. Once it did, she'd probably flip the tables and rule the afterlife too.

"That's true." Ayana let out a small laugh. "Okay, that's it. We *really* need to stop talking about morbid stuff over the holidays. If my parents were here, they'd slap me on the head for it." She twined her fingers through mine and pulled me toward where the preview was starting. "They're so excited to see you again, by the way. Expect lots of food and board games for the next two weeks."

We were spending Christmas and New Year's with her entire extended family in D.C. We were scheduled to leave in two days.

I smiled. *Looking forward it.*

I meant it. With Willow retired and living in Oregon, spending time with the Kidanes was the closest I'd felt to having a family since mine died.

Ayana and I took our seats. The lights dimmed, and the preview started. I really didn't care about fashion, but I loved Ayana's gasps and laughs of delight at the outfits on display.

"Which one is your favorite so far?" she whispered toward the end of the show.

They all looked the same to me. Lots of red and gold and sparkles.

I shrugged. *I guess that lacy thing with the bow. You'd look great in it.*

"Is that your way of saying you want to see me in holiday lingerie?" she teased.

I want to see you in everything. Anything. A wicked smile. *Nothing.*

Her breath caught with an audible hitch. The air heated around us, and when the show ended, we didn't say a word. We simply stood and left the main floor in unison, our silence punctuated by the occasional breathless laugh until I successfully locked us in the private owners' bathroom upstairs.

Xavier and I were the only people who had access. Clean marble counters. Polished floors. Backlit mirrors.

Much nicer than the club's public restrooms, and much better suited for the activities I had in mind.

"We shouldn't be doing this here," Ayana breathed when I picked her up and set her on the counter. "We should be downstairs with—*oh*."

While she'd been talking, I'd hiked her dress up and pulled down her underwear. I knelt before her and teased her clit with a gentle lick. "You were saying?"

"Um." She sounded dazed. "We shouldn't...downstairs...oh, *God yes!*"

Satisfaction filled my chest as I drew her clit in between my lips and sucked. She went fucking wild, and I didn't hold back as I ate her out right there in the club bathroom. I didn't stop until she gushed all over my face in a screaming orgasm.

There was no sweeter sound in the world.

I rose to my feet and undid my belt. Lust streaked from the head of my cock down to my aching balls. No matter how many times we were together, it always felt like the first time.

Ayana was still shuddering from the throes of her climax when I gripped her hips and lined the tip of my cock up with her entrance. She was on birth control now, and we rarely used condoms anymore.

Thank God. I didn't have any on me, and if I had to wait one more second to be inside her, I was going to explode.

I groaned at the slick, bare feel of her when I finally sank balls deep into her clenching pussy. She wrapped her arms around my neck and held on for dear life while I fucked her, sweet and slow and then hard and fast, until we were both drenched in sweat and lazy, post-coital contentment.

It said something that I would rather be in a nightclub bathroom with Ayana than anywhere else on the planet without her. Sex or not, I would've been happy as long as we were alone.

"Merry early Christmas, *srce moje,*" I murmured.

Ayana smiled, her face glowing with such happiness it made my heart squeeze. "Merry early Christmas, my love."

I stilled. *My love.*

We'd avoided using the L word so far, not because I didn't feel it—she'd been the only woman for me since the moment I set eyes on her, even if I hadn't known it at the time—but because I didn't want her to be pressured into saying it back until she was ready.

More than a month had passed since her kidnapping, but she was still grappling with the events of that day. She saw her therapist twice a week, and sometimes, nightmares plagued her in the darkness. I had saved her life, and I didn't want her to conflate that with love.

Ayana framed my face with her hands, her eyes bright. "I love you," she said. "Not because you saved my life but because you're *you*." It was as if she'd read my mind. "Grumpy, sweet, smart, loyal...a little stabby at times, but no one's perfect." She smiled at my small huff. "I'm *in love* with every part of you, Vuk Markovic, and I've been meaning to tell you for a while. Tonight just happened to be the night I found the courage to do so."

I love you. Words no one had ever uttered to me before—not in the romantic sense. It didn't matter because I'd never cared to hear those words from anyone else.

They only held power coming from one person's mouth.

"Say it again." My voice was so thick and rough I hardly recognized it as mine.

"I love you," Ayana repeated huskily. Her eyes shimmered beneath the lights.

I love you I love you I love you.

Nothing had ever felt so right.

I dropped my forehead to hers. "I don't deserve you, Ayana Kidane," I whispered. "But fuck, I love you too."

If hearing those words lit me up, saying them out loud set me ablaze in the best way possible. These flames were sweet and exquisite, not destructive, as they swept away the ugliness from last month to make space for new memories.

And as Ayana and I kissed again, our tongues sweet with the taste of our words, I had a feeling there would plenty of new memories to come.

CHAPTER 55

Vuk

Ten months later

I LOVED AYANA. I REALLY DID.

But over the course of our relationship, I realized that dating her encompassed one aspect of life that I did not love: social events.

There were dinner parties and charity galas and industry networking events. There were parties for things I didn't think you could have parties for, like a pet's birthday. It confounded me as to why my staff insisted on celebrating Shadow's birthday when we didn't even know when it was; I'd rescued the damn thing off the street.

Jeremiah said they made up a date for him, which completely destroyed the point of a birthday. No one else seemed to think so when I pointed that out, so here we were, singing Happy Birthday to a fucking cat.

"Oh, look at him! He is just so cute!" Maya gushed after the song finished and everyone clapped. She snapped a photo of a preening Shadow as everyone showered him with pets and treats. "Whose idea was the cake?"

"Vuk's," Ayana said before I could pin the blame on her. She'd officially moved into my house over the summer, and she and my staff often ganged up on me on all things Shadow-related. "Don't let his surliness fool you. He's totally into this party. He called the baker so much over the past week that the man threatened to quit if Vuk didn't stop asking him whether he was sure the cake was cat-friendly."

I frowned. *I am not surly.*

Ayana patted my hand. "Of course not, dear."

What was I supposed to do? Let him poison my cat? We would be the ones who'd have to clean up the mess.

I'd ordered a custom mouse-shaped sweet potato cake. We didn't let Shadow eat sweet potatoes often because it wasn't good for him, but it was a special occasion—or so people kept telling me.

I'd never used that particular baker before, so excuse me for doing my due diligence. Ayana was the one who'd finally convinced me to throw a huge party, hence why so many friends and business associates were here; she should be happy I didn't shove a bowl of dry cat food in front of Shadow and call it a day.

"Of course not," she said reassuringly. "I'm positive the baker understands why you were, uh, so *insistent* on checking in every day."

"I kind of want a cat now, but my mom would kill me." Maya sighed. "She's allergic."

"Vuk." A cool, familiar voice interrupted our conversation. Dominic appeared with his wife Alessandra by his side. "Can we speak for a moment? Privately."

"I wanted to talk to you too," Alessandra told Ayana with a smile. They were acquainted with each other since Alessandra's mother used to be Ayana's unofficial model mentor. "My mom's in the city, and she wanted to see if we could all get together…"

While the women conversed, I slipped away to speak with Dominic. We stepped into the hall outside the dining room, where the main party was held.

I hadn't told him about my involvement with Roman, nor had I revealed his role in bringing down Emmanuelle to anyone else. There was no point in doing either when they would only cause more complications.

"I'm calling in my favor," Dominic said. "I have personal news to share with someone, but I need help tracking them down. I've tried on my own, but I haven't been successful. I heard you have...other resources that might be helpful."

Oh, fuck. I had a feeling I knew who that "someone" was, but I kept my expression neutral and typed out my reply on my phone. *Send me the details. I'll take care of it.*

I hadn't heard a peep from Roman since last fall. I couldn't think of anyone else Dominic would want to share personal news with that he couldn't track down, and I wasn't eager to make contact with the new Brotherhood leader again.

But a favor owed was a favor owed, and I always kept my promises.

Relief flickered across Dominic's face. "Thank you."

When we returned to the party, it had devolved into chaos. Maya was dancing with a bemused-looking Shadow; Xavier and Sloane were lording over an impromptu poker game using cards with different pictures of Shadow printed on the back—where the fuck had those come from? I didn't remember ordering them—and Jordan was explaining the latest viral internet meme to Jeremiah.

Loud music. Loud laughter. Loud *everything*.

My skin prickled.

While Dominic beelined straight back to his wife's side, I took in the scene and contemplated whether murder at a party I was hosting would be bad form. Then I contemplated whether or not I cared if it was bad form.

Answer: I didn't.

"You're thinking of murder, aren't you?" Ayana came up beside me, her face a portrait of amusement.

Possibly. Cannot confirm or deny.

She laughed and wrapped her arms around my neck. "Seriously, thank you for doing this. I'm pretty sure half our friends collapsed with shock when they received their first party invitation from *the* Vuk Markovic."

I snorted. *First and last.*

Until…well, that was another type of occasion for another time.

"Oh, come on. You're telling me you're not enjoying yourself?" Ayana unlooped one of her arms and pinched her thumb and forefinger together. "Not even a *liiittle*?"

Define enjoy. I lowered my head so only she could hear me. "I enjoy spending time with you," I said. "I enjoy seeing you happy. That's what I enjoy."

Her expression softened. "It's Shadow's birthday, not mine," she said with a smile in her voice. "One year to the day you found him."

"I got him a sweet potato cake. That's enough." Though I supposed it was nice to see him so energetic. Maybe if Maya kept him busy, he would stop scratching the shit out of priceless furniture. "Can we kick everyone out now? It's been an hour."

Ayana grinned. "I recommend giving it another two hours or so. They did trek all this way for our cat's birthday party."

"Most of them live less than ten minutes away."

"Vuk."

"Fine," I said. "Two more hours. You should be glad I love you so much."

"I am." She pressed a light kiss to my lips. "Don't worry. I'll show you just how glad I am later."

My body sparked to life. "If that's supposed to make me want people around more, it's having the opposite effect."

"The anticipation enhances the fun," she said with a wink. "Now, come on. Let's see if we can't win some money off Xavier and Sloane."

We rejoined the rest of the party. Despite my grumbles, I did enjoy myself, especially after I beat Xavier at poker.

Most importantly, Ayana was enjoying herself, and I would do anything to make her smile—including hosting and *staying* at a feline birthday party.

And hours later, after everyone had left and it was only us in our bedroom, she made good on her promise to show me exactly how glad she was.

She'd been right—the anticipation did enhance the fun.

Ayana

Two months later

"I'm not sure those shoes are a good idea."

I planted my hands on my hips. "You should know better than to underestimate my ability to walk in impractical footwear."

Vuk arched an eyebrow at the high-heeled, weatherproof boots, which I'd bought specifically for this trip.

"We're walking through snow, *srce*," he said. "Your feet are going to freeze."

"They're snow boots."

"I've never seen snow boots with heels."

"You also think ecru and beige are the same color, so as much as I love you, I will have to respectfully decline your opinions on fashion."

He shook his head with a laugh. "Fine. It's your toes."

It was early December, and we were spending a week at Finland's newest luxury resort in Lapland. Our "room" was a giant igloo with a glass dome ceiling and spectacular views of the skies above. Tonight, the gorgeous lights of the Aurora Borealis shimmered above and cast an ethereal feel over the setting.

Views aside, the resort also boasted a world-class spa, a hot chocolate concierge, and private guides for activities ranging from husky sledding to reindeer safaris. Basically, it was the snowy winter wonderland of my dreams, and I never wanted to leave.

"We should've brought Shadow," I said as Vuk and I left our room for the private perfume-making workshop he'd arranged. "He would love this."

"That cat does not need an all-expenses paid vacation to Europe," Vuk said dryly. "The staff spoil him enough."

I didn't point out that he was the one who'd booked Shadow a day at a luxury cat spa just last weekend.

I also didn't admit that he was right—my toes *were* freezing. I made it halfway to the activity pavilion before I started slowing down. I shivered, the ice creeping up from my feet to my arms and chest.

Weatherproof, my ass. I was never buying from this brand again.

"You okay?" he asked when he noticed me lagging.

"Mmhmm."

His mouth quirked. "It's your shoes, isn't it?"

"Well, not *exactly,* but—Vuk!" I squealed when he swept me up off the ground. The world tilted, and my laughter bounced off the snow-dusted pines as he carried me the rest of the way. "What are you doing? Put me down!"

"Once we're inside. We have two more days here, *srce*. You're not going to spend them with frostbitten toes."

"Don't be dramatic," I huffed. But I couldn't stop smiling.

We arrived at the activity lodge soon after. Our workshop instructor didn't blink an eye at our unconventional entrance, and she greeted us warmly before she kicked things off.

Vuk and I each got to create and take home our own fragrance. Our instructor explained the different fragrance notes and how to combine them for the perfect balance. She also guided us through the process of selecting the right ingredients for our individual tastes.

Vuk was strangely subdued compared to his earlier teasing. He was always quiet around people he didn't know, but tonight he seemed almost...nervous? He would hate if I asked him about it in front of our instructor though, so I filed my questions away for later.

After much deliberation, I selected a scent combo that would remind me of this trip: a minty opening note that blossomed into a gentle musk infused with iris, snowdrops, and lily of the valley, topped with a dash of woody vanilla.

"Excellent choice," the instructor said. "Let me box up your fragrances for you. One moment please." She disappeared into a back room and returned a minute later with two bags. "Please, stay as long as you'd like. The activity lodge is yours for the night." She handed the bags to me with a smile. "I hope you enjoyed the workshop. Have a wonderful rest of your trip."

I blinked, a little stunned by the speed with which she left.

"That was weird," I said. "Why would we need the lodge for the rest of the night? The workshop's over."

"I have no idea." Vuk sounded oddly strained. Then again, he was always a bit grumpy after social outings.

"What notes did you put in your cologne?" I asked. He'd refused to let me see his final combination, and I was dying of curiosity. "I hope you chose that first woody base. It smells amazing on you."

A smile pulled on his lips. "Why don't you look in the box and see for yourself?"

Our fragrances included custom-printed labels on the back that listed their scent notes and creation date.

Vuk pushed his hands in his pockets and waited, his jaw taut, while I retrieved his cologne from his bag. I turned the bottle around, expecting to see a combination of woods and vanillas on the label.

I didn't. In fact, I didn't see any scent notes at all. There was only one sentence printed in vintage typewriter font:

Will you marry me?

The breath evaporated from my lungs. My palms grew so slick and hot, the bottle would've slipped from my grasp and crashed to the floor had I not been clutching it so tightly.

When I looked up, my throat burning with unshed tears, Vuk was already on one knee in front of me. The most breathtaking ring I'd ever seen glittered in his hand. The flawless pear-shaped diamond rested on a bed of black velvet. It was set in gold and adorned with an exquisite scattering of tiny emeralds.

"When I first told you about this workshop, you asked why it was so late at night," he said. A wash of pink colored his cheekbones, and there was a small shake in his normally cool, steady voice. "It's because I wanted to do this under the Northern Lights. Last year, when we were in D.C., you told me you never got to see the Lights, and I wanted you to experience them. I want you to experience everything beautiful in this world, Ayana, and I hope you'll give me the honor of being by your side for it all." Vuk swallowed. "I originally had a much longer speech planned, but I'm not the best with words. We've never needed them much anyway; we've always known what was in each other's hearts. So I only have one question to ask. Ayana Kidane, will you marry me?"

My tears had spilled out before he finished his first sentence, and they came faster and harder now as his question hung in the air.

"*Yes*. Oh my God, yes!" I sobbed. "Of course I'll marry you!"

I thought I saw his shoulders sag with relief, but honestly, I couldn't see much past the veil of tears.

The world was a blur as he slid the ring on my finger, and then we were kissing and laughing and kissing some more.

I should've known he had something up his sleeve when he'd suggested a "spontaneous" trip to Finland, but I also wouldn't have been surprised if he'd brought me here simply because I'd told him I wanted to come back.

Vuk was stoic, grumpy, and possessed the occasional murderous tendency, but deep in his heart, he was a good person. We fit in a way that was uniquely us—light and dark, sea and snow, flame and ice.

Before we met, I'd spent years bemoaning my lack of a love life, but my sighs had just been the universe whispering to me, *Wait a while longer. Your perfect match will come.*

He had.

And he was worth every second of the wait.

Thank you for reading *King of Envy*! If you enjoyed this book,
I would be grateful if you could leave a review
on the platform(s) of your choice.

Reviews are like tips for authors, and every one helps!

Much love,
Ana

P.S. Want to discuss my books and other fun shenanigans with
like-minded readers? Join my exclusive reader group Ana's
Twisted Squad!

Can't get enough of Vuk & Ayana?

Download their bonus scene at
anahuang.com/bonus-scenes

Keep in Touch
with Ana Huang

Reader Group: facebook.com/groups/anastwistedsquad
Website: anahuang.com
BookBub: bookbub.com/profile/ana-huang
Instagram: instagram.com/authoranahuang
TikTok: tiktok.com/@authoranahuang
Goodreads: goodreads.com/anahuang

Acknowledgments

It's been a while since I've written a morally gray, unhinged hero, which is probably why I had so much fun with Vuk and Ayana's story! A dangerous MMC who's so down bad, he'll burn the world for her? Yes, please.

This book also had a little more action and suspense than previous volumes of the Kings of Sin series, so thank you to everyone on Team Ana for rolling with it!

To Becca—It took us a while to get into this couple's heads, but we did it! Moving you-know-what to you-know-where in the story was absolutely the right move. Plus, Jordan lived to see another day.

To my alpha readers Brittney, Rebecca, and Salma—We have another completed novel on the books! Thank you for being both my rocks and my cheerleaders throughout this process.

To my specialty alphas Marijana, Efrata, and Hayley—Thank you for sharing your knowledge and translation wizardry with me. I learned so much, and I couldn't have done this without you.

To my sensitivity and beta readers Chelé, Erica, Aishah, Emma, Jessie, Sonali, Malia, and Nina—Thank you for all your thoughtful feedback. I truly appreciate the time and care you put into your notes. You helped make this story shine!

To Britt—Thank you for your proofreading magic. Another tight deadline met!

To Cat—"Think python, not garden snake." IYKYK. Thank you for being a great designer and a great friend.

To Christa, Madison, and the rest of the Bloom team—I can't believe we're already on the fifth book of this series! I love working with you, and I'm so excited for what lies ahead.

To Gina, Ellie, and the rest of the Piatkus team—Thank you for all the work you've put into this release. It's such a joy to see my books in stores around the world, and that wouldn't be possible without you.

To Kimberly, Aimee, Joy, and the rest of the Park, Fine and Brower team—I am so grateful to have you in my corner. You're all rockstars!

To Jess—Thank you for all your hard work behind the scenes! You made release week so smooth, and I couldn't do half the things I do without you.

To my readers—Your excitement for *King of Envy* has been incredible to see. Thank you for your support throughout the years. You are truly the best readers I could ask for, and I'm so honored to be part of this community with you.

Much love,
Ana

**Look out for the new
King of Sin . . .**

KING
OF
GLUTTONY

**She's his greatest rival . . . and his
greatest weakness.**

Continue your *Kings of Sin* journey
with Sebastian & Maya's story.

Coming soon from

PIATKUS

**Don't miss the next
God of the Game . . .**

*THE
DEFENDER*

**He has to play by the rules . . . but
for her, he'd break them all.**

Continue your *Gods of the Game* journey with
Vincent and Brooklyn's story.

Coming soon from

PIATKUS